CLEA

CLEA

a novel

by

LAWRENCE
DURRELL

FABER AND FABER

24 Russell Square

London

First published in this edition mcmlxi
by Faber and Faber Limited
24 Russell Square London W.C.1
Printed in Great Britain by
Latimer Trend & Co Ltd Whitstable

© *Lawrence Durrell*
1960

AUTHOR'S NOTE

This is the fourth volume of a group of novels intended to be judged as a single work. It is a sequel to JUSTINE, BALTHAZAR, *and* MOUNT-OLIVE. *Together the four novels constitute "The Alexandria Quartet"; a suitable descriptive subtitle would be "a word continuum". The prefatory note to* BALTHAZAR *has already described my intentions as far as the form of the books is concerned.*

Among the workpoints at the end of this volume I have sketched a number of possible ways of continuing to deploy these characters and situations in further instalments—but this is only to suggest that even if the series were extended indefinitely the result would never become a roman fleuve *(an expansion of the matter in serial form) but would remain strictly part of the present word-continuum. If the axis has been well and truly laid down in the quartet it should be possible to radiate in any direction without losing the strictness and congruity of the continuum. But to all intents and purposes the present set of four volumes may be judged as a completed whole.*

L.D.

The Primary and most beautiful of Nature's qualities is motion, which agitates her at all times, but this motion is simply the perpetual consequence of crimes, it is conserved by means of crimes alone.

(D. A. F. de Sade)

To
MY FATHER

BOOK I

I

The oranges were more plentiful than usual that year. They glowed in their arbours of burnished green leaf like lanterns, flickering up there among the sunny woods. It was as if they were eager to celebrate our departure from the little island—for at last the long-awaited message from Nessim had come, like a summons back to the Underworld. A message which was to draw me back inexorably to the one city which for me always hovered between illusion and reality, between the substance and the poetic images which its very name aroused in me. A memory, I told myself, which had been falsified by the desires and intuitions only as yet half-realised on paper. Alexandria, the capital of memory! All the writing which I had borrowed from the living and the dead, until I myself had become a sort of postscript to a letter which was never ended, never posted. . . .

How long had I been away? I could hardly compute, though calendar-time gives little enough indication of the aeons which separate one self from another, one day from another; and all this time I had been living there, truly, in the Alexandria of my heart's mind. And page by page, heartbeat by heartbeat, I had been surrendering myself to the grotesque organism of which we had all once been part, victors and vanquished alike. An ancient city changing under the brush-strokes of thoughts which besieged meaning, clamouring for identity; somewhere there, on the black thorny promontories of Africa the aromatic truth of the place lived on, the bitter unchewable herb of the past, the pith of memory. I had set out once to store, to codify, to annotate the past before it was utterly lost—that at least was a task I had set myself. I had failed in it (perhaps it was hopeless?)—for no sooner had I embalmed one aspect of it in words than the intrusion of new knowledge disrupted the frame of reference, everything flew asunder, only to reassemble again in unforeseen, unpredictable patterns. . . .

"To re-work reality" I had written somewhere; temeritous, presumptuous words indeed—for it is reality which works and reworks us on its slow wheel. Yet if I had been enriched by the experience of this island interlude, it was perhaps because of this total failure to record the inner truth of the city. I had now come face to face with the nature of time, that ailment of the human psyche. I had been forced to admit defeat on paper. Yet curiously enough the act of writing had in itself brought me another sort of increase; by the very *failure* of words, which sink one by one into the measureless caverns of the imagination and gutter out. An expensive way to begin living, yes; but then we artists are driven towards personal lives nourished in these strange techniques of self-pursuit.

But then . . . if I had changed, what of my friends—Balthazar, Nessim, Justine, Clea? What new aspects of them would I discern after this time-lapse, when once more I had been caught up in the ambience of a new city, a city now swallowed by a war? Here was the rub. I could not say. Apprehension trembled within me like a lodestar. It was hard to renounce the hard-won territory of my dreams in favour of new images, new cities, new dispositions, new loves. I had come to hug my own dreams of the place like a monomaniac. . . . Would it not, I wondered, be wiser to stay where I was? Perhaps. Yet I knew I must go. Indeed *this very night* I should be gone! The thought itself was so hard to grasp that I was forced to whisper it aloud to myself.

We had passed the last ten days since the messenger called in a golden hush of anticipation; and the weather had matched it, turning up a succession of perfectly blue days, windless seas. We stood between the two landscapes, unwilling to relinquish the one yet aching to encounter the other. Poised, like gulls upon the side of a cliff. And already the dissimilar images

12

mixed and baulked in my dreams. This island house, for example, its smoke-silvered olives and almonds where the red-footed partridge wandered . . . silent glades where only the goat-face of a Pan might emerge. Its simple and lucent perfection of form and colour could not mix with the other premonitions crowding in upon us. (A sky full of falling-stars, emerald wash of tides on lonely beaches, crying of gulls on the white roads of the south.) This Grecian world was already being invaded by the odours of the forgotten city—promontories where the sweating sea-captains had boozed and eaten until their intestines cracked, had drained their bodies, like kegs, of every lust, foundering in the embrace of black slaves with spaniels' eyes. (The mirrors, the heart-rending sweetness of the voices of blinded canaries, the bubble of *narguilehs* in their rose-water bowls, the smell of patchouli and joss.) They were eating into one another, these irreconcilable dreams. And I saw my friends once again (not as names now), irradiated anew by the knowledge of this departure. They were no longer shadows of my own writing but refreshed anew—even the dead. At night I walked again those curling streets with Melissa (situated now somewhere beyond regrets, for even in my dreams I knew she was dead), walking comfortably arm in arm; her narrow legs like scissors gave her a swaying walk. The habit of pressing her thigh to mine at every step. I could see everything with affection now—even the old cotton frock and cheap shoes which she wore on holidays. She had not been able to powder out the faint blue lovebite on her throat. . . . Then she vanished and I awoke with a cry of regret. Dawn was breaking among the olives, silvering their still leaves.

Somewhere along the road I had recovered my peace of mind. This handful of blue days before saying farewell—I treasured them, luxuriating in their simplicity: fires of olive-wood blazing in the old hearth whose painting of Justine would be the last item to be packed, jumping and gleaming on the battered table and chair, on the blue enamel bowl of early cyclamen. What

13

had the city to do with all this—an Aegean spring hanging upon a thread between winter and the first white puffs of almond blossom? It was a word merely, and meant little, being scribbled on the margins of a dream, or being repeated in the mind to the colloquial music of time, which is only desire expressed in heartbeats. Indeed, though I loved it so much, I was powerless to stay; the city which I now knew I hated held out something different for me—a new evaluation of the experience which had marked me. I must return to it once more in order to be able to leave it forever, to shed it. If I have spoken of time it is because the writer I was becoming was learning at last to inhabit those deserted spaces which time misses— beginning to live between the ticks of the clock, so to speak. The continuous present, which is the real history of that collective anecdote, the human mind; when the past is dead and the future represented only by desire and fear, what of that adventive moment which can't be measured, can't be dismissed? For most of us the so-called Present is snatched away like some sumptuous repast, conjured up by fairies—before one can touch a mouthful. Like the dead Pursewarden I hoped I might soon be truthfully able to say: "I do not write for those who have never asked themselves this question: 'at what point does real life begin?'"

Idle thoughts passing through the mind as I lay on a flat rock above the sea, eating an orange, perfectly circumscribed by a solitude which would soon be engulfed by the city, the ponderous azure dream of Alexandria basking like some old reptile in the bronze Pharaonic light of the great lake. The master-sensualists of history abandoning their bodies to mirrors, to poems, to the grazing flocks of boys and women, to the needle in the vein, to the opium-pipe, to the death-in-life of kisses without appetite. Walking those streets again in my imagination I knew once more that they spanned, not merely human history, but the whole biological scale of the heart's affections —from the painted ecstasies of Cleopatra (strange that the vine

14

should be discovered here, near Taposiris) to the bigotry of Hypatia (withered vine-leaves, martyr's kisses). And stranger visitors: Rimbaud, student of the Abrupt Path, walked here with a belt full of gold coins. And all those other swarthy dream-interpreters and politicians and eunuchs were like a flock of birds of brilliant plumage. Between pity, desire and dread, I saw the city once more spread out before me, inhabited by the faces of my friends and subjects. I knew that I must re-experience it once more and this time forever.

Yet it was to be a strange departure, full of small unforeseen elements—I mean the messenger being a hunchback in a silver suit, a flower in his lapel, a perfumed handkerchief in his sleeve! And the sudden springing to life of the little village which had for so long tactfully ignored our very existence, save for an occasional gift of fish or wine or coloured eggs which Athena brought us, folded in her red shawl. She, too, could hardly bear to see us go; her stern old wrinkled mask crumpled into tears over each item of our slender baggage. But "They will not let you leave without a hospitality" she repeated stubbornly. "The village will not let you go like that." We were to be offered a farewell banquet!

As for the child I had conducted the whole rehearsal of this journey (of her whole life, in truth) in images from a fairy story. Many repetitions had not staled it. She would sit staring up at the painting and listening attentively. She was more than prepared for it all, indeed almost ravenous to take up her own place in the gallery of images I had painted for her. She had soaked up all the confused colours of this fanciful world to which she had once belonged by right and which she would now recover—a world peopled by those presences—the father, a dark pirate-prince, the stepmother a swarthy imperious queen. . . .

"She is like the playing-card?"

"Yes. The Queen of Spades."

"And her name is Justine."

"Her name is Justine."

"In the picture she is smoking. Will she love me more than my father or less?"

"She will love you both."

There had been no other way to explain it to her, except in terms of myth or allegory—the poetry of infant uncertainty. I had made her word-perfect in this parable of an Egypt which was to throw up for her (enlarged to the size of gods or magi) the portraits of her family, of her ancestors. But then is not life itself a fairy-tale which we lose the power of apprehending as we grow? No matter. She was already drunk upon the image of her father.

"Yes, I understand everything." With a nod and a sigh she would store up these painted images in the treasure-box of her mind. Of Melissa, her dead mother, she spoke less often, and when she did I answered her in the same fashion from the story-book; but she had already sunk, pale star, below the horizon into the stillness of death, leaving the foreground to those others—the playing-card characters of the living.

The child had thrown a tangerine into the water and now leaned to watch it roll softly down to the sandy floor of the grotto. It lay there, flickering like a small flame, nudged by the swell and fall of the currents.

"Now watch me fetch it up."

"Not in this icy sea, you'll die of cold."

"It isn't cold to-day. Watch."

By now she could swim like a young otter. It was easy, sitting here on the flat rock above the water, to recognise in her the dauntless eyes of Melissa, slanted a little at the edges; and sometimes, intermittently, like a forgotten grain of sleep in the corners, the dark supposing look (pleading, uncertain) of her father Nessim. I remembered Clea's voice saying once, in another world, long ago: "Mark, if a girl does not like dancing and swimming she will never be able to make love." I smiled and wondered if the words were true as I watched the little creature turn over smoothly in the water and flow gracefully

16

downwards to the target with the craft of a seal, toes pressed back against the sky. The glimmer of the little white purse between her legs. She retrieved the tangerine beautifully and spiralled to the surface with it gripped in her teeth.

"Now run and dry quickly."

"It isn't cold."

"Do as you are told. Be off. Hurry."

"And the man with the hump?"

"He has gone."

Mnemjian's unexpected appearance on the island had both started and thrilled her—for it was he who brought us Nessim's message. It was strange to see him walking along the shingle beach with an air of grotesque perturbation, as if balancing on corkscrews. I think he wished to show us that for years he had not walked on anything but the finest pavements. He was literally unused to terra firma. He radiated a precarious and overbred finesse. He was clad in a dazzling silver suit, spats, a pearl tie-pin, and his fingers were heavily ringed. Only the smile, the infant smile was unchanged, and the oiled spitcurl was still aimed at the frontal sinus.

"I have married Halil's widow. I am the richest barber in all Egypt to-day, my dear friend."

He blurted this out all in one breath, leaning on a silver-knobbed walking-stick to which he was clearly as unaccustomed. His violet eye roved somewhat disdainfully round our somewhat primitive cottage, and he refused a chair, doubtless because he did not wish to crease those formidable trousers. "You have a hard style of life here, eh? Not much *luxe*, Darley." Then he sighed and added, "But now you will be coming to us again." He made a vague gesture with the stick intended to symbolise the hospitality we should once more enjoy from the city. "Myself I cannot stay. I am on my way back. I did this purely as a favour to Hosnani." He spoke of Nessim with a sort of pearly grandeur, as if he were now his equal socially; then he caught sight of my smile and had the grace to giggle once before becoming serious again. "There is no time, anyway" he said, dusting his sleeves.

This had the merit of being true, for the Smyrna boats stays only long enough to unload mail and occasional merchandise—a few cases of macaroni, some copper sulphate, a pump. The wants of the islanders are few. Together we walked back towards the village, across the olive-groves, talking as we went. Mnemjian still trudged with that slow turtle-walk. But I was glad, for it enabled me to ask him a few questions about the city, and from his answers to gain some inkling of what I was to find there in the matter of changed dispositions, unknown factors.

"There are many changes since this war. Dr. Balthazar has been very ill. You know about the Hosnani intrigue in Palestine? The collapse? The Egyptians are trying to sequestrate. They have taken much away. Yes, they are poor now, and still in trouble. She is still under house-detention at Karm Abu Girg. Nobody has seen her for an age. He works by special permission as an ambulance driver in the docks, twice a week. Very dangerous. And there was a bad air-raid; he lost one eye and a finger."

"Nessim?" I was startled. The little man nodded self-importantly. This new, this unforeseen image of my friend struck me like a bullet. "Good God" I said, and the barber nodded as if to approve the appropriateness of the oath. "It was bad" he said. "It is the war, Darley." Then suddenly a happier thought came into his mind and he smiled the infant smile once more which reflected only the iron material values of the Levant. Taking my arm he continued: "But the war is also good business. My shops are cutting the armies' hair day and night. Three saloons, twelve assistants! You will see, it is superb. And Pombal says, as a joke, 'Now you are shaving the dead while they are still alive.'" He doubled up with soundless refined laughter.

"Is Pombal back there?"

"Of course. He is a high man of the Free French now. He has conferences with Sir Mountolive. He is also still there.

Many have remained from your time, Darley, you will see."

Mnemjian seemed delighted to have been able to astonish me so easily. Then he said something which made my mind do a double somersault. I stood still and asked him to repeat it, thinking that I had misheard him. "I have just visited Capodistria." I stared at him with utter incredulity. Capodistria! "But he *died*!" I exclaimed in surprise.

The barber leaned far back, as if on a rocking-horse, and tittered profusely. It was a very good joke this time and lasted him a full minute. Then at last, still sighing luxuriously at the memory of it, he slowly took from his breast-pocket a postcard such as one buys upon any Mediterranean seafront and held it out to me, saying: "Then who is this?"

It was a murky enough photograph with the heavy developing-marks which are a feature of hasty street-photography. It depicted two figures walking along a seafront. One was Mnemjian. The other . . . I stared at it in growing recognition. . . .

Capodistria was clad in tubular trousers of an Edwardian style and very pointed black shoes. With this he wore a long academician's topcoat with a fur collar and cuffs. Finally, and quite fantastically, he was sporting a *chapeau melon* which made him look rather like a tall rat in some animal cartoon. He had grown a thin Rilkean moustache which drooped a little at the corner of his mouth. A long cigarette-holder was between his teeth. It was unmistakably Capodistria. "What on earth . . ." I began, but the smiling Mnemjian shut one eye and laid a finger across his lips. "Always" he said "there are mysteries"; and in the act of guarding them he swelled up toad-like, staring into my eyes with a mischievous content. He would perhaps have deigned to explain but at that minute a ship's siren rang out from the direction of the village. He was flustered. "Quickly"; he began his trudging walk. "I mustn't forget to give you the letter from Hosnani." It was carried doubled in his breast pocket and he fished it out at last. "And now goodbye" he said. "All is arranged. We will meet again."

19

I shook his hand and stood looking after him for a moment, surprised and undecided. Then I turned back to the edge of the olive grove and sat down on a rock to read the letter from Nessim. It was brief and contained the details of the travel arrangements he had made for us. A little craft would be coming to take us off the island. He gave approximate times and instructions as to where we should wait for it. All this was clearly set out. Then, as a postscript Nessim added in his tall hand: "It will be good to meet again, without reserves. I gather that Balthazar has recounted all our misadventures. You won't exact an unduly heavy repentance from people who care for you so much? I hope not. Let the past remain a closed book for us all."

That was how it fell out.

For those last few days the island regaled us nobly with the best of its weather and those austere Cycladean simplicities which were like a fond embrace—for which I knew I should be longing when once more the miasma of Egypt had closed over my head.

On the evening of departure the whole village turned out to give us the promised farewell dinner of lamb on the spit and gold *rezina* wine. They spread the tables and chairs down the whole length of the small main street and each family brought its own offerings to the feast. Even those two proud dignitaries were there—mayor and priest—each seated at one end of the long table. It was cold to sit in the lamplight thus, pretending that it was really a summer evening, but even the moon collaborated, rising blindly out of the sea to shine upon the white tablecloths, polish the glasses of wine. The old burnished faces, warmed by drink, glowed like copperware. Ancient smiles, archaic forms of address, traditional pleasantries, courtesies of the old world which was already fading, receding from us. The old sea-captains of the sponge-fleets sucking their bounty of wine from blue enamel cans, their warm embraces smelt like wrinkled crab-apples, their great moustaches tanned by tobacco curled towards their ears.

At first I had been touched, thinking all this ceremony was for me; I was not the less so to find that it was for my country. To be English when Greece had fallen was to be a target for the affection and gratitude of every Greek, and the humble peasants of this hamlet felt it no less keenly than Greeks everywhere. The shower of toasts and pledges echoed on the night, and all the speeches flew like kites, in the high style of Greek, orotund and sonorous. They seemed to have the cadences of immortal poetry—the poetry of a desperate hour; but of course they were only words, the wretched windy words which war so easily breeds and which the rhetoricians of peace would soon wear out of use.

But tonight the war lit them up like tapers, the old men, giving them a burning grandeur. Only the young men were not there to silence and shame them with their hangdog looks—for they had gone to Albania to die among the snows. The women spoke shrilly, in voices made coarsely thrilling with unshed tears, and among the bursts of laughter and song fell their sudden silences—like so many open graves.

It had come so softly towards us over the waters, this war; gradually, as clouds which quietly fill in a horizon from end to end. But as yet it had not broken. Only the rumour of it gripped the heart with conflicting hopes and fears. At first it had seemed to portend the end of the so-called civilised world, but this hope soon proved vain. No, it was to be as always simply the end of kindness and safety and moderate ways; the end of the artist's hopes, of nonchalance, of joy. Apart from this everything else about the human condition would be confirmed and emphasised; perhaps even a certain truthfulness had already begun to emerge from behind appearances, for death heightens every tension and permits us fewer of the half-truths by which we normally live.

This was all we had known of it, to date, this unknown dragon whose claws had already struck elsewhere. All? Yes, to be sure, once or twice the upper sky had swollen with the slur

21

of invisible bombers, but their sounds could not drown the buzzing, nearer at hand, of the island bees: for each household owned a few whitewashed hives. What else? Once (this seemed more real) a submarine poked up a periscope in the bay and surveyed the coastline for minutes on end. Did it see us bathing on the point? We waved. But a periscope has no arms with which to wave back. Perhaps on the beaches to the north it had discovered something else more rare—an old bull seal dozing in the sun like a Moslem on his prayer-mat. But this again could have had little to do with war.

Yet the whole business became a little more real when the little *caique* which Nessim had sent fussed into the dusk-filled harbour that night, manned by three sullen-looking sailors armed with automatics. They were not Greek, though they spoke the tongue with waspish authority. They had tales to tell of shattered armies and death by frostbite, but in a sense it was already too late, for the wine had fuddled the wits of the old men. Their stories palled rapidly. Yet they impressed me, these three leather-faced specimens from an unknown civilisation called "war". They sat uneasily in such good fellowship. The flesh was stretched tight over their unshaven cheek-bones as if from fatigue. They smoked gluttonously, gushing the blue smoke from mouth and nostrils like voluptuaries. When they yawned they seemed to fetch their yawns up from the very scrotum. We confided ourselves to their care with misgiving for they were the first unfriendly faces we had seen for a long time.

At midnight we slipped out slantwise from the bay upon a high moonlight—the further darkness made more soft, more confiding, by the warm incoherent goodbyes which poured out across the white beaches towards us. How beautiful are the Greek words of greeting and farewell!

We shuttled for a while along the ink-shadowed line of cliffs where the engine's heartbeats were puckered up and thrown back at us in volleys. And so at last outwards upon the main deep, feeling the soft swelling unction of the water's rhythms

22

begin to breast us up, cradle and release us, as if in play. The night was superlatively warm and fine. A dolphin broke once, twice at the bow. A course was set.

Exultation mixed with a profound sadness now possessed us; fatigue and happiness in one. I could taste the good salt upon my lips. We drank some warm sage-tea without talking. The child was struck speechless by the beauties of this journey—the quivering phosphorescence of our wake, combed out behind us like a comet's hair, flowing and reviving. Above us, too, flowed the plumed branches of heaven, stars scattered as thick as almond-blossom on the enigmatic sky. So at last, happy with these auguries and lulled by pulses of the water and the even vibrations of the engine, she fell asleep with a smile upon parted lips, with the olive-wood doll pressed against her cheek.

How could I help but think of the past towards which we were returning across the dense thickets of time, across the familiar pathways of the Greek sea? The night slid past me, an unrolling ribbon of darkness. The warm sea-wind brushed my cheek—soft as the brush of a fox. Between sleep and waking I lay, feeling the tug of memory's heavy plumb-line: tug of the leaf-veined city which my memory had peopled with masks, malign and beautiful at once. I should see Alexandria again, I knew, in the elusive temporal fashion of a ghost—for once you become aware of the operation of a time which is not calendar-time you become in some sort a ghost. In this other domain I could hear the echoes of words uttered long since in the past by other voices. Balthazar saying: "This world represents the promise of a unique happiness which we are not well-enough equipped to grasp." The grim mandate which the city exercised over its familiars, crippling sentiment, steeping everything in the vats of its own exhausted passions. Kisses made more passionate by remorse. Gestures made in the amber light of shuttered rooms. The flocks of white doves flying upwards among the minarets. These pictures seemed to me to represent the city as I would see it again. But I was wrong—for each new approach is different. Each time we deceive ourselves that it will be the same. The Alexandria I now saw, the first vision of it from the sea, was something I could not have imagined.

It was still dark when we lay up outside the invisible harbour with its remembered outworks of forts and anti-submarine nets. I tried to paint the outlines on the darkness with my mind. The boom was raised only at dawn each day. An all-obliterating darkness reigned. Somewhere ahead of us lay the invisible coast of Africa, with its "kiss of thorns" as the Arabs say. It was intolerable to be so aware of them, the towers and minarets of the city, and yet to be unable to will them to appear. I could not see my own fingers before my face. The sea had become a vast empty ante-room, a hollow bubble of blackness.

Then suddenly there passed a sudden breath, a whiff like a wind passing across a bed of embers, and the nearer distance glowed pink as a sea-shell, deepening gradually into the rose-richness of a flower. A faint and terrible moaning came out across the water towards us, pulsing like the wing-beats of some fearful prehistoric bird—sirens which howled as the damned must howl in limbo. One's nerves were shaken like the branches of a tree. And as if in response to this sound lights began to prick out everywhere, sporadically at first, then in ribbons, bands, squares of crystal. The harbour suddenly out-lined itself with complete clarity upon the dark panels of heaven, while long white fingers of powder-white light began to stalk about the sky in ungainly fashion, as if they were the legs of some awkward insect struggling to gain a purchase on the slippery black. A dense stream of coloured rockets now began to mount from the haze among the battleships, emptying on the sky their brilliant clusters of stars and diamonds and smashed pearl snuff-boxes with a marvellous prodigality. The air shook in strokes. Clouds of pink and yellow dust arose with the maroons to shine upon the greasy buttocks of the barrage bal-loons which were flying everywhere. The very sea seemed to tremble. I had had no idea that we were so near, or that the city

24

could be so beautiful in the mere saturnalia of a war. It had begun to swell up, to expand like some mystical rose of the darkness, and the bombardment kept it company, overflowing the mind. To our surprise we found ourselves shouting at each other. We were staring at the burning embers of Augustine's Carthage, I thought to myself, we were observing the fall of city man.

It was as beautiful as it was stupefying. In the top left-hand corner of the tableau the searchlights had begun to congregate, quivering and sliding in their ungainly fashion, like daddy-long-legs. They intersected and collided feverishly, and it was clear that some signal had reached them which told of the struggles of some trapped insect on the outer cobweb of darkness. Again and again they crossed, probed, merged, divided. Then at last we saw what they were bracketing: six tiny silver moths moving down the skylanes with what seemed unbearable slowness. The sky had gone mad around them yet they still moved with this fatal languor; and languidly too curled the curving strings of hot diamonds which spouted up from the ships, or the rank lacklustre sniffs of cloudy shrapnel which marked their progress.

And deafening as was the roaring which now filled our ears it was possible to isolate many of the separate sounds which orchestrated the bombardment. The crackle of shards which fell back like a hailstorm upon the corrugated roofs of the waterside cafés: the scratchy mechanical voices of ships' signallers repeating, in the voices of ventriloquists' dummies, semi-intelligible phrases which sounded like "Three o'clock red, Three o'clock red". Strangely too, there was music somewhere at the heart of all the hubbub, jagged quartertones which stabbed; then, too, the foundering roar of buildings falling. Patches of light which disappeared and left an aperture of darkness at which a dirty yellow flame might come and lap like a thirsty animal. Nearer at hand (the water smacked the echo out) we could hear the rich harvest of spent cannon-shells pour-

25

ing upon the decks from the Chicago Pianos: an almost continuous splashing of golden metal tumbling from the breeches of the skypointed guns.

So it went on, feasting the eye yet making the vertebrae quail before the whirlwind of meaningless power it disclosed. I had not realised the impersonality of war before. There was no room for human beings or thought of them under this vast umbrella of coloured death. Each drawn breath had become only a temporary refuge.

Then, almost as suddenly as it had started, the spectacle died away. The harbour vanished with theatrical suddenness, the string of precious stones was turned off, the sky emptied, the silence drenched us, only to be broken once more by that famished crying of the sirens which drilled at the nerves. And then, nothing—a nothingness weighing tons of darkness out of which grew the smaller and more familiar sounds of water licking at the gunwales. A faint shore-wind crept out to invest us with the alluvial smells of an invisible estuary. Was it only in my imagination that I heard from far away the sounds of wildfowl on the lake?

We waited thus for a long time in great indecision; but meanwhile from the east the dawn had begun to overtake the sky, the city and desert. Human voices, weighted like lead, came softly out, stirring curiosity and compassion. Children's voices—and in the west a sputum-coloured meniscus on the horizon. We yawned, it was cold. Shivering, we turned to one another, feeling suddenly orphaned in this benighted world between light and darkness.

But gradually it grew up from the eastern marches, this familiar dawn, the first overflow of citron and rose which would set the dead waters of Mareotis a-glitter; and fine as a hair, yet so indistinct that one had to stop breathing to verify it, I heard (or thought I heard) the first call to prayer from some as yet invisible minaret.

Were there, then, still gods left to invoke? And even as the

26

question entered my mind I saw, shooting from the harbour-mouth, the three small fishing-boats—sails of rust, liver and blue plum. They heeled upon a freshet and stooped across our bows like hawks. We could hear the rataplan of water lapping their prows. The small figures, balanced like riders, hailed us in Arabic to tell us that the boom was up, that we might enter harbour.

This we now did with circumspection, covered by the apparently deserted batteries. Our little craft trotted down the main channel between the long lines of ships like a *vaporetto* on the Grand Canal. I gazed around me. It was all the same, yet at the same time unbelievably different. Yes, the main theatre (of the heart's affections, of memory, of love?) was the same; yet the differences of detail, of décor stuck out obstinately. The liners now grotesquely dazzle-painted in cubist smears of white, khaki and North-Sea greys. Self-conscious guns, nesting awkwardly as cranes in incongruous nests of tarpaulin and webbing. The greasy balloons hanging in the sky as if from gibbets. I compared them to the ancient clouds of silver pigeon which had already begun to climb in wisps and puffs among the palms, diving upwards into the white light to meet the sun. A troubling counterpoint of the known and the unknown. The boats, for example, drawn up along the slip at the Yacht Club, with the remembered dew thick as sweat upon their masts and cordage. Flags and coloured awnings alike hanging stiffly, as if starched. (How many times had we not put out from there, at this same hour, in Clea's small boat, loaded with bread and oranges and wicker-clothed wine?) How many old sailing-days spent upon this crumbling coast, landmarks of affection now forgotten? I was amazed to see with what affectionate emotion one's eye could travel along a line of inanimate objects tied to a mossy wharf, regaling itself with memories which it was not conscious of having stored. Even the French warships (though now disgraced, their breech-blocks confiscated, their crews in nominal internment aboard) were exactly where I had last seen

27

them in that vanished life, lying belly-down upon the dawn murk like malevolent tomb-stones: and still, as always, backed by the paper-thin mirages of the city, whose fig-shaped minarets changed colour with every lift of the sun.

Slowly we passed down the long green aisle among the tall ships, as if taking part in some ceremonial review. The surprises among so much that was familiar, were few but choice: an ironclad lying dumbly on its side, a corvette whose upper works had been smeared and flattened by a direct hit—gun-barrels split like carrots, mountings twisted upon themselves in a contortion of scorched agony. Such a large package of grey steel to be squashed at a single blow, like a paper bag. Human remains were being hosed along the scuppers by small figures with a tremendous patience and quite impassively. This was surprising as it might be for someone walking in a beautiful cemetery to come upon a newly dug grave. ("It is beautiful" said the child.) And indeed it was so—the great forests of masts and spires which rocked and inclined to the slight swell set up by water-traffic, the klaxons mewing softly, the reflections dissolving and reforming. There was even some dog-eared jazz flowing out upon the water as if from a waste-pipe somewhere. To her it must have seemed appropriate music for a triumphal entry into the city of childhood. *"Jamais de la vie"* I caught myself humming softly in my own mind, amazed how ancient the tune sounded, how dated, how preposterously without concern for myself! She was looking into the sky for her father, the image which would form like a benevolent cloud above us and envelop her.

Only at the far end of the great dock were there evidences of the new world to which we were coming: long lines of trucks and ambulances, barriers, and bayonets, manned by the blue and khaki races of men like gnomes. And here a slow, but purposeful and continuous activity reigned. Small troglodytic figures emerged from iron cages and caverns along the wharves, busy upon errands of differing sorts. Here too there were ships split apart in geometrical sections which exposed their steaming intestines, ships laid open in Caesarian section: and into these wounds crawled an endless ant-like string of soldiers and blue-jackets humping canisters, bales, sides of oxen on blood-stained shoulders. Oven doors opened to expose to the firelight white-capped men feverishly dragging at oven-trays of bread. It was somehow unbelievably slow, all this activity, yet immense in compass. It belonged to the instinct of a race rather than to its appetites. And while silence here was only of comparative value small sounds became concrete and imperative—sentries stamping iron-shod boots upon the cobbles, the yowl of a tug, or the buzz of a liner's siren like the sound of some giant blue-bottle caught in a web. All this was part of the newly acquired city to which I was henceforth to belong.

We drew nearer and nearer, scouting for a berth among the small craft in the basin; the houses began to go up tall. It was a moment of exquisite delicacy, too, and my heart was in my mouth (as the saying goes) for I had already caught sight of the figure which I knew would be there to meet us—away across the wharves there. It was leaning against an ambulance, smoking. Something in its attitude struck a chord and I knew it was Nessim, though I dared not as yet be sure. It was only when the ropes went out and we berthed that I saw, with beating heart (recognising him dimly through his disguise as I had with Capodistria), that it was indeed my friend. Nessim!

He wore an unfamiliar black patch over one eye. He was dressed in a blue service greatcoat with clumsy padded shoulders and very long in the knee. A peaked cap pulled well down over his eyes. He seemed much taller and slimmer than I remembered—perhaps it was this uniform which was half chauffeur's livery, half airman's rig. I think he must have felt the force of my recognition pressing upon him for he suddenly stood upright, and after peering briefly about him, spotted us. He threw the cigarette away and walked along the quay with his swift and graceful walk, smiling nervously. I waved but he did not respond, though he half nodded as he moved towards us. "Look" I said, not without apprehension. "Here he comes at last, your father." She watched with wide and frozen eyes following the tall figure until it stood smiling at us, not six feet away. Sailors were busy with ropes. A gang plank went down with a bang. I could not decide whether that ominous black patch over his eye added to or subtracted from, the old distinction. He took off his cap and still smiling, shyly and somewhat ruefully, stroked his hair into place before putting it on again. "Nessim" I called, and he nodded, though he did not respond. A silence seemed to fall upon my mind as the child stepped out upon the plank. She walked with an air of bemused rapture, spellbound by the image rather than the reality. (Is poetry, then, more real than observed truth?) And putting out her arms like a sleepwalker she walked chuckling into his embrace. I came hard on her heels, and as he still laughed and hugged her Nessim handed me the hand with the missing finger. It had become a claw, digging into mine. He uttered a short dry sob disguised as a cough. That was all. And now the child crawled up like a sloth into a tree-trunk and wound her legs about his hips. I did not quite know what to say, gazing into that one all-comprehending dark eye. His hair was quite white at the temples. You cannot squeeze a hand with a missing finger as hard as you would like.

"And so we meet again."

He backed away briskly and sat down upon a bollard, groping for his cigarette case to offer me the unfamiliar delicacy of a French cigarette. We were both dumb. The matches were damp and only struck with difficulty. "Clea was to have come" he said at last, "but she turned tail at the last moment. She has gone to Cairo. Justine is out at Karm!" Then ducking his head he said under his breath "You know about it eh?" I nodded and he looked relieved. "So much the less to explain. I came off duty half an hour ago and waited for you to take you out. But perhaps. . . ."

But at this moment a flock of soldiers closed on us, verifying our identities and checking on our destinations. Nessim was busy with the child. I unpacked my papers for the soldiers. They studied them gravely, with a certain detached sympathy even, and hunted for my name upon a long sheet of paper before informing me that I should have to report to the Consulate, for I was a "refugee national". I returned to Nessim with the clearance slips and told him of this. "As a matter of fact it does not fall badly. I had to go there anyway to fetch a suitcase I left with all my respectable suits in it . . . how long ago, I wonder?"

"A lifetime" he smiled.

"How shall we arrange it?"

We sat side by side smoking and reflecting. It was strange and moving to hear around us all the accents of the English shires. A kindly corporal came over with a tray full of tin mugs, steaming with that singular brew, Army tea, and decorated with slabs of white bread smeared with margarine. In the middle distance a stretcher-party walked apathetically offstage with a sagging load from a bombed building. We ate hungrily and became suddenly aware of our swimming knees. At last I said: "Why don't you go on and take her with you? I can get a tram at the dock-gate and visit the Consul. Have a shave. Some lunch. Come out this evening to Karm if you will send a horse to the ford."

"Very well" he said, with a certain relief, and hugging the child suggested this plan to her, whispering in her ear. She offered no objection, indeed seemed eager to accompany him— for which I felt thankful. And so we walked, with a feeling of unreality, across the slimy cobbles to where the little ambulance was parked, and Nessim climbed into the driver's seat with the child. She smiled and clapped her hands, and I waved them away, delighted that the transition was working so smoothly. Nevertheless it was strange to find myself thus, alone with the city, like a castaway on a familiar reef. 'Familiar'—yes! For once one had left the semi-circle of the harbour nothing had changed whatsoever. The little tin tram groaned and wriggled along its rusty rails, curving down those familiar streets which spread on either side of me images which were absolute in their fidelity to my memories. The barbers' shops with their fly-nets drawn across the door, tingling with coloured beads: the cafés with their idlers squatting at the tin tables (by El Bab, still the crumbling wall and the very table where we had sat motionless, weighed down by the blue dusk). Just as he let in the clutch Nessim had peered at me sharply and said: "Darley, you have changed very much", though whether in reproof or commendation I could not tell. Yes, I had: seeing the old crumbled arch of El Bab I smiled, remembering a now prehistoric kiss upon my fingers. I remembered the slight flinch of the dark eyes as she uttered the sad brave truth: "One learns nothing from those who return our love." Words which burnt like surgical spirit on an open wound, but which cleansed, as all truth does. And busy with these memories as I was, I saw with another part of my mind the whole of Alexandria unrolling once more on either side of me—its captivating detail, its insolence of colouring, its crushing poverty and beauty. The little shops, protected from the sun by bits of ragged awning in whose darkness was piled up every kind of merchandise from live quail to honeycombs and lucky mirrors. The fruit-stalls with their brilliant stock made doubly brilliant by being displayed upon brighter papers; the warm gold of oranges lying on brilliant slips of magenta and crimson-lake. The smoky glitter of the coppersmiths' caves. Gaily tasselled camel-saddlery. Pottery and blue jade beads against the Evil Eye. All this given a sharp prismatic brilliance by the crowds milling back and forth, the blare of the café radios, the hawkers' long sobbing cries, the imprecations of street-arabs, and the demented ululations of distant mourners setting forth at a jog-trot behind the corpse of some notable sheik. And here, strolling in the foreground of the painting with the insolence of full possession, came plum-blue Ethiopians in snowy turbans, bronze Sudanese with puffy charcoal

32

lips, pewter-skinned Lebanese and Bedouin with the profiles of kestrels, woven like brilliant threads upon the monotonous blackness of the veiled women, the dark Moslem dream of the hidden Paradise which may only be glimpsed through the key-hole of the human eye. And lurching down these narrow streets with their packs scraping the mud walls plunged the sumpter camels with cargoes of green clover, putting down their huge soft pads with infinite delicacy. I suddenly remembered Scobie giving me a lesson on the priority of salutation: "You must realise that it's a question of form. They're regular Britishers for politeness, my boy. No good throwing your *Salaam Aleikum* around just anyhow. It must be given first by a camel-rider to a man on a horse, by a horseman to a man on a donkey, by a donkey-rider to a man on foot, by a man walking to a man seated, by a small party to a large one, by the younger to the older. . . . It's only in the great schools at home they teach such things. But here every nipper has it at his fingers' ends. Now repeat the order of battle after me!" It was easier to repeat the phrase than to remember the order at this remove in time. Smiling at the thought, I strove to re-establish those forgotten priorities from memory, while I gazed about me. The whole toybox of Egyptian life was still there, every figure in place—street-sprinkler, scribe, mourner, harlot, clerk, priest—untouched, it seemed, by time or by war. A sudden melancholy invaded me as I watched them, for they had now become a part of the past. My sympathy had discovered a new element inside itself—detachment. (Scobie used to say, in an expansive moment: "Cheer up, me boyo, it takes a lifetime to grow. People haven't the patience any more. *My* mother waited nine months for me!" A singular thought.)

Jolting past the Goharri Mosque I remembered finding one-eyed Hamid there one afternoon rubbing a slice of lemon on a pilaster before sucking it. This, he had said, was an infallible specific against the stone. He used to live somewhere in this quarter with its humble cafés full of native splendours like rose-scented drinking water and whole sheep turning on spits, stuffed with pigeons, rice, nuts. All the paunch-beguiling meals which delighted the ventripotent pachas of the city!

Somewhere up here, skirting the edge of the Arab quarter the tram gives a leap and grinds round abruptly. You can for one moment look down through the frieze of shattered buildings into the corner of the harbour reserved for craft of shallow draught. The hazards of the war at sea had swollen their numbers to overflowing. Framed by the coloured domes there lay feluccas and lateen-rig giassas, wine-caiques, schooners, and brigantines of every shape and size, from all over the Levant. An anthology of masts and spars and haunting Aegean eyes; of names and rigs and destinations. They lay there coupled to their reflections with the sunlight on them in a deep water-trance. Then abruptly they were snatched away and the Grande Corniche began to unroll, the magnificent long sea-parade which frames the modern city, the Hellenistic capital of the bankers and cotton-visionaries—all those European bagmen whose enterprise had re-ignited and ratified Alexander's dream of conquest after the centuries of dust and silence which Amr had imposed upon it.

Here, too, it was all relatively unchanged save for the dull khaki clouds of soldiers moving everywhere and the rash of new bars which had sprung up everywhere to feed them. Outside the Cecil long lines of transport-trucks had overflowed the taxi-ranks. Outside the Consulate an unfamiliar naval sentry with rifle and bayonet. I could not say it was all irremediably changed, for these visitors had a shiftless and temporary look, like countrymen visiting a capital for a fair. Soon a sluice gate would open and they would be drawn off into the great reservoir of the desert battles. But there were surprises. At the Consulate, for example, a very fat man who sat like a king prawn at his desk, pressing white hands together whose long filbert nails had been carefully polished that morning, and who addressed me with familiarity. "My task may seem invidious" he fluted, "yet it is necessary. We are trying to grab everyone who has a special aptitude before the Army gets them. I have been sent your name by the Ambassador who had designated you for the censorship department which we have just opened, and which is grotesquely understaffed."

"The Ambassador?" It was bewildering.

"He's a friend of yours is he not?"

"I hardly know him."

"Nevertheless I am bound to accept his direction, even though I am in charge of this operation."

There were forms to be filled in. The fat man, who was not unamiable, and whose name was Kenilworth, obliged by helping me. "It is a bit of mystery" I said. He shrugged his shoulders and spread his white hands. "I suggest you discuss it with him when you meet."

"But I had no intention . . ." I said. But it seemed pointless to discuss the matter further until I discovered what lay behind it. How could Mountolive. . . ? But Kenilworth was talking again. "I suppose you might need a week to find yourself lodgings here before you settle in. Shall I tell the department so?"

"If you wish" I said in bewilderment. I was dismissed and spent some time in the cellars unearthing my battered cabin-trunk and selecting from it a few respectable city-clothes. With these in a brown paper parcel I walked slowly along the Corniche towards the Cecil, where I purposed to take a room, have a bath and shave, and prepare myself for the visit to the country-house. This had begun to loom up rather in my mind, not exactly with anxiety but with the disquiet which suspense always brings. I stood for a while staring down at the still sea, and it was while I was standing thus that the silver Rolls with the daffodil hub-caps drew up and a large bearded personage jumped out and came galloping towards me with hands out-stretched. It was only when I felt his arms hugging my shoulders and the beard brushing my cheek in a Gallic greeting that I was able to gasp "Pombal!"

35

"Darley". Still holding my hands as tenderly, and with tears in his eyes, he drew me to one side and sat down heavily on one of the stone benches bordering the marine parade. Pombal was in the most elegant *tenue*. His starched cuffs rattled crisply. The dark beard and moustache gave him an imposing yet somehow forlorn air. Inside all these trappings he seemed quite unchanged. He peered through them, like a Tiberius in fancy-dress. We gazed at each other for a long moment of silence, with emotion. Both knew that the silence we observed was one of pain for the fall of France, an event which symbolised all too clearly the psychic collapse of Europe itself. We were like mourners at an invisible cenotaph during the two minutes' silence which commemorates an irremediable failure of the human will. I felt in his handclasp all the shame and despair of this graceless tragedy and I sought desperately for the phrase which might console him, might reassure him that France itself could never truly die so long as artists were being born into the world. But this world of armies and battles was too intense and too concrete to make the thought seem more than of secondary importance—for art really means freedom, and it was this which was at stake. At last the words came. "Never mind. To-day I've seen the little blue cross of Lorraine flowering everywhere."

"You understand" he murmured and squeezed my hand again. "I knew you would understand. Even when you most criticised her you knew that she meant as much to you as to us." He blew his nose suddenly, with startling loudness, in a clean handkerchief and leaned back on the stone bench. With amazing suddenness he had become his old self again, the timid, fat, irrepressible Pombal of the past. "There is so much to tell you. You will come with me now. At once. Not a word. Yes, it is Nessim's car. I bought it to save it from the Egyptians. Mountolive has fixed you an excellent post. I am still in the old flat, but now we have taken the building. You can have the whole top floor. It will be like old times again." I was carried

36

off my feet by his volubility and by the bewildering variety of prospects he described so rapidly and confidently, without apparently expecting comment. His English had become practically perfect.

"Old times" I stammered.

But here an expression of pain crossed his fat countenance and he groaned, pressing his hands between his knees as he uttered the word: "Fosca!" He screwed up his face comically and stared at me. "You do not know." He looked almost terrified. "I am in love with her."

I laughed. He shook his head rapidly. "No. Don't laugh."

"I must, Pombal."

"I beseech you." And leaning forward with a look of despair on his countenance he lowered his voice and prepared to confide something to me. His lips moved. It was clearly something of tragic importance. At last he brought it out, and the tears came into his eyes as he spoke the words: "You don't understand. *Je suis fidèle malgré moi.*" He gasped like a fish and repeated "*Malgré moi.* It has never happened before, *never.*" And then abruptly he broke into a despairing whinny with the same look of awed bewilderment on his face. How could I forbear to laugh? At a blow he had restored Alexandria to me, complete and intact—for no memory of it could be complete without the thought of Pombal in love. My laughter infected him. He was shaking like a jelly. "Stop" he pleaded at last with comic pathos, interjecting into the forest of bearded chuckles the words. "And I have never slept with her, not once. That is the insane thing." This made us laugh more than ever.

But the chauffeur softly sounded the horn, recalling him to himself abruptly, reminding him that he had duties to perform. "Come" he cried. "I have to take a letter to Pordre before nine. Then I'll have you dropped at the flat. We can lunch together. Hamid is with me, by the way; he'll be delighted. Hurry up." Once more my doubts were not given time to formulate themselves. Clutching my parcel I accompanied him to the familiar car, noticing with a pang that its upholstery now smelt of expensive cigars and metal-polish. My friend talked rapidly all the way to the French Consulate, and I was surprised to find that his whole attitude to the Chief had changed. All the old bitterness and resentment had vanished. They had both, it seemed, abandoned their posts in different capitals (Pombal in Rome) in order to join the Free French in Egypt. He spoke of Pordre now with tender affection. "He is like a father to me. He has been marvellous" said my friend rolling his expressive dark eye. This somewhat puzzled me until I saw them both together and understood in a flash that the fall of their country had created this new bond. Pordre had become quite white-haired; his frail and absent-minded gentleness had given place to the calm resolution of someone grappling with responsibilities which left no room for affectation. The two men treated each other with a courtesy and affection which in truth made them seem like father and son rather than colleagues. The hand that Pordre placed so lovingly on Pombal's shoulder, the face he turned to him, expressed a wistful and lonely pride.

But the situation of their new Chancery was a somewhat unhappy one. The broad windows looked out over the harbour, over the French Fleet which lay there at anchor like a symbol of all that was malefic in the stars which governed the destiny of France. I could see that the very sight of it lying there idle was a perpetual reproach to them. And there was no escaping it. At every turn taken between the high old-fashioned desks and the white wall their eyes fell upon this repellent array of ships. It was like a splinter lodged in the optic nerve. Pordre's eye kindled with self-reproach and the zealot's hot desire to reform these cowardly followers of the personage whom Pombal (in his less diplomatic moments) was henceforward to refer to as *"ce vieux Putain"*. It was a relief to vent feelings so intense by the simple substitution of a letter. The three of us stood there, looking down into the harbour at this provoking sight, and suddenly the old man burst out: "Why don't you British intern them? Send them to India with the Italians. I shall never understand it. Forgive me. But do you realise that they are allowed to keep their small arms, mount sentries, take shore leave, just as if they were a neutral fleet? The admirals wine and dine in the town, all intriguing for Vichy. There are endless *bagarres* in the cafés between our boys and their sailors." I could see that it was a subject which was capable of making them quite beside themselves with fury. I tried to change it, since there was little consolation I could offer.

I turned instead to Pombal's desk on which stood a large framed photograph of a French soldier. I asked who it was and both men replied simultaneously: "He saved us." Later of course I would come to recognise this proud, sad Labrador's head as that of de Gaulle himself.

Pombal's car dropped me at the flat. Forgotten whispers stirred in me as I rang the bell. One-eyed Hamid opened to me, and after a moment of surprise he performed a curious little jump in the air. The original impulse of this jump must have been an embrace which he repressed just in time. But he put two fingers on my wrist and jumped like a solitary penguin on an ice-floe before retreating to give himself room for the more elaborate and formal greeting. "Ya Hamid" I cried, as delighted as he was. We crossed ourselves ceremonially at each other.

The whole place had been transformed once more, repainted and papered and furnished in massive official fashion. Hamid led me gloatingly from room to room while I mentally tried to reconstruct its original appearance from memories which had by now become faded and transposed. It was hard to see Melissa shrieking, for example. On the exact spot now stood a handsome sideboard crowded with bottles. (Pursewarden had once gesticulated from the far corner.) Bits of old furniture came back to mind. "Those old things must be knocking about somewhere" I thought in quotation from the poet of the city.* The only recognisable item was Pombal's old gout-chair

39

which had mysteriously reappeared in its old place under the window. Had he perhaps flown back with it from Rome? That would be like him. The little box-room where Melissa and I. . . . It was now Hamid's own room. He slept on the same uncomfortable bed which I looked at with a kind of shrinking feeling, trying to recapture the flavour and ambience of those long enchanted afternoons when. . . . But the little man was talking. He must prepare lunch. And then he rummaged in a corner and thrust into my hand a crumpled snapshot which he must at some time have stolen from Melissa. It was a street-photograph and very faded. Melissa and I walked arm in arm talking down Rue Fuad. Her face was half turned away from me, smiling—dividing her attention between what I was saying so earnestly and the lighted shop-windows we passed. It must have been taken, this snapshot, on a winter afternoon around the hour of four. What on earth could I have been telling her with such earnestness? For the life of me I could not recall the time and place; yet there it was, in black and white, as they say. Perhaps the words I was uttering were momentous, significant—or perhaps they were meaningless! I had a pile of books under my arm and was wearing the dirty old mackintosh which I finally gave to Zoltan. It was in need of a dry-clean. My hair, too, seemed to need cutting at the back. Impossible to restore this vanished afternoon to mind! I gazed carefully at the circumstantial detail of the picture like someone bent upon restoring an irremediably faded fresco. Yes, it was winter, at four o'clock. She was wearing her tatty sealskin and carried a handbag which I had not ever seen in her possession. "Sometime in August—was it August?" I mentally quoted to myself again.*

Turning back to the wretched rack-like bed again I whispered her name softly. With surprise and chagrin I discovered that she had *utterly vanished*. The waters had simply closed over her head. It was as if she had never existed, never inspired in me the pain and pity which (I had always told myself) would live on, transmuted into other forms perhaps—but live triumph-antly on forever. I had worn her out *like an old pair of socks,* and the utterness of this disappearance surprised and shocked me. Could "love" simply wear out like this? "Melissa" I said again, hearing the lovely word echo in the silence. Name of a sad herb, name of a pilgrim to Eleusis. Was she less now than a scent or a flavour? Was she simply a nexus of literary cross-references scribbled in the margins of a minor poem? And had my love dissolved her in this strange fashion, or was it simply the literature I had tried to make out of her? Words, the acid-bath of words! I felt guilty. I even tried (with that lying self-deception so natural to sentimentalists) to *force* her to reappear by an act of will, to re-evoke a single one of those afternoon kisses which had once been for me the sum of the city's many meanings. I even tried deliberately to squeeze the tears into my eyes, to hypnotise memory by repeating her name like a charm. The experiment yielded nothing. Her name had been utterly worn out of use! It was truly shameful not to be able to evoke the faintest tribute to so all-engulfing an unhappiness. Then like the chime of a distant bell I heard the tart voice of the dead Pursewarden saying "But our unhappiness was sent to regale us. We were intended to revel in it, enjoy it to the full." Melissa had been simply one of the many costumes of love!

I was bathed and changed by the time Pombal hurried in to an early lunch, full of the incoherent rapture of his new and remarkable state of mind. Fosca, the cause of it, was, he told me, a refugee married to a British officer. "How could it have come about, this sudden passionate understanding?" He did not know. He got up to look at his own face in the hanging mirror. "I who believed so many things about love" he went on moodily, half addressing his own reflection and combing his beard with his fingers, "but never something like this. Even a year ago had you said what I am just saying I would have answered: *'Pouagh!* It is simply a Petrarchian obscenity. Med-iaeval rubbish!'. I even used to think that continence was

41

medically unhealthy, that the damned thing would atrophy or fall off if it were not frequently used. Now look at your un-happy—no *happy* friend! I feel bound and gagged by Fosca's very existence. Listen, the last time Keats came in from the desert we went out and got drunk. He took me to Golfo's tavern. I had a sneaking desire—sort of experimental—to *ramoner une poule*. Don't laugh. Just to see what had gone wrong with my feelings. I drank five Armagnacs to liven them up. I began to feel quite like it theoretically. Good, I said to myself, I will crack this virginity. I will *dépuceler* this romantic image once and for all lest people begin to talk and say that the great Pombal is unmanned. But what happened? I became panic-stricken! My feelings were quite quite *blindés* like a bloody tank. The sight of all those girls made me memorise Fosca in detail. Everything, even her hands in her lap with her knitting! I was cooled as if by an ice cream down my collar. I emptied my pockets on the table and fled in a hail of slippers and a torrent of cat-calls from my old friends. I was swearing, of course. Not that Fosca expects it, no. She tells me to go ahead and have a girl if I must. Perhaps this very freedom keeps me in prison? Who knows? It is a complete mystery to me. It is strange that this girl should drag me by the hair down the paths of honour like this—an unfamiliar place."

Here he struck himself softly on the chest with a gesture of reproof mixed with a certain doubtful self-commendation. He came and sat down once more saying moodily: "You see, she is pregnant by her husband and her sense of honour would not permit her to trick a man on active service, who may be killed at any time. Specially when she is bearing his child. *Ça se conçoit.*"

We ate in silence for a few moments, and then he burst out: "But what have I to do with such ideas? Tell me please. We only talk, yet it is enough." He spoke with a touch of self-contempt.

"And he?"

Pombal sighed: "He is an extremely good and *kind* man, with that national kindliness which Pursewarden used to say was a kind of compulsion neurosis brought on by the almost suicidal boredom of English life! He is handsome, gay, speaks three languages. And yet . . . it is not that he is *froid*, exactly, but he is *tiède*—I mean somewhere in his inner nature. I am not sure if he is typical or not. At any rate he seems to embody notions of honour which would do credit to a troubadour. It isn't that we Europeans lack honour, of course, but we don't stress things unnaturally. I mean self-discipline should be more than a concession to a behaviour-pattern. I sound confused. Yes, I am a little confused in thinking of their relationship. I mean something like this: in the depths of his national conceit he really believes foreigners incapable of fidelity in love. Yet in being so truthful and so faithful she is only doing what comes naturally to her, without a false straining after a form. *She acts as she feels.* I think if he really loved her in the sense I mean he would not appear always to have merely condescended to rescue her from an intolerable situation. I think somewhere inside herself, though she is not aware of it, the sense of injustice rankles a little bit; she is faithful to him . . . how to say? Slightly contemptuously? I don't know. But she does love him in this peculiar fashion, the only one he permits. She is a girl of delicate feelings. But what is strange is that our own love—which neither doubts, and which we have confessed and accepted—has been coloured in a curious way by these circumstances. If it has made me happy it has also made me a little uncertain of myself; at times I get rebellious. I feel that our love is beginning to wear a penitential air—this glorious adventure. It gets coloured by his own grim attitude which is like one of atonement. I wonder if love for a *femme galante* should be quite like this. As for him he also is a *chevalier* of the middle class, as incapable of inflicting pain as of giving physical pleasure I should say. Yet withal gentle and quite overwhelming in his kindness and uprightness. But *merde*, one cannot love

43

judicially, out of a sense of justice, can one? Somewhere along the line he fails her without being conscious of the fact. Nor do I think she *knows* this, at any rate in her conscious mind. But when they are together you feel in the presence of something incomplete, something which is not cemented but just soldered together by good manners and convention. I am aware that I sound unkind, but I am only trying to describe exactly what I see. For the rest we are good friends and indeed I really admire him; when he comes on leave we all go out to dinner and talk politics! Ouf!"

He lay back in his chair, exhausted by this exposition, and yawned heavily before consulting his watch. "I suppose" he went on with resignation "that you will find it all very strange, these new aspects of people; but then everything sounds strange here, eh? Pursewarden's sister, Liza, for example—you don't know her? She is stone blind. It seems to us all that Mountolive is madly in love with her. She came out originally to collect his papers and also to find materials for a book about him. Allegedly. Anyway she has stayed on at the Embassy ever since. When he is in Cairo on duty he visits her every week-end! He looks somehow unhappy now—perhaps I do too?" He once more consulted the mirror and shook his head decisively. Apparently he did not. "Well anyway" he conceded "I am probably wrong."

The clock on the mantelpiece struck and he started up. "I must get back to the office for a conference" he said. "What about you?" I told him of my projected trip to Karm Abu Girg. He whistled and looked at me keenly. "You will see Justine again, eh?" He thought for a moment and then shrugged his shoulders doubtfully. "A recluse now, isn't she? Put under house-arrest by Memlik. Nobody has seen her for ages. I don't know what's going on with Nessim either. They've quite broken with Mountolive and as an official I have to take his line, so we would never even try to meet: even if it were allowed, I mean. Clea sees him sometimes. I'm sorry for

44

Nessim. When he was in hospital she could not get permission to visit him. It is all a merry-go-round, isn't it? Like a Paul Jones. New partners until the music stops! But you'll come back, won't you, and share this place? Good. Then I'll tell Hamid. I must be off. Good luck."

I had only intended to lie down for a brief sieasta before the car came, but such was my fatigue that I plunged into a heavy sleep the moment my head touched the pillow; perhaps I should have slept the clock round had not the chauffeur awakened me. Half-dazed as yet I sat in the familiar car and watched the unreal lakelands grow up around with their palms and water-wheels—the Egypt which lives outside the cities, ancient, pastoral and veiled by mists and mirages. Old memories stirred now, some bland and pleasing, others rough as old cicatrices. Scar-tissue of old emotions which I should soon be shedding. The first momentous step would be to encounter Justine again. Would she help or hinder me in the task of controlling and evaluating these precious "reliques of sensation" as Coleridge calls them? It was hard to know. With every succeeding mile I felt anxiety and expectation running neck and neck. The Past!

o   o   o   o   o

45

II

Ancient lands, in all their prehistoric intactness: lake-solitudes hardly brushed by the hurrying feet of the centuries where the uninterrupted pedigrees of pelican and ibis and heron evolve their slow destinies in complete seclusion. Clover-patches of green baize swarming with snakes and clouds of mosquitoes. A landscape devoid of songbirds yet full of owls, hoopoes and kingfishers hunting by day, pluming themselves on the banks of the tawny waterways. The packs of half-wild dogs foraging, the blindfolded water-buffaloes circling the water-wheels in an eternity of darkness. The little wayside chancels built of dry mud and floored with fresh straw where the pious traveller might say a prayer as he journeyed. Egypt! The goose-winged sails scurrying among the freshets with perhaps a human voice singing a trailing snatch of song. The click-click of the wind in the Indian corn, plucking at the coarse leaves, shumbling them. Liquid mud exploded by rainstorms in the dust-laden air throwing up mirages everywhere, despoiling perspectives. A lump of mud swells to the size of a man, a man to the size of a church. Whole segments of the sky and land displace, open like a lid, or heel over on their side to turn upside down. Flocks of sheep walk in and out of these twisted mirrors, appearing and disappearing, goaded by the quivering nasal cries of invisible shepherds. A great confluence of pastoral images from the forgotten history of the old world which still lives on side by side with the one we have inherited. The clouds of silver winged ants floating up to meet and incandesce in the sunlight. The clap of a horse's hoofs on the mud floors of this lost world echo like a pulse and the brain swims among these veils and melting rainbows.

And so at last, following the curves of the green embankments you come upon an old house built sideways upon an intersection of violet canals, its cracked and faded shutters tightly fastened, its rooms hung with dervish trophies, hide shields, bloodstained spears and magnificent carpets. The gardens desolate and untended. Only the little figures on the wall move their celluloid wings—scarecrows which guard against the Evil Eye. The silence of complete desuetude. But then the whole countryside of Egypt shares this melancholy feeling of having been abandoned, allowed to run to seed, to bake and crack and moulder under the brazen sun.

Turn under an arch and clatter over the cobbles of a dark courtyard. Will this be a new point of departure or a return to the starting-point?

It is hard to know.

o   o   o   o   o

III

She stood at the very top of the long outer staircase looking down into the dark courtyard like a sentinel and holding in her right hand a branch of candles which threw a frail circle of light around her. Very still, as if taking part in a *tableau vivant*. It seemed to me that the tone in which she first uttered my name had been deliberately made flat and unemphatic, copied perhaps from some queer state of mind which she had imposed upon herself. Or perhaps, uncertain that it was I, she was merely interrogating the darkness, trying to unearth me from it like some obstinate and troublesome memory which had slipped out of place. But the familiar voice was to me like the breaking of a seal. I felt like someone at last awakened from a sleep which had lasted centuries and as I walked slowly and circumspectly up the creaking wooden stairway I felt, hovering over me, the breath of a new self-possession. I was halfway up when she spoke again, sharply this time, with something almost comminatory in her tone. "I heard the horses and went all-overish suddenly. I've spilt scent all over my dress. I stink, Darley. You will have to forgive me."

She seemed to have become very much thinner. Holding the candle high she advanced a step to the stairhead, and after gazing anxiously into my eyes placed a small cold kiss upon my right cheek. It was as cold as an obituary, dry as leather. As she did so I smelt the spilt perfume. She did indeed give off overpowering waves of it. Something in the enforced stillness of her attitude suggested an inner unsteadiness and the idea crossed my mind that perhaps she had been drinking. I was a trifle shocked too to see that she had placed a bright patch of rouge on each cheek-bone which showed up sharply against a dead white, overpowered face. If she was beautiful still it was the passive beauty of some Propertian mummy which had been clumsily painted to give the illusion of life, or a photograph carelessly colour-tinted. "You must not look at my eye" she next said, sharply, imperatively: and I saw that her left eyelid drooped slightly, threatening to transform her expression into something like a leer—and most particularly the welcoming smile which she was trying to adopt at this moment. "Do you understand?" I nodded. Was the rouge, I wondered, designed to distract attention from that drooping eyelid? "I had a small stroke" she added under her breath, as if explaining to herself. And as she still stood before me with the raised branch of candles she seemed to be listening to some other sound. I took her hand and we stood together for a long moment thus, staring at one another.

"Have I changed very much?"

"Not at all."

"Of course I have. We all have." She spoke now with a contemptuous shrillness. She raised my hand briefly and put it to her cheek. Then nodding with a puzzled air she turned and drew me towards the balcony, walking with a stiff proud step. She was clad in a dress of dark taffeta which whispered loudly at every movement. The candlelight jumped and danced upon the walls. We stopped before a dark doorway and she called out "Nessim" in a sharp tone which shocked me, for it was the tone in which one would call a servant. After a moment Nessim appeared from the shadowy bedroom, obedient as a djinn.

"Darley's here" she said, with the air of someone handing over a parcel, and placing the candles on a low table reclined swiftly in a long wicker chair and placed her hand over her eyes.

Nessim had changed into a suit of a more familiar cut, and he came nodding and smiling towards me with the accustomed expression of affection and solicitude. Yet it was somehow different again; he wore a faintly cowed air, shooting little

D   49

glances sideways and downwards towards the figure of Justine, and speaking softly as one might in the presence of someone asleep. A constraint had suddenly fallen upon us as we seated ourselves on that shadowy balcony and lit cigarettes. The silence locked like a gear which would not disengage.

"The child is in bed, delighted with the palace as she calls it, and the promise of a pony of her own. I think she will be happy."

Justine suddenly sighed deeply and without uncovering her eyes said slowly: "He says we have not changed."

Nessim swallowed and continued as if he had not heard the interruption in the same low voice: "She wanted to stay awake till you came but she was too tired."

Once again the reclining figure in the shadowy corner interrupted to say: "She found Narouz' little circumcision cap in the cupboard. I found her trying it on." She gave a short sharp laugh, like a bark, and I saw Nessim wince suddenly and turn away his face.

"We are short of servants" he said in a low voice, hastily as if to cement up the holes made in the silence by her last remark.

His air of relief was quite patent when Ali appeared and bade us to dinner. He picked up the candles and led us into the house. It had a somewhat funereal flavour—the white-robed servant with his scarlet belt leading, holding aloft the candles in order to light Justine's way. She walked with an air of pre-occupation, of remoteness. I followed next with Nessim close behind me. So we went in Indian file down the unlighted corridors, across high-ceilinged rooms with their walls covered in dusty carpets, their floors of rude planks creaking under our feet. And so we came at last to a supper-room, long and narrow, and suggesting a forgotten sophistication which was Ottoman perhaps; say, a room in a forgotten winter palace of Abdul Hamid, its highly carved window-screens of filigree looking out upon a neglected rose-garden. Here the candlelight with its luminous shadows was ideal as an adjunct to furnishings which were, in themselves, strident. The golds and the reds and the violets would in full light have seemed unbearable. By candlelight they had a subdued magnificence.

We seated ourselves at the supper-table and once more I became conscious of the almost cowed expression of Nessim as he gazed around him. It is perhaps not the word. It was as if he expected some sudden explosion, expected some unforeseen reproach to break from her lips. He was mentally prepared to parry it, to fend it off with a tender politeness. But Justine ignored us. Her first act was to pour out a glass of red wine. This she raised to the light as if to verify its colour. Then she dipped it ironically to each of us in turn like a flag and drank it off all in one motion before replacing the glass on the table. The touches of rouge gave her an enflamed look which hardly matched the half-drowsy stupefaction of her glance. She was wearing no jewelry. Her nails were painted with gold polish. Putting her elbows on the table she propped her chin for a long moment as she studied us keenly, first one and then the other. Then she sighed, as if replete, and said: "Yes, we have all changed", and turning swiftly like an accuser she stabbed her finger at her husband and said: "*He* has lost an eye."

Nessim pointedly ignored this, passing some item of table fare towards her as if to distract her from so distressing a topic. She sighed again and said: "Darley, you look much better, but your hands are cracked and calloused. I felt it on my cheek."

"Wood-cutting I expect."

"Ah. So! But you look well, very well."

(A week later she would telephone Clea and say: "Dear God, how coarse he has become. What little trace of sensibility he had has been swamped by the peasant.")

In the silence Nessim coughed nervously and fingered the black patch over his eye. Clearly he misliked the tone of her voice, distrusted the weight of the atmosphere under which one could feel, building up slowly like a wave, the pressure of a hate which was the newest element among so many novelties of speech and manner. Had she really turned into a shrew? Was she ill? It was difficult to disinter the memory of that magical dark mistress of the past whose every gesture, however ill-advised and ill-considered, rang with the newly minted splendour of complete generosity. ("So you come back" she was saying harshly "and find us all locked up in Karm. Like old figures in a forgotten account book. Bad debts, Darley. Fugitives from justice, eh Nessim?")

There was nothing to be said in answer to such bitter sallies. We ate in silence under the quiet ministration of the Arab servant. Nessim addressed an occasional hurried remark to me on some neutral topic, brief, monosyllabic. Unhappily we felt the silence draining out around us, emptying like some great reservoir. Soon we should be left there, planted in our chairs like effigies. Presently the servant came in with two charged thermos flasks and a package of food which he placed at the end of the table. Justine's voice kindled with a kind of insolence as she said: "So you are going back tonight?"

Nessim nodded shyly and said: "Yes, I'm on duty again." Clearing his throat he added to me: "It is only four times a week. It gives me something to do."

"Something to do" she said clearly, derisively. "To lose his eye and his finger gives him something to do. Tell the truth, my dear, you would do anything to get away from this house." Then leaning forward towards me she said: "To get away from me, Darley. I drive him nearly mad with my scenes. That is what he says." It was horribly embarrassing in its vulgarity.

The servant came in with his duty clothes carefully pressed and ironed, and Nessim rose, excusing himself with a word and a wry smile. We were left alone. Justine poured out a glass of wine. Then, in the act of raising it to her lips she surprised me with a wink and the words: "Truth will out."

"How long have you been locked up here?" I asked.

"Don't speak of it."

52

"But is there no way. . . ."

"He has managed to partly escape. Not me. Drink, Darley, drink your wine."

I drank in silence, and in a few minutes Nessim appeared once more, in uniform and evidently ready for his night journey. As if by common consent we all rose, the servant took up the candles and once more conducted us back to the balcony in lugubrious procession. During our absence one corner had been spread with carpets and divans while extra candlesticks and smoking materials stood upon inlaid side-tables. The night was still, and almost tepid. The candle-flames hardly moved. Sounds of the great lake came ebbing in upon us from the outer darkness. Nessim said a hurried good-bye and we heard the diminishing clip of his horse's hoofs gradually fade as he took the road to the ford. I turned my head to look at Justine. She was holding up her wrists at me, her face carved into a grimace. She held them joined together as if by invisible manacles. She exhibited these imaginary handcuffs for a long moment before dropping her hands back into her lap, and then, abruptly, swift as a snake, she crossed to the divan where I lay and sat down at my feet, uttering as she did so, in a voice vibrating with remorseful resentment, the words: "Why, Darley? O why?" It was as if she were interrogating not merely destiny or fate but the very workings of the universe itself in these thrilling poignant tones. Some of the old beauty almost flashed out in this ardour to trouble me like an echo. But the perfume! At such close quarters the spilled perfume was over-powering, almost nauseating.

Yet suddenly now all our constraint vanished and we were at last able to talk. It was as if this outburst had exploded the bubble of listlessness in which we had been enveloped all evening. "You see a different me" she cried in a voice almost of triumph. "But once again the difference lies in you, in what you imagine you see!" Her words rattled down like a hail of sods on an empty coffin. "How is it that you can feel no

53

resentment against me? To forgive such treachery so easily—
why, it is unmanly. Not to hate such a vampire? It is un-
natural. Nor could you ever understand my sense of humiliation
at not being able to regale, yes *regale* you, my dear, with the
treasures of my inner nature as a mistress. And yet, in truth, I
enjoyed deceiving you, I must not deny it. But also there was
regret in only offering you the pitiful simulacrum of a love
(Ha! that word again!) which was sapped by deceit. I suppose
this betrays the bottomless female vanity again: to desire the
worst of two worlds, of both words—love and deceit. Yet it is
strange that now, when you know the truth, and I am free to
offer you affection, I feel only increased self-contempt. Am I
enough of a woman to feel that the real sin against the Holy
Ghost is dishonesty in love? But what pretentious rubbish—for
love admits of no honesty by its very nature."

So she went on, hardly heeding me, arguing my life away,
moving obsessively up and down the cobweb of her own
devising, creating images and beheading them instantly before
my eyes. What could she hope to prove? Then she placed her
head briefly against my knee and said: "Now that I am free to
hate or love it is comical to feel only fury at this new self-
possession of yours! You have escaped me somewhere. But
what else was I to expect?"

In a curious sort of way this was true. To my surprise I now
felt the power to wound her for the first time, even to sub-
jugate her purely by my indifference! "Yet the truth" I said
"is that I feel no resentment for the past. On the contrary I
am full of gratitude because an experience which was perhaps
banal in itself (even perhaps disgusting for you) was for me
immeasurably enriching!" She turned away saying harshly:
"Then we should both be laughing now."

Together we sat staring out into the darkness for a long
while. Then she shivered, lighted a cigarette and resumed the
thread of her interior monologue. "The post-mortems of the
undone! What could you have seen in it all I wonder? We are

after all totally ignorant of one another, presenting selected fictions to each other! I suppose we all observe each other with the same immense ignorance. I used, in my moments of guilt long afterwards, to try and imagine that we might one day become lovers again, on a new basis. What a farce! I pictured myself making it up to you, expiating my deceit, repaying my debt. But . . . I knew that you would always prefer your own mythical picture, framed by the five senses, to anything more truthful. But now, then, tell me—which of us was the greater liar? I cheated you, you cheated yourself."

These observations, which at another time, in another context, might have had the power to reduce me to ashes, were now vitally important to me in a new way. "However hard the road, one is forced to come to terms with truth at last" wrote Pursewarden somewhere. Yes, but unexpectedly I was discovering that truth was nourishing—the cold spray of a wave which carried one always a little further towards self-realisation. I saw now that my own Justine had indeed been an illusionist's creation, raised upon the faulty armature of misinterpreted words, actions, gestures. Truly there was no blame here; the real culprit was my love which had invented an image on which to feed. Nor was there any question of dishonesty, for the picture was coloured after the necessities of the love which invented it. Lovers, like doctors, colouring an unpalatable medicine to make it easier for the unwary to swallow! No, this could not have been otherwise, I fully realised.

Something more, fully as engrossing: I also saw that lover and loved, observer and observed, throw down a field about each other ("Perception is shaped like an embrace—the poison enters with the embrace" as Pursewarden writes). They then infer the properties of their love, judging it from this narrow field with its huge margins of unknown ("the refraction"), and proceed to refer it to a generalised conception of something constant in its qualities and universal in its operation. How valuable a lesson this was, both to art and to life! I had only

55

been attesting, in all I had written, to the power of an image which I had created involuntarily by the *mere act of seeing* Justine. There was no question of true or false. Nymph? Goddess? Vampire? Yes, she was all of these, and none of them. She was, like every woman, everything that the mind of a man (let us define "man" as a poet perpetually conspiring against himself) —that the mind of man wished to imagine. She was there forever, and she had never existed! Under all these masks there was only another woman, every woman, like a lay figure in a dressmaker's shop, waiting for the poet to clothe her, breathe life into her. In understanding all this for the first time I began to realise with awe the enormous reflexive power of woman—the fecund passivity with which, like the moon, she borrows her second-hand light from the male sun. How could I help but be anything but grateful for such vital information? What did they matter, the lies, deceptions, follies, in comparison to this truth?

Yet while this new knowledge compelled my admiration for her more than ever—as symbol of woman, so to speak—I was puzzled to explain the new element which had crept in here: a flavour of disgust for her personality and its attributes. The scent! Its cloying richness half sickened me. The touch of the dark head against my knee stirred dim feelings of revulsion in me. I was almost tempted to embrace her once more in order to explore this engrossing and inexplicable novelty of feeling further! Could it be that a few items of information merely, *facts* like sand trickling into the hour-glass of the mind, had irrevocably altered the image's qualities—turning it from something once desirable to something which now stirred disgust? Yes, the same process, the very same love-process, I told myself. This was the grim metamorphosis brought about by the acid-bath of truth—as Pursewarden might say.

Still we sat together on that shadowy balcony, prisoners of memory, still we talked on: and still it remained unchanged, this new disposition of selves, the opposition of new facts of mind.

At last she took a lantern and a velvet cloak and we walked about for a while in that tideless night, coming at last to a great *nubk* tree whose branches were loaded with votive offerings. Here Nessim's brother had been found dead. She held the lantern high to light the tree, reminding me that the "nubk" forms the great circular palisade of trees which encircles the Moslem Paradise. "As for Narouz, his death hangs heavy on Nessim because people say that he ordered it himself —the Copts say so. It has become like a family curse to him. His mother is ill, but she will never return to this house, she says. Nor does he wish her to. He gets quite cold with rage when I speak of her. He says he wishes she would die! So here we are cooped up together. I sit all night reading—guess what? —a big bundle of love-letters to her which she left behind! Mountolive's love-letters! More confusion, more unexplored corners!" She raised the lantern and looked closely into my eyes: "Ah, but this unhappiness is not just ennui, spleen. There is also a desire to swallow the world. I have been experimenting with drugs of late, the sleep-givers!"

And so back in silence to the great rustling house with its dusty smells.

"He says we will escape one day and go to Switzerland where at least he still has money. But when, but when? And now this war! Pursewarden said that my sense of guilt was atrophied. It is simply that I have no power to decide things now, any more. I feel as if my will had snapped. But it will pass." Then suddenly, greedily she grasped my hand and said: "But thank God, you are here. Just to talk is such a *soulagement*. We spend whole weeks together without exchanging a word."

We were seated once more on the clumsy divans by the light of candles. She lit a silver-tipped cigarette and smoked with short decisive inspirations as the monologue went on, unrolling on the night, winding away in the darkness like a river.

"When everything collapsed in Palestine, all our dumps discovered and captured, the Jews at once turned on Nessim

57

accusing him of treachery, because he was friendly with Mount-olive. We were between Memlik and the hostile Jews, in disgrace with both. The Jews expelled me. This was when I saw Clea again; I so badly needed news and yet I couldn't confide in her. Then Nessim came over the border to get me. He found me like a mad woman. I was in despair! And he thought it was because of the failure of our plans. It was, of course, it was; but there was another and deeper reason. While we were conspirators, joined by our work and its dangers, I could feel truly passionate about him. But to be under house-arrest, compelled to idle away my time alone with him, in his company. . . . I knew I should die of boredom. My tears, my lamentations were those of a woman forced against her will to take the veil. Ah but you will not understand, being a northerner. How could you? To be able to love a man fully, but only in a single posture, so to speak. You see, when he does not act, Nessim is nothing; he is completely flavourless, not in touch with himself at any point. Then he has no real self to interest a woman, to grip her. In a word he is really a pure idealist. When a sense of destiny consumes him he becomes truly splendid. It was as an actor that he magnetised me, illuminated me for myself. But as a fellow prisoner, in defeat—he predisposes to ennui, migraine, thoughts of utter banality like suicide! That is why from time to time I drive my claws into his flesh. In despair!"

"And Pursewarden?"

"Ah! Pursewarden. That is something different again. I cannot think of him without smiling. There my failure was of a totally different order. My feeling for him was—how shall I say?—almost incestuous, if you like; like one's love for a beloved, an incorrigible elder brother. I tried so hard to penetrate into his confidences. He was too clever, or perhaps too egotistical. He defended himself against loving me by *making me laugh*. Yet I achieved with him, even so very briefly, a tantalising inkling that there might be other ways of living open to me if only I could find them. But he was a tricky one. He used to

58

say: 'An artist saddled with a woman is like a spaniel with a tick in its ear; it itches, it draws blood, one cannot reach it. Will some kindly grown-up please. . . ?' Perhaps he was utterly lovable because quite out of reach? It is hard to say these things. One word 'love' has to do service for so many different kinds of the same animal. It was he, too, who reconciled me to that whole business of the rape, remember? All that nonsense of Arnauti's in *Moeurs*, all those psychologists! His single observation stuck like a thorn. He said: 'Clearly you enjoyed it, as any child would, and probably even invited it. You have wasted all this time trying to come to terms with an imaginary conception of damage done to you. Try dropping this invented guilt and telling yourself that the thing was both pleasurable and meaningless. Every neurosis is made to measure!' It was curious that a few words like this, and an ironic chuckle, could do what all the others could not do for me. Suddenly everything seemed to lift, get lighter, move about. Like cargo shifting in a vessel. I felt faint and rather sick, which puzzled me. Then later on a space slowly cleared. It was like feeling creeping back into a paralysed hand again."

She was silent for a moment before going on. "I still do not quite know how he saw us. Perhaps with contempt as the fabricators of our own misfortunes. One can hardly blame him for clinging to his own secrets like a limpet. Yet he hardly kept them, for he had a so-called Check hardly less formidable than mine, something which had plucked and gutted all sensation for him; so really in a way perhaps his strength was really a great weakness! You are silent, have I wounded you? I hope not, I hope your self-esteem is strong enough to face these truths of our old relationship. I should like to get it *all* off my chest, to come to terms with you—can you understand? To confess everything and wipe the slate clean. Look, even that first, that very first afternoon when I came to you —remember? You told me once how momentous it was. When you were ill in bed with sunburn, remember? Well, I had just been kicked out of his hotel-room against my will and was quite beside myself with fury. Strange to think that every word I then addressed to you was spoken mentally to him, to Pursewarden! In your bed it was he I embraced and subjugated in my mind. And yet again, in another dimension, *everything* I felt and did then was really for Nessim. At the bottom of my rubbish heap of a heart there was really Nessim, and the plan. My innermost life was rooted in this crazy adventure. Laugh now, Darley! Let me see you laugh for a change. You look rueful, but why should you? We are all in the grip of the emotional field which we throw down about one another—you yourself have said it. Perhaps our only sickness is to desire a truth which we cannot bear rather than to rest content with the fictions we manufacture out of each other.''

She suddenly uttered a short ironic laugh and walked to the balcony's edge to drop the smouldering stub of her cigarette out into the darkness. Then she turned, and standing in front of me with a serious face, as if playing a game with a child, she softly patted her palms together, intoning the names, "Pursewarden and Liza, Darley and Melissa, Mountolive and Leila, Nessim and Justine, Narouz and Clea. . . . Here comes a candle to light them to bed, and here comes a chopper to chop off their heads. The sort of pattern we make should be of interest to someone; or is it just a meaningless display of coloured fireworks, the actions of *human* beings or of a set of dusty puppets which could be hung up in the corner of a writer's mind? I suppose you ask yourself the question.''

"Why did you mention Narouz?''

"After he died I discovered some letters to Clea; in his cupboard along with the old circumcision-cap there was a huge nosegay of wax flowers and a candle the height of a man. As you know a Copt proposes with these. But he never had the courage to send them! How I laughed!''

"You laughed?''

"Yes, laughed until the tears ran down my cheeks. But I was really laughing at myself, at you, at all of us. One stumbles over it at every turn of the road, doesn't one; under every sofa the same corpse, in every cupboard the same skeleton? What can one do but laugh?"

It was late by now, and she lighted my way to the gaunt guest-bedroom where I found a bed made up for me, and placed the candles on the old-fashioned chest of drawers. I slept almost at once.

It must have been at some time not far off dawn when I awoke to find her standing beside the bed naked, with her hands joined in supplication like an Arab mendicant, like some beggar-woman of the streets. I started up. "I ask nothing of you" she said, "nothing at all but only to lie in your arms for the comfort of it. My head is bursting tonight and the medicines won't bring sleep. I do not want to be left to the mercies of my own imagination. Only for the comfort, Darley. A few strokes and endearments, that is all I beg you."

I made room for her listlessly, still half asleep. She wept and trembled and muttered for a long time before I was able to quieten her. But at last she fell asleep with her dark head on the pillow beside me.

I lay awake for a long time to taste, with perplexity and wonder, the disgust that had now surged up in me, blotting out every other feeling. From where had it come? The perfume! The unbearable perfume and the smell of her body. Some lines from a poem of Pursewarden's drifted through my mind.

> "Delivered by her to what drunken caresses,
> Of mouths half eaten like soft rank fruit,
> From which one takes a single bite,
> A mouthful of the darkness where we bleed."

The once magnificent image of my love lay now in the hollow of my arm, defenceless as a patient on an operating table, hardly breathing. It was useless even to repeat her name which

61

once held so much fearful magic that it had the power to slow the blood in my veins. She had become a woman at last, lying there, soiled and tattered, like a dead bird in a gutter, her hands crumpled into claws. It was as if some huge iron door had closed forever in my heart.

I could hardly wait for that slow dawn to bring me release. I could hardly wait to be gone.

o o o o o

IV

Walking about the streets of the summer capital once more, walking by spring sunlight, and a cloudless skirmishing blue sea—half-asleep and half-awake—I felt like the Adam of the mediaeval legends: the world-compounded body of a man whose flesh was soil, whose bones were stones, whose blood water, whose hair was grass, whose eyesight sunlight, whose breath was wind, and whose thoughts were clouds. And weightless now, as if after some long wasting illness, I found myself turned adrift again to float upon the shallows of Mareotis with its old tide-marks of appetites and desires refunded into the history of the place: an ancient city with all its cruelties intact, pitched upon a desert and a lake. Walking down with remembered grooves of streets which extended on every side, radiating out like the arms of a starfish from the axis of its founder's tomb. Footfalls echoing in the memory, forgotten scenes and conversations springing up at me from the walls, the café tables, the shuttered rooms with cracked and peeling ceilings. Alexandria, princess and whore. The royal city and the *anus mundi*. She would never change so long as the races continued to seethe here like must in a vat; so long as the streets and squares still gushed and spouted with the fermentation of these diverse passions and spites, rages and sudden calms. A fecund desert of human loves littered with the whitening bones of its exiles. Tall palms and minarets marrying in the sky. A hive of white mansions flanking those narrow and abandoned streets of mud which were racked all night by Arab music and the cries of girls who so easily disposed of their body's wearisome baggage (which galled them) and offered to the night the passionate kisses which money could not disflavour. The sadness and beatitude of this human conjunction which perpetuated itself to eternity, an endless cycle of rebirth and annihilation which alone could teach and reform by its destructive power. ("One makes love only to confirm one's loneliness" said Pursewarden, and at another time Justine added like a coda "A woman's best love letters are always written to the man she is betraying" as she turned an immemorial head on a high balcony, hanging above a lighted city where the leaves of the trees seemed painted by the electric signs, where the pigeons tumbled as if from shelves. . . .) A great honeycomb of faces and gestures.

"We become what we dream" said Balthazar, still hunting among these grey paving stones for the key to a watch which is Time. "We achieve in reality, in substance, only the pictures of the imagination." The city makes no answer to such propositions. Unheeding it coils about the sleeping lives like some great anaconda digesting a meal. Among those shining coils the pitiable human world went its way, unaware and unbelieving, repeating to infinity its gestures of despair, repentance, and love. Demonax the philosopher said: "Nobody wishes to be evil" and was called a cynic for his pains. And Pursewarden in another age, in another tongue replied: "Even to be half-awake among sleep-walkers is frightening at first. Later one learns to dissimulate!"

I could feel the ambience of the city on me once more, its etiolated beauties spreading their tentacles out to grasp at my sleeve. I felt more summers coming, summers with fresh despairs, fresh onslaughts of the "bayonets of time". My life would rot away afresh in stifling offices to the tepid whirl of electric fans, by the light of dusty unshaded bulbs hanging from the cracked ceilings of renovated tenements. At the Café Al Aktar, seated before a green *menthe*, listening to the sulky bubbles in the *narguilehs* I would have time to catechise the silences which followed the cries of the hawkers and the clatter of backgammon-boards. Still the same phantoms would pass and repass in the Nebi Daniel, the gleaming limousines of the bankers would bear their choice freight of painted ladies to distant bridge-tables, to the synagogue, the fortune-teller, the smart café. Once all this had power to wound. And now? Snatches of a quartet squirted from a café with scarlet awnings reminded me of Clea once saying: "Music was invented to confirm human loneliness." But if I walked here with attention and even a certain tenderness it was because for me the city was something which I myself had deflowered, at whose hands I had learned to ascribe some particular meaning to fortune. These patched and faded walls, the lime wash cracking into a million oyster-coloured patches, only imitated the skins of the lepers who whined here on the edge of the Arab quarter; it was simply the hide of the place itself, peeling and caking away under the sun.

Even the war had come to terms with the city, had indeed stimulated its trade with its bands of aimless soldiers walking about with that grim air of unflinching desperation with which Anglo-Saxons embark upon their pleasures; their own demagnetised women were all in uniform now which gave them a ravenous air—as if they could drink the blood of the innocents while it was still warm. The brothels had over-flowed and gloriously engulfed a whole quarter of the town around the old square. If anything the war had brought an air of tipsy carnival rather than anything else; even the nightly bombardments of the harbour were brushed aside by day, shrugged away like nightmares, hardly remembered as more than an inconvenience. For the rest, nothing had fundamentally changed. The brokers still sat on the steps of the Mohammed Ali club sipping their newspapers. The old horse-drawn gharries still clopped about upon their listless errands. The crowds still thronged the white Corniche to take the frail spring sunlight. Balconies crowded with wet linen and tittering girls. The Alexandrians still moved inside the murex-tinted cyclorama of the life they imagined. ("Life is more complicated

E   65

than we think, yet far simpler than anyone dares to imagine.'')
Voices of girls, stabbing of Arab quarter-tones, and from the
synagogue a metallic drone punctuated by the jingle of a sis-
trum. On the floor of the Bourse they were screaming like one
huge animal in pain. The money-changers were arranging their
currencies like sweets upon the big squared boards. Pashas in
scarlet flower-pots reclining in immense cars like gleaming
sarcophagi. A dwarf playing a mandolin. An immense eunuch
with a carbuncle the size of a brooch eating pastry. A legless
man propped on a trolley, dribbling. In all this furious
acceleration of the mind I thought suddenly of Clea—her thick
eyelashes fragmenting every glance of the magnificent eyes—
and wondered vaguely when she would appear. But in the
meantime my straying footsteps had led me back to the narrow
opening of the Rue Lepsius, to the worm-eaten room with the
cane chair which creaked all night, and where once the old
poet of the city had recited 'The Barbarians'. I felt the stairs
creak again under my tread. On the door was a notice in
Arabic which said 'Silence'. The latch was hooked back.

Balthazar's voice sounded strangely thin and far away as he
bade me to enter. The shutters were drawn and the room was
shrouded in half-darkness. He was lying in bed. I saw with a
considerable shock that his hair was quite white which made
him look like an ancient version of himself. It took me a
moment or two to realise that it was not dyed. But how he had
changed! One cannot exclaim to a friend: "My God, how
much you have aged!" Yet this is what I almost did, quite
involuntarily.

"Darley!" he said feebly, and held up in welcome hands
swollen to the size of boxing-gloves by the bandages which
swathed them.

"What on earth have you been doing to yourself?"

He drew a long sad sigh of vexation and nodded towards a
chair. The room was in great disorder. A mountain of books
and papers on the floor by the window. An unemptied chamber-

66

pot. A chessboard with the pieces all lying in confusion. A newspaper. A cheese-roll on a plate with an apple. The wash-basin full of dirty plates. Beside him in a glass of some cloudy fluid stood a glittering pair of false teeth on which his feverish eye dwelt from time to time with confused perplexity. "You have heard nothing? That surprises me. Bad news, news of a scandal, travels so fast and so far I should have thought that by now you had heard. It is a long story. Shall I tell you and provoke the look of tactful commiseration with which Mount-olive sits down to play chess with me every afternoon?"

"But your hands. . . ."

"I shall come to those in due course. It was a little idea I got from your manuscript. But the real culprits are these, I think, these false teeth in the glass. Don't they glitter bewitchingly? I am sure it was the teeth which set me off. When I found that I was about to lose my teeth I suddenly began to behave like a woman at the change of life. How else can I explain falling in love like a youth?" He cauterised the question with a dazed laugh.

"First the Cabal—which is now disbanded; it went the way of all words. Mystagogues arose, theologians, all the resource-ful bigotry that heaps up around a sect and spells dogma! But the thing had to me a special meaning, a mistaken and un-conscious meaning, but nevertheless a clear one. I thought that slowly, by degrees, I should be released from the bondage of my appetites, of the flesh. I should at last, I felt, find a philo-sophic calm and balance which would expunge the passional nature, sterilise my actions. I thought of course that I had no such *préjugés* at the time; that my quest for truth was quite pure. But unconsciously I was using the Cabal to this precise end—instead of letting it use me. First miscalculation! Pass me some water from the pitcher over there." He drank thirstily through his new pink gums. "Now comes the absurdity. I found I must lose my teeth. This caused the most frightful up-heaval. It seemed to me like a death-sentence, like a confirma-

67

tion of growing old, of getting beyond the reach of life itself. I have always been fastidious about mouths, always hated rank breath and coated tongues; but most of all false teeth! Unconsciously, then, I must have somehow pushed myself to this ridiculous thing—as if it were a last desperate fling before old age settled over me. Don't laugh. *I fell in love* in a way that I have never done before, at least not since I was eighteen. 'Kisses sharp as quills' says the proverb; or as Pursewarden might say 'Once more the cunning gonads on the prowl, the dragnet of the seed, the old biological terror'. But my dear Darley, this was no joke. I still had my own teeth! But the object of my choice, a Greek actor, was the most disastrous that anyone could hit upon. To look like a god, to have a charm like a shower of silver arrows—and yet to be simply a small-spirited, dirty, venal and empty personage: that was Panagiotis! I knew it. It seemed to make no difference whatsoever. I cursed myself in the mirror. But I was powerless to behave otherwise. And, in truth, all this might have passed off as so much else had he not pushed me to outrageous jealousies, terrific scenes of recrimination. I remember that old Pursewarden used to say: 'Ah! you Jews, you have the knack of suffering' and I used to reply with a quotation from Mommsen about the bloody Celts: 'They have shaken all states and founded none. They nowhere created a great state or developed a distinctive culture of their own.' No, this was not simply an expression of minority-fever: this was the sort of murderous passion of which one has read, and for which our city is famous! Within a matter of months I became a hopeless drunkard. I was always found hanging about the brothels. I obtained drugs under prescription for him to sell. Anything, lest he should leave me. I became as weak as a woman. A terrific scandal, rather a series of them, made my practice dwindle until it is now non-existent. Amaril is keeping the clinic going out of kindness until I can pick myself off the floor. I was dragged across the floor of the club, holding on to his coat and imploring him not to leave me! I was knocked down in Rue Fuad, thrashed with a cane outside the French Consulate. I found myself surrounded by long-faced and concerned friends who did everything they could to avert disaster. Useless. I had become quite impossible! All this went on, this ferocious life—and really I enjoyed being debased in a queer way, being whipped and scorned, reduced to a wreck! It was as if I wanted to swallow the world, to drain the sore of love until it healed. I was pushed to the very extremity of myself, yet I myself was doing the pushing: or was it the teeth?" He cast a sulky furious look in their direction and sighed, moving his head about as if with inner anguish at the memory of these misdeeds.

"Then of course it came to an end, as everything does, even presumably life! There is no merit in suffering as I did, dumbly like a pack animal, galled by intolerable sores it cannot reach with its tongue. It was then that I remembered a remark in your manuscript about the ugliness of my hands. Why did I not cut them off and throw them in the sea as you had so thoughtfully recommended? This was the question that arose in my mind. At the time I was so numb with drugs and drink that I did not imagine I would feel anything. However I made an attempt, but it is harder than you imagine, all that gristle! I was like those fools who cut their throats and come bang up against the oesophagus. They always live. But when I desisted with pain I thought of another writer, Petronius. (The part that literature plays in our lives!) I lay down in a hot bath. But the blood wouldn't run, or perhaps I had no more. The colour of bitumen it seemed, the few coarse drops I persuaded to trickle. I was about to try other ways of alleviating the pain when Amaril appeared at his most abusive and brought me to my senses by giving me a deep sedation of some twenty hours during which he tidied up my corpse as well as my room. Then I was very ill, with shame I believe. Yes, it was chiefly shame, though of course I was much weakened by the absurd excesses to which I had been pushed. I submitted to Pierre Balbz who removed the teeth and provided me with this set of glittering snappers—*art nouveau*! Amaril tried in his clumsy way to analyse me—but what is one to say of this very approximate science which has carelessly overflowed into anthropology on one side, theology on the other? There is much they do not know as yet: for instance that one kneels in church because one kneels to enter a woman, or that circumcision is derived from the clipping of the vine, without which it will run to leaf and produce no fruit! I had no philosophic system on which to lean as even Da Capo did. Do you remember Capodistria's exposition of the nature of the universe? 'The world is a biological phenomenon which will only come to an end when every single man has had all the women, every woman all the men. Clearly this will take some time. Meanwhile there is nothing to do but to help forward the forces of nature by treading the grapes as hard as we can. As for an afterlife—what will it consist of but satiety? The play of shadows in Paradise—pretty *hanoums* flitting across the screens of memory, no longer desired, no longer desiring to be desired. Both at rest at last. But clearly it cannot be done all at once. Patience! *Avanti!*' Yes, I did a lot of slow and careful thinking as I lay here, listening to the creak of the cane chair and the noises from the street. My friends were very good and often visited me with gifts and conversations that left me headaches. So I gradually began to swim up to the surface again, with infinite slowness. I said to myself 'Life is the master. We have been living against the grain of our intellects. The real teacher is endurance.' I had learned something, but at what a cost!

"If only I had had the courage to tackle my love whole-heartedly I would have served the ideas of the Cabal better. A paradox, you think? Perhaps. Instead of letting my love poison my intellect and my intellectual reservations my love. Yet though I am rehabilitated, and ready once more to enter the world, everything in nature seems to have disappeared! I still awake crying out: 'He has gone away forever. True lovers exist for the sake of love.' "

He gave a croaky sob and crawled out from between the sheets, looking ridiculous in his long woollen combinations, to hunt for a handkerchief in the chest of drawers. To the mirror he said: "The most tender, the most tragic of illusions is perhaps to believe that our actions can add or subtract from the total quantity of good and evil in the world." Then he shook his head gloomily and returned to his bed, settling the pillows at his back and adding: "And that fat brute Father Paul talks of acceptance! Acceptance of the world can only come from a full recognition of its measureless extents of good and evil; and to really inhabit it, explore it to the full uninhibited extent of this finite human understanding—that is all that is necessary in order to accept it. But what a task! One lies here with time passing and wonders about it. Every sort of time trickling through the hour-glass, 'time immemorial' and 'for the time being' and 'time out of mind'; the time of the poet, the philosopher, the pregnant woman, the calendar. . . . Even 'time is money' comes into the picture; and then, if you think that money is excrement for the Freudian, you understand that time must be also! Darley you have come at the right moment, for I am to be rehabilitated tomorrow by my friends. It was a touching thought which Clea first had. The shame of having to put in a public appearance again after all my misdeeds has been weighing on me very heavily. How to face the city again—that is the problem. It is only in moments like this that you realise who your friends are. Tomorrow a little group is coming here to find me dressed, my hands less conspicuously bandaged, my new teeth in place. I shall of course wear dark glasses. Mountolive, Amaril, Pombal and Clea, two on each arm. We will walk the whole length of Rue Fuad thus and take a lengthy public coffee on the pavement outside Pastroudi. Mountolive has booked the largest lunch table at the Mohammed Ali and proposes to offer me a lunch of twenty people to celebrate my resurrection from the dead. It is a wonderful gesture of solidarity, and will certainly quell spiteful tongues and sneers. In the evening the Cervonis have asked me to dinner. With such lucky help I feel I may be able in the long run to repair my damaged confidence and that of my old patients. Is it not fine of them—and in the traditions of the city? I may live to smile again, if not to love—a fixed and glittering smile which only Pierre will gaze at with affection—the affection of the artificer for his handiwork." He raised his white boxing-gloves like a champion entering the ring and grimly saluted an imaginary crowd. Then he flopped back on his pillows once more and gazed at me with an air of benign sorrow.

"Where has Clea gone?" I asked.

"Nowhere. She was here yesterday afternoon asking for you."

"Nessim said she had gone somewhere."

"Perhaps to Cairo for the afternoon; where have you been?"

"Out to Karm for the night."

There was a long silence during which we eyed each other. There were clearly questions in his mind which he tactfully did not wish to inflict on me; and for my part there was little that I felt I could explain. I picked up an apple and took a bite from it.

"And the writing?" he said after a long silence.

"It has stopped. I don't seem to be able to carry it any further for the moment. I somehow can't match the truth to the illusions which are necessary to art without the gap showing—you know, like an unbasted seam. I was thinking of it at Karm, confronted again by Justine. Thinking how despite the factual falsities of the manuscript which I sent you the portrait was somehow poetically true—psychographically if you like. But an artist who can't solder the elements together falls short somewhere. I'm on the wrong track."

"I don't see why. In fact this very discovery should encourage rather than hamper you. I mean about the mutability of all truth. Each fact can have a thousand motivations, all equally

72

valid, and each fact a thousand faces. So many truths which have little to do with fact! Your duty is to hunt them down. At each moment of time all multiplicity waits at your elbow. Why, Darley, this should thrill you and give your writing the curves of a pregnant woman.''

"On the contrary, it has faulted me. For the moment anyway. And now that I am back here in the real Alexandria from which I drew so many of my illustrations I don't feel the need for more writing—or at any rate writing which doesn't fulfil the difficult criteria I see lurking behind art. You remember Pursewarden writing: 'A novel should be an act of divination by entrails, not a careful record of a game of pat-ball on some vicarage lawn!' ''

"Yes."

"And so indeed it should. But now I am confronted once more with my models I am ashamed to have botched them up. If I start again it will be from another angle. But there is still so much I don't know, and presumably never will, about all of you. Capodistria, for example, where does he fit in?"

"You sound as if you knew he was alive!"

"Mnemjian told me so."

"Yes. The mystery isn't a very complicated one. He was working for Nessim and compromised himself by a serious slip. It was necessary to clear out. Conveniently it happened at a time when he was all but bankrupt financially. The insurance money was most necessary! Nessim provided the setting and I provided the corpse. You know we get quite a lot of corpses of one sort or another. Paupers. People who donate their bodies, or actually sell them in advance for a fixed sum. The medical schools need them. It wasn't hard to obtain a private one, relatively fresh. I tried to hint at the truth to you once but you did not take my meaning. Anyway the thing's worked smoothly. Da Capo now lives in a handsomely converted Martello tower, dividing his time between studying black magic and working on certain schemes of Nessim's about which I

73

know nothing. Indeed I see Nessim only rarely, and Justine not at all. Though guests are permitted by special police order they never invite anyone out to Karm. Justine telephones people from time to time for a chat, that is all. You have been privileged, Darley. They must have got you a permit. But I am relieved to see you cheerful and undesponding. You have made a step forward somewhere, haven't you?"

"I don't know. I worry less."

"But you will be happy this time, I feel it; much has changed but much has remained the same. Mountolive tells me he has recommended you for a censorship post, and that you will probably live with Pombal, until you have had a chance to look round a bit."

"Another mystery! I hardly know Mountolive. Why has he suddenly constituted himself my benefactor?"

"I don't know, possibly because of Liza."

"Pursewarden's sister?"

"They are up at the summer legation for a few weeks. I gather you will be hearing from him, from them both."

There was a tap at the door and a servant entered to tidy the flat; Balthazar propped himself up and issued his orders. I stood up to take my leave.

"There is only one problem" he said "which occupies me. Shall I leave my hair as it is? I look about two hundred and seventy when it isn't dyed. But I think on the whole it would be better to leave it to symbolise my return from the dead with a vanity chastened by experience, eh? Yes, I shall leave it. I think I shall definitely leave it."

"Toss a coin."

"Perhaps I will. This evening I must get up for a couple of hours and practise walking about; extraordinary how weak one feels simply from lack of practice. After a fortnight in bed one loses the power of one's legs. And I mustn't fall down to-morrow or people will think I am drunk again and that would never do. As for you, you must find Clea."

74

"I'll go round to the studio and see if she is working."

"I'm glad you are back."

"In a strange way so am I."

And in the desultory brilliant life of the open street it was hard not to feel like an ancient inhabitant of the city, returning from the other side of the grave to visit it. Where would I find Clea?

o   o   o   o   o

V

She was not at the flat, though her letter-box was empty, which suggested that she had already collected her mail and gone out to read it over a *café crème*, as had been her wont in the past. There was nobody at the studio either. It fitted in with my mood to try and track her down in one of the familiar cafés and so I dutifully walked down Rue Fuad at a leisurely pace towards Baudrot, the Café Zoltan and the Coquin. But there was no sign of her. There was one elderly waiter at the Coquin who remembered me however, and he had seen her walking down Rue Fuad earlier in the morning with a portfolio. I continued my circuit, peering into the shop-windows, examining the stalls of second-hand books, until I reached the Select on the seafront. But she was not there. I turned back to the flat and found a note from her saying that she would not be able to make contact before the later afternoon, but that she would call there for me; it was annoying, for it meant that I should have to pass the greater part of the day alone, yet it was also useful, for it enabled me to visit Mnemjian's redecorated emporium and indulge in a post-Pharaonic haircut and shave. ("The natron-bath" Pursewarden used to call it.) It also gave me time to unpack my belongings.

But we met by chance, not design. I had gone out to buy some stationery, and had taken a short cut through the little square called Bab El Fedan. My heart heeled half-seas over for a moment, for she was sitting where once (that first day) Melissa had been sitting, gazing at a coffee cup with a wry reflective air of amusement, with her hands supporting her chin. The exact station in place and time where I had once found Melissa, and with such difficulty mustered enough courage at last to enter the place and speak to her. It gave me a

76

strange sense of unreality to repeat this forgotten action at such a great remove of time, like unlocking a door which had remained closed and bolted for a generation. Yet it was in truth Clea and not Melissa, and her blonde head was bent with an air of childish concentration over her coffee cup. She was in the act of shaking the dregs three times and emptying them into the saucer to study them as they dried into the contours from which fortune-tellers "skry"—a familiar gesture.

"So you haven't changed. Still telling fortunes."

"Darley." She sprang up with a cry of pleasure and we embraced warmly. It was with a queer interior shock, almost like a new recognition, that I felt her warm laughing mouth on mine, her hands upon my shoulders. As though somewhere a window had been smashed, and the fresh air allowed to pour into a long-sealed room. We stood thus embracing and smiling for a long moment. "You startled me! I was just coming on to the flat to find you."

"You've had me chasing my tail all day."

"I had work to do. But Darley, how you've changed! You don't stoop any more. And your spectacles. . . ."

"I broke them by accident ages ago, and then found I didn't really need them."

"I'm delighted for you. Bravo! Tell me, do you notice my wrinkles? I'm getting some I fear. Have I changed very much would you say?"

She was more beautiful than I could remember her to have been, slimmer, and with a subtle range of new gestures and expressions suggesting a new and troubling maturity.

"You've grown a new laugh."

"Have I?"

"Yes. It's deeper and more melodious. But I must not flatter you! A nightingale's laugh—if they do laugh."

"Don't make me self-conscious because I so much want to laugh with you. You'll turn it into a croak."

"Clea, why didn't you come and meet me?"

She wrinkled up her nose for a moment, and putting her hand on my arm, bent her head once more to the coffee grounds which were drying fast into little whorls and curves like sand-dunes. "Light me a cigarette" she said pleadingly.

"Nessim said you turned tail at the last moment."

"Yes, I did, my dear."

"Why?"

"I suddenly felt it might be inopportune. It might have been a complication somehow. You had old accounts to render, old scores to settle, new relationships to explore. I really felt powerless to do anything about you until . . . well, until you had seen Justine. I don't know why. Yes, I do though. I wasn't sure that the cycle would really change, I didn't know how much you had or hadn't changed yourself. You are such a bloody correspondent I hadn't any way of judging about your inside state of mind. Such a long time since you wrote, isn't it? And then the child and all that. After all, people sometimes get stuck like an old disc and can't move out of a groove. That might have been your fate with Justine. So it wasn't for me to intrude, since my side of you. . . . Do you see? I had to give you air."

"And supposing I have stuck like some old disc?"

"No it hasn't turned out like that."

"How can you tell?"

"From your face, Darley. I could tell in a flash!"

"I don't know quite how to explain. . . ."

"You don't *need* to" her voice curved upwards with elation and her bright eyes smiled. "We have such totally different claims upon each other. We are free to *forget*! You men are the strangest creatures. Listen, I have arranged this first day together like a tableau, like a charade. Come first and see the queer immortality one of us has gained. Will you put yourself in my hands? I have been so looking forward to acting as drago-man on . . . but no, I won't tell you. Just let me pay for this coffee."

"What does your fortune say in the grounds?"

"Chance meetings!"

"I think you invent."

The afternoon had been overcast and dusk fell early. Already the sunset violets had begun to tamper with the perspectives of the streets along the seafront. We took an old horse-drawn gharry which was standing forlornly in a taxi rank by Ramleh Station. The ancient jarvey with his badly cicatriced face asked hopefully if we wished for a "carriage of love" or an "ordinary carriage", and Clea, giggling, selected the latter variety of the same carriage as being cheaper. "O son of truth!" she said. "What woman would take a lusty husband in such a thing when she has a good bed at home which costs nothing."

"Merciful is God" said the old man with sublime resignation.

So we set off down the white curving Esplanade with its fluttering awnings, the quiet sea spreading away to the right of us to a blank horizon. In the past we had so often come this way to visit the old pirate in his shabby rooms in Tatwig Street.

"Clea, where the devil are we going?"

"Wait and see."

I could see him so clearly, the old man. I wondered for a moment if his shabby ghost still wandered about those dismal rooms, whistling to the green parrot and reciting: "*Taisez-vous, petit babouin.*" I felt Clea's arm squeeze mine as we sheered off left and entered the smoking ant-heap of the Arab town, the streets choked with smoke from the burning refuse-heaps, or richly spiced with cooking meat and whiffs of baking bread from the bakeries.

"Why on earth are you taking me to Scobie's rooms?" I said again as we started to clip-clop down the length of the familiar street. Her eyes shone with a mischievous delight as putting her lips to my ear she whispered: "Patience. You shall see."

It was the same house all right. We entered the tall gloomy archway as we had so often in the past. In the deepening dusk it looked like some old faded daguerrotype, the little court-yard, and I could see that it had been much enlarged. Several supporting walls of neighbouring tenements had been razed or had fallen down and increased its mean size by about two hundred square feet. It was just a shattered and pock-marked no-man's-land of red earth littered with refuse. In one corner stood a small shrine which I did not remember having re-marked before. It was surrounded by a huge ugly modern grille of steel. It boasted a small white dome and a withered tree, both very much the worse for wear. I recognised in it one of the many *Maquams* with which Egypt is studded, spots made sacred by the death of a hermit or holy man and where the faithful repair to pray or solicit his help by leaving ex-votos. This little shrine looked as so many do, utterly shabby and forlorn, as if its existence had been overlooked and forgotten for centuries. I stood looking around me, and heard Clea's clear voice call: "Ya Abdul!" There was a note in it which suggested suppressed amusement but I could not for the life of me tell why. A man advanced towards us through the shadows peering. "He is almost blind. I doubt if he'll recognise you."

"But who is it?" I said, almost with exasperation at all this mystery. "Scobie's Abdul" she whispered briefly and turned away to say: "Abdul, have you the key of the *Maquam* of El Scob?"

He greeted her in recognition making elaborate passes over his breast, and produced a clutch of tall keys saying in a deep voice: "At once O lady" rattling the keys together as all guardians of shrines must do to scare the djinns which hang about the entrances to holy places.

"Abdul!" I exclaimed with amazement in a whisper. "But he was a youth." It was quite impossible to identify him with this crooked and hunched anatomy with its stooping centenarian's gait and cracked voice. "Come" said Clea hurriedly, "explanations later. Just come and look at the shrine." Still bemused I followed in the guardian's footsteps. After a very thorough rattling and banging to scare the djinns he unlocked the rusty portals and led the way inside. It was suffocatingly hot in that little airless tomb. A single wick somewhere in a recess had been lighted and gave a wan and trembling yellow light. In the centre lay what I presumed must be the tomb of the saint. It was covered with a green cloth with an elaborate design in gold. This Abdul reverently removed for my inspection, revealing an object under it which was so surprising that I uttered an involuntary exclamation. It was a galvanised iron bath-tub on one leg of which was engraved in high relief the words: " 'The Dinky Tub' Crabbe's. Luton." It had been filled with clean sand and its four hideous crocodile-feet heavily painted with the customary anti-djinn blue colour. It was an astonishing object of reverence to stumble upon in such surroundings, and it was with a mixture of amusement and dismay that I heard the now completely unrecognisable Abdul, who was the object's janitor, muttering the conventional prayers in the name of El Scob, touching as he did so the ex-votos which hung down from every corner of the wall like little white tassels. These were, of course, the slips of cloth which women tear from their underclothes and hang up as offerings to a saint who, they believe, will cure sterility and enable them to conceive. The devil! Here was old Scobie's bath-tub apparently being invoked to confer fertility upon the childless—and with success, too, if one could judge by the great number of the offerings.

"El Scob was a holy one?" I said in my halting Arabic.

The tired, crooked bundle of humanity with its head encircled in a tattered shawl nodded and bowed as he croaked: "From far away in Syria he came. Here he found his rest. His name enlightens the just. He was a student of harmlessness!"

I felt as if I were dreaming. I could almost hear Scobie's voice say: "Yes, it's a flourishing little shrine as shrines go. Mind you, I don't make a fortune, but I do give service!" The laughter began to pile up inside me as I felt the trigger of

Clea's fingers on my elbow. We exchanged delighted squeezes as we retired from that fuggy little hole into the dusky court-yard, while Abdul reverently replaced the cloth over the bath-tub, attended to the oil wick, and then joined us. Carefully he locked the iron grille, and accepting a tip from Clea with many hoarse gratitudes, shuffled away into the shadows, leaving us to sit down upon a heap of tumbled masonry.

"I didn't come right in" she said. "I was afraid we'd start laughing and didn't want to risk upsetting Abdul."

"Clea! Scobie's *bath-tub*!"

"I know."

"How the devil did this happen?"

Clea's soft laughter!

"You must tell me."

"It is a wonderful story. Balthazar unearthed it. Scobie is now officially El Yacoub. At least that is how the shrine is registered on the Coptic Church's books. But as you have just heard he is really El Scob! You know how these saints' *Maquams* get forgotten, overlooked. They die, and in time people completely forget who the original saint was; sometimes a sand-dune buries the shrine. But they also spring alive again. Suddenly one day an epileptic is cured there, or a prophecy is given by the shrine to some mad woman—and presto! the saint wakes up, revives. Well, all the time our old pirate was living in this house El Yacoub was there, at the end of the garden, though nobody knew it. He had been bricked in, surrounded by haphazard walls—you know how crazily they build here. He was utterly forgotten. Meanwhile Scobie, after his death, had become a figure of affectionate memory in the neighbourhood. Tales began to circulate about his great gifts. He was clever at magic potions (like Mock Whisky?). A cult began to blossom around him. They said he was a necromancer. Gamblers swore by his name. 'El Scob spit on this card' became quite a proverb in the quarter. They also said that he had been able to change himself into a woman at will (!) and by sleeping with impotent

82

men regenerate their forces. He could also make the barren conceive. Some women even called their children after him. Well, in a little while he had already joined the legendary of Alexandrian saints, but of course he had no actual shrine—because everyone knew with one half of his mind that Father Paul had stolen his body, wrapped it in a flag, and buried it in the Catholic cemetery. They knew because many of them had been there for the service and much enjoyed the dreadful music of the police band of which I believe Scobie had once been a member. I often wonder whether he played any instrument and if so what. A slide trombone? Anyway, it was during this time, while his sainthood was only, so to speak, awaiting a Sign, a Portent, a Confirmation, that that wall obligingly fell down and revealed the (perhaps indignant?) Yacoub. Yes, but there was no tomb in the shrine. Even the Coptic Church which has at last reluctantly taken Yacoub on their books knows nothing of him except that he came from Syria. They are not even sure whether he was a Moslem or not! He sounds distinctly Jewish to me. However they diligently questioned the oldest inhabitants of the quarter and at least established his name. But nothing more. And so one fine day the neighbourhood found that it had an empty shrine free for Scobie. He must have a local habitation to match the power of his name. A spontaneous festival broke out at which his bath-tub which had been responsible for so many deaths (great is Allah!) was solemnly enshrined and consecrated after being carefully filled with holy sand from the Jordan. Officially the Copts could not concede Scob and insisted on sticking to Yacoub for official purposes; but Scob he remained to the faithful. It might have been something of a dilemma, but being magnificent diplomatists, the clergy turned a blind eye to El Scob's reincarnation; they behave *as if* they thought it was really El Yacoub in a local pronunciation. So everyone's face is saved. They have, in fact, even—and here is that marvellous tolerance which exists no-where else on earth—formally registered Scobie's birthday, I

83

suppose because they do not know Yacoub's. Do you know that he is even to have a yearly *mulid* in his honour on St. George's Day? Abdul must have remembered his birthday because Scobie always hung up from each corner of his bed a string of coloured flags-of-all-nations which he borrowed from the newsagent. And he used to get rather drunk, you told me once, and sing sea-chanties and recite 'The Old Red Duster' until the tears flowed!"

"What a marvellous immortality to enjoy."

"How happy the old pirate must be."

"How happy! To be the patron saint of his own *quartier*! O Darley I knew you'd enjoy it. I often come here at this time in the dusk and sit on a stone and laugh inwardly, rejoicing for the old man."

So we sat together for a long time as the shadows grew up around the shrine, quietly laughing and talking as people should at the shrine of a saint! Reviving the memory of the old pirate with the glass eye whose shade still walked about those mouldering rooms on the second floor. Vaguely glimmered the lights of Tatwig Street. They shone, not with their old accustomed brilliance, but darkly—for the whole harbour quarter had been placed under blackout and one sector of it included the famous street. My thoughts were wandering.

"And Abdul" I said suddenly. "What of him?"

"Yes, I promised to tell you; Scobie set him up in a barber's shop, you remember. Well, he was warned for not keeping his razors clean, and for spreading syphilis. He didn't heed the warnings perhaps because he believed that Scobie would never report him officially. But the old man did, with terrible results. Abdul was nearly beaten to death by the police, lost an eye. Amaril spent nearly a year trying to tidy him up. Then he got some wasting disease on top of it and had to abandon his shop. Poor man. But I'm not sure that he isn't the appropriate guardian for the shrine of his master."

"El Scob! Poor Abdul!"

"But now he has taken consolation in religion and does some mild preaching and reciting of the Suras as well as this job. Do you know I believe that he has forgotten the real Scobie. I asked him one evening if he remembered the old gentleman on the upper floor and he looked at me vaguely and muttered something; as if he were reaching far back in his memory for something too remote to grasp. The real Scobie had disappeared just like Yacoub, and El Scob had taken his place."

"I feel rather as one of the Apostles must have—I mean to be in on the birth of a saint, a legend; think, we actually knew the real El Scob! We heard his voice. . . ."

To my delight Clea now began to mimic the old man quite admirably, copying the desultory scattered manner of his conversation to the life; perhaps she was only repeating the words from memory?

"Yes, mind you, on St. George's Day I always get a bit carried away for England's sake as well as my own. Always have a sip or two of the blushful, as Toby would say, even bubbly if it comes my way. But, bless you, I'm no horse-drawn conveyance—always stay on my two pins. It's the cup that cheers and not in . . . in . . . inebriates for me. Another of Toby's expressions. He was full of literary illustrations. As well he might be—for why? *Ber*corse he was never without a book under his arm. In the Navy he was considered quite queer, and several times had rows. 'What yer got there?' they used to shout, and Toby who could be pert at times used to huff up and answer quite spontaneous. 'What d'yer think, Puffy? Why me marriages lines of course.' But it was always some heavy book which made *my* head swim though I love reading. One year it was Stringbag's Plays, a Swedish author as I understand it. Another year it was Goitre's 'Frowst'. Toby said it was a liberal education. My education just wasn't up to his. The school of life, as you might say. But then my mum and dad were killed off early on and we were left, three perishing little orphans. They had destined us for high things, my father had;

85

one for the church, one for the army, one for the navy. Quite shortly after this my two brothers were run over by the Prince Regent's private train near Sidcup. That was the end of *them*. But it was in all the papers and the Prince sent a wreath. But there I was left quite alone. I had to make my own way without influence—otherwise I should have been an Admiral I expect by now. . . ."

The fidelity of her rendering was absolutely impeccable. The little old man stepped straight out of his tomb and began to stalk about in front of us with his lopsided walk, now toying with his telescope on the cake-stand, now opening and shutting his battered Bible, or getting down on one creaking knee to blow up his fire with the tiny pair of bellows. His birthday! I recalled finding him one birthday evening rather the worse for brandy, but dancing around completely naked to music of his own manufacture on a comb and paper.

Recalling this celebration of his Name Day I began, as it were, to mimic him back to Clea, in order to hear once more this thrilling new laugh she had acquired. "O! it's you, Darley! You gave me quite a turn with your knock. Come in, I'm just having a bit of a dance round in my *tou tou* to recall old times. It's my birthday, yes. I always dwell a bit on the past. In my youth I was a proper spark, I don't mind admitting. I was a real dab at the Velouta. Want to watch me? Don't laugh, just *ber*corse I'm *in puris*. Sit on the chair over there and watch. Now, advance, take your partners, shimmy, bow, reverse! It looks easy but it isn't. The smoothness is deceptive. I could do them all once, my boy, Lancers, Caledonians, Circassian Circle. Never seen a *demi-chaine Anglais*, I suppose? Before your time I think. Mind you, I loved dancing, and for years I kept up to date. I got up as far as the Hootchi-Kootchi—have you ever seen that? Yes, the haitch is haspirated as in 'otel. It's got some fetching little movements they call oriental allurements. Undulations, like. You take off one veil after another until all is revealed. The suspense is terrific, but you have to waggle as you

86

glide, see?" Here he took up a posture of quite preposterous oriental allurement and began to revolve slowly, wagging his behind and humming a suitable air which quite faithfully copied the lag and fall of Arab quartertones. Round and round the room he went until he began to feel dizzy and flopped back triumphantly on his bed, chuckling and nodding with self-approval and self-congratulation, and reaching out for a swig of *arak*, the manufacture of which was also among his secrets. He must have found the recipe in the pages of Postlethwaite's Vade Mecum For Travellers in Foreign Lands, a book which he kept under lock and key in his trunk and by which he absolutely swore. It contained, he said, everything that a man in Robinson Crusoe's position ought to know—even how to make fire by rubbing sticks together; it was a mine of marvellous information. ("To achieve Bombay arrack dissolve two scruples of flowers of benjamin in a quart of good rum and it will impart to the spirit the fragrance of arrack.") That was the sort of thing. "Yes" he would add gravely, "old Postlethwaite can't be bettered. There's something in him for every sort of mind and every sort of situation. He's a genius I might say."

Only once had Postlethwaite failed to live up to his reputation, and that was when Toby said that there was a fortune to be made in Spanish Fly if only Scobie could secure a large quantity of it for export. "But the perisher didn't explain what it was or how, and it was the only time Postlethwaite had me beat. D'you know what he says about it, under Cantharides? I found it so mysterious I memorised the passage to repeat to Toby when next he came through. Old Postle says this: 'Cantharides when used internally are diuretic and stimulant; when applied externally they are epispastic and rubefacient.' Now what the devil can he mean, eh? And how does this fit in with Toby's idea of a flourishing trade in the things? Sort of worms, they must be. I asked Abdul but I don't know the Arabic word."

87

Refreshed by the interlude he once more advanced to the mirror to admire his wrinkled old tortoise-frame. A sudden thought cast a gloom over his countenance. He pointed at a portion of his own wrinkled anatomy and said: "And to think that *that* is what old Postlethwaite describes as '*merely* erectile tissue'. Why the *merely*, I always ask myself. Sometimes these medical men are a puzzle in their language. Just a sprig of erectile tissue indeed! And think of all the trouble it causes. Ah me; if you'd seen what I've seen you wouldn't have half the nervous energy I've got today."

And so the saint prolonged his birthday celebrations by putting on pyjamas and indulging in a short song-cycle which included many old favourites and one curious little ditty which he only sang on birthdays. It was called "The Cruel Cruel Skipper" and had a chorus which ended:

> *So he was an old sky plant, tum tum,*
> *So he was an old meat loaf, tum tum,*
> *So he was an old cantankeroo.*

And now, having virtually exhausted his legs by dancing and his singing-voice with song, there remained a few brief conundrums which he enunciated to the ceiling, his arms behind his head.

"Where did King Charles' executioner dine, and what did he order?"

"I don't know."

"Give in?"

"Yes."

"Well he took a chop at the King's Head."

Delighted clucks and chuckles!

"When may a gentleman's property be described as feathers?"

"I don't know."

"Give in?"

"Yes."

"When his estates are all entails (hen-tails, see?)"

The voice gradually fading, the clock running down, the eyes closing, the chuckles trailing away languorously into sleep. And it was thus that the saint slept at last, with his mouth open, upon St. George's Day.

So we walked back, arm in arm, through the shadowy archway, laughing the compassionate laughter which the old man's image deserved—laughter which in a way regilded the ikon, refuelled the lamps about the shrine. Our footfalls hardly echoed on the streets' floor of tamped soil. The partial blackout of the area had cut off the electric light which so brilliantly illuminated it under normal conditions, and had been replaced by the oil lamps which flickered wanly everywhere, so that we walked in a dark forest by glow-worm light which made more than ever mysterious the voices and the activities in the buildings around us. And at the end of the street, where the rickety gharry stood awaiting us, came the stirring cool breath of the night-sea which would gradually infiltrate the town and disperse the heavy breathless damps from the lake. We climbed aboard, the evening settling itself about us cool as the veined leaves of a fig.

"And now I must dine you, Clea, to celebrate the new laughter!"

"No. I haven't finished yet. There is another tableau I want you to see, of a different kind. You see, Darley, I wanted to sort of recompose the city for you so that you could walk back into the painting from another angle and feel quite at home— though that is hardly the word for a city of exiles, is it? Anyhow . . ." And leaning forward (I felt her breath on my cheek) she said to the jarvey, "Take us to the Auberge Bleue!"

"More mysteries."

"No. Tonight the Virtuous Semira makes her first appearance on the public stage. It is rather like a *vernissage* for me— you know, don't you, that Amaril and I are the authors of her lovely nose? It has been a tremendous adventure, these long months; and she has been very patient and brave under the

89

bandages and grafts. Now it's complete. Yesterday they were married. Tonight all Alexandria will be there to see her. We shouldn't absent ourselves, should we? It characterises something which is all too rare in the city and which you, as an earnest student of the matter, will appreciate. *Il s'agit de* Romantic Love with capital letters. My share in it has been a large one so let me be a bit boastful; I have been part duenna, part nurse, part artist, all for the good Amaril's sake. You see, she isn't very clever, Semira, and I have had to spend hours with her sort of preparing her for the world. Also brushing up her reading and writing. In short, trying to educate her a bit. It is curious in a way that Amaril does not regard this huge gap in their different educations as an obstacle. He loves her the more for it. He says: 'I know she is rather simple-minded. That is what makes her so exquisite.'

"This is the purest flower of romantic logic, no? And he has gone about her rehabilitation with immense inventiveness. I should have thought it somewhat dangerous to play at Pygmalion, but only now I begin to understand the power of the image. Do you know, for example, what he has devised for her in the way of a profession, a skill of her own? It shows brilliance. She would be too simple-minded to undertake anything very specialised so he has trained her, with my help, to be a doll's surgeon. His wedding-present to her is a smart little surgery for children's dolls which has already become tremendously fashionable though it won't officially open until they come back from the honeymoon. But this new job Semira has really grasped with both hands. For months we have been cutting up and repairing dolls together in preparation for this! No medical student could have studied harder. 'It is the only way' says Amaril 'to hold a really stupid woman you adore. Give her something of her own to do.' "

So we swayed down the long curving Corniche and back into the lighted area of the city where the blue street-lamps came up one by one to peer into the gharry at us as we talked; and all at once it seemed that past and present had joined again without any divisions in it, and that all my memories and impressions had ordered themselves into one complete pattern whose metaphor was always the shining city of the disinherited —a city now trying softly to spread the sticky prismatic wings of a new-born dragon-fly on the night. Romantic Love! Pursewarden used to call it "The Comic Demon".

The Auberge had not changed at all. It remained a lasting part of the furniture of my dreams, and here (like faces in a dream) were the Alexandrians themselves seated at flower-decked tables while a band softly punctuated their idleness with the Blues. The cries of welcome recalled vanished generosities of the old city. Athena Trasha with the silver crickets in her ears, droning Pierre Balbz who drank opium because it made the "bones blossom", the stately Cervonis and the rash dexterous Martinengo girls, they were all there. All save Nessim and Justine. Even the good Pombal was there in full evening-dress so firmly ironed and starched as to give him the air of a monumental relief executed for the tomb of François Premier. With him was Fosca, warm and dark of colouring, whom I had not met before. They sat with their knuckles touching in a curious stiff rapture. Pombal was perched quite upright, attentive as a rabbit, as he gazed into her eyes—the eyes of this handsome young matron. He looked absurd. ("She calls him 'Georges-Gaston' which for some reason quite delights him" said Clea.)

So we made our slow way from table to table, greeting old friends as we had often done in the past until we came to the little alcove table with its scarlet celluloid reservation card marked in Clea's name, where to my surprise Zoltan the waiter materialised out of nothing to shake my hand with warmth. He was now the resplendent *maître d'hôtel* and was in full fig, his hair cut *en brosse*. It seemed also that he was fully in the secret for he remarked under his breath to Clea that everything had been prepared in complete secrecy, and even went so far as to wink. "I have Anselm outside watching. As soon as he sees Dr. Amaril's car he will signal. Then the music will play —Madame Trasha has asked for the old 'Blue Danube'." He clasped his hands together in ecstasy and swallowed like a toad. "O what a good idea of Athena's. Bravo!" cried Clea. It was indeed a gesture of affection for Amaril was the best Viennese waltzer in Alexandria, and though not a vain man was always absurdly delighted by his own prowess as a dancer. It could not fail to please him.

Neither had we long to wait; anticipation and suspense had hardly had time to become wearying when the band, which had been softly playing with one ear cocked for the sound of a car, so to speak, fell silent. Anselm appeared at the corner of the vestibule waving his napkin. They were coming! The musicians struck out one long quivering arpeggio such as normally brings a tzigane melody to a close, and then, as the beautiful figure of Semira appeared among the palms, they swung softly and gravely into the waltz measure of 'The Blue Danube'. I was suddenly quite touched to see the shy way that Semira hesitated on the threshold of that crowded ballroom; despite the magnificence of her dress and grooming those watching eyes intimidated her, made her lose her self-possession. She hovered with a soft indecision which reminded me of the way a sailing boat hangs pouting when the painter is loosed, the jib shaken out—as if slowly meditating for a long moment before she turns, with an almost audible sigh, to take the wind upon her cheek. But in this moment of charming irresolution Amaril came up behind her and took her arm. He himself looked, I thought, rather white and nervous despite the customary foppishness of his attire. Caught like this, in a moment of almost panic, he looked indeed absurdly young. Then he registered the waltz and stammered something to her with trembling lips, at the same time leading her down gravely among the tables to the edge of the floor where with a slow and perfectly turned movement they began to dance.

With the first full figure of the waltz the confidence poured into them both—one could almost see it happening. They calmed, became still as leaves, and Semira closed her eyes while Amaril recovered his usual gay, self-confident smile. And everywhere the soft clapping welled up around them from every corner of the ballroom. Even the waiters seemed moved and the good Zoltan groped for a handkerchief, for Ameril was much-beloved.

Clea too looked quite shaken with emotion. "O quick, let's have a drink" she said "for I've a huge lump in my throat and if I cry my make-up will run."

The batteries of champagne-bottles opened up from every corner of the ballroom now, and the floor filled with waltzers, the lights changed colour. Now blue now red now green I saw the smiling face of Clea over the edge of her champagne glass turned towards me with an expression of happy mockery. "Do you mind if I get a little tipsy tonight to celebrate her successful nose? I think we can drink to their future without reserve for they will never leave each other; they are drunk with the knightly love one reads about in the Arthurian legends— knight and rescued lady. And pretty soon there will be children all bearing my lovely nose."

"Of that you can't be sure."

"Well, let me believe it."

"Let's dance a while."

And so we joined the thronging dancers in the great circle which blazed with spinning prismatic light hearing the soft drum-beats punctuate our blood, moving to the slow grave rhythms like the great wreaths of coloured seaweed swinging in some under-water lagoon, one with the dancers and with each other.

We did not stay late. As we came out into the cold damp air she shivered and half-fell against me, catching my arm.

"What is it?"

"I felt faint all of a sudden. It's passed."

So back into the city along the windless seafront, drugged by the clop of the horse's hooves on the macadam, the jingle of harness, the smell of straw, and the dying strains of music which flowed out of the ballroom and dwindled away among the stars. We paid off the cab at the Cecil and walked up the winding deserted street towards her flat arm-in-arm, hearing our own slow steps magnified by the silence. In a bookshop window there were a few novels, one by Pursewarden. We stopped for a moment to peer into the darkened shop and then resumed our leisurely way to the flat. "You'll come in for a moment?" she said.

Here, too, the air of celebration was apparent, in the flowers and the small supper-table on which stood a champagne-bucket. "I did not know we'd stay to dine at the Auberge, and prepared to feed you here if necessary" said Clea, dipping her fingers in the ice-water; she sighed with relief. "At least we can have a night-cap together."

Here at least there was nothing to disorient or disfigure memory, for everything was exactly as I remembered it; I had stepped back into this beloved room as one might step into some favourite painting. Here it all was, the crowded book-shelves, heavy drawing-boards, small cottage piano, and the corner with the tennis racquet and fencing foils; on the writing desk, with its disorderly jumble of letters, drawings and bills, stood the candlesticks which she was now in the act of lighting. A bundle of paintings stood against the wall. I turned one or two round and stared at them curiously.

"My God! You've gone abstract, Clea."

"I know! Balthazar hates them. It's just a phase I expect, so don't regard it as irrevocable or final. It's a different way of mobilising one's feelings about paint. Do you loathe them?"

"No, they are stronger I think."

"Hum. Candle-light flatters them with false chiaroscuro."

"Perhaps."

"Come, sit down; I've poured us a drink."

As if by common consent we sat facing each other on the carpet as we had so often done in the past, cross-legged like "Armenian tailors", as she had once remarked. We toasted each other in the rosy light of the scarlet candles which stood unwinking in the still air defining with their ghostly radiance the smiling mouth and candid features of Clea. Here, too, at last, on this memorable spot on the faded carpet, we embraced each other with—how to say it?—a momentous smiling calm, as if the cup of language had silently overflowed into these eloquent kisses which replaced words like the rewards of silence itself, perfecting thought and gesture. They were like soft cloud-formations which had distilled themselves out of a novel innocence, the veritable ache of desirelessness. My steps had led me back again, I realised, remembering the night so long ago when we had slept dreamlessly in each other's arms, to the locked door which had once refused me admission to her. Led me back once more to that point in time, that threshold, behind which the shade of Clea moved, smiling and irresponsible as a flower, after a huge arid detour in a desert of my own imaginings. I had not known then how to find the key to that door. Now of its own accord it was slowly opening. Whereas the other door which had once given me access to Justine had now locked irrevocably. Did not Pursewarden say something once about "sliding-panels"? But he was talking of books, not of the human heart. In her face now there was neither guile nor premeditation mirrored, but only a sort of magnificent mischief which had captured the fine eyes, expressed itself in the firm and thoughtful way she drew my hands up inside her sleeves to offer herself to their embrace with the uxorious gesture of a woman offering her body to some priceless cloak. Or else to catch my hand, place it upon her heart and whisper "Feel! It has stopped beating!" So we lingered, so we might have stayed, like rapt figures in some forgotten painting, unhurriedly savouring the happiness given to those who set out to enjoy each other without reservations or self-contempts, without the premeditated costumes of selfishness—the invented limitations of human love: but that suddenly the dark air of the night outside grew darker, swelled up with the ghastly tumescence of a sound which, like the frantic wing-beats of some prehistoric bird, swallowed the whole room, the candles, the figures. She shivered at the first terrible howl of the sirens but did not move; and all around us the city stirred to life like an ants' nest. Those streets which had been so dark and silent now began to echo with the sound of feet as people made their way to the air-raid shelters, rustling like a gust of dry autumn leaves whirled by the wind. Snatches of sleepy conversation, screams, laughter, rose to the silent window of the little room. The street had filled as suddenly as a dry river-bed when the spring rains fall.

"Clea, you should shelter."

But she only pressed closer, shaking her head like someone drugged with sleep, or perhaps by the soft explosion of kisses which burst like bubbles of oxygen in the patient blood. I shook her softly, and she whispered: "I am too fastidious to die with a lot of people in a shelter like an old rats' nest. Let us go to bed together and ignore the loutish reality of the world."

So it was that love-making itself became a kind of challenge to the whirlwind outside which beat and pounded like a thunder-storm of guns and sirens, igniting the pale skies of the city with the magnificence of its lightning-flashes. And kisses themselves became charged with the deliberate affirmation which can come only from the foreknowledge and presence of death. It would have been good to die at any moment then, for love and death had somewhere joined hands. It was an expression of her pride, too, to sleep there in the crook of my arm like a wild bird exhausted by its struggles with a limed twig, for all the world as if it were an ordinary summer night of peace. And lying awake at her side, listening to the infernal racket of gunfire and watching the stabbing and jumping of light behind the blinds I remembered how once in the remote past she had reminded me of the limitations which love illuminated in us: saying something about its capacity being limited to an iron ration for each soul and adding gravely: "The love you feel for Melissa, the same love, is trying to work itself out through Justine." Would I, by extension, find this to be true also of Clea? I did not like to think so—for these fresh and spontaneous embraces were as pristine as invention, and not like ill-drawn copies of past actions. They were the very improvisations of the heart itself—or so I told myself as I lay there trying so hard to recapture the elements of the feelings I had once woven around those other faces. Yes, improvisations upon reality itself, and for once devoid of the bitter impulses of the will. We had sailed into this calm water completely without premeditation, all canvas crowded on; and for the first time it felt natural to be where I was, drifting into sleep with her calm body lying beside me. Even the long rolling cannonades which shook the houses so, even the hail of shards which swept the streets, could not disturb the dreaming silence we harvested together. And when we awoke to find everything silent once more she lit a single candle and we lay by its flickering light, looking at each other, and talking in whispers.

"I am always so bad the first time, why is it?"

"So am I."

"Are you afraid of me?"

"No. Nor of myself."

"Did you ever imagine this?"

"We must both have done. Otherwise it would not have happened."

"Hush! Listen."

Rain was now falling in sheets as it so often did before dawn in Alexandria, chilling the air, washing down the stiffly clicking leaves of the palms in the Municipal Gardens, washing the iron grilles of the banks and the pavements. In the Arab town the earthen streets would be smelling like a freshly dug graveyard.

The flower-sellers would be putting out their stocks to catch the freshness. I remembered their cry of "Carnations, sweet as the breath of a girl!" From the harbour the smells of tar, fish and briny nets flowing up along the deserted streets to meet the scentless pools of desert air which would later, with the first sunlight, enter the town from the east and dry its damp façades. Somewhere, briefly, the hushing of the rain was pricked by the sleepy pang of a mandoline, inscribing on it a thoughtful and melancholy little air. I feared the intrusion of a single thought or idea which, inserting itself between these moments of smiling peace, might inhibit them, turn them to instruments of sadness. I thought too of the long journey we made from this very bed, since last we lay here together, through so many climates and countries, only to return once more to our starting-point again, captured once more by the gravitational field of the city. A new cycle which was opening upon the promise of such kisses and dazed endearments as we could now exchange—where would it carry us? I thought of some words of Arnauti, written about another woman, in another context: "You tell yourself that it is a woman you hold in your arms, but watching the sleeper you see all her growth in time, the unerring unfolding of cells which group and dispose themselves into the beloved face which remains always and for ever mysterious—repeating to infinity the soft boss of the human nose, an ear borrowed from a sea-shell's helix, an eyebrow thought-patterned from ferns, or lips invented by bivalves in their dreaming union. All this process is human, bears a name which pierces your heart, and offers the mad dream of an eternity which time disproves in every drawn breath. And if human personality is an illusion? And if, as biology tells us, every single cell in our bodies is replaced every seven years by another? At the most I hold in my arms something like a fountain of flesh, continuously playing, and in my mind a rainbow of dust." And like an echo from another point of the compass I heard the sharp voice of Pursewarden saying: "There is no

Other; there is only oneself facing forever the problem of one's self discovery!"

I had drifted into sleep again; and when I woke with a start the bed was empty and the candle had guttered away and gone out. She was standing at the drawn curtains to watch the dawn break over the tumbled roofs of the Arab town, naked and slender as an Easter lily. In that spring sunrise, with its dense dew, sketched upon the silence which engulfs a whole city before the birds awaken it, I caught the sweet voice of the blind *muezzin* from the mosque reciting the *Ebed*—a voice hanging like a hair in the palm-cooled upper airs of Alexandria. "I praise the perfection of God, the Forever existing; the perfection of God, the desired, the Existing, the Single, the Supreme; the Perfection of God, the One, the Sole". . . . The great prayer wound itself in shining coils across the city as I watched the grave and passionate intensity of her turned head where she stood to observe the climbing sun touch the minarets and palms with light: rapt and awake. And listening I smelt the warm odour of her hair upon the pillow beside me. The buoyancy of a new freedom possessed me like a draught from what the Cabal once called "The Fountain of All Existing Things". I called "Clea" softly, but she did not heed me; and so once more I slept. I knew that Clea would share everything with me, withholding nothing—not even the look of complicity which women reserve only for their mirrors.

o   o   o   o   o

BOOK II

I

So the city claimed me once more—the same city made now somehow less poignant and less terrifying than it had been in the past by new displacements in time. If some parts of the old fabric had worn away, others had been restored. In the first few weeks of my new employment I had time to experience both a sense of familiarity and one of alienation, measuring stability against change, past against present tense. And if the society of my friends remained relatively the same, new influences had entered, new winds had sprung up; we had all begun, like those figures on revolving turntables in jewellers' shops, to turn new facets of ourselves towards each other. Circumstances also helped to provide a new counterpoint, for the old, apparently unchanged city had now entered the penumbra of a war. For my part I had come to see it as it must always have been—a shabby little seaport built upon a sand-reef, a moribund and spiritless backwater. True this unknown factor "war" had given it a specious sort of modern value, but this belonged to the invisible world of strategies and armies, not to ourselves, the inhabitants; it had swollen its population by many thousands of refugees in uniform and attracted those long nights of dull torment which were only relatively dangerous, for as yet the enemy was confining his operations strictly to the harbour area. Only a small area of the Arab quarter came under direct fire; the upper town remained relatively untouched, except perhaps for an occasional error of judgement. No, it was only the harbour at which the enemy scratched and scratched, like a dog at an inflamed scab. A mile away from it the bankers conducted their affairs by day as if from the immunity of New York. Intrusions into their world were rare and accidental. It came as a painful surprise to confront a shop-front which had been blasted in, or a lodging-house blown inside out with all its inhabitants' clothes hanging in festoons from the neighbouring trees. This was not part of the normal expectation of things; it had the shocking rarity value merely of some terrible street accident.

How had things changed? It was not danger, then, but a less easily analysable quality which made the notion of war distinctive; a sensation of some change in the specific gravity of things. It was as if the oxygen content of the air we breathed were being steadily, invisibly reduced day by day; and side by side with this sense of inexplicable blood-poisoning came other pressures of a purely material kind brought about by the huge shifting population of soldiers in whom the blossoming of death released the passions and profligacies which lie buried in every herd. Their furious gaiety tried hard to match the gravity of the crisis in which they were involved; at times the town was racked by the frenetic outbursts of their disguised spleen and boredom until the air became charged with the mad spirit of carnival; a saddening and heroic pleasure-seeking which disturbed and fractured the old harmonies on which personal relationships had rested, straining the links which bound us. I am thinking of Clea, and her loathing for the war and all it stood for. She feared, I think, that the vulgar blood-soaked reality of this war world which spread around her might one day poison and infect our own kisses. "Is it fastidious to want to keep your head, to avoid this curious sexual rush of blood to the head which comes with war, exciting the women beyond endurance? I would not have thought the smell of death could be so exciting to them! Darley, I don't want to be a part of this mental saturnalia, these overflowing brothels. And all these poor men crowded up here. Alexandria has become a huge orphanage, everyone grabbing at the last chance of life. You haven't been long enough yet to feel the strain. The disorientation. The city was always perverse, but it took its pleasures with style at an old-fashioned tempo, even in rented beds: never up against a wall or a tree or a truck! And now at times the town seems to be like some great public urinal. You step over the bodies of drunkards as you walk home at night. I suppose the sunless have been robbed even of sensuality and drink compensates them for the loss! But there is no place in all this for me. I cannot see these soldiers as Pombal does. He gloats on them like a child—as if they were bright lead soldiers—because he sees in them the only hope that France will be freed. I only feel ashamed for them, as one might to see friends in convict garb; out of shame and sympathy I feel like turning my face away. O Darley, it isn't very sensible, and I know I am doing them a grotesque injustice. Possibly it is just selfishness. So I force myself to serve them teas at their various canteens, roll bandages, arrange concerts. But inside myself I shrink smaller every day. Yet I always believed that a love of human beings would flower more strongly out of a common misfortune. It isn't true. And now I am afraid that you too will begin to like me the less for these absurdities of thought, these revulsions of feeling. To be here, just the two of us, sitting by candle-light is almost a miracle in such a world. You can't blame me for trying to hoard and protect it against the intrusive world outside can you? Curiously, what I hate most about it all is the sentimentality which spells violence in the end!"

I understood what she meant, and what she feared; and yet from the depths of my own inner selfishness I was glad of these external pressures, for they circumscribed our world perfectly, penned us up more closely together, isolated us! In the old world I would have had to share Clea with a host of other friends and admirers. Not now.

Curiously, too, some of these external factors around us, involving us in its death-struggles—gave our newest passion a fulfilment not based on desperation yet nevertheless built just as certainly upon the sense of impermanence. It was of the same order, though different in kind to the dull orgiastic rut of the various armies; it was quite impossible to repudiate the truth, namely, that death (not even at hand, but in the air) sharpens kisses, adds unbearable poignance to every smile and handclasp. Even though I was no soldier the dark question mark hovered over our thoughts, for the real issues of the heart were influenced by something of which we were all, however reluctantly, part: a whole world. If the war did not mean a way of dying, it meant a way of ageing, of tasting the true staleness in human things, and of learning to confront change bravely. No-one could tell what lay beyond the closed chapter of every kiss. In those long quiet evenings before the bombardment began we would sit upon that small square of carpet by the light of candles, debating these matters, punctuating our silences with embraces which were the only inadequate answer we could offer to the human situation. Nor, lying in each other's arms during those long nights of fitful sleep broken by the sirens, did we ever (as if by a silent convention) speak of love. To have uttered the word might acknowledge a more rare yet less perfect variety of the state which now bewitched us, perfected this quite unpremeditated relationship. Somewhere in *Moeurs* there is a passionate denunciation of the word. I cannot remember into whose mouth the speech has been put—perhaps Justine's. "It may be defined as a cancerous growth of unknown origin which may take up its site anywhere without the subject knowing or wishing it. How often have you tried to love the 'right' person in vain, even when your heart knows it has found him after so much seeking? No, an eyelash, a perfume, a haunting walk, a strawberry on the neck, the smell of almonds on the breath— these are the accomplices the spirit seeks out to plan your overthrow."

Thinking of such passages of savage insight—and they are many in that strange book—I would turn to the sleeping Clea and study her quiet profile in order to . . . to ingest her, drink the whole of her up without spilling a drop, mingle my very heart-beats with hers. "However near we would wish to be, so far exactly do we remain from each other" wrote Arnauti. It seemed to be no longer true of our condition. Or was I simply deluding myself once more, refracting truth by the disorders inherent in my own vision? Strangely enough I neither knew nor cared now; I had stopped rummaging through my own mind, had learned to take her like a clear draught of spring water.

"Have you been watching me asleep?"

"Yes."

"Unfair! But what thinking?"

"Many things."

"Unfair to watch a sleeping woman, off her guard."

"Your eyes have changed colour again. Smoke."

(A mouth whose paint blurred slightly under kisses. The two small commas, which were almost cusps, almost ready to turn into dimples when the lazy smiles broke surface. She stretches and places her arms behind her head, pushing back the helmet of fair hair which captures the sheen of the candle-light. In the past she had not possessed this authority over her own beauty. New gestures, new tendrils had grown, languorous yet adept to express this new maturity. A limpid sensuality which was now undivided by hesitations, self-questionings. A transformation of the old "silly goose" into this fine, indeed impressive, personage, quite at one with her own body and mind. How had this come about?)

I: "That commonplace book of Pursewarden's. How the devil did you come by it? I took it to the office today."

She: "Liza. I asked her for something to remember him by. Absurd. As if one could forget the brute! He's everywhere. Did the notes startle you?"

I: "Yes. It was as if he had appeared at my elbow. The first thing I fell upon was a description of my new chief, Maskelyne by name. It seems Pursewarden worked with him once. Shall I read it to you?"

She: "I know it."

("Like most of my compatriots he had a large hand-illu-

107

minated sign hanging up on the front of his mind reading
ON NO ACCOUNT DISTURB. At some time in the
distant past he had been wound up and set like a quartz clock.
He will run his course unfaltering as a metronome. Do not let
the pipe alarm you. It is intended to give a judicial air. White
man smoke puff puff, white man ponder puff puff. In fact
white man is deeply deeply asleep under the badges of office,
the pipe, the nose, the freshly starched handkerchief sticking
out of his sleeve.'')

She: "Did you read it to Maskelyne?"

I: "Naturally not."

She: "There are wounding things about all of us in it; perhaps
that is why I took a fancy to it! I could hear the brute's voice
as he uttered them. You know, my dear, I think I am the only
person to have loved old Pursewarden for himself while he was
alive. I got his wavelength. I loved him for himself, I say,
because strictly he *had* no self. Of course he could be tiresome,
difficult, cruel—like everyone else. But he exemplified something—a grasp on something. That is why his work will live
and go on giving off light, so to speak. Light me a cigarette. He
had cut a foothold in the cliff a bit higher than I could dare to
go—the point where one looks at the top because one is afraid
to look down! You tell me that Justine also says something like
this. I suppose she got the same thing in a way—but I suspect
her of being merely grateful to him, like an animal whose
master pulls a thorn from its paw. His intuition was very
feminine and much sharper than hers—and you know that
women instinctively like a man with plenty of female in him;
there, they suspect, is the only sort of lover who can sufficiently
identify himself with them to . . . deliver them of being just
women, catalysts, strops, oil-stones. Most of us have to be
content to play the role of *machine à plaisir!*"

I: "Why do you laugh, suddenly like that?"

"I was remembering making a fool of myself with Pursewarden. I suppose I should feel ashamed of it! You will see

what he says about me in the notebook. He calls me 'a juicy Hanoverian goose, the only truly kallipygous girl in the city'! I cannot think what possessed me, except that I was so worried about my painting. It had dried up on me. I couldn't get any further somehow, canvas gave me a headache. I finally decided that the question of my own blasted virginity was the root cause of the business. You know it is a terrible business to be a virgin—it is like not having one's Matric or Bac. You long to be delivered from it yet . . . at the same time this valuable experience should be with someone whom you care for, otherwise it will be without value to your inside self. Well, there I was, stuck. So with one of those characteristic strokes of fancy which in the past confirmed for everyone my stupidity I decided —guess what? To offer myself grimly to the only artist I knew I could trust, to put me out of my misery. Pursewarden, I thought, might have an understanding of my state and some consideration for my feelings. I'm amused to remember that I dressed myself up in a very heavy tweed costume and flat shoes, and wore dark glasses. I was timid, you see, as well as desperate. I walked up and down the corridor of the hotel outside his room for ages in despair and apprehension, my dark glasses firmly on my nose. He was inside. I could hear him whistling as he always did when he was painting a water colour; a maddening tuneless whistle! At last I burst in on him like a fireman into a burning building, startling him, and said with trembling lips: 'I have come to ask you to *dépuceler* me, please, because I cannot get any further with my work unless you do.' I said it in French. It would have sounded dirty in English. He was startled. All sorts of conflicting emotions flitted across his face for a second. And then, as I burst into tears and sat down suddenly on a chair he threw his head back and roared with laughter. He laughed until the tears ran down his cheeks while I sat there in my dark glasses sniffing. Finally he collapsed exhausted on his bed and lay staring at the ceiling. Then he got up, put his arms on my shoulders, removed my glasses, kissed me, and put them back.

Then he put his hands on his hips and laughed again. 'My dear Clea' he said, 'it would be anyone's dream to take you to bed, and I must confess that in a corner of my mind I have often allowed the thought to wander but . . . dearest angel, you have spoilt everything. *This* is no way to enjoy you, and no way for you to enjoy yourself. Forgive my laughing! You have effectively spoiled my dream. Offering yourself *this* way, without *wanting* me, is such an insult to my male vanity that I simply would not be able to comply with your demand. It is, I suppose, a compliment that you chose me rather than someone else—but my vanity is larger than that! In fact your request is like a pailful of slops emptied over my head! I shall always treasure the compliment and regret the refusal but . . . if only you had chosen some other way to do it, how glad I would have been to oblige! Why did you have to let me see that you really did not care for *me*?'

"He blew his nose gravely in a corner of the sheet, took my glasses and placed them on his own nose to examine himself in the mirror. Then he came and stared at me until the comedy overflowed again and we both started laughing. I felt an awful sense of relief. And when I had repaired my damaged make-up in the mirror he allowed me to take him to dinner to discuss the problem of paint with magnificent, generous honesty. The poor man listened with such patience to my rigmarole! He said: 'I can only tell you what I know, and it isn't much. First you have to know and understand intellectually what you want to do—then you have to sleep-walk a little to reach it. The real obstacle is oneself. I believe that artists are composed of vanity, indolence and self-regard. Work-blocks are caused by the swelling-up of the ego on one or all of these fronts. You get a bit scared about the imaginary importance of what you are doing! Mirror-worship. My solution would be to slap a poultice on the inflamed parts—tell your ego to go to hell and not make a misery of what should be essentially *fun*, *joy*.' He said many other things that evening, but I have forgotten the rest; but the funny thing was that just talking to him, just being talked to, seemed to clear the way ahead again. I started work again, clear as a bell, the next morning. Perhaps in a funny sort of way he did *dépuceler* me? I regretted not being able to reward him as he deserved, but I realised that he was right. I would have to wait for a tide to turn. And this did not happen until later, in Syria. There was something bitter and definitive about it when it came, and I made the usual mistakes one makes from inexperience and paid for them. Shall I tell you?"

I: "Only if you wish."

She: "I found myself suddenly and hopelessly entangled with someone I had admired some years before but never quite imagined in the context of a lover. Chance brought us together for a few short months. I think that neither of us had foreseen this sudden *coup de foudre*. We both caught fire, as if somewhere an invisible burning glass had been playing on us without our being aware. It is curious that an experience so wounding can also be recognised as good, as positively nourishing. I suppose I was even a bit eager to be wounded—or I would not have made the mistakes I did. He was somebody already committed to someone else, so there was never, from the beginning, any pretence of permanence in our liaison. Yet (and here comes my famous stupidity again) I very much wanted to have a child by him. A moment's thought would have shown me that it would have been impossible; but the moment's thought only supervened when I was already pregnant. I did not, I thought, care that he must go away, marry someone else. I would at least have his child! But when I confessed it—at the very moment the words left my lips—I suddenly woke up and realised that this would be to perpetuate a link with him to which I had no right. To put it plainly I should be taking advantage of him, creating a responsibility which would shackle him throughout his marriage. It came to me in a flash, and I swallowed my tongue. By the greatest luck he had not heard my words. He was lying like you are now, half asleep, and had not caught my whisper.

'What did you say?' he said. I substituted another remark, made up on the spur of the moment. A month later he left Syria. It was a sunny day full of the sound of bees. I knew I should have to destroy the child. I bitterly regretted it, but there seemed no other honourable course to take in the matter. You will probably think I was wrong, but even now I am glad I took the course I did, for it would have perpetuated something which had no right to exist outside the span of these few golden months. Apart from that I had nothing to regret. I had been immeasurably grown-up by the experience. I was full of gratitude, and still am. If I am generous now in my love-making it is perhaps because I am paying back the debt, refunding an old love in a new. I entered a clinic and went through with it. Afterwards the kindly old anaesthetist called me to the dirty sink to show me the little pale homunculus with its tiny nails and members. I wept bitterly. It looked like a smashed yolk of an egg. The old man turned it over curiously with a sort of spatula—as one might turn over a rasher of bacon in a frying-pan. I could not match his cold scientific curiosity and felt rather sick. He smiled and said: 'It is all over. How relieved you must feel!' It was true, with my sadness there was a very real relief at having done what I recognised as the right thing. Also a sense of loss; my heart felt like a burgled swallow's nest. And so back to the mountains, to the same easel and white canvas. It is funny but I realised that precisely what wounded me most as a woman nourished me most as an artist. But of course I missed him for a long time: just a physical being whose presence attaches itself without one's knowing, like a piece of cigarette paper to the lip. It hurts to pull it away. Bits of the skin come off! But hurt or not, I learned to bear it and even to cherish it, for it allowed me to come to terms with another illusion. Or rather to see the link between body and spirit in a new way—for the physique is only the outer periphery, the contours of the spirit, its solid part. Through smell, taste, touch we apprehend each other, ignite each other's minds;

information conveyed by the body's odours after orgasm, breath, tongue-taste—through these one 'knows' in quite primeval fashion. Here was a perfectly ordinary man with no exceptional gifts but in his elements, so to speak, how good for me; he gave off the odours of good natural objects: like newly baked bread, roasting coffee, cordite, sandalwood. In this field of *rapport* I missed him like a skipped meal—I know it sounds vulgar! Paracelsus says that thoughts are acts. Of them all, I suppose, the sex act is the most important, the one in which our spirits most divulge themselves. Yet one feels it is a sort of clumsy paraphrase of the poetic, the noetic, *thought* which shapes itself into a kiss or an embrace. Sexual love *is* knowledge, both in etymology and in cold fact; 'he knew her' as the Bible says! Sex is the joint or coupling which unites the male and female ends of knowledge merely—a cloud of unknowing! When a culture goes bad in its sex all knowledge is impeded. We women know that. That was when I wrote to you asking if I should come to visit you in your island. How grateful I am that you did not answer me! It would have been a wrong move at the time. Your silence saved me! Ah! my dear, forgive me if I bore you with my wanderings, for I see that you are looking some-what sleepy! But with you it is such a pleasure to talk away the time between love-making! It is a novelty for me. Apart from you there is only dear Balthazar—whose rehabilitation, by the way, is going on apace. But he has told you? He has been inun-dated with invitations since the Mountolive banquet, and it seems will have little difficulty in rebuilding the clinic practice again."

I: "But he is far from reconciled to his teeth."

She: "I know. And he is still rather shaken and hysterical—as who would not be. But everything goes forward steadily, and I think he will not lapse."

I: "But what of this sister of Pursewarden's?"

She: "Liza! I think you will admire her, though I can't tell if you will like her. She is rather impressive, indeed perhaps just a little bit frightening. The blindness does not seem like an incapacity, rather it gives an expression of double awareness. She listens to one as if one were music, an extra intentness which makes one immediately aware of the banality of most of one's utterances. She's unlike him, yet very beautiful though deathly pale, and her movements are swift and absolutely certain, unlike most blind people. I have never seen her miss a doorhandle or trip on a mat, or pause to get her bearings in a strange place. All the little errors of judgement the blind make, like talking to a chair which has just been vacated by its owner . . . they are absent. One wonders sometimes if she really is blind. She came out here to collect his effects and to gather material about him for a biography."

I: "Balthazar hinted at some sort of mystery."

She: "There is little doubt that David Mountolive is hopelessly in love with her; and from what he told Balthazar it began in London. It is certainly an unusual liaison for someone so correct, and it obviously gives them both a great deal of pain. I often imagine them, the snow falling in London, suddenly finding themselves face to face with the Comic Demon! Poor David! And yet why should I utter such a patronising phrase? Lucky David! Yes, I can tell you a little, based on a scrap of Balthazar's conversation. Suddenly, in a moribund taxi speeding away to the suburbs she turned her face to him and told him that she had been told to expect him many years ago; that the moment she heard his voice she knew that he was the dark princely stranger of the prophecy. He would never leave her. And she only asked leave to verify it, pressing her cold fingers to his face to feel it all over, before sinking back on the cold cushions with a sigh! Yes, it was he. It must have been strange to feel the fingers of the blind girl pressing one's features with a sculptor's touch. David said that a shudder ran through him, all the blood left his face, and his teeth began to chatter! He groaned aloud and clenched them together. So they sat there, hand in hand, trembling while the snowlit suburbs shuttled by

the windows. Later she placed his finger upon the exact configuration in her hand which portended an altered life, and the
emergence of this unexpected figure which would dominate it!
Balthazar is sceptical of such prophecies, as you are, and he
cannot avoid a note of amused irony in recounting the story.
But so far the enchantment seems to have lasted, so perhaps you
will concede something to the power of prophecy, sceptic that
you are! And well: with her brother's death she arrived here,
has been sorting out papers and manuscripts, as well as inter-
viewing people who knew him. She came here once or twice to
talk to me; it wasn't altogether easy for me, though I told her
all that I could remember of him. But I think the question
which really filled her mind was one which she did not actually
utter, namely, had I ever been Pursewarden's mistress? She
circled round and round it warily. I think, no, I am sure that
she thought me a liar because what I had to tell her was so
inconsequent. Indeed perhaps its vagueness suggested that I had
something to conceal. In the studio I still have the plaster
negative of the death-mask which I showed Balthazar how to
make. She held it to her breast for a moment as if to suckle it,
with an expression of intense pain, her blind eyes seeming to
grow larger and larger until they overflowed the whole face, and
turned it into a cave of interrogation. I was horribly embar-
rassed and sad to suddenly notice, sticking in the plaster, a few
little shreds of his moustache. And when she tried to place the
negative together and apply it to her own features I almost
caught her hand lest she feel them. An absurdity! But her
manner startled and upset me. Her questions put me on edge.
There was something shamefully inconclusive about these inter-
views, and I was mentally apologising to Pursewarden all the
time in my mind for not making a better showing; one should,
after all, be able to find something sensible to say of a great
man whom one fully recognised in his lifetime. Not like poor
Amaril who was so furious to see Pursewarden's death-mask
lying near that of Keats and Blake in the National Portrait

Gallery. It was all he could do, he says, to prevent himself from giving the insolent thing a smack with his hand. Instead he abused the object, saying: *'Salaud!'* Why did you not tell me you were a great man passing through my life? I feel defrauded in not noticing your existence, like a child whom someone forgot to tell, and who missed the Lord Mayor riding by in his coach!' I had no such excuse myself, and yet what could I find to say? You see, I think a cardinal factor in all this is that Liza lacks a sense of humour; when I said that in thinking of Pursewarden I found myself instinctively smiling she put on a puzzled frown of interrogation merely. It is possible that they never laughed together, I told myself; yet their only real similarity in the physical sense is in the alignment of teeth and the cut of the mouth. When she is tired she wears the rather insolent expression which, on his face, heralded a witticism! But I expect you too will have to see her, and tell her what you know, what you can remember. It is not easy, facing those blind eyes, to know where to begin! As for Justine, she has luckily been able to escape Liza so far; I suppose the break between Mountolive and Nessim has presented an effective enough excuse. Or perhaps David has convinced her that any contact might be compromising to him officially. I do not know. But I am certain that she has not seen Justine. Perhaps you will have to supply her with a picture, for the only references in Pursewarden's notes are cruel and perfunctory. Have you reached the passages yet in the commonplace book? No. You will. I'm afraid none of us gets off very lightly there! As for any really profound mystery I think Balthazar is wrong. Essentially I think that the problem which engulfs them is simply the effect upon him of her blindness. In fact I am sure from the evidence of my own eyes. Through the old telescope of Nessim . . . yes, the same one! It used to be in the Summer Palace, do you recall? When the Egyptians began to expropriate Nessim all Alexandria got busy to defend its darling. We all bought things from him, intending to hold them for him until everything had blown over. The Cervonis bought the Arab stock, Ganzo the car, which he resold to Pombal, and Pierre Balbz the telescope. As he had nowhere to house it Mountolive let him put it on the verandah of the summer legation, an ideal site. One can sweep the harbour, and most of the town, and in the summer dinner guests can do a little mild star-gazing. Well, I went up there one afternoon and was told that they were both out for a walk, which by the way was a daily custom all winter with them. They would take the car down to the Corniche and walk along the Stanley Bay front arm in arm for half an hour. As I had time to kill I started to fool with the telescope, and idly trained it on the far corner of the bay. It was a blowy day, with high seas running, and the black flags out which signalled dangerous bathing. There were only a few cars about in that end of the town, and hardly anyone on foot. Quite soon I saw the Embassy car come round the corner and stop on the sea-front. Liza and David got down and began to walk away from it towards the beach end. It was amazing how clearly I could see them; I had the impression that I could touch them by just putting out a hand. They were arguing furiously, and she had an expression of grief and pain on her face. I increased the magnification until I discovered with a shock that I could literally lip-read their remarks! It was startling, indeed a little frightening. I could not 'hear' him because his face was half turned aside, but Liza was looking into my telescope like a giant image on a cinema screen. The wind was blowing her dark hair back in a shock from her temples, and with her sightless eyes she looked like some strange Greek statue come to life. She shouted through her tears, 'No, you *could* not have a blind Ambassadress', turning her head from side to side as if trying to find a way of escaping this fearful truth—which I must admit had not occurred to me until the words registered. David had her by the shoulders and was saying something very earnestly, but she wasn't heeding. Then with a sudden twist she broke free and with a single jump cleared the parapet like a stag, to land upon the sand. She began to run towards the sea. David shouted something, and stood for a second gesticulating at the top of the stone steps to the beach. I had such a distinct picture of him then, in that beautifully cut suit of pepper and salt, the flower in his button-hole and the old brown waistcoat he loves with its gun-metal buttons. He looked a strangely ineffectual and petulant figure, his moustache flying in the wind as he stood there. After a second of indecision he too jumped down on to the sand and started after her. She ran very fast right into the water which splashed up, darkening her skirt about her thighs and braking her. Then she halted in sudden indecision and turned back, while he, rushing in after her, caught her by the shoulders and embraced her. They stood for a moment—it was so strange—with the waves thumping their legs; and then he drew her back to the shore with a strange look of gratitude and exultation on his face—as if he were simply delighted by this strange gesture. I watched them hurry back to the car. The anxious chauffeur was standing in the road with his cap in his hand, obviously relieved not to have been called upon to do any life-saving. I thought to myself then: 'A blind Ambassadress? Why not? If David were a meaner-spirited man he might think to himself: "The originality alone would help rather than hinder my career in creating for me artificial sympathies to re-place the respectful admiration which I dare only to claim by virtue of my position!" But he would be too single-minded for any such thoughts to enter his mind.'

"Yet when they arrived back for tea, soaked, he was strangely elated. 'We had a little accident' he called gaily as he retired with her for a change of clothes. And of course there was no further reference to the escapade that evening. Later he asked me if I would undertake a portrait of Liza and I agreed. I do not know quite why I felt a sense of misgiving about it. I could not refuse, yet I have found several ways of delaying the busi-ness and would like to put it off indefinitely if I could. It is curious to feel as I do, for she would be a splendid subject and

118

perhaps if she had several sittings we might get to know each other a little and ease the constraint I feel when I am with her. Besides, I would really like to do it for his sake, for he has always been a good friend. But there it is. . . . I shall be curious to know what she has to ask you about her brother. And curious to see what you will find to say about him."

I: "He seems to change shape so quickly at every turn of the road that one is forced to revise each idea about him almost as soon as it is formulated. I'm beginning to wonder about one's right to pronounce in this fashion on unknown people."

She: "I think, my dear, you have a mania for exactitude and an impatience with partial knowledge which is . . . well, unfair to knowledge itself. How can it be anything but imperfect? I don't suppose reality ever bears a close resemblance to human truth as, say, El Scob to Yacoub. Myself I would like to be content with the poetic symbolism it presents, the shape of nature itself as it were. Perhaps this was what Pursewarden was trying to convey in those outrageous attacks upon you—have you come to the passages called 'My silent conversations with Brother Ass'?"

I: "Not yet."

She: "Don't be too wounded by them. You must exonerate the brute with a good-natured laugh, for after all he was one of us, one of the tribe. Relative size of accomplishment doesn't matter. As he himself says: 'There is not enough faith, charity or tenderness to furnish this world with a single ray of hope—yet so long as that strange sad cry rings out over the world, the birth-pangs of an artist—all cannot be lost! This sad little squeak of rebirth tells us that all still hangs in the balance. Heed me, reader, for the artist is you, all of us—the statue which must disengage itself from the dull block of marble which houses it and start to live. But when? But when? And then in another place he says: 'Religion is simply art bastardised out of all recognition'—a characteristic remark. It was the central point of his difference with Balthazar and the Cabal.

Pursewarden had turned the whole central proposition upside down."

I: "To suit his private ends."

She: "No. To suit his own immortal needs. There was nothing dishonest about it all. If you are born of the artist tribe it is a waste of time to try and function as a priest. You have to be faithful to your angle of vision, and at the same time fully recognise its partiality. There is a kind of perfection to be achieved in matching oneself to one's capacities—at every level. This must, I imagine, do away with striving, and with illusions too. I myself always admired old Scobie as a thoroughly successful example of this achievement in his own way. He was quite successfully himself, I thought."

I: "Yes, I suppose so. I was thinking of him today. His name cropped up at the office in some connection. Clea, imitate him again. You do it so perfectly that I am quite dumb with admiration."

She: "But you know all his stories."

I: "Nonsense. They were inexhaustible."

She: "And I wish I could imitate his expression! That look of portentous owlishness, the movement of the glass eye! Very well; but close your eyes and hear the story of Toby's downfall, one of his many downfalls. Are you ready?"

I: "Yes."

She: "He told it to me in the course of a dinner-party just before I went to Syria. He said he had come into some money and insisted on taking me to the Lutetia in ceremonial fashion where we dined on *scampi* and Chianti. It began like this in a low confidential tone. 'Now the thing about Toby that characterised him was a superb effrontery, the fruit of perfect breeding! I told you his father was an M.P.? No? Funny, I thought I mentioned it in passing. Yes, he was very highly placed, you might say. But Toby never boasted of it. In fact, and *this* shows you, he actually asked me to treat the matter with discretion and not mention it to his shipmates. He didn't want any favours, he said. He didn't want people sucking up to him neither, just because his father was an M.P. He wanted to go through life incognito, he said, and make his own career by hard work. Mind you, he was almost continuously in trouble with the upper deck. It was his religious convictions more than anything, I think. He had a remorseless taste for the cloth did old Toby. He was vivid. The only career he wanted was to be a sky-pilot. But somehow he couldn't get himself ordained. *They* said he drank too much. But *he* said it was because his vocation was so strong that it pushed him to excesses. If only they'd ordain him, he said, everything would be all right. He'd come right off the drink. He told me this many a time when he was on the Yokohama run. When he was drunk he was always trying to hold services in Number One hold. Naturally people complained and at Goa the captain made a bishop come aboard to reason with him. It was no go. "Scurvy" he used to say to me, "Scurvy, I shall die a martyr to my vocation, that's what." But there's nothing in life like determination. Toby had plenty of it. And I wasn't at all surprised one day, after many years, to see him come ashore ordained. Just how he'd squeezed into the Church he never would tell. But one of his mates said that he got a slightly tainted Chinese Catholic bishop to ordain him on the sly in Hong Kong. Once the articles were all signed sealed and wrapped up there was nothing anyone could do, so the Church had to put a good face on it, taint and all. After that he became a holy terror, holding services everywhere and distributing cigarette cards of the saints. The ship he was serving on got fed up and paid him off. They framed him up; said he had been seen going ashore carrying a lady's handbag! Toby denied it and said it was something religious, a chasuble or something that they mistook for a handbag. Anyway he turned up on a passenger-ship next carrying pilgrims. He said that at last he had fulfilled himself. Services all day long in "A" Lounge, and no one to hinder the word of the Lord. But I noticed with alarm that he was drinking more heavily than before and he had a funny cracked sort of laugh. It wasn't the old Toby. I wasn't surprised to hear he had been in trouble again. Apparently he had been suspected of being drunk on duty and of having made an unflattering reference to a bishop's posterior. Now this shows his superb cleverness, for when he came up for court martial he had the perfect answer ready. I don't quite know how they do court martials in the Church, but I suppose this pilgrim boat was full of bishops or something and they did it drum-head fashion in "A" Lounge. But Toby was too fast for them with his effrontery. There's nothing like breeding to make you quick at answering. His defence was that if anyone *had* heard him breathing heavily at Mass it was his asthma; and secondly he hadn't never mentioned anyone's posterior. He had talked about a bishop's *fox terrier*! Isn't it dazzling? It was the smartest thing he ever did, old Toby, though I've never known him at a loss for a clever answer. Well, the bishops were so staggered that they let him off with a caution and a thousand Ave Marias as a penance. This was pretty easy for Toby; in fact it was no trouble at all because he'd bought a little Chinese prayer-wheel which Budgie had fixed up to say Ave Marias for him. It was a simple little device, brilliantly adapted to the times as you might say. One revolution was an Ave Maria or fifty beads. It simplified prayer, he said; in fact one could go on praying without thinking. Later someone told on him and it was confiscated by the head bloke. Another caution for poor Toby. But nowadays he treated everything with a toss of the head and a scornful laugh. He was riding for a fall, you see. He had got a bit above himself. I couldn't help noticing how much he'd changed because he touched here nearly every week with these blinking pilgrims. I think they were Italians visiting the Holy Places. Back and forth they went, and with them Toby. But he had changed. He was always in trouble now, and seemed to have thrown off all restraint. He had gone completely fanciful. Once he called on me dressed as a cardinal with a red beret and a sort of lampshade in his hand. "Cor!" I gasped.

"You aren't half orchidaceous, Toby!" Later he got very sharply told off for dressing above his rank, and I could see that it was only a matter of time before he fell out of the balloon, so to speak. I did what I could as an old friend to reason with him but somehow I couldn't bring him to see the point. I even tried to get him back on to beer but it wasn't any go at all. Nothing but fire water for Toby. Once I had to have him carried back aboard by the police. He was all figged up in a prelate's costume. I think they call it a shibboleth. And he tried to pronounce an anathema on the city from "A" Boat Deck. He was waving an apse or something. The last thing I saw of him was a lot of real bishops restraining him. They were nearly as purple as his own borrowed robes. My, how those Italians carried on! Then came the crash. They nabbed him in fragrant delicto swigging the sacramental wine. You know it has the Pope's Seal on it, don't you? You buy it from Cornford's, the Ecclesiastical Retailers in Bond Street, ready sealed and blessed. Toby had *broken the seal*. He was finished. I don't know whether they ex-communicate or what, but anyway he was struck off the register properly. The next time I saw him he was a shadow of his old self and dressed as an ordinary seaman. He was still drinking heavily but in a different way now, he said. "Scurvy" he said. "Now I simply drink to expiate my sins. I'm drinking as a punishment now, not a pleasure." The whole tragedy had made him very moody and restless. He talked of going off to Japan and becoming a religious body there. The only thing that prevented him was that there you have to shave your head and he couldn't bear to part with his hair which was long, and was justly admired by his friends. "No" he said, after discussing the idea, "no, Scurvy old man, I couldn't bring myself to go about as bald as an egg, after what I've been through. It would give me a strangely roofless appearance at my age. Besides once when I was a nipper I got ringworm and lost my crowning glory. It took ages to grow again. It was so slow that I feared it never would come into

123

bloom again. Now I couldn't bear to be parted from it. Not for anything." I saw his dilemma perfectly, but I didn't see any way out for him. He would always be a square peg would old Toby, swimming against the stream. Mind you, it was a mark of his originality. For a little while he managed to live by blackmailing all the bishops who'd been to confession while he was O.C. Early Mass, and twice he got a free holiday in Italy. But then other troubles came his way and he shipped to the Far East, working in Seamen's Hostels when he was ashore, and telling everyone that he was going to make a fortune out of smuggled diamonds. I see him very rarely now, perhaps once every three years, and he never writes; but I'll never forget old Toby. He was always such a gentleman in spite of his little mishaps, and when his father dies he expects to have a few hundred a year of his own. Then we're going to join forces in Horsham with Budgie and put the earth-closet trade on a real economic basis. Old Budgie can't keep books and files. That's a job for me with my police training. At least so old Toby always said. I wonder where he is now?' "

The recital ended, the laughter suddenly expired and a new expression appeared on Clea's face which I did not remember ever having seen before. Something between a doubt and an apprehension which played about the mouth like a shadow. She added with a studied naturalness which was somehow strained: "Afterwards he told my fortune. I know you will laugh. He said he could only do it with certain people and at certain times. Will you believe me if I tell you that he described with perfect fidelity and in complete detail the whole Syrian episode?" She turned her face to the wall with an abrupt movement and to my surprise I saw her lips were trembling. I put my hand up her warm shoulder and said "Clea" very softly. "What is it?" Suddenly she cried out: "O leave me alone. Can't you see I want to sleep?"

o   o   o   o   o

II

MY CONVERSATIONS WITH BROTHER ASS
(being extracts from Pursewarden's Notebook)

With what a fearful compulsion we return to it
again and again—like a tongue to a hollow
tooth—this question of writing! Can writers
talk nothing but shop then? No. But with old
Darley I am seized with a sort of convulsive vertigo for, while
we have everything in common, I find I cannot talk to him at
all. But wait. I mean that I do talk: endlessly, passionately,
hysterically without uttering a word aloud! There is no way to
drive a wedge between his ideas which, *ma foi*, are thoughtful,
orderly, the very essence of "soundness". Two men propped on
bar-stools thoughtfully gnawing at the universe as if at a stick
of sugar-cane! The one speaks in a low, modulated voice, using
language with tact and intuition; the other shifts from buttock
to listless buttock shamefacedly shouting in his own mind, but
only answering with an occasional affirmative or negative to
these well-rounded propositions which are, for the most part,
incontestably valuable and true! This would perhaps make the
germ of a short story? ("But Brother Ass, there is a whole
dimension lacking to what you say. How is it possible for one
to convey this in Oxford English?") Still with sad penitential
frowns the man on the high bar-stool proceeds with his exposition about the problem of the creative act—I ask you! From
time to time he shoots a shyish sideways glance at his tor-
mentor—for in a funny sort of way I do seem to torment him;
otherwise he would not always be at me, aiming the button of
his foil at the chinks in my self-esteem, or at the place where
he believes I must keep my heart. No, we would be content

with simpler conversational staples like the weather. In me he scents an enigma, something crying out for the probe. ("But Brother Ass, I am as clear as a bell—a sancing bell! The problem is there, here, nowhere!") At times while he is talking like this I have the sudden urge to jump on his back and ride him frantically up and down Rue Fuad, thrashing him with a Thesaurus and crying: "Awake, moon-calf! Let me take you by your long silken jackass's ears and drive you at a gallop through the waxworks of our literature, among the clicking of Box Brownies each taking its monochrome snapshots of so-called reality! Together we will circumvent the furies and become celebrated for our depiction of the English scene, of English life which moves to the stately rhythm of an autopsy! Do you hear me, Brother Ass?"

He does not hear, he will not hear. His voice comes to me from a great way off, as if over a faulty land-line. "Hullo! Can you hear me?" I cry, shaking the receiver. I hear his voice faintly against the roaring of Niagara Falls. "What is that? Did you say that you wished to contribute to English literature? What, to arrange a few sprigs of parsley over this dead turbot? To blow diligently into the nostrils of this corpse? Have you mobilised your means, Brother Ass? Have you managed to annul your early pot-training? Can you climb like a cat-burglar with loosened sphincters? But then what will you say to people whose affective life is that of hearty Swiss hoteliers? I will tell you. I will say it and save all you artists the trouble. A simple word. *Edelweiss*. Say it in a low well-modulated voice with a refined accent, and lubricate it with a sigh! The whole secret is there, in a word which grows above snowline! And then, having solved the problem of ends and means you will have to face another just as troublesome—for if by any chance a work of art should cross the Channel it would be sure to be turned back at Dover on the grounds of being improperly dressed! It is not easy, Brother Ass. (Perhaps it would be wisest to ask the French for intellectual asylum?) But I see you will not heed me. You continue in the same unfaltering tone to describe for me the literary scene which was summed up once and for all by the poet Gray in the line 'The lowing herd winds slowly o'er the lea'! Here I cannot deny the truth of what you say. It is cogent, it is prescient, it is carefully studied. But I have taken my own precautions against a nation of mental grannies. Each of my books bears a scarlet wrapper with the legend: *NOT TO BE OPENED BY OLD WOMEN OF EITHER SEX.* (Dear D.H.L. so wrong, so right, so great, may his ghost breathe on us all!)"

He puts down his glass with a little click and sighing runs his fingers through his hair. Kindness is no excuse, I tell myself. Disinterested goodness is no exoneration from the basic demands of the artist's life. You see, Brother Ass, there is my life and then the life of my life. They must belong as fruit and rind. I am not being cruel. It is simply that I am not indulgent!

"How lucky not to be interested in writing" says Darley with a touch of plaintive despair in his tone. "I envy you." But he does not, really, not at all. Brother Ass, I will tell you a short story. A team of Chinese anthropologists arrived in Europe to study our habits and beliefs. Within three weeks they were all dead. They died of uncontrollable laughter and were buried with full military honours! What do you make of that? We have turned ideas into a paying form of tourism.

Darley talks on with slanting eye buried in his gin-sling. I reply wordlessly. In truth I am deafened by the pomposity of my own utterances. They echo in my skull like the reverberating eructations of Zarathustra, like the wind whistling through Montaigne's beard. At times I mentally seize him by the shoulders and shout: "Should literature be a path-finder or a bromide? Decide! Decide!"

He does not heed, does not hear me. He has just come from the library, from the pot-house, or from a Bach concert (the gravy still running down his chin). We have aligned our shoes upon the polished brass rail below the bar. The evening has begun to yawn around us with the wearisome promise of girls to be ploughed. And here is Brother Ass discoursing upon the book he is writing and from which he has been thrown, as from a horse, time and time again. It is not really art which is at issue, it is ourselves. Shall we always be content with the ancient tinned salad of the subsidised novel? Or the tired ice-cream of poems which cry themselves to sleep in the refrigerators of the mind? If it were possible to adopt a bolder scansion, a racier rhythm we might all breathe more freely! Poor Darley's books—will they always be such painstaking descriptions of the soul-states of . . . the human omelette? (Art occurs at the point where a form is sincerely honoured by an awakened spirit.)

"This one's on me."

"No, old man, on me"

"No. No; I insist."

"No. It's my turn."

This amiable quibble allows me just the split second I need to jot down the salient points for my self-portrait on a rather ragged cuff. I think it covers the whole scope of the thing with admirable succinctness. Item one. "Like all fat men I tend to be my own hero." Item two. "Like all young men I set out to be a genius, but mercifully laughter intervened." Item three. "I always hoped to achieve the Elephant's Eye view." Item four. "I realised that to become an artist one must shed the whole complex of egotisms which led to the choice of self-expression as the only means of growth! This because it is impossible I call The Whole Joke!"

Darley is talking of disappointments! But Brother Ass, disenchantment is the essence of the game. With what high hopes we invaded London from the provinces in those old dead days, our manuscripts bagging out suitcases. Do you recall? With what emotion we gazed over Westminster Bridge, reciting Wordsworth's indifferent sonnet and wondering if his daughter grew up less beautiful for being French. The whole metropolis seemed to quiver with the portent of our talent, our skill, our discernment. Walking along the Mall we wondered who all those men were—tall hawk-featured men perched on balconies and high places, scanning the city with heavy binoculars. What were they seeking so earnestly? Who were they—so composed and steely-eyed? Timidly we stopped a policeman to ask him. "They are publishers" he said mildly. Publishers! Our hearts stopped beating. "They are on the look out for new talent." Great God! It was for *us* they were waiting and watching! Then the kindly policeman lowered his voice confidentially and said in hollow and reverent tones: *"They are waiting for the new Trollope to be born!"* Do you remember, at these words, how heavy our suitcases suddenly felt? How our blood slowed, our footsteps lagged? Brother Ass, we had been bashfully thinking of a kind of illumination such as Rimbaud dreamed of—a nagging poem which was not didactic or expository but which *infected*—was not simply a rationalised intuition, I mean, clothed in isinglass! We had come to the wrong shop, with the wrong change! A chill struck us as we saw the mist falling in Trafalgar Square, coiling around us its tendrils of ectoplasm! A million muffin-eating moralists were waiting, not for us, Brother Ass, but for the plucky and tedious Trollope! (If you are dissatisfied with your form, reach for the *curette*.) Now do you wonder if I laugh a little off-key? Do you ask yourself what has turned me into nature's bashful little aphorist?

> *Disguised as an eiron, why who should it be*
> *But tuft-hunting, dram-drinking, toad-eating Me!*

We who are, after all, simply poor co-workers in the psyche of our nation, what can we expect but the natural automatic rejection from a public which resents interference? And quite right too. There is no injustice in the matter, for I also resent interference, Brother Ass, just as you do. No, it is not a question of being aggrieved, it is a question of being unlucky. Of the ten thousand reasons for my books' unpopularity I shall only bother to give you the first, for it includes all the others.

A puritan culture's conception of art is of something which will endorse its morality and flatter its patriotism. Nothing else. I see you raise your eyebrows. Even you, Brother Ass, realise the basic unreality of this proposition. Nevertheless it explains everything. A puritan culture, *argal*, does not know what art is—how can it be expected to care? (I leave religion to the bishops—there it can do most harm!)

> No croked legge, no blered eye,
> no part deformed out of kinde
> Nor yet so onolye half can be
> As is the inward suspicious minde.

> The wheel is patience on to which I'm bound.
> Time is this nothingness within the round.

Gradually we compile our own anthologies of misfortune, our dictionaries of verbs and nouns, our copulas and gerundives. That symptomatic policeman of the London dusk first breathed the message to us! That kindly father-figure put the truth in a nutshell. And here we are both in a foreign city built of smegma-tinted crystal and tinsel whose *moeurs*, if we described them, would be regarded as the fantasies of our disordered brains. Brother Ass, we have the hardest lesson of all to learn as yet—that truth cannot be forced but must be allowed to plead for itself! Can you hear me? The line is faulty again, your voice has gone far away. I hear the water rushing!

> Be bleak, young man, and let who will be sprightly,
> And honour Venus if you can twice nightly.
> All things being equal you should not refuse
> To ring the slow sad cowbell of the English muse!

> Art's Truth's Nonentity made quite explicit.
> If it ain't this then what the devil is it?

Writing in my room last night I saw an ant upon the table.

It crossed near the inkwell, and I saw it hesitate at the whiteness of a sheet of paper on which I had written the word "Love"; my pen faltered, the ant turned back, and suddenly my candle guttered and went out. Clear octaves of yellow light flickered behind my eyeballs. I had wanted to start a sentence with the words "Proponents of love"—but the thought had guttered out with the candle! Later on, just before dropping off to sleep an idea struck me. On the wall above my bed I wrote in pencil the words: "What is to be done when one cannot share one's own opinions about love?" I heard my own exasperated sigh as I was dropping off to sleep. In the morning I awoke, clear as a perforated appendix, and wrote my own epitaph on the mirror with my shaving-stick:

> "*I never knew which side my art was buttered*"
> *Were the Last Words that poor Pursewarden uttered!*

As for the proponents of love, I was glad they had vanished for they would have led me irresistibly in the direction of sex— that bad debt which hangs upon my compatriots' consciences. The quiddity! The veritable nub and quiddity of this disordered world, and the only proper field for the deployment of our talents, Brother Ass. But one true, honest unemphatic word in this department will immediately produce one of those neighing and whinnying acts peculiar to our native intellectuals! For them sex is either a Gold Rush or a Retreat from Moscow. And for us? No, but if we are to be a moment serious I will explain what I mean. (Cuckow, Cuckow, a merry note, unpleasing to the pigskin ear.) I mean more than they think. (The strange sad hermaphrodite figure of the London dusk—the Guardsman waiting in Ebury Street for the titled gent.) No, quite another region of enquiry which cannot be reached without traversing this *terrain vague* of the partial spirits. Our topic, Brother Ass, is the same, always and irremediably the same—I spell the word for you: l-o-v-e. Four letters, each letter a volume! The *point faible* of the human psyche, the very site of

131

the carcinoma maxima! How, since the Greeks, has it got mixed up with the cloaca maxima? It is a complete mystery to which the Jews hold the key unless my history is faulty. For this gifted and troublesome race which has never known art, but exhausted its creative processes purely in the construction of ethical systems, has fathered on us all, literally impregnated the Western European psyche with, the whole range of ideas based on "race" and sexual containment in the furtherance of the race! I hear Balthazar growling and lashing his tail! But where the devil do these fantasies of purified bloodstreams come from? Am I wrong to turn to the fearful prohibitions listed in Leviticus for an explanation of the manic depressive fury of Plymouth Brethren and a host of other dismal sectarians? We have had our testicles pinched for centuries by the Mosaic Law; hence the wan and pollarded look of our young girls and boys. Hence the mincing effrontery of adults willed to perpetual adolescence! Speak, Brother Ass! Do you need me? If I am wrong you have only to say so! But in my conception of the four-letter word—which I am surprised has not been black-listed with the other three by the English printer—I am some-what bold and sweeping. I mean the *whole bloody range*—from the little greenstick fractures of the human heart right up to its higher spiritual connivance with the . . . well, the absolute ways of nature, if you like. Surely, Brother Ass, this is the improper study of man? The main drainage of the soul? We could make an atlas of our sighs!

> *Zeus gets Hera on her back*
> *But finds that she has lost the knack.*
> *Extenuated by excesses*
> *She is unable, she confesses.*

> *Nothing daunted Zeus, who wise is,*
> *Tries a dozen good disguises.*
> *Eagle, ram, and bull and bear*
> *Quickly answer Hera's prayer.*

> *One knows a God should be prolix,*
> *But . . . think of all those different ******!*

But I break off here in some confusion, for I see that I am in danger of not taking myself as seriously as I should! And this is an unpardonable offence. Moreover I missed your last remark which was something about the choice of a style. Yes, Brother Ass, the choice of a style is most important; in the market garden of our domestic culture you will find strange and terrible blooms with every stamen standing erect. O to write like Ruskin! When poor Effie Grey tried to get to his bed, he shoo'd the girl away! O to write like Carlyle! Haggis of the mind. When a Scotsman comes to toun Can Spring be far behind? No. Everything you say is truthful and full of point; relative truth, and somewhat pointless point, but nevertheless I will try and think about this invention of the scholiasts, for clearly style is as important to you as matter to me.

How shall we go about it? Keats, the word-drunk, searched for resonance among vowel-sounds which might give him an echo of his inner self. He sounded the empty coffin of his early death with patient knuckles, listening to the dull resonances given off by his certain immortality. Byron was off-hand with English, treating it as master to servant; but the language, being no lackey, grew up like tropic lianas between the cracks of his verses, almost strangling the man. He really lived, his life was truly imaginary; under the figment of the passional self there is a mage, though he himself was not aware of the fact. Donne stopped upon the exposed nerve, jangling the whole cranium. Truth should make one wince, he thought. He hurts us, fearing his own facility; despite the pain of the stopping his verse must be chewed to rags. Shakespeare makes all Nature hang its head. Pope, in an anguish of method, like a constipated child, sandpapers his surfaces to make them slippery for our feet. Great stylists are those who are least certain of their effects. The secret lack in their matter haunts them without knowing it!

133

Eliot puts a cool chloroform pad upon a spirit too tightly braced by the information it has gathered. His honesty of measure and his resolute bravery to return to the headsman's axe is a challenge to us all; but where is the smile? He induces awkward sprains at a moment when we are trying to dance! He has chosen greyness rather than light, and he shares his portion with Rembrandt. Blake and Whitman are awkward brown paper parcels full of vessels borrowed from the temple which tumble all over the place when the string breaks. Longfellow heralds the age of invention for he first thought out the mechanical piano. You pedal, it recites. Lawrence was a limb of the genuine oak-tree, with the needed girth and span. Why did he show them that it mattered, and so make himself vulnerable to their arrows? Auden also always talks. He has manumitted the colloquial. . . .

But here, Brother Ass, I break off; for clearly this is not higher or even lower criticism! I do not see this sort of fustian going down at our older universities where they are still painfully trying to extract from art some shadow of justification for their way of life. Surely there must be a grain of hope, they ask anxiously? After all, there must be a grain of hope for decent honest Christian folk in all this rigmarole which is poured out by our tribe from generation to generation. Or is art simply the little white stick which is given to the blind man and by the help of which he tap tap taps along a road he cannot see but which he is certain is there? Brother Ass, it is for you to decide!

When I was chided by Balthazar for being equivocal I replied, without a moment's conscious thought: "Words being what they are, people being what they are, perhaps it would be better always to say the opposite of what one means?" Afterwards, when I reflected on this view (which I did not know that I held) it seemed to me really eminently sage! So much for conscious thought: you see, we Anglo-Saxons are incapable of thinking *for* ourselves; *about*, yes. In thinking *about* ourselves we put up every kind of pretty performance in every sort of voice, from cracked Yorkshire to the hot-potato-in-the-mouth voice of the BBC. There we excel, for we see ourselves at one remove from reality, as a subject under a microscope. This idea of objectivity is really a flattering extension of our sense of humbug. When you start to think *for* yourself it is impossible to *cant*—and we live by cant! Ah! I hear you say with a sigh, another of those English writers, eminent jailors of the soul! How they weary and disturb us! Very true and very sad.

> *Hail! Albion drear, fond home of cant!*
> *Pursewarden sends thee greetings scant.*
> *Thy notions he's turned back to front*
> *Abhorring cant, adoring* ****

But if you wish to enlarge the image turn to Europe, the Europe which spans, say, Rabelais to de Sade. A progress from the belly-consciousness to the head-consciousness, from flesh and food to sweet (sweet!) reason. Accompanied by all the inter-changing ills which mock us. A progress from religious ecstasy to duodenal ulcer! (It is probably healthier to be entirely brain-less.) But, Brother Ass, this is something which you did not take into account when you chose to compete for the Heavy-weight Belt for Artists of the Millennium. It is too late to complain. You thought you would somehow sneak by the penal-ties without being called upon to do more than demonstrate your skill with words. But words . . . they are only an Aeolian harp, or a cheap xylophone. Even a sea-lion can learn to balance a football on its nose or to play the slide trombone in a circus. What lies beyond. . . ?

No, but seriously, if you wished to be—I do not say original but merely contemporary—you might try a four-card trick in the form of a novel; passing a common axis through four stories, say, and dedicating each to one of the four winds of heaven. A continuum, forsooth, embodying not a *temps retrouvé* but a *temps délivré*. The curvature of space itself would give you stereoscopic narrative, while human personality seen across a

135

continuum would perhaps become prismatic? Who can say? I throw the idea out. I can imagine a form which, if satisfied, might raise in human terms the problems of causality or indeterminacy. . . . And nothing very *recherché* either. Just an ordinary Girl Meets Boy story. But tackled in this way you would not, like most of your contemporaries, be drowsily cutting along a dotted line!

That is the sort of question which you will one day be forced to ask yourself ("We will never get to Mecca!" as the Tchekhov sisters remarked in a play, the title of which I have forgotten.)

> *Nature he loved, and next to nature nudes,*
> *He strove with every woman worth the strife,*
> *Warming both cheeks before the fire of life,*
> *And fell, doing battle with a million prudes.*

Who dares to dream of capturing the fleeting image of truth in all its gruesome multiplicity? (No, no, let us dine cheerfully off scraps of ancient discarded poultice and allow ourselves to be classified by science as wet and dry bobs.)

Whose are the figures I see before me, fishing the brackish reaches of the C. of E.?

One writes, Brother Ass, for the spiritually starving, the castaways of the soul! They will always be a majority even when everyone is a state-owned millionaire. Have courage, for here you will always be master of your audience! Genius which cannot be helped should be politely ignored.

Nor do I mean that it is useless to master and continuously practise your craft. No. A good writer should be able to write anything. But a great writer is the servant of compulsions which are ordained by the very structure of the psyche and cannot be disregarded. Where is he? Where is he?

Come, let us collaborate on a four- or five-decker job, shall we? "Why the Curate Slipped" would be a good title. Quick, they are waiting, those hypnagogic figures among the London minarets, the *muezzin* of the trade. "Does Curate get girl *as well*

136

as stipend, or *only* stipend? Read the next thousand pages and find out!" English life in the raw—like some pious melodrama acted by criminal churchwardens sentenced to a lifetime of sexual misgivings! In this way we can put a tea-cosy over reality to our mutual advantage, writing it all in the plain prose which is only just distinguishable from galvanised iron. In this way we will put a lid on a box with no sides! Brother Ass, let us conciliate a world of listless curmudgeons who read to verify, not their intuitions, but their prejudices!

I remember old Da Capo saying one afternoon: "Today I had five girls. I know it will seem excessive to you. I was not trying to prove anything to myself. But if I said that I had merely blended five teas to suit my palate or five tobaccos to suit my pipe, you would not give the matter a second thought. You would, on the contrary, admire my eclecticism, would you not?"

The belly-furbished Kenilworth at the F.O. once told me plaintively that he had "just dropped in" on James Joyce out of curiosity, and was surprised and pained to find him rude, arrogant and short-tempered. "But" I said "he was paying for his privacy by giving lessons to niggers at one and six an hour! He might have been entitled to feel safe from ineffables like yourself who imagine that art is something to which a good education automatically entitles you; that it is a part of a social equipment, class aptitude, like painting water-colours was for a Victorian gentlewoman! I can imagine his poor heart sinking as he studied your face, with its expression of wayward condescension—the fathomless self-esteem which one sees occasionally flit across the face of a goldfish with a hereditary title!" After this we never spoke, which was what I wanted. The art of making necessary enemies! Yet one thing I liked in him: he pronounced the word 'Civilisation' as if it had an S-bend in it.

(Brother Ass is on symbolism now, and really talking good sense, I must admit.) Symbolism! The abbreviation of language into poem. The heraldic aspect of reality! Symbolism is the great repair-outfit of the psyche, Brother Ass, the *fond de pouvoir*

137

of the soul. The sphincter-loosening music which copies the ripples of the soul's progress through human flesh, playing in us like electricity! (Old Parr, when he was drunk, said once: "Yes, but it *hurts* to realise!")

Of course it does. But we know that the history of literature is the history of laughter and pain. The imperatives from which there is no escape are: *Laugh till it hurts, and hurt till you laugh!*

The greatest thoughts are accessible to the least of men. Why do we have to struggle so? Because understanding is a function not of ratiocination but of the psyche's stage of growth. There, Brother Ass, is the point at which we are at variance. No amount of explanation can close the gap. Only realisation! One day you are going to wake from your sleep shouting with laughter. *Ecco!*

About Art I always tell myself: while they are watching the firework display, yclept Beauty, you must smuggle the truth into their veins like a filter-passing virus! This is easier said than done. How slowly one learns to embrace the paradox! Even I am not there as yet; nevertheless, like that little party of explorers, "Though we were still two days' march from the falls we suddenly heard their thunder growing up in the distance"! Ah! those who merit it may one day be granted a rebirth-certificate by a kindly Government Department. This will entitle them to receive everything free of charge—a prize reserved for those who want nothing. Celestial economics, about which Lenin is strangely silent! Ah! the gaunt faces of the English muses! Pale distressed gentlewomen in smocks and beads, dispensing tea and drop-scones to the unwary!

> *The foxy faces*
> *Of Edwardian Graces*
> *Horse-faces full of charm*
> *With strings of beads*
> *And a packet of seeds*
> *And an ape-tuft under each arm!*

Society! Let us complicate existence to the point of drudgery so that it acts as a drug against reality. Unfair! Unfair! But, my dear Brother Ass, the sort of book I have in mind will be characterised by the desired quality which will make us rich and famous: it will be characterised by a *total lack of codpiece*!

When I want to infuriate Balthazar I say: "Now if the Jews would only *assimilate* they would give us a valuable lead in the matter of breaking down puritanism everywhere. For they are the licence-holders and patentees of the closed system, the ethical response! Even our absurd food prohibitions and inhibitions are copied from their melancholy priest-ridden rigmarole about flesh and fowl. Aye! We artists are not interested in policies but in values—this is our field of battle! If once we could loosen up, relax the terrible grip of the so-called Kingdom of Heaven which has made the earth such a blood-soaked place, we might rediscover in sex the key to a metaphysical search which is our *raison d'être* here below! If the closed system and the moral exclusiveness on divine right were relaxed a little what could we not do?" What indeed? But the good Balthazar smokes his Lakadif gloomily and shakes his shaggy head. I think of the black velvet sighs of Juliet and fall silent. I think of the soft white knosps—unopened flower-shapes—which decorate the tombs of Moslem women! The slack, soft insipid mansuetude of these females of the mind! No, clearly my history is pretty weak. Islam also libs as the Pope does.

Brother Ass, let us trace the progress of the European artist from problem-child to case-history, from case-history to cry-baby! He has kept the psyche of Europe alive by his ability to be wrong, by his continual cowardice—this is his function! Cry-baby of the Western World! Cry-babies of the world unite! But let me hasten to add, lest this sounds cynical or despairing, that I am full of hope. For always, at every moment of time, there is a chance that the artist will stumble upon what I can only call The Great Inkling! Whenever this happens he is at once free to enjoy his fecundating rôle; but it can never

139

really happen as fully and completely as it deserves until the miracle comes about—the miracle of Pursewarden's Ideal Commonwealth! Yes, I believe in this miracle. Our very existence as artists affirms it! It is the act of yea-saying about which the old poet of the city speaks in a poem you once showed me in translation.* The *fact* of an artist being born affirms and reaffirms this in every generation. The miracle is there, on ice so to speak. One fine day it will blossom: then the artist suddenly grows up and accepts the full responsibility for his origins in the people, and when *simultaneously* the people recognise his peculiar significance and value, and greet him as the unborn child in themselves, the infant Joy! I am certain it will come. At the moment they are like wrestlers nervously circling one another, looking for a hold. But when it comes, this great blinding second of illumination—only then shall we be able to dispense with hierarchy as a social form. The new society—so different from anything we can imagine now—will be born around the small strict white temple of the infant Joy! Men and women will group themselves around it, the proto-plasmic growth of the village, the town, the capital! Nothing stands in the way of this Ideal Commonwealth, save that in every generation the vanity and laziness of the artist has always matched the self-indulgent blindness of the people. But prepare, prepare! It is on the way. It is here, there, nowhere!

The great schools of love will arise, and sensual and intel-lectual knowledge will draw their impetus from each other. The human animal will be uncaged, all his dirty cultural straw and coprolitic refuse of belief cleaned out. And the human spirit, radiating light and laughter, will softly tread the green grass like a dancer; will emerge to cohabit with the time-forms and give children to the world of the elementaries—undines and salamanders, sylphs and sylvestres, Gnomi and Vulcani, angels and gnomes.

Yes, to extend the range of physical sensuality to embrace mathematics and theology: to nourish not to stunt the intuitions. For culture means sex, the root-knowledge, and where the faculty is derailed or crippled, its derivatives like religion come up dwarfed or contorted—instead of the emblematic mystic rose you get Judaic cauliflowers like Mormons or Vegetarians, instead of artists you get cry-babies, instead of philosophy semantics.

The sexual and the creative energy go hand in hand. They convert into one another—the solar sexual and the lunar spiritual holding an eternal dialogue. They ride the spiral of time together. They embrace the whole of the human motive. The truth is only to be found in our own entrails—the truth of Time.

"Copulation is the lyric of the mob!" Aye, and also the university of the soul: but a university at present without endowments, without books or even students. No, there are a few.

How wonderful the death-struggle of Lawrence: to realise his sexual nature fully, to break free from the manacles of the Old Testament; flashing down through the firmament like a great white struggling man-fish, the last Christian martyr. His struggle is ours—to rescue Jesus from Moses. For a brief moment it looked possible, but St. Paul restored the balance and the iron handcuffs of the Judaic prison closed about the growing soul forever. Yet in *The Man Who Died* he tells us plainly what must be, what the reawakening of Jesus should have meant—the true birth of free man. Where is he? What has happened to him? Will he ever come?

My spirit trembles with joy as I contemplate this city of light which a divine accident might create before our very eyes at any moment! Here art will find its true form and place, and the artist can play like a fountain without contention, without even trying. For I see art more and more clearly as a sort of manuring of the psyche. It has no intention, that is to say no *theology*. By nourishing the psyche, by dunging it up, it helps it to find its own level, like water. That level is an original inno-

141

cence—who invented the perversion of Original Sin, that filthy obscenity of the West? Art, like a skilled masseur on a playing-field, is always standing by to help deal with casualties; and just as a masseur does, its ministrations ease up the tensions of the psyche's musculature. That is why it always goes for the sore places, its fingers pressing upon the knotted muscles, the tendon afflicted with cramp—the sins, perversions, displeasing points which we are reluctant to accept. Revealing them with its harsh kindness it unravels the tensions, relaxes the psyche. The other part of the work, if there is any other work, must belong to religion. Art is the purifying factor merely. It predicates nothing. It is the handmaid of silent content, essential only to joy and to love! These strange beliefs, Brother Ass, you will find lurking under my mordant humours, which may be described simply as a technique of therapy. As Balthazar says: "A good doctor, and in a special sense the psychologist, makes it quite deliberately, slightly harder for the patient to recover too easily. You do this to see if his psyche has any real bounce in it, for the secret of healing is in the patient and not the doctor. The only measure is the reaction!"

I was born under Jupiter, Hero of the Comic Mode! My poems, like soft music invading the encumbered senses of young lovers left alone at night. . . . What was I saying? Yes, the best thing to do with a great truth, as Rabelais discovered, is to bury it in a mountain of follies where it can comfortably wait for the picks and shovels of the elect.

Between infinity and eternity stretches the thin hard tightrope human beings must walk, joined at the waist! Do not let these unamiable propositions dismay you, Brother Ass. They are written down in pure joy, uncontaminated by a desire to preach! I am really writing for an audience of the blind—but aren't we all? Good art points, like a man too ill to speak, like a baby! But if instead of following the direction it indicates you take it for a thing in itself, having some sort of absolute value, or as a thesis upon something which can be paraphrased, surely you miss the point; you lose yourself at once among the barren abstractions of the critic? Try to tell yourself that its fundamental object was only to invoke the ultimate healing silence—and that the symbolism contained in form and pattern is only a frame of reference through which, as in a mirror, one may glimpse the idea of a universe at rest, a universe in love with itself. Then like a babe in arms you will "milk the universe at every breath"! We must learn to read between the lines, between the lives.

Liza used to say: "But its very perfection makes one sure that it will come to an end." She was right; but women will not accept time and the dictates of the death-divining second. They do not see that a civilisation is simply a great metaphor which describes the aspirations of the individual soul in collective form—as perhaps a novel or a poem might do. The struggle is always for greater consciousness. But alas! Civilisations die in the measure that they become conscious of themselves. They realise, they lose heart, the propulsion of the unconscious motive is no longer there. Desperately they begin to copy themselves in the mirror. It is no use. But surely there is a catch in all this? Yes, Time is the catch! Space is a concrete idea, but Time is abstract. In the scar tissue of Proust's great poem you see that so clearly; his work is the great academy of the time-consciousness. But being unwilling to mobilise the meaning of time he was driven to fall back on memory, the ancestor of hope!

Ah! but being a Jew he had hope—and with Hope comes the irresistible desire to meddle. Now we Celts mate with despair out of which alone grows laughter and the desperate romance of the eternally hopeless. We hunt the attainless, and for us there is only a search unending.

For him it would mean nothing, my phrase "the prolongation of childhood into art". Brother Ass, the diving-board, the trapeze, lie just to the eastward of this position! A leap through the firmament to a new status—only don't miss the ring!

Why for example don't they recognise in Jesus the great Ironist that he is, the comedian? I am sure that two-thirds of the Beatitudes are jokes or squibs in the manner of Chuang Tzu. Generations of mystagogues and pedants have lost the sense. I am sure of it however because he must have known that Truth disappears with the telling of it. It can only be conveyed, not stated; irony alone is the weapon for such a task.

Or let us turn to another aspect of the thing; it was you, just a moment ago, who mentioned our poverty of observation in all that concerns each other—the limitations of sight itself. Bravely spoken! But translated spiritually you get the picture of a man walking about the house, hunting for the spectacles which are on his forehead. To see is to imagine! And what, Brother Ass, could be a better illustration than your manner of seeing Justine, fitfully lit up in the electric signs of the imagination? It is not the same woman evidently who set about besieging me and who was finally driven off by my sardonic laughter. What you saw as soft and appealing in her seemed to me a specially calculated hardness, not which she invented, but which you evoked in her. All that throaty chatter, the compulsion to exteriorise hysteria, reminded me of a feverish patient plucking at a sheet! The violent necessity to incriminate life, to *explain* her soul-states, reminded me of a mendicant soliciting pity by a nice exhibition of sores. Mentally she always had me scratching myself! Yet there was much to admire in her and I indulged my curiosity in exploring the outlines of her character with some sympathy—the configurations of an unhappiness which was genuine, though it always smelt of grease paint! The child, for example!

"I found it, of course. Or rather Mnemjian did. In a brothel. It died from something, perhaps meningitis. Darley and Nessim came and dragged me away. All of a sudden I realised that I could not bear to find it; all the time I hunted I lived on the hope of finding it. But this thing, once dead, seemed suddenly to deprive me of all purpose. I recognised it, but my inner mind kept crying out that it was not true, refusing to let me recognise it, even though I already had consciously done so!"

The mixture of conflicting emotions was so interesting that I jotted them down in my notebook between a poem and a recipe for angel bread which I got from El Kalef. Tabulated thus:

1. Relief at end of search.
2. Despair at end of search; no further motive force in life.
3. Horror at death.
4. Relief at death. What future possible for it?
5. Intense shame (don't understand this).
6. Sudden desire to continue search uselessly rather than admit truth.
7. Preferred to continue to feed on false hopes!

A bewildering collection of fragments to leave among the analects of a moribund poet! But here was the point I was trying to make. She said: "Of course neither Nessim nor Darley noticed anything. Men are so stupid, they never do. I would have been able to forget it even perhaps, and dream that I had never really discovered it, but for Mnemjian, who wanted the reward, and was so convinced of the truth of his case that he made a great row. There was some talk of an autopsy by Balthazar. I was foolish enough to go to his clinic and offer to bribe him to say it was not my child. He was pretty astonished. I wanted him to deny a truth which I so perfectly knew to be true, *so that I should not have to change my outlook.* I would not be deprived of my sorrow, if you like; I wanted it to go on—to go on passionately searching for what I did not dare to find. I even frightened Nessim and incurred his suspicions with my antics over his private safe. So the matter passed off, and for a long time I still went on automatically searching until underneath I could stand the strain of the truth and come to terms with it. I see it so clearly, the divan, the tenement."

Here she put on her most beautiful expression, which was one of intense sadness, and put her hands upon her breasts.

Shall I tell you something? *I suspected her of lying*; it was an unworthy thought but then . . . I am an unworthy person.

I: "Have you ever been back to the place?"

She: "No. I have often wanted to, but did not dare." She shuddered a little. "In my memory I have become attached to that old divan. It must be knocking about somewhere. You see, I am still half convinced it was all a dream."

At once I took up my pipe, violin and deerstalker like a veritable Sherlock. I have always been a X-marks-the-spot man. "Let us go and revisit it," I said briskly. At the worst, I thought, such a visitation would be cathartic. It was in fact a supremely practical thing to suggest, and to my surprise she at once rose and put on her coat. We walked silently down through the western edges of the town, arm in arm.

There was some kind of festival going on in the Arab town which was blazing with electric light and flags. Motionless sea, small high clouds, and a moon like a disapproving archimandrite or another faith. Smell of fish, cardamon seed and frying entrails packed with cummin and garlic. The air was full of the noise of mandolines scratching their little souls out on the night, as if afflicted with fleas—scratching scratching until the blood came on the lice-intoxicated night! The air was heavy. Each breath invisibly perforated it. You felt it come in and out of the lungs as if in a leather bellows. Eheu! It was grisly all that light and noise, I thought. And they talk of the romance of the East! Give me the Metropole at Brighton any day! We traversed this sector of light with quick deliberate step. She walked unerringly, head bent, deep in thought. Then gradually the streets grew darker, faded into the violet of darkness, became narrower, twisted and turned. At last we came to a great empty space with starlight. A dim great barrack of a building. She moved slowly now, with less certainty, hunting for a door. In a whisper she said "This place is run by old Mettrawi. He is bedridden. The door is always open. But he hears everything from his bed. Take my hand." I was never a great fire-eater and

146

I must confess to a certain uneasiness as we walked into this bandage of total blackness. Her hand was firm and cool, her voice precise, unmarked by any range of emphasis, betraying neither excitement nor fear. I thought I heard the scurrying of immense rats in the rotten structure around me, the very rafters of night itself. (Once in a thunderstorm among the ruins I had seen their fat wet glittering bodies flash here and there as they feasted on garbage.) "Please God, remember that even though I am an English poet I do not deserve to be eaten by rats" I prayed silently. We had started to walk down a long corridor of blackness with the rotten wooden boards creaking under us; here and there was one missing, and I wondered if we were not walking over the bottomless pit itself! The air smelt of wet ashes and that unmistakable odour of black flesh when it is sweating. It is quite different from white flesh. It is dense, foetid, like the lion's cage at the Zoo. The Darkness itself was sweating—and why not? The Darkness must wear Othello's skin. Always a timorous fellow, I suddenly wanted to go to the lavatory but I crushed the thought like a blackbeetle. Let my bladder wait. On we went, and round two sides of a . . . piece of darkness floored with rotten boards. Then suddenly she whispered: "I think we are there!" and pushed open a door upon another piece of impenetrable darkness. But it was a room of some size for the air was cool. One felt the space though one could see nothing whatsoever. We both inhaled deeply.

"Yes" she whispered thoughtfully and, groping in her velvet handbag for a box of matches, hesitantly struck one. It was a tall room, so tall that it was roofed by darkness despite the yellow flapping of the match-flame; one huge shattered window faintly reflected starlight. The walls were of verdigris, the plaster peeling everywhere, and their only decoration was the imprint of little blue hands which ran round the four walls in a haphazard pattern. As if a lot of pygmies had gone mad with blue paint and then galloped all over the walls standing on their hands! To the left, a little off centre, reposed a large gloomy divan, floating upon the gloom like a Viking catafalque; it was a twice-chewed relic of some Ottoman calif, riddled with holes. The match went out. "There it is" she said and putting the box into my hand she left my side. When I lit up again she was sitting beside the divan with her cheek resting upon it, softly stroking it with the palm of her hand. She was completely composed. She stroked it with a calm voluptuous gesture and then crossed her paws on it, reminding me of a lioness sitting astride its lunch. The moment had a kind of weird tension, but this was not reflected on her face. (Human beings are like pipe-organs, I thought. You pull out a stop marked "Lover" or "Mother" and the requisite emotions are unleashed—tears or sighs or endearments. Sometimes I try and think of us all as habit-patterns rather than human beings. I mean, wasn't the idea of the individual soul grafted on us by the Greeks in the wild hope that, by its sheer beauty, it would "take"—as we say of vaccination? That we might grow up to the size of the concept and grow the heavenly flame in each of our hearts? *Has* it taken or hasn't it? Who can say? Some of us still have one, but how vestigial it seems. Perhaps. . . .)

"They have heard us."

Somewhere in the darkness there was a thin snarl of voice, and the silence became suddenly padded out with the scamper of feet upon rotted woodwork. In the expiring flicker of the match I saw, as if somewhere very far away, a bar of light—like a distant furnace door opening in heaven. And voices now, the voices of ants! The children came through a sort of hatch or trap-door made of darkness, in their cotton nightgowns, absurdly farded. With rings on their fingers and bells on their toes. She shall have music wherever she goes! One of them carried a waxlight floating in a saucer. They twanged nasally about us, interrogating our needs with blasting frankness—but they were surprised to see Justine sitting beside the Viking catafalque, her head (now smiling) half turned towards them.

148

"I think we should leave" I said in a low voice, for they smelt dreadfully these tiny apparitions, and they showed a disagreeable tendency to twine their skinny arms about my waist as they wheedled and intoned. But Justine turned to one and said: "Bring the light here, where we can all see." And when the light was brought she suddenly turned herself, crossed her legs under her, and in the high ringing tone of the street story-teller she intoned: "Now gather about me, all ye blessed of Allah, and hear the wonders of the story I shall tell you." The effect was electric; they settled about her like a pattern of dead leaves in a wind, crowding up close together. Some even climbed on to the old divan, chuckling and nudging with delight. And in the same rich triumphant voice, saturated with unshed tears, Justine began again in the voice of the professional story-teller: "Ah, listen to me, all ye true believers, and I will unfold to you the story of Yuna and Aziz, of their great many-petalled love, and of the mishaps which befell them from the doing of Abu Ali Saraq el-Maza. In those days of the great Califate, when many heads fell and armies marched. . . ."

It was a wild sort of poetry for the place and the time—the little circle of wizened faces, the divan, the flopping light; and the strangely captivating lilt of the Arabic with its heavy damascened imagery, the thick brocade of alliterative repetitions, the nasal twanging accents, gave it a laic splendour which brought tears to my eyes—gluttonous tears! It was such a rich diet for the soul! It made me aware how thin the fare is which we moderns supply to our hungry readers. The epic contours, that is what her story had! I was envious. How rich these beggar children were. And I was envious too of her audience. Talk of suspended judgement! They sank into the imagery of her story like plummets. One saw, creeping out like mice, their true souls—creeping out upon those painted masks in little expressions of wonder, suspense and joy. In that yellow gloaming they were expressions of a terrible truth. You saw how they would be in middle age—the witch, the good wife, the gossip, the shrew.

The poetry had stripped them to the bone and left only their natural selves to flower thus in expressions faithfully portraying their tiny stunted spirits!

How could I help but admire her for giving me one of the most significant and memorable moments of a writer's life? I put my arm about her shoulders and sat, as rapt as any of them, following the long sinuous curves of the immortal story as it unfolded before our eyes.

They could hardly bear to part with us when at last the story came to an end. They clung to her, pleading for more. Some picked the hem of her skirt and kissed it in an agony of pleading. "There is no time" she said, smiling calmly. "But I will come again, my little ones." They hardly heeded the money she distributed but thronged after us along the dark corridors to the blackness of the square. At the corner I looked back but could only see the flicker of shadows. They said farewell in voices of heartbreaking sweetness. We walked in deep contented silence across the shattered, time-corrupted town until we reached the cool seafront; and stood for a long time leaning upon the cold stone piers above the sea, smoking and saying nothing! At last she turned to me a face of tremendous weariness and whispered: "Take me home, now. I'm dead tired." And so we hailed a pottering gharry and swung along the Corniche as sedately as bankers after a congress. "I suppose we are all hunting for the secrets of growth!" was all she said as we parted.

It was a strange remark to make at parting. I watched her walk wearily up the steps to the great house groping for her key. I still felt drunk with the story of Yuna and Aziz!

Brother Ass, it is a pity that you will never have a chance to read all this tedious rigmarole; it would amuse me to study your puzzled expression as you did so. Why should the artist always be trying to saturate the world with his own anguish, you asked me once. Why indeed? I will give you another phrase: emotional gongorism! I have always been good at polite phrase-making.

Loneliness and desire,
Lord of the Flies,
Are thy unholy empire and
The self's inmost surprise!
Come to these arms, my dear old Dutch
And firmly bar the door
I could not love thee, dear, so much
Loved I not ******* more!

And later, aimlessly walking, who should I encounter but the slightly titubating Pombal just back from the Casino with a chamber-pot full of paper money and a raging thirst for a last beaker of champagne which we took together at the Étoile. It was strange that I had no taste for a girl that night; somehow Yuna and Aziz had barred the way. Instead I straggled back to Mount Vulture with a bottle in my mackintosh pocket, to confront once more the ill-starred pages of my book which, twenty years from now, will be the cause of many a thrashing among the lower forms of our schools. It seemed a disastrous sort of gift to be offering to the generations as yet unborn; I would rather have left them something like Yuna and Aziz, but it hasn't been possible since Chaucer; the sophistication of the laic audience is perhaps to blame? The thought of all those smarting little bottoms made me close my notebooks with a series of ill-tempered snaps. Champagne is a wonderfully soothing drink, however, and prevented me from being too cast-down. Then I stumbled upon the little note which you, Brother Ass, had pushed under the door earlier in the evening: a note which complimented me on the new series of poems which the Anvil was producing (a misprint per line); and writers being what they are I thought most kindly of you, I raised my glass to you. In my eyes you had become a critic of the purest discernment; and once more I asked myself in exasperated tones why the devil I had never wasted more time on you? It was really remiss of me. And falling asleep I made a mental note to take you to dinner the next evening and talk your jackass's head off—about writing, of course, what else? Ah! but that is the point. Once a writer seldom a talker; I knew that, speechless as Goldsmith, I should sit hugging my hands in my armpits while *you* did the talking!

In my sleep I dug up a mummy with poppy-coloured lips, dressed in the long white wedding dress of the Arab sugar-dolls. She smiled but would not awake, though I kissed her and talked to her persuasively. Once her eyes half opened; but they closed again and she lapsed back into smiling sleep. I whispered her name which was Yuna, but which had unaccountably become Liza. And as it was no use I interred her once more among the shifting dunes where (the wind-shapes were changing fast) there would be no trace remaining of the spot. At dawn I woke early and took a gharry down to the Rushdi beach to cleanse myself in the dawn-sea. There was not a soul about at that time save Clea, who was on the far beach in a blue bathing-costume, her marvellous hair swinging about her like a blonde Botticelli. I waved and she waved back, but showed no inclination to come and talk which made me grateful. We lay, a thousand yards apart, smoking and wet as seals. I thought for an instant of the lovely burnt coffee of her summer flesh, with the little hairs on her temples bleached to ash. I inhaled her metaphorically, like a whiff of roasting coffee, dreaming of the white thighs with those small blue veins in them! Well, well . . . she would have been worth taking trouble over had she not been so beautiful. That brilliant glance exposed everything and forced me to take shelter from her.

One could hardly ask her to bandage them in order to be made love to! And yet . . . like the black silk stockings some men insist on! Two sentences ending with a preposition! What is poor Pursewarden coming to?

> *His prose created grievous lusts*
> *Among the middle classes*

152

His propositions were decried
As dangerous for the masses

His major works were classified
Among the noxious gases
                    England awake!

Brother Ass, the so-called act of living is really an act of the imagination. The world—which we always visualise as "the outside" World—yields only to self-exploration! Faced by this cruel, yet necessary paradox, the poet finds himself growing gills and a tail, the better to swim against the currents of unenlightenment. What appears to be perhaps an arbitrary act of violence is precisely the opposite, for by reversing process in this way, he unites the rushing, heedless stream of humanity to the still, tranquil, motionless, odourless, tasteless plenum from which its own motive essence is derived. (Yes, but it *hurts* to realise!) If he were to abandon his rôle all hope of gaining a purchase on the slippery surface of reality would be lost, and everything in nature would disappear! But this act, the poetic act, will cease to be necessary when everyone can perform it for himself. What hinders them, you ask? Well, we are all naturally afraid to surrender our own pitifully rationalised morality —and the poetic jump I'm predicating lies the other side of it. It is only terrifying because we refuse to recognise in ourselves the horrible gargoyles which decorate the totem poles of our churches—murderers, liars, adulterers and so on. (Once recognised, these papier-mâché masks fade.) Whoever makes this enigmatic leap into the heraldic reality of the poetic life discovers that truth has its own built-in morality! There is no need to wear a truss any longer. Inside the penumbra of this sort of truth morality can be disregarded because it is a *donnée*, a part of the thing, and not simply a brake, an inhibition. It is there to be lived out and not thought out! Ah, Brother Ass, this will seem a far cry to the "purely literary" preoccupations which beset you; yet unless you tackle this corner of the field with your sickle you will never reap the harvest in yourself, and so fulfil your true function here below.

But how? you ask me plaintively. And truly here you have me by the short hairs, for the thing operates differently with each one of us. I am only suggesting that you have not become desperate enough, determined enough. Somewhere at the heart of things you are still lazy of spirit. But then, why struggle? If it is to happen to you it will happen of its own accord. You may be quite right to hang about like this, waiting. I was too proud. I felt I must take it by the horns, this vital question of my birthright. For me it was grounded in an act of will. So for people like me I would say: "Force the lock, batter down the door. Outface, defy, disprove the Oracle in order to become the poet, the darer!"

But I am aware the test may come under any guise, perhaps even in the physical world by a blow between the eyes or a few lines scribbled in pencil on the back of an envelope left in a café. The heraldic reality can strike from any point, above or below: it is not particular. But without it the enigma will remain. You may travel round the world and colonise the ends of the earth with your lines and yet never hear the singing yourself.

o   o   o   o   o

III

I found myself reading these passages from Pursewarden's
notebooks with all the attention and amusement they
deserved, and without any thought of "exoneration"—
to use the phrase of Clea. On the contrary, it seemed to
me that his observation was not lacking in accuracy and whatever whips and scorpions he had applied to my image were well
justified. It is, moreover, useful as well as salutary to see oneself portrayed with such blistering candour by someone one
admires! Yet I was a trifle surprised not to feel even a little
wounded in my self-esteem. Not only were no bones broken,
but at times, chuckling aloud at his sallies, I found myself
addressing him under my breath as if he were actually present
before me, uttering rather than writing down these unpalatable
home-truths. "You bastard" I said under my breath. "You just
wait a little bit." Almost as if one day I might right the
reckoning with him, pay off the score! It was troubling to raise
my head and realise suddenly that he had already stepped
behind the curtains, vanished from the scene; he was so much
of a presence, popping up everywhere, with the strange mixture
of strengths and weaknesses which made up his enigmatic
character.

"What are you chuckling at?" said Telford, always anxious
to share a jocose exchange of office wit provided it had the
requisite moribund point.

"A notebook."

Telford was a large man draped in ill-cut clothes and a
spotted blue bow tie. His complexion was blotchy and of the
kind which tears easily under a razor-blade; consequently there
was always a small tuft of cotton wool sticking to chin or ear,
stanching a wound. Always voluble and bursting with the

wrong sort of expansive *bonhomie* he gave the impression of being at war with his dentures, which were ill-fitting. He gobbled and gasped, biting on loose stoppings, or swallowing a soft palate, gasping like a fish as he uttered his pleasantries or laughed at his own jokes like a man riding a bone-shaker, his top set of teeth bumping up and down on his gums. "I say, old fruit, that was rich" he would exclaim. I did not find him too disagreeable an inmate of the office which we shared at the censorship, for the work was not exacting and he, as an old hand, was always ready to give me advice or help with it; I enjoyed too his obstinately recurring stories of the mythical "old days", when he, Little Tommy Telford, had been a personage of great importance, second only in rank and power to the great Maskelyne, our present Chief. He always referred to him as "The Brig", and made it very clear that the department, which had once been Arab Bureau, had seen better times, had in fact been downgraded to a mere censorship department dealing with the ebb and flow of civilian correspondence over the Middle East. A menial rôle compared to "Espionage" which he pronounced in four separate syllables.

Stories of this ancient glory, which had now faded beyond recall, formed part of the Homeric Cycle, so to speak, of office life: to be recited wistfully during intervals between snatches of work or on afternoons when some small mishap like a broken fan had made concentration in those airless buildings all but impossible. It was from Telford that I learned of the long internecine struggle between Pursewarden and Maskelyne—a struggle which was, in a sense, continuing on another plane between the silent Brigadier and Mountolive, for Maskelyne was desperately anxious to rejoin his regiment and shed his civilian suit. This desire had been baulked. Mountolive, explained Telford with many a gusty sigh (waving chapped and podgy hands which were stuffed with bluish clusters of veins like plums in a cake)—Mountolive had "got at" the War Office and persuaded them not to countenance Maskelyne's resignation. I must say the Brigadier, whom I saw perhaps twice a week, did convey an impression of sullen, saturnine fury at being penned up in a civilian department while so much was going on in the desert, but of course any regular soldier would. "You see" said Telford ingenuously, "when a war comes along there's bags of promotion, old thing, bags of it. The Brig has a right to think of his career like any other man. It is different for us. We were born civilians, so to speak." He himself had spent many years in the currant trade in the Eastern Levant residing in places like Zante and Patras. His reasons for coming to Egypt were obscure. Perhaps he found life more congenial in a large British colony. Mrs. Telford was a fattish little duck who used mauve lipstick and wore hats like pincushions. She only appeared to live for an invitation to the Embassy on the King's birthday. ("Mavis loves her little official 'do', she does.")

But if the administrative war with Mountolive was so far empty of victory there were consolations, said Telford, from which the Brig could derive a studied enjoyment: for Mountolive was very much in the same boat. This made him (Telford) "chortle"—a characteristic phrase which he often used. Mountolive, it seemed, was no less eager to abandon his post, and had indeed applied several times for a transfer from Egypt. Unluckily, however, the war had intervened with its policy of "freezing personnel" and Kenilworth, no friend of the Ambassador, had been sent out to execute this policy. If the Brigadier was pinned down by the intrigues of Mountolive, the latter had been pinned down just as certainly by the newly appointed Personnel Adviser—pinned down "for the duration"! Telford rubbed unctuous hands as he retailed all this to me! "It's a case of the biter bit all right" he said. "And if you ask me the Brig will manage to get away sooner than Sir David. Mark my words, old fruit." A single solemn nod was enough to satisfy him that his point had been taken.

Telford and Maskelyne were united by a curious sort of bond which intrigued me. The solitary monosyllabic soldier

157

and the effusive bagman—what on earth could they have had in common? (Their very names on the printed duty rosters irresistibly suggested a music-hall team or a firm of respectable undertakers!) Yet I think the bond was one of admiration, for Telford behaved with a grotesque wonder and respect when in the presence of his Chief, fussing around him anxiously, eagerly, longing to anticipate his commands and so earn a word of commendation. His heavily salivated "Yes, sir" and "No, sir" popped out from between his dentures with the senseless regularity of cuckoos from a clock. Curiously enough there was nothing feigned in this sycophancy. It was in fact something like an administrative love-affair, for even when Maskelyne was not present Telford spoke of him with the greatest possible reverence, the profoundest hero-worship—compounded equally of social admiration for his rank and deep respect for his character and judgement. Out of curiosity I tried to see Maskelyne through my colleague's eyes but failed to discern more than a rather bleak and well-bred soldier of narrow capacities and a clipped world-weary public school accent. Yet . . . "The Brig is a real cast-iron gentleman" Telford would say with an emotion so great that it almost brought tears to his eyes. "He's as straight as string, is the old Brig. Never stoop to do anything beneath him." It was perhaps true, yet it did not make our Chief less unremarkable in my eyes.

Telford had several little menial duties which he himself had elected to perform for his hero—for example, to buy the week-old *Daily Telegraph* and place it on the great man's desk each morning. He adopted a curious finicky walk as he crossed the polished floor of Maskelyne's empty office (for we arrived early at work): almost as if he were afraid of leaving footprints behind him. He positively stole across to the desk. And the tenderness with which he folded the paper and ran his fingers down the creases before laying it reverently on the green blotter reminded me of a woman handling a husband's newly starched and ironed shirt.

Nor was the Brigadier himself unwilling to accept the burden of this guileless admiration. I imagine few men could resist it. At first I was puzzled by the fact that once or twice a week he would visit us, clearly with no special matter in mind, and would take a slow turn up and down between our desks, occasionally uttering an informal monochrome pleasantry—indicating the recipient of it by pointing the stem of his pipe at him lightly, almost shyly. Yet throughout these visitations his swarthy greyhound's face, with its small crowsfeet under the eyes, never altered its expression, his voice never lost its studied inflections. At first, as I say, these appearances somewhat puzzled me, for Maskelyne was anything but a convivial soul and could seldom talk of anything but the work in hand. Then one day I detected, in the slow elaborate figure he traced between our desks, the traces of an unconscious coquetry—I was reminded of the way a peacock spreads its great studded fan of eyes before the female, or of the way a mannequin wheels in an arabesque designed to show off the clothes she is wearing. Maskelyne had in fact simply come to be admired, to spread out the riches of his character and breeding before Telford. Was it possible that this easy conquest provided him with some inner assurance he lacked? It would be hard to say. Yet he was inwardly basking in his colleague's wide-eyed admiration. I am sure it was quite unconscious—this gesture of a lonely man towards the only whole-hearted admirer he had as yet won from the world. From his own side, however, he could only reciprocate with the condescension bred by his education. Secretly he held Telford in contempt for not being a gentleman. "Poor Telford" he would be heard to sigh when out of the other's hearing. "Poor Telford". The commiserating fall of the voice suggested pity for someone who was worthy but hopelessly uninspired.

These, then, were my office familiars during the whole of that first wearing summer, and their companionship offered me no problem. The work left me easy and untroubled in mind.

My ranking was a humble one and carried with it no social obligations whatsoever. For the rest we did not frequent each other outside the office. Telford lived somewhere near Rushdi in a small suburban villa, outside the centre of the town, while Maskelyne seldom appeared to stir from the gaunt bedroom on the top floor of the Cecil. Once free from the office, therefore, I felt able to throw it off completely and once more resume the life of the town, or what was left of it.

With Clea also the new relationship offered no problems, perhaps because deliberately we avoided defining it too sharply, and allowed it to follow the curves of its own nature, to fulfil its own design. I did not, for example, always stay at her flat— for sometimes when she was working on a picture she would plead for a few days of complete solitude and seclusion in order to come to grips with her subject, and these intermittent intervals, sometimes of a week or more, sharpened and refreshed affection without harming it. Sometimes, however, after such a compact we would stumble upon each other by accident and out of weakness resume the suspended relationship before the promised three days or a week was up! It wasn't easy.

Sometimes at evening I might come upon her sitting absently alone on the little painted wooden terrace of the Café Baudrot, gazing into space. Her sketching blocks lay before her, unopened. Sitting there as still as a coney, she had forgotten to remove from her lips the tiny moustache of cream from her *café viennois*! At such a moment it needed all my self-possession not to vault the wooden balustrade and put my arms round her, so vividly did this touching detail seem to light up the memory of her; so childish and serene did she look. The loyal and ardent image of Clea the lover rose up before my eyes and all at once separation seemed unendurable! Conversely I might suddenly (sitting on a bench in a public garden, reading) feel cool hands pressed over my eyes and turn suddenly to embrace her and inhale once more the fragrance of her body through her crisp summer frock. At other times, and very often at moments when

I was actually thinking of her, she would walk miraculously into the flat saying: "I felt you calling me to come" or else "It suddenly came over me to need you very much." So these encounters had a breathless sharp sweetness, unexpectedly re-igniting our ardour. It was as if we had been separated for years instead of days.

This self-possession in the matter of planned absences from each other struck a spark of admiration from Pombal, who could no more achieve the same measure in his relations with Fosca than climb to the moon. He appeared to wake in the morning with her name on his lips. His first act was to tele-phone her anxiously to find out if she were well—as if her ab-sence had exposed her to terrible unknown dangers. His official day with its various duties was a torment. He positively gal-loped home to lunch in order to see her again. In all justice I must say that his attachment was fully reciprocated for all that their relationship was like that of two elderly retired pensioners in its purity. If he were kept late at an official dinner she would work herself into a fever of apprehension. ("No, it is not his fidelity that worries me, it is his safety. He drives so carelessly, as you know.") Fortunately during this period the nightly bombardment of the harbour acted upon social activities almost like a curfew, so that it was possible to spend almost every evening together, playing chess or cards, or reading aloud. Fosca I found to be a thoughtful, almost intense young woman, a little lacking in humour but devoid of the priggishness which I had been inclined to suspect from Pombal's own description of her when first we met. She had a keen and mobile face whose premature wrinkles suggested that perhaps she had been marked by her experiences as a refugee. She never laughed aloud, and her smile had a touch of reflective sadness in it. But she was wise, and always had a spirited and thoughtful answer ready—indeed the quality of *esprit* which the French so rightly prize in a woman. The fact that she was nearing the term of her pregnancy only seemed to make Pombal more attentive and adoring—indeed he behaved with something like complacence about the child. Or was he simply trying to suggest that it was his own: as a show of face to a world which might think that he was "unmanned"? I could not decide. In the summer afternoons he would float about the harbour in his cutter while Fosca sat in the stern trailing one white hand in the sea. Sometimes she sang for him in a small true voice like a bird's. This transported him, and he wore the look of a good *bourgeois papa de famille* as he beat time with his finger. At night they sat out the bombardment for preference over a chess board—a somewhat singular choice; but as the infernal racket of gunfire gave him nervous head-aches he had skilfully constructed ear plugs for them both by cutting the filter-tips from cigarettes. So they were able to sit, concentrating in silence!

But once or twice this peaceful harmony was overshadowed by outside events which provoked doubts and misgivings under-standable enough in a relationship which was so nebulous—I mean so much *discussed* and anatomised and not acted out. One day I found him padding about in a dressing-gown and slippers looking suspiciously distraught, even a little red-eyed. "Ah, Darley!" he sighed gustily, falling into his gout chair and catching his beard in his fingers as if he were about to dismantle it completely. "We will never understand them, never. Women! What bad luck. Perhaps I am just stupid. Fosca! Her husband!"

"He has been killed?" I asked.

Pombal shook his head sadly. "No. Taken prisoner and sent to Germany."

"Well why the fuss?"

"I am ashamed, that is all. I did not fully realise until this news came, neither did she, that we were really *expecting* him to be killed. Unconsciously, of course. Now she is full of self disgust. But the whole plan for *our* lives was unconsciously built upon the notion of him surrendering his own. It is monstrous. His death would have freed us; but now the whole problem is deferred perhaps for years, perhaps forever. . . ."

He looked quite distracted and fanned himself with a news-paper, muttering under his breath. "Things take the strangest turns" he went on at last. "For if Fosca is too honourable to confess the truth to him while he is at the front, she would equally never do it to a poor prisoner. I left her in tears. Every-thing is put off till the *end of the war*."

He ground his back teeth together and sat staring at me. It was difficult to know what one could say by way of consolation.

"Why doesn't she write and tell him?"

"Impossible! Too cruel. And with the child coming on? Even I, Pombal, would not wish her to do such a thing. Never. I found her in *tears*, my friend, holding the telegram. She said in tones of anguish: 'O Georges-Gaston for the first time I feel ashamed of my love, when I realise that we were wishing him to die rather than get captured this way.' It may sound compli-cated to you, but her emotions are so fine, her sense of honour and pride and so on. Then a queer thing happened. So great was our mutual pain that in trying to console her I slipped and we began to make real love without noticing it. It is a strange picture. And not an easy operation. Then when we came to our-selves she began to cry all over again and said: 'Now for the first time I have a feeling of hate for you, Georges-Gaston, be-cause now our love is on the same plane as everyone else's. We have cheapened it.' Women always put you in the wrong some-how. I was so full of joy to have at last. . . . Suddenly her words plunged me into despair. I rushed away. I have not seen her for *five hours*. Perhaps this is the end of everything? Ah but it could have been the beginning of something which would at least sustain us until the whole problem sees the light of day."

"Perhaps she is too stupid."

Pombal was aghast. "How can you say that! All this comes from her exquisite finesse of spirit. That is all. Don't add to my misery by saying foolish things about one so fine."

"Well, telephone her."

"Her phone is out of order. Aie! It is worse than toothache.

I have been toying with the idea of suicide for the first time in my life. That will show you to what a point I've been driven."

But at this moment the door opened and Fosca stepped into the room. She too had been crying. She stopped with a queer dignity and held out her hands to Pombal who gave an inarticulate growling cry of delight and bounded across the room in his dressing-gown to embrace her passionately. Then he drew her into the circle of his arm and they went slowly down the corridor to his room together and locked themselves in.

Later that evening I saw him coming down Rue Fuad towards me, beaming. "Hurrah!" he shouted and threw his expensive hat high into the air. *"Je suis enfin là"*!

The hat described a large parabola and settled in the middle of the road where it was immediately run over by three cars in rapid succession. Pombal clasped his hands together and beamed as if the sight gave him the greatest joy. Then he turned his moon-face up into the sky as if searching for a sign or portent. As I came abreast of him he caught my hands and said: "Divine logic of women! Truly there is nothing so wonderful on earth as the sight of a woman thinking out her feelings. I adore it. I adore it. Our love. . . . Fosca! It is complete now. I am so astonished, truthfully, I am *astonished*. I would never have been able to think it out so accurately. Listen, she could not bring herself to deceive a man who was in hourly danger of death. Right. But now that he is safely behind bars it is different. We are free to normalise ourselves. We will not, of course, hurt him by telling him as yet. We will simply help ourselves from the pantry, as Pursewarden used to say. My dear friend, isn't it wonderful? Fosca is an angel."

"She sounds like a woman after all."

"A Woman! The word, magnificent as it is, is hardly enough for a spirit like hers."

He burst into a whinny of laughter and punched me affectionately on the shoulder. Together we walked down the long street. "I am going to Pierantoni to buy her an expensive present . . . I, who never give a woman presents, never in my life. It always seemed absurd. I once saw a film of penguins in the mating season. The male penguin, than which nothing could more ludicrously resemble man, collects stones and places them before the lady of his choice when he proposes. It must be seen to be appreciated. Now I am behaving like a male penguin. Never mind. Never mind. Now our story cannot help but have a happy ending."

Fateful words which I have so often recalled since, for within a few months Fosca was to be a problem no more.

o   o   o   o   o

IV

For some considerable time I heard nothing of Purse-warden's sister, though I knew that she was still up at the summer legation. As for Mountolive, his visits were recorded among the office memoranda, so that I knew he came up from Cairo for the night about every ten days. For a while I half expected a signal from him, but as time wore on I almost began to forget his existence as presumably he had forgotten mine. So it was that her voice, when first it floated over the office telephone, came as an unexpected intrusion—a surprise in a world where surprises were few and not unwelcome. A curiously disembodied voice which might have been that of uncertain adolescence, saying: "I think you know of me. As a friend of my brother I would like to talk to you." The invitation to dinner the following evening she described as "private, informal and unofficial" which suggested to me that Mountolive himself would be present. I felt the stirring of an unusual curiosity as I walked up the long drive with its very English hedges of box, and through the small coppice of pines which encircled the summer residence. It was an airless hot night—such as must presage the gathering of a *khamseen* somewhere in the desert which would later roll its dust clouds down the city's streets and squares like pillars of smoke. But as yet the night air was harsh and clear.

I rang the bell twice without result, and was beginning to think that perhaps it might be out of order when I heard a soft swift step inside. The door opened and there stood Liza with an expression of triumphant eagerness on her blind face. I found her extraordinarily beautiful at first sight, though a little on the short side. She wore a dress of some dark soft stuff with a collar cut very wide, out of which her slender throat and head rose as if out of the corolla of a flower. She stood before me with her face thrown upwards, forwards—with an air of spectral bravery —as if presenting her lovely neck to an invisible executioner. As I uttered my own name she smiled and nodded and repeated it back to me in a whisper tense as a thread. "Thank goodness, at last you have come" she said, as though she had lived in the expectation of my visit for years! As I stepped forward she added quickly "Please forgive me if I. . . . It is my only way of knowing." And I suddenly felt her soft warm fingers on my face, moving swiftly over it as if spelling it out, I felt a stirring of some singular unease, composed of sensuality and disgust, as these expert fingers travelled over my cheeks and lips. Her hands were small and well-shaped; the fingers conveyed an extraordinary impression of delicacy, for they appeared to turn up slightly at the ends to present their white pads, like antennae, to the world. I had once seen a world-famous pianist with just such fingers, so sensitive that they appeared to grow into the keyboard as he touched it. She gave a small sigh, as if of relief, and taking me by the wrist drew me across the hall and into the living-room with its expensive and featureless official furniture where Mountolive stood in front of the fireplace with an air of uneasy concern. Somewhere a radio softly played. We shook hands and in his handclasp I felt something infirm, indecisive which was matched by the fugitive voice in which he excused his long silence. "I had to wait until Liza was ready" he said, rather mysteriously.

Mountolive had changed a good deal, though he still bore all the marks of the superficial elegance which was a prerequisite for his work, and his clothes were fastidiously chosen—for even (I thought grimly) informal undress is still a uniform for a diplomat. His old kindness and attentiveness were still there. Yet he had aged. I noticed that he now needed reading-glasses, for they lay upon a copy of *The Times* beside the sofa. And he had grown a moustache which he did not trim and which had altered the shape of his mouth, and emphasised a certain finely bred feebleness of feature. It did not seem possible to imagine him ever to have been in the grip of a passion strong enough to qualify the standard responses of an education so definitive as his. Nor now, looking from one to the other, could I credit the suspicions which Clea had voiced about his love for this strange blind witch who now sat upon the sofa staring sightlessly at me, with her hands folded in her lap—those rapacious, avaricious hands of a musician. Had she coiled herself, like a small hateful snake, at the centre of his peaceful life? I accepted a drink from his fingers and found, in the warmth of his smile, that I remembered having liked and admired him. I did so still.

"We have both been eager to see you, and particularly Liza, because she felt that you might be able to help her. But we will talk about all that later." And with an abrupt smoothness he turned away from the real subject of my visit to enquire whether my post pleased me, and whether I was happy in it. An exchange of courteous pleasantries which provoked the neutral answers appropriate to them. Yet here and there were gleams of new information. "Liza was quite determined you should stay here; and so we got busy to arrange it!" Why? Simply that I should submit to a catechism about her brother, who in truth I could hardly claim to have known, and who grew more and more mysterious to me every day—less important as a personage, more and more so as an artist? It was clear that I must wait until she chose to speak her mind. Yet it was baffling to idle away the time in the exchange of superficialities.

Yet these smooth informalities reigned, and to my surprise the girl herself said nothing—not a word. She sat there on the sofa, softly and attentively, as if on a cloud. She wore, I noticed, a velvet ribbon on her throat. It occurred to me that her pallor, which had so much struck Clea, was probably due to not being able to make-up in the mirror. But Clea had been right about the shape of her mouth, for once or twice I caught an expression, cutting and sardonic, which was a replica of her brother's.

Dinner was wheeled in by a servant, and still exchanging small talk we sat down to eat it; Liza ate swiftly, as if she were hungry, and quite unerringly, from the plate which Mountolive filled for her. I noticed when she reached for her wineglass that her expressive fingers trembled slightly. At last, when the meal was over, Mountolive rose with an air of scarcely disguised relief and excused himself. "I'm going to leave you alone to talk shop to Liza. I shall have to do some work in the Chancery this evening. You will excuse me won't you?" I saw an apprehensive frown shadow Liza's face for a moment, but it vanished almost at once and was replaced by an expression which suggested something between despair and resignation. Her fingers picked softly, suggestively at the tassel of a cushion. When the door had closed behind him she still sat silent, but now preternaturally still, her head bent downwards as if she were trying to decipher a message written in the palm of her hand. At last she spoke in a small cold voice, pronouncing the words incisively as if to make her meaning plain.

"I had no idea it would be difficult to explain when first I thought of asking your help. This book. . . ."

There was a long silence. I saw that little drops of perspiration had come out on her upper lip and her temples looked as if they had tightened under stress. I felt a certain compassion for her distress and said: "I can't claim to have known him well, though I saw him quite frequently. In truth, I don't think we liked each other very much."

"Originally" she said sharply, cutting across my vagueness with impatience "I thought I might persuade you to do the book about him. But now I see that you will have to know everything. It is not easy to know where to begin. I myself doubt whether the facts of his life are possible to put down and publish. But I have been driven to think about the matter, first because his publishers insist on it—they say there is a great public demand; but mostly because of the book which this shabby journalist is writing, or has written. Keats."

"Keats" I echoed with surprise.

"He is here somewhere I believe; but I do not know him. He has been put up to the idea by my brother's wife. She hated him, you know, after she found out; she thought that my brother and I had between us ruined her life. Truthfully I am afraid of her. I do not know what she has told Keats, or what he will write. I see now that my original idea in having you brought here was to get you to write a book which would . . . disguise the truth somehow. It only became clear to me just now when I was confronted by you. It would be inexpressibly painful to me if anything got out which harmed my brother's memory."

Somewhere to the east I heard a grumble of thunder. She stood up with an air of panic and after a moment's hesitation crossed to the grand piano and struck a chord. Then she banged the cover down and turned once more to me, saying: "I am afraid of thunder. Please may I hold your hand in a firm grip." Her own was deathly cold. Then, shaking back her black hair she said: "We were lovers, you know. That is really the meaning of his story and mine. He tried to break away. His marriage foundered on this question. It was perhaps dishonest of him not to have told her the truth before he married her. Things fall out strangely. For many years we enjoyed a perfect happiness, he and I. That it ended tragically is nobody's fault I suppose. He could not free himself from my inside hold on him, though he tried and struggled. I could not free myself from him, though truthfully I never wished to until . . . until the day arrived which he had predicted so many years before when the man he always called 'the dark stranger' arrived. He saw him so clearly when he gazed into the fire. It was David Mountolive. For a little while I did not tell him that I had fallen in love, the fated love. (David would not let me. The only person we told was Nessim's mother. David asked my permission.) But my brother knew it quite unerringly and wrote after a long silence asking me if the stranger had come. When he got my letter he seemed suddenly to realise that our relationship might be endangered or crushed in the way his had been with his wife—not by anything we did, no, but by the simple fact of my existence. So he committed suicide. He explained it all so clearly in his last letter to me. I can recite it by heart. He said: 'For so many years I have waited in anguished expectation for your letter. Often, often I wrote it for you in my own head, spelling it out word by magical word. I knew that in your happiness you would at once turn to me to express a passionate gratitude for what I had given you—for learning the meaning of all love through mine: so that when the stranger came you were ready. . . . And today it came! this long-awaited message, saying that he had read the letters, and I knew for the first time a sense of inexpressible relief as I read the lines. And joy—such joy as I never hoped to experience in my life—to think of you suddenly plunging into the full richness of life at last, no longer tied, manacled to the image of your tormented brother! Blessings tumbled from my lips. But then, gradually, as the cloud lifted and dispersed I felt the leaden tug of another truth, quite unforeseen, quite unexpected. The fear that, so long as I was still alive, still somewhere existing in the world, you would find it impossible truly to escape from the chains in which I have so cruelly held you all these years. At this fear my blood has turned chill—for I know that truthfully something much more definitive is required of me if you are ever to renounce me and start living. I must really abandon you, really remove myself from the scene in a manner which would permit no further equivocation in our vacillating hearts. Yes, I had anticipated the joy, but not that it would bring with it such a clear representation of certain death. This was a huge novelty! Yet it is the completest gift I can offer you as a wedding present! And if you look beyond the immediate pain you will see how perfect the logic of love seems to one who is ready to die for it.' "

She gave a short clear sob and hung her head. She took the handkerchief from the breast pocket of my coat and pressed it to her trembling lip. I felt stupefied by the sad weight of all this calamitous information. I felt, in the ache of pity for Pursewarden, a new recognition of him growing up, a new enlightenment. So many things became clearer. Yet there were no words of consolation or commiseration which could do justice to so tragic a situation. She was talking again.

"I will give you the private letters to read so that you can advise me. These are the letters which I was not to open but was to keep until David came. He would read them to me and we would destroy them—or so he said. Is it strange—his certainty? The other ordinary letters were of course read to me in the usual way; but these private letters, and they are very many, were all pierced with a pin in the top left-hand corner. So that I could recognise them and put them aside. They are in that suitcase over there. I would like you to take them away and study them. O Darley, you have not said a word. Are you prepared to help me in this dreadful predicament? I wish I could read your expression."

"Of course I will help you. But just how and in what sense?"

"Advise me what to do! None of this would have arisen had not this shabby journalist intervened and been to see his wife."

"Did your brother appoint a literary executor?"

"Yes. I am his executor."

"Then you have a right to refuse to allow any of his unsold writings to be published while they're in copyright. Besides, I do not see how such facts could be made public without your own permission, even in an unauthorised biography. There is no cause whatsoever to worry. No writer in his senses could touch such material; no publisher in the world would undertake to print it if he did. I think the best thing I can do is to try and find out something about this book of Keats's. Then at least you will know where you stand."

"Thank you, Darley. I could not approach Keats myself because I knew he was working for her. I hate and fear her—perhaps unjustly. I suppose too that I have a feeling of having wronged her without wishing it. It was a deplorable mistake on his part, not to tell her before their marriage; I think he recognised it, too, for he was determined that I should not make the same mistake when at last David appeared. Hence the private letters, which leave no one in doubt. Yet it all fell out exactly as he had planned it, had prophesied it. That very first night when I told David I took him straight home to read them. We sat on the carpet in front of the gas-fire and he read them to me one by one in that unmistakable voice—the stranger's voice."

She gave a queer blind smile at the memory and I had a sudden compassionate picture of Mountolive sitting before the fire, reading these letters in a slow faltering voice, stunned by the revelation of his own part in this weird masque, which had been planned for him years before, without his knowing. Liza sat beside me, lost in deep thought, her head hanging. Her lips moved slowly as if she were spelling something out in her own mind, following some interior recitation. I shook her hand softly, as if to awaken her. "I should leave you now" I said softly. "And why should I see the private letters at all? There is no need."

"Now that you know the worst and best I would like you to advise me about destroying them. It was his wish. But David feels that they belong to his writings, and that we have a duty to preserve them. I cannot make up my mind about this. You are a writer. Try and read them as a writer, as if you had written them, and then tell me whether you would wish them preserved or not. They are all together in that suitcase. There are one or two other fragments which you might help me edit if you have time or if you think them suitable. He always puzzled me— except when I had him in my arms."

A sudden expression of savage resentment passed across her white face. As if she had been goaded by a sudden disagreeable memory. She passed her tongue over her dry lips and as we stood up together she added in a small husky voice: "There is one thing more. Since you have seen so far into out lives why should you not look right to the bottom? I always keep this close to me." Reaching down into her dress she took out a snapshot and handed it to me. It was faded and creased. A small child with long hair done up in ribbons sat upon a park bench, gazing with a melancholy and wistful smile at the camera and holding out a white stick. It took me a moment or so to identify those troubling lines of mouth and nose as the features of Pursewarden himself and to realise that the little girl was blind.

"Do you see her?" said Liza in a thrilling whisper that shook the nerves by its strange tension, its mixture of savagery, bitterness and triumphant anguish. "Do you see her? She was our child. It was when she died that he was overcome with remorse for a situation which had brought us nothing but joy before. Her death suddenly made him guilty. Our relationship foundered there; and yet it became in another way even more intense, closer. We were united by our guilt from that moment. I have often asked myself why it should be so. Tremendous unbroken happiness and then . . . one day, like an iron shutter falling, *guilt*."

The word dropped like a falling star and expired in the silence. I took this unhappiest of all relics and pressed it into her cold hands.

"I will take the letters" I said.

"Thank you" she replied with an air now of dazed exhaustion. "I knew we had a friend in you. I shall count on your help."

As I softly closed the front-door behind me I heard a chord struck upon the piano—a single chord which hung in the silent air, its vibrations diminishing like an echo. As I crossed among the trees I caught a glimpse of Mountolive sneaking towards the side door of the house. I suddenly divined that he had been walking up and down outside the house in an agony of apprehension, with the air of a schoolboy waiting outside his housemaster's study to receive a beating. I felt a pang of sympathy for him, for his weakness, for the dreadful entanglement in which he had found himself.

I found to my surprise that it was still early. Clea had gone to Cairo for the day and was not expected back. I took the little suitcase to her flat and sitting on the floor unpacked it.

In that quiet room, by the light of her candles, I began to read the private letters with a curious interior premonition, a stirring of something like fear—so dreadful a thing is it to explore the inmost secrets of another human being's life. Nor did this feeling diminish as I proceeded, rather it deepened into a sort of terror, almost a horror of what might be coming next. The letters! Ferocious, sulky, brilliant, profuse—the torrent of words in that close hand flowed on and on endlessly, studded with diamond-hard images, a wild self-analytical frenzy of despair, remorse and passion. I began to tremble as one must in the presence of a great master, to tremble and mutter. With an interior shock I realised that there was nothing in the whole length and breadth of our literature with which to compare them! Whatever other masterpieces Pursewarden may have written these letters outshone them all in their furious, un-premeditated brilliance and prolixity. Literature, I say! But these were life itself, not a studied representation of it in a form —life itself, the flowing undivided stream of life with all its pitiable will-intoxicated memories, its pains, terrors and sub-missions. Here illusion and reality were fused in one single blinding vision of a perfect incorruptible passion which hung over the writer's mind like a dark star—the star of death! The tremendous sorrow and beauty which this man expressed so easily—the terrifying abundance of his gifts—filled me with helpless despair and joy at once. The cruelty and the richness! It was as if the words poured from every pore in his body— execrations, groans, mixed tears of joy and despair—all welded to the fierce rapid musical notation of a language perfected by its purpose. Here at last the lovers confronted one another, stripped to the bone, stripped bare.

In this strange and frightening experience I caught a glimpse, for a moment, of the true Pursewarden—the man who had always eluded me. I thought with shame of the shabby passages in the Justine manuscript which I had devoted to him—to my image of him! I had, out of envy or unconscious jealousy, invented a Pursewarden to criticise. In everything I had written there I had accused him only of my own weaknesses—even down to completely erroneous estimates of qualities like social inferiorities which were mine, had never been his. It was only now, tracing out the lines written by that rapid unfaltering pen, that I realised that poetic or transcendental knowledge somehow cancels out purely relative knowledge, and that his black humours were simply ironies due to this enigmatic knowledge whose field of operation was above, beyond that of the relative fact-finding sort. There *was* no answer to the questions I had raised in very truth. He had been quite right. Blind as a mole, I had been digging about in the graveyard of relative fact piling up data, more information, and completely missing the mythopoeic reference which underlies fact. I had called this searching for truth! Nor was there any way in which I might be instructed in the matter—save by the ironies I had found so wounding. For now I realised that his irony was really tenderness turned inside out like a glove! And seeing Pursewarden thus, for the first time, I saw that through his work he had been seeking for the very tenderness of logic itself, of the Way Things Are; not the logic of syllogism or the tide-marks of emotions, but the real essence of fact-finding, the *naked* truth, the *Inkling* . . . the whole pointless Joke. Yes, Joke! I woke up with a start and swore.

If two or more explanations of a single human action are as good as each other then what does action mean but an illusion —a gesture made against the misty backcloth of a reality made palpable by the delusive nature of human division merely? Had any novelist before Pursewarden considered this question? I think not.

And in brooding over these terrible letters I also suddenly stumbled upon the true meaning of my own relationship to Pursewarden, and through him to all writers. I saw, in fact, that we artists form one of those pathetic human chains which human beings form to pass buckets of water up to a fire, or to bring in a lifeboat. An uninterrupted chain of humans born to explore the inward riches of the solitary life on behalf of the unheeding unforgiving community; manacled together by the same gift.

I began to see too that the real "fiction" lay neither in Arnauti's pages nor Pursewarden's—nor even my own. It was life itself that was a fiction—we were all saying it in our different ways, each understanding it according to his nature and gift.

It was now only that I began to see how mysteriously the configuration of my own life had taken its shape from the properties of those elements which lie outside the relative life—in the kingdom which Pursewarden calls the "heraldic universe". We were three writers, I now saw, confided to a mythical city from which we were to draw our nourishment, in which we were to confirm our gifts. Arnauti, Pursewarden, Darley—like Past, Present and Future tense! And in my own life (the staunchless stream flowing from the wounded side of Time!) the three women who also arranged themselves as if to represent the moods of the great verb, Love: Melissa, Justine and Clea.

And realising this I was suddenly afflicted by a great melancholy and despair at recognising the completely limited nature of my own powers, hedged about as they were by the limitations of an intelligence too powerful for itself, and lacking in sheer word-magic, in propulsion, in passion, to achieve this other world of artistic fulfilment.

I had just locked those unbearable letters away and was sitting in melancholy realisation of this fact when the door opened and Clea walked in, radiant and smiling. "Why, Darley, what are you doing sitting in the middle of the floor in that rueful attitude? And my dear there are tears in your eyes." At once she was down beside me on her knees, all tenderness.

"Tears of exasperation" I said, and then, embracing her, "I have just realised that I am not an artist at all. There is not a shred of hope of my ever being one."

"What on earth have you been up to?"

"Reading Pursewarden's letters to Liza."

"Did you see her?"

"Yes. Keats is writing some absurd book——"

"But I just ran into him. He's back from the desert for the night."

I struggled to my feet. It seemed to me imperative that I should find him and discover what I could about his project. "He spoke" said Clea "about going round to Pombal's for a bath. I expect you'll find him there if you hurry."

Keats! I thought to myself as I hurried down the street towards the flat; he was also to play his part in this shadowy representation, this tableau of the artist's life. For it is always a Keats that is chosen to interpret, to drag his trail of slime over the pitiful muddled life out of which the artist, with such pain, recaptures these strange solitary jewels of self-enlightenment. After those letters it seemed to me more than ever necessary that people like Keats should if possible be kept away from interfering in matters beyond their normal concerns. As a journalist with a romantic story (suicide is the most romantic act for an artist) he doubtless felt himself to be in the presence of what he, in the old days, would have called "A stunner. A Story in a Million". I thought that I knew my Keats—but of course once more I had completely forgotten to take into account the operations of Time, for Keats had changed as we all had, and my meeting with him turned out to be as unexpected as everything else about the city.

I had mislaid my key and had to ring for Hamid to open the door for me. Yes, he said, Mr. Keats was there, in the bath. I traversed the corridor and tapped at the door behind which

178

came the sound of rushing water and a cheerful whistling. "By God, Darley, how splendid" he shouted in answer to my call. "Come in while I dry. I heard you were back."

Under the shower stood a Greek god! I was so surprised at the transformation that I sat down abruptly on the lavatory and studied this . . . apparition. Keats was burnt almost black, and his hair had bleached white. Though slimmer, he looked in first-class physical condition. The brown skin and ashen hair had made his twinkling eyes bluer than ever. He bore absolutely *no resemblance* to my memories of him! "I just sneaked off for the night" he said, speaking in a new rapid and confident voice. "I'm developing one of those blasted desert sores on my elbow, so I got a chit and here I am. I don't know what the hell causes them, nobody does; perhaps all the tinned muck we eat up there in the desert! But two days in Alex and an injection and presto! The bloody thing clears up again! I say, Darley, what fun to meet again. There's so much to tell you. This war!" He was bubbling over with high spirits. "God, this water is a treat. I've been revelling."

"You look in tremendous shape."

"I am. I am." He smacked himself exuberantly on the buttocks. "Golly though, it is good to come into Alex. Contrasts make you appreciate things so much better. Those tanks get so hot you feel like frying whitebait. Reach my drink, there's a good chap." On the floor stood a tall glass of whisky and soda with an ice cube in it. He shook the glass, holding it to his ear like a child. "Listen to the ice tinkling" he cried in ecstasy. "Music to the soul, the tinkle of ice." He raised his glass, wrinkled up his nose at me and drank my health. "You look in quite good shape, too" he said, and his blue eyes twinkled with a new mischievous light. "Now for some clothes and then . . . my dear chap, I'm rich. I'll give you a slap-up dinner at the Petit Coin. No refusals, I'll not be baulked. I particularly wanted to see you and talk to you. I have news."

He positively skipped into the bedroom to dress and I sat

on Pombal's bed to keep him company while he did so. His high spirits were quite infectious. He seemed hardly able to keep still. A thousand thoughts and ideas bubbled up inside him which he wanted to express simultaneously. He capered down the stairs into the street like a schoolboy, taking the last flight at a single bound. I thought he would break into a dance along Rue Fuad. "But seriously" he said, squeezing my elbow so hard that it hurt. "*Seriously*, life is wonderful" and as if to illustrate his seriousness he burst into ringing laughter. "When I think how we used to brood and worry." Apparently he included me in this new euphoric outlook on life. "How slowly we took everything, I feel ashamed to remember it!"

At the Petit Coin we secured a corner table after an amiable altercation with a naval lieutenant, and he at once took hold of Menotti and commanded champagne to be brought. Where the devil had he got this new laughing authoritative manner which instantly commanded sympathetic respect without giving offence?

"The desert!" he said, as if in answer to my unspoken question. "The desert, Darley, old boy. That is something to be seen." From a capacious pocket he produced a copy of the *Pickwick Papers*. "Damn!" he said. "I mustn't forget to get this copy replaced. Or the crew will bloody well fry me." It was a sodden, dog-eared little book with a bullet hole in the cover, smeared with oil. "It's our only library, and some bastard must have wiped himself on the middle third. I've sworn to replace it. Actually there's a copy at the flat. I don't suppose Pombal would mind my pinching it. It's absurd. When there isn't any action we lie about reading it aloud to one another, under the stars! Absurd, my dear chap, but then everything is more absurd. More and more absurd every day."

"You sound so happy" I said, not without a certain envy.

"Yes" he said in a smaller voice, and suddenly, for the first time, became relatively serious. "I am. Darley, let me make you a confidence. Promise not to groan."

"I promise."

He leaned forward and said in a whisper, his eyes twinkling, "I've become a writer at last!" Then suddenly he gave his ringing laugh. "You promised not to groan" he said.

"I didn't groan."

"Well, you looked groany and supercilious. The proper response would have been to shout 'Hurrah!' "

"Don't shout so loud or they'll ask us to leave."

"Sorry. It came over me."

He drank a large bumper of champagne with the air of someone toasting himself and leaned back in his chair, gazing at me quizzically with the same mischievous sparkle in his blue eyes.

"What have you written?" I asked.

"Nothing" he said, smiling. "Not a word as yet. It's all up here." He pointed a brown finger at his temple. "But now at least I know it is. Somehow whether I do or don't actually write isn't important—it isn't, if you like, the whole point about becoming a writer at all, as I used to think."

In the street outside a barrel organ began playing with its sad hollow iteration. It was a very ancient English barrel organ which old blind Arif had found on a scrap heap and had fixed up in a somewhat approximate manner. Whole notes misfired and several chords were hopelessly out of tune.

"Listen" said Keats, with deep emotion, "just listen to old Arif." He was in that delicious state of inspiration which only comes when champagne supervenes upon a state of fatigue—a melancholy tipsiness which is wholly inspiriting. "Gosh!" he went on in rapture, and began to sing in a very soft husky whisper, marking time with his finger, '*Taisez-vous petit babouin*". Then he gave a great sigh of repletion, and chose himself a cigar from Menotti's great case of specimens, sauntering back to the table where he once more sat before me, smiling rapturously. "This war" he said at last, "I really must tell you. . . . It is quite different to what I imagined it must be like."

Under his champagne-bedizened tipsiness he had become relatively grave all at once. He said: "Nobody seeing it for the first time could help crying out with the whole of his rational mind in protest at it: crying out 'It must stop!' My dear chap, to see the ethics of man *at his norm* you must see a battlefield. The general idea may be summed up in the expressive phrase: 'If you can't eat it or **** it, then **** on it.' Two thousand years of civilisation! It peels off in a flash. Scratch with your little finger and you reach the woad or the ritual war paint under the varnish! Just like that!" He scratched the air between us languidly with his expensive cigar. "And yet—you know what? The most unaccountable and baffling thing. It has made a man of me, as the saying goes. More, a writer! My soul is quite clear. I suppose you could regard me as permanently disfigured! I have begun it at last, that bloody joyful book of mine. Chapter by chapter it is forming in my old journalist's noddle—no, not a journalist's any more, a *writer's*." He laughed again as if at the preposterous notion. "Darley when I look around that . . . battlefield at night, I stand in an ecstasy of shame, revelling at the coloured lights, the flares wallpapering the sky, and I say: 'All this had to be brought about so that poor Johnny Keats could grow into a man.' That's what. It is a complete enigma to me, yet I am absolutely certain of it. No other way would have helped me because I was too damned *stupid*, do you see?" He was silent for a while and somewhat distrait, drawing on his cigar. It was as if he were going over this last piece of conversation in his mind to consider its validity, word by word, as one tests a piece of machinery. Then he added, but with care and caution, and a certain expression of bemused concentration, like a man handling unfamiliar terms: "The man of action and the man of reflection are really the same man, operating on two different fields. But to the same end! Wait, this is beginning to sound silly." He tapped his temple reproachfully and frowned. After a moment's thought he went on, still frowning: "Shall I tell you my notion about it . . . the war? What I have come to believe? I believe the desire for war was first lodged in the instincts as a biological shock-mechanism to precipitate a spiritual crisis which couldn't be done any other how in limited people. The less sensitive among us can hardly visualise death, far less live joyfully with it. So the powers that arranged things for us felt they must concretise it, in order to lodge death in the actual present. Purely helpfully, if you see what I mean!" He laughed again, but ruefully this time. "Of course it is rather different now that the bystander is getting hit harder than the front-line bloke. It is unfair to the men of the tribe who would like to leave the wife and kids in relative safety before stumping off to this primitive ordination. For my part I think the instinct has somewhat atrophied, and may be on the way out altogether; but what will they put in its place—that's what I wonder? As for me, Darley, I can only say that no half-dozen French mistresses, no travels round the globe, no adventures in the peace-time world we knew could have grown me up so thoroughly in half the time. You remember how I used to be? Look, I'm really an adult now—but of course ageing fast, altogether too fast! It will sound damn silly to you, but the presence of death out there as a normal feature of life—only in full acceleration so to speak—has given me an inkling of Life Everlasting! And there was no other way I could have grasped it, damn it. Ah! well, I'll probably get bumped off up there in full possession of my imbecility, as you might say."

He burst out laughing once more, and gave himself three noiseless cheers, raising his cigar-hand ceremoniously at each cheer. Then he winked carefully at me and filled his glass once more, adding with an air of vagueness the coda: "Life only has its full meaning to those who co-opt death!" I could see that he was rather drunk by now, for the soothing effects of the hot shower had worn off and the desert-fatigue had begun to reassert itself.

"And Pursewarden?" I said, divining the very moment at

183

which to drop his name, like a hook, into the stream of our conversation.

"Pursewarden!" he echoed on a different note, which combined a melancholy sadness and affection. "But my dear Darley, it was something like this that he was trying to tell me, in his own rather bloody way. And I? I still blush with shame when I think of the questions I asked him. And yet his answers, which seemed so bloody enigmatic then, make perfect sense to me *now*. Truth is double-bladed, you see. There is no way to express it in terms of language, this strange bifurcated medium with its basic duality! Language! What is the writer's struggle except a struggle to use a medium as precisely as possible, but knowing fully its basic imprecision? A hopeless task, but none the less rewarding for being hopeless. Because the task itself, the act of wrestling with an insoluble problem, grows the writer up! This was what the old bastard realised. You should read his letters to his wife. For all their brilliance how he whined and cringed, how despicably he presented himself—like some Dostoievskian character beset by some nasty compulsion neurosis! It is really staggering what a petty and trivial soul he reveals there." This was an amazing insight into the tormented yet wholly complete being of the letters which I myself had just read!

"Keats" I said, "for goodness' sake tell me. Are you writing a book about him?"

Keats drank slowly and thoughtfully and replaced his glass somewhat unsteadily before saying: "No." He stroked his chin and fell silent.

"They say you are writing something" I persisted. He shook his head obstinately and contemplated his glass with a blurred eye. "I wanted to" he admitted at last, slowly. "I did a long review of the novels once for a small mag. The next thing I got a letter from his wife. *She* wanted a book done. A big rawboned Irish girl, very hysterical and sluttish: handsome in a big way, I suppose. Always blowing her nose in an old envelope.

Always in carpet slippers. I must say I felt for him. But I tumbled straight into a hornets' nest there. She *loathed* him, and there seemed to be plenty to loathe, I must say. She gave me a great deal of information, and simply masses of letters and manuscripts. Treasure trove all right. But, my dear chap, I couldn't use this sort of stuff. If for no other reason than that I respect his memory and his work. No. No. I fobbed her off. Told her she would never get such things published. She seemed to want to be publicly martyred in print just to get back at him—old Pursewarden! I couldn't do such a thing. Besides the material was quite hair-raising! I don't want to talk about it. Really, I would never repeat the truth to a soul."

We sat looking thoughtfully, even watchfully at each other, for a long moment before I spoke again.

"Have you ever met his sister, Liza?"

Keats shook his head slowly. "No. What was the point? I abandoned the project right away, so there was no need to try and hear her story. I know she has a lot of manuscript stuff, because the wife told me so. But. . . . She is here isn't she?" His lip curled with the faintest suggestion of disgust. "Truthfully I don't want to meet her. The bitter truth of the matter seems to me that the person old Pursewarden most loved—I mean purely spiritually—did not at all understand the state of his soul, so to speak, when he died: or even have the vaguest idea of the extent of his achievement. No, she was busy with a vulgar intrigue concerned with legalising her relations with Mountolive. I suppose she feared that her marriage to a diplomat might be imperilled by a possible scandal. I may be wrong, but that is the impression I gathered. I believe she was going to try and get a whitewashing book written. But now, in a sense, I have my own Pursewarden, my own copy of him, if you like. It's enough for me. What do the details matter, and why should I meet his sister? It is his work and not his life which is necessary to us—which offers one of the many meanings of the word with four faces!"

185

I had an impulse to cry out "Unfair", but I restrained it. It is impossible in this world to arrange for full justice to be done to everyone. Keats's eyelids drooped. "Come" I said, calling for the bill, "it's time you went home and got some sleep."

"I do feel rather tired" he mumbled.

"Avanti."

There was an old horse-drawn gharry in a side-street which we were glad to find. Keats protested that his feet were beginning to hurt and his arm to pain him. He was in a pleasantly exhausted frame of mind, and slightly tipsy after his potations. He lay back in the smelly old cab and closed his eyes. "D'you know, Darley" he said indistinctly, "I meant to tell you but forgot. Don't be angry with me, old fellow-bondsman, will you. I know that you and Clea. . . . Yes, and I'm glad. But I have the most curious feeling that one day I am going to marry her. Really. Don't be silly about it. Of course I would never breathe a word, and it would happen years after this silly old war. But somewhere along the line I feel I'm bound to hitch up with her."

"Now what do you expect me to say?"

"Well, there are a hundred courses open. Myself I would start yelling and screaming at once if you said such a thing to me. I'd knock your block off, push you out of the cab, anything. I'd punch me in the eye."

The gharry drew up with a jolt outside the house. "Here we are" I said, and helped my companion down into the road. "I'm not as drunk as all that" he cried cheerfully, shaking off my help, "'tis but fatigue, dear friend." And while I argued out the cost of the trip with the driver he went round and held a long private confabulation with the horse, stroking its nose. "I was giving it some maxims to live by" he explained as we wound our weary way up the staircase. "But the champagne had muddled up my quotation-box. What's that thing of Shakespeare's about the lover and the cuckold all compact, seeking the bubble reputation e'en in the cannon's mouth." The last phrase he pronounced in the strange (man-sawing-wood) delivery of Churchill. "Or something about swimmers into cleanness leaping—a pre-fab in the eternal mind no less!"

"You are murdering them both."

"Gosh I'm tired. And there seems to be no bombardment tonight."

"They are getting less frequent."

He collapsed on his bed fully dressed, slowly untying his suède desert boots and wriggling with his toes until they slid slowly off and plopped to the floor. "Did you ever see Pursewarden's little book called *Select Prayers for English Intellectuals*? It was funny. 'Dear Jesus, please keep me as eighteenth century as possible—but without the c*******d. . . .'" He gave a sleepy chuckle, put his arms behind his head and started drifting into smiling sleep. As I turned out the light he sighed deeply and said: "Even the dead are overwhelming us all the time with kindnesses."

I had a sudden picture of him as a small boy walking upon the very brink of precipitous cliffs to gather seabirds' eggs. One slip. . . .

But I was never to see him again. *Vale!*

o   o   o   o   o

V

Ten thirsty fingers of my blind Muse
Confer upon my face their sensual spelling

The lines ran through my head as I pressed the bell of the summer residence the following evening. In my hand I held the green leather suitcase which contained the private letters of Pursewarden—that brilliant sustained fusillade of words which still exploded in my memory like a firework display, scorching me. I had telephoned to Liza from my office in the morning to make the rendezvous. She opened the door and stood before me with a pale graven expression of expectancy. "Good" she whispered as I murmured my name and "Come". She turned and walked before me with a stiff upright expressive gait which reminded me of a child dressed up as Queen Elizabeth for a charade. She looked tired and strained, and yet in a curious way proud. The living-room was empty. Mountolive, I knew, had returned to Cairo that morning. Rather surprisingly, for it was late in the year, a log-fire burned in the chimney-piece. She took up her stand before it, arching her back to the warmth, and rubbing her hands as if she were chilled.

"You have been quick, very quick" she said, almost sharply, almost with a hint of implied reproach in her tone. "But I am glad." I had already told her by telephone the gist of my conversation with Keats about the non-existent book. "I am glad, because now we can decide something, finally. I couldn't sleep last night. I kept imagining you reading them, the letters. I kept imagining him writing them."

"They are marvellous. I have never read anything like them in my whole life." I felt a note of chagrin in my own tones.

188

"Yes" she said, and fetched a deep sigh. "And yet I was afraid you would think so; *afraid* because you would share David's opinion of them and advise me that they should be preserved *at all costs*. Yet *he* expressly told me to burn them."

"I know."

"Sit down, Darley. Tell me what you really think."

I sat down, placing the little suitcase on the floor beside me, and said: "Liza, this is not a literary problem unless you choose to regard it as one. You need take nobody's advice. Naturally nobody who has read them could help but regret the loss."

"But Darley, if they had been yours, written to someone you . . . loved?"

"I should feel relief to know that my instructions had been carried out. At least I presume that is what *he* would feel, wherever he might be now."

She turned her lucid blind face to the mirror and appeared to explore her own reflection in it earnestly, resting the tips of her frilly fingers on the mantelpiece. "I am as superstitious as he was" she said at last. "But it is more than that. I was always obedient because I knew that he saw farther than I and understood more than I did."

> *This caged reflection gives her nothing back*
> *That women drink like thirsty stags from mirrors*

How very much of Pursewarden's poetry became crystal-clear and precise in the light of all this new knowledge! How it gathered consequence and poignance from the figure of Liza exploring her own blindness in the great mirror, her dark hair thrown back on her shoulders!

At last she turned back again, sighing once more, and I saw a look of tender pleading on her face, made the more haunting and expressive by the empty sockets of her eyes. She took a step forward and said: "Well, then, it is decided. Only tell me you will help me burn them. They are very many. It will take a little time."

189

"If you wish."

"Let us sit down beside the fire together."

So we sat facing each other on the carpet and I placed the suitcase between us, pressing the lock so that the cover released itself and sprang up with a snap.

"Yes" she said. "This is how it must be. I should have known all along that I must obey him." Slowly, one by one I took up the pierced envelopes, unfolded each letter in turn and handed it to her to place upon the burning logs.

"We used to sit like this as children with our playbox between us, before the fire, in the winter. So often, and always together. You would have to go back very far into the past to understand it all. And even then I wonder if you would understand. Two small children left alone in an old rambling farmhouse among the frozen lakes, among the mists and rains of Ireland. We had no resources except in each other. He converted my blindness into poetry, I saw with his brain, he with my eyes. So we invented a whole imperishable world of poetry together—better by far than the best of his books, and I have read them all with my fingers, they are all at the institute. Yes I read and re-read them looking for a clue to the guilt which had transformed everything. Nothing had affected us before, everything conspired to isolate us, keep us together. The death of our parents happened when we were almost too small to comprehend it. We lived in this ramshackle old farmhouse in the care of an eccentric and deaf old aunt who did the work, saw that we were fed, and left us to our own devices. There was only one book there, a Plutarch, which we knew by heart. Everything else he invented. This was how I became the strange mythological queen of his life, living in a vast palace of sighs— as he used to say. Sometimes it was Egypt, sometimes Peru, sometimes Byzantium. I suppose I must have known that really it was an old farmhouse kitchen, with shabby deal furniture and floors of red tile. At least when the floors had been washed with carbolic soap with its peculiar smell I *knew*, with half my mind, that it was a farmhouse floor, and not a palace with magnificent tessellated floors brilliant with snakes and eagles and pygmies. But at a word he brought me back to reality, as he called it. Later, when he started looking for justifications for our love instead of just simply being proud of it, he read me a quotation from a book. 'In the African burial rites it is the sister who brings the dead king back to life. In Egypt as well as Peru the king, who was considered as God, took his sister to wife. But the motive was ritual and not sexual, for they symbolised the moon and the sun in their conjunction. The king marries his sister because he, as God the star, wandering on earth, is immortal and may therefore not propagate himself in the children of a strange woman, any more than he is allowed to die a natural death.' That is why he was pleased to come here to Egypt, because he felt, he said, an interior poetic link with Osiris and Isis, with Ptolemy and Arsinoë—the race of the sun and the moon!''

Quietly and methodically she placed letter after letter on the burning pyre, talking in a sad monotone, as much to herself as to me.

"No it would not be possible to make it all comprehensible to those who were not of our race. But when the guilt entered the old poetic life began to lose its magic—not for me: but for him. It was he who made me dye my hair black, so that I could pretend to be a step-sister of his, not a sister. It hurt me deeply to realise suddenly that he was guilty all of a sudden; but as we grew up the world intruded more and more upon us, new lives began to impinge on our solitary world of palaces and kingdoms. He was forced to go away for long periods. When he was absent I had nothing whatsoever except the darkness and what my memory of him could fill it with; somehow the treasures of his invention went all lustreless until he came back, his voice, his touch. All we knew of our parents, the sum of our knowledge, was an old oak cupboard full of their clothes. They seemed enormous to us when we were small—the clothes of giants, the shoes of giants. One day he said they oppressed him, these clothes. We did not need parents. And we took them out into the yard and made a bonfire of them in the snow. We both wept bitterly, I do not know why. We danced round the bonfire singing an old hunting song with savage triumph and yet weeping."

She was silent for a long moment, her head hanging in profound concentration over this ancient image, like a soothsayer gazing fixedly into the dark crystal of youth. Then she sighed and raised her head, saying: "I know why you hesitate. It is the last letter, isn't it? You see I counted them. Give it to me, Darley."

I handed it to her without a word and she softly placed it in the fire saying: "It is over at last."

o o o o o

BOOK III

I

As the summer burned away into autumn, and autumn into winter once more we became slowly aware that the war which had invested the city had begun slowly to ebb, to flow gradually away along the coast-roads fringing the desert, releasing its hold upon us and our pleasures. For receding like a tide it left its strange coprolitic trophies along the beaches which we had once used, finding them always white and deserted under the flying gulls. War had denied them to us for a long time; but now, when we rediscovered them, we found them littered with pulped tanks and twisted guns, and the indiscriminate wreckage of temporary supply harbours abandoned by the engineers to rot and rust under the desert sun, to sink gradually into the shifting dunes. It gave one a curious melancholy reassurance to bathe there now—as if among the petrified lumber of a Neolithic age: tanks like the skeletons of dinosaurs, guns standing about like outmoded furniture. The minefields constituted something of a hazard, and the Bedouin were often straying into them in the course of pasturing; once Clea swerved—for the road was littered with glistening fragments of shattered camel from some recent accident. But such occasions were rare, and as for the tanks themselves, though burned out they were tenantless. There were no human bodies in them. These had presumably been excavated and decently buried in one of the huge cemeteries which had grown up in various unexpected corners of the western desert like townships of the dead. The city, too, was finding its way back to its normal habits and rhythms, for the bombardments had now ceased altogether and the normal night-life of the Levant had begun once more to flower. And though uniforms were less abundant the bars and night clubs still plied a splendid trade with servicemen on leave.

My own eventless life, too, seemed to have settled itself into a natural routine-fed pattern, artificially divided by a private life which I had surrendered to my complete absorption in Clea, and an office life which, though not onerous, had little meaning to me. Little had changed: but yes, Maskelyne had at last managed to break his bonds and escape back to his regiment. He called on us, resplendent in uniform, to say goodbye, shyly pointing—not his pipe but a crisp new swagger-stick—at his tail-wagging colleague. "I told you he'd do it" said Telford with a triumphant sadness in his voice. "I always knew it." But Mountolive stayed on, apparently still "frozen" in his post.

From time to time by arrangement I revisited the child at Karm Abu Girg to see how she was faring. To my delight I found that the transplantation, about which I had had many misgivings, was working perfectly. The reality of her present life apparently chimed with the dreams I had invented for her. It was all as it should be—the coloured playing-card characters among whom she could now number herself! If Justine remained a somewhat withdrawn and unpredictable figure of moods and silences it only added, as far as I could see, to the sombre image of a dispossessed empress. In Nessim she had realised a father. His image had gained definition by greater familiarity because of his human tendernesses. He was a delightful companion-father now, and together they explored the desert lands around the house on horseback. He had given her a bow and arrows, and a little girl of about her own age, Taor, as a body-servant and *amah*. The so-called palace, too, which we had imagined together, stood the test of reality magnificently. Its labyrinth of musty rooms and its ramshackle treasures were a perpetual delight. Thus with her own horses and servants, and a private palace to play in, she was an Arabian Nights queen indeed. She had almost forgotten the island now, so absorbed was she among these new treasures. I did not see Justine during these visits, nor did I try to do so. Sometimes however Nessim

196

was there, but he never accompanied us on our walks or rides, and usually the child came to the ford to meet me with a spare horse.

In the Spring Balthazar, who had by now quite come to himself and had thrown himself once more into his work, invited Clea and myself to take part in a ceremony which rather pleased his somewhat ironic disposition. This was the ceremonial placing of flowers on Capodistria's grave on the anniversary of the Great Porn's birthday. "I have the express authority of Capodistria himself" he explained. "Indeed he himself always pays for the flowers every year." It was a fine sunny day for the excursion and Balthazar insisted that we should walk. Though somewhat hampered by the nosegay he carried he was in good voice. His vanity in the matter of his hair had become too strong to withstand, and he had duly submitted to Mnemjian's ministrations, thus "rubbing out his age", as he expressed it. Indeed the change was remarkable. He was now, once more, the old Balthazar, with his sapient dark eyes turned ironically on the doings of the city. And no less on Capodistria from whom he had just received a long letter. "You can have no idea what the old brute is up to over the water. He has taken the Luciferian path and plunged into Black Magic. But I'll read it to you. His graveside is, now I come to think of it, a most appropriate place to read his account of his experiments!"

The cemetery was completely deserted in the sunshine. Capodistria had certainly spared no expense to make his grave imposing and had achieved a fearsome vulgarity of decoration which was almost mind-wounding. Such cherubs and scrolls, such floral wreaths. On the slab was engraved the ironic text: "Not Lost But Gone Before". Balthazar chuckled affectionately as he placed his flowers upon the grave and said "Happy Birthday" to it. Then he turned aside, removing coat and hat for the sun was high and bright, and together we sat on a bench under a cypress tree while Clea ate toffees and he groped in his pockets for the bulky typewritten packet which contained

197

Capodistria's latest and longest letter. "Clea" he said, "you must read it to us. I've forgotten my reading glasses. Besides, I would like to hear it through once, to see if it sounds less fantastic or more. Will you?"

Obediently she took the close-typed pages and started reading.

"My dear M.B."

"The initials" interposed Balthazar "stand for the nickname which Pursewarden fastened on me—Melancholia Borealis, no less. A tribute to my alleged Judaic gloom. Proceed, my dear Clea."

The letter was in French.

"I have been conscious, my dear friend, that I owed you some account of my new life here, yet though I have written you fairly frequently I have got into the habit of evading the subject. Why? Well, my heart always sank at the thought of your derisive laugh. It is absurd, for I was never a sensitive man or quick to worry about the opinion of my neighbours. Another thing. It would have involved a long and tiresome explanation of the unease and unfamiliarity I always felt at the meetings of the Cabal which sought to drench the world in its abstract goodness. I did not know then that my path was not the path of Light but of Darkness. I would have confused it morally or ethically with good and evil at that time. Now I recognise the path I am treading as simply the counterpoise—the bottom end of the see-saw, as it were—which keeps the light side up in the air. Magic! I remember you once quoting to me a passage (quite nonsensical to me then) from Paracelsus. I think you added at the time that even such gibberish must mean something. It does! 'True Alchemy which teaches how to make (or ⊙ out of the five imperfect metals, requires no other materials but only the metals. The perfect metals are made out of the imperfect metals, through them and with them alone; for with other things is *Luna* (phantasy) but in the metals is *Sol* (wisdom).'

"I leave a moment's pause for your peculiar laugh, which in

198

the past I would not have been slow to echo! What a mountain of rubbish surrounding the idea of the *tinctura physicorum*, you would observe. Yes but. . . .

"My first winter in this windy tower was not pleasant. The roof leaked. I did not have my books to solace me as yet. My quarters seemed rather cramped and I wondered about extending them. The property on which the tower stands above the sea had also a straggle of cottages and outbuildings upon it; here lodged the ancient, deaf couple of Italians who looked after my wants, washed and cleaned and fed me. I did not want to turn them out of their quarters but wondered whether I could not convert the extra couple of barns attached to their abode. It was then that I found, to my surprise, that they had another lodger whom I had never seen, a strange and solitary creature who only went abroad at night, and wore a monk's cassock. I owe all my new orientation to my meeting with him. He is a defrocked Italian monk, who describes himself as a Rosicrucian and an alchemist. He lived here among a mountain of masonic manu-scripts—some of very great age—which he was in the process of studying. It was he who first convinced me that this line of enquiry was (despite some disagreeable aspects) concerned with increasing man's interior hold on himself, on the domains which lie unexplored within him; the comparison with every-day science is not fallacious, for the form of this enquiry is based as firmly on method—only with different premises! And if, as I say, it has some disagreeable aspects, why so has formal science—vivisection for instance. Anyway, here I struck up a rapport, and opened up for myself a field of study which grew more and more engrossing as the months went by. I also dis-covered at last something which eminently fitted my nature! Truthfully, everything in this field seemed to nourish and sus-tain me! Also I was able to be of considerable practical assistance to the Abbé F. as I will call him, for some of these manuscripts (stolen from the secret lodges on Athos I should opine) were in Greek, Arabic and Russian—languages which he did not know well. Our friendship ripened into a partnership. But it was many months before he introduced me to yet another strange, indeed formidable figure who was also dabbling in these matters. This was an Austrian Baron who lived in a large mansion inland and who was busy (no, do not laugh) on the obscure problem which we once discussed—is it in *De Natura Rerum*? I think it is—the *generatio homunculi?* He had a Turkish butler and famulus to help him in his experiments. Soon I became *persona grata* here also and was allowed to help them to the best of my ability.

"Now this Baron—whom you would certainly find a strange and imposing figure, heavily bearded and with big teeth like the seeds of a corn-cob—this Baron had . . . ah! my dear Balthazar, had *actually produced* ten homunculi which he called his 'prophesying spirits'. They were preserved in the huge glass canisters which they use hereabouts for washing olives or to preserve fruit, and they lived in water. They stood on a long oaken rack in his studio or laboratory. They were produced or 'patterned', to use his own expression, in the course of five weeks of intense labour of thought and ritual. They were exquisitely beautiful and mysterious objects, floating there like sea-horses. They consisted of a king, a queen, a knight, a monk, a nun, an architect, a miner, a seraph, and finally a blue spirit and a red one! They dangled lazily in these stout glass jars. A tapping fingernail seemed to alarm them. They were only about a span long, and as the Baron was anxious for them to grow to a greater size, we helped him to bury them in several cartloads of horse-manure. This great midden was sprinkled daily with an evil-smelling liquid which was prepared with great labour by the Baron and his Turk, and which contained some rather disgusting ingredients. At each sprinkling the manure began to steam as if heated by a subterranean fire. It was almost too hot to place one finger in it. Once every three days the Abbé and the Baron spent the whole night praying and fumigating the midden with incense. When at last the Baron deemed this process complete the bottles were carefully removed and returned to the laboratory shelves. All the homunculi had grown in size to such an extent that the bottles were now hardly big enough for them, and the male figures had come into possession of heavy beards. The nails of their fingers and toes had grown very long. Those which bore a human representation wore clothes appropriate to their rank and style. They had a kind of beautiful obscenity floating there with an expression on their faces such as I have only once seen before—on the face of a Peruvian pickled human head! Eyes turned up into the skull, pale fish's lips drawn back to expose small perfectly formed teeth! In the bottles containing respectively the red and blue spirit there was nothing to be seen. All the bottles, by the way, were heavily sealed with oxbladders and wax bearing the imprint of a magic seal. But when the Baron tapped with his fingernail on the bottles and repeated some words in Hebrew the water clouded and began to turn red and blue respectively. The homunculi began to show their faces, to develop cloudily like a photographic print, gradually increasing in size. The blue spirit was as beautiful as any angel, but the red wore a truly terrifying expression.

"These beings were fed every three days by the Baron with some dry rose-coloured substance which was kept in a silver box lined with sandalwood. Pellets about the size of a dried pea. Once every week, too, the water in the bottles had to be emptied out; they had to be refilled (the bottles) with fresh rainwater. This had to be done very rapidly because during the few moments that the spirits were exposed to the air they seemed to get weak and unconscious, as if they were about to die like fish. But the blue spirit was never fed; while the red one received once a week a thimbleful of the fresh blood of some animal—a chicken I think. This blood disappeared at once in the water without colouring or even troubling it. As soon as this bottle was opened it turned turbid and dark and gave off the odour of rotten eggs!

"In the course of a couple of months these homunculi reached their full stature, the stage of prophecy—as the Baron calls it; then every night the bottles were carried into a small ruined chapel, situated in a grove at some distance from the house, and here a service was held and the bottles 'interrogated' on the course of future events. This was done by writing questions in Hebrew on slips of paper and pressing them to the bottle before the eyes of the homunculus; it was rather like exposing sensitized photographic paper to light. I mean it was not as if the beings read but divined the questions, slowly, with much hesitation. They spelled out their answers, drawing with a finger on the transparent glass, and these responses were copied down immediately by the Baron in a great commonplace book. Each homunculus was only asked questions appropriate to his station, and the red and blue spirits could only answer with a smile or a frown to indicate assent or dissent. Yet they seemed to know everything, and any question at all could be put to them. The King could only touch on politics, the monk religion . . . and so on. In this way I witnessed the compilation of what the Baron called 'the annals of Time' which is a document at least as impressive as that left behind him by Nostradamus. So many of these prophecies have proved true in these last short months that I can have little doubt about the rest also proving so. It is a curious sensation to peer thus into the future!

"One day, by some accident, the glass jar containing the monk fell to the stone flags and was broken. The poor monk died after a couple of small painful respirations, despite all the efforts made by the Baron to save him. His body was buried in the garden. There was an abortive attempt to 'pattern' another monk but this was a failure. It produced a small leech-like object without vitality which died within a few hours.

"A short while afterwards the King managed to escape from his bottle during the night; he was found sitting upon the bottle containing the Queen, scratching with his nails to get the seal away! He was beside himself, and very agile, though weakening desperately from his exposure to the air. Neverthe-less he led us quite a chase among the bottles—which we were afraid of overturning. It was really extraordinary how nimble he was, and had he not become increasingly faint from being out of his native element I doubt whether we could have caught him. We did however and he was pushed, scratching and biting, back into his bottle, but not before he had severely scratched the Abbé's chin. In the scrimmage he gave off a curious odour, as of a hot metal plate cooling. My finger touched his leg. It was of a wet and rubbery consistency, and sent a shiver of apprehension down my spine.

"But now a mishap occurred. The Abbé's scratched face be-came inflamed and poisoned and he went down with a high fever and was carried off to hospital where he lies at present, convalescing. But there was more to follow, and worse; the Baron, being Austrian, had always been something of a curi-osity here, and more especially now when the spy-mania which every war brings has reached its height. It came to my ears that he was to be thoroughly investigated by the authorities. He received the news with despairing calmness, but it was clear that he could not afford to have unauthorised persons poking about in his laboratory. It was decided to 'dissolve' the homun-culi and bury them in the garden. In the absence of the Abbé I agreed to help him. I do not know what it was he poured into the bottles but all the flames of hell leaped up out of them until the whole ceiling of the place was covered in soot and cobwebs. The beings shrank now to the size of dried leeches, or the dried navel-cords which sometimes village folk will preserve. The Baron groaned aloud from time to time, and the sweat stood out on his forehead. The groans of a woman in labour. At last the process was complete and at midnight the bottles were taken out and interred under some loose flags in the little chapel where, presumably, they must still be. The Baron has been interned, his books and papers sealed by the Custodians of Property. The Abbé lies, as I said, in hospital. And I? Well, my

Greek passport has made me less suspect than most people hereabouts. I have retired for the moment to my tower. There is still the mass of masonic data in the barns which the Abbé inhabited; I have taken charge of these. I have written to the Baron once or twice but he has not, perhaps out of tact, replied to me; believing perhaps that my association with him might lead to harm. And so . . . well, the war rolls on about us. Its end and what follows it—right up to the end of this century— I know: it lies here beside me as I write, in question and answer form. But who would believe me if I published it all—and much less you, doctor of the empiric sciences, sceptic and ironist? As for the war—Paracelsus has said: 'Innumerable are the *Egos* of man; in him are angels and devils, heaven and hell, the whole of the animal creation, the vegetable and mineral kingdoms; and just as the little individual man may be diseased, so the great universal man has his diseases, which manifest themselves as the ills which affect humanity as a whole. Upon this fact is based the prediction of future events.' And so, my dear friend, I have chosen the Dark Path towards my own light. I know now that I must follow it wherever it leads! Isn't that something to have achieved? Perhaps not. But for me it truthfully seems so. But I hear that laughter!

"Ever your devoted Da Capo".*

"Now" said Clea "oblige with the laughter!"

"What Pursewarden" I said, "called 'the melancholy laughter of Balthazar which betokens solipsism'."

Balthazar did indeed laugh now, slapping his knee and doubling himself up like a jack knife. "That damned rogue, Da Capo" he said. "And yet, *soyons raisonnables* if that is indeed the expression—he wouldn't tell a pack of lies. Or perhaps he might. No, he wouldn't. Yet can you bring yourself to believe in what he says—you two?"

"Yes" said Clea, and here we both smiled for her bondage to the soothsayers of Alexandria would naturally give her a predisposition towards the magic arts. "Laugh" she said quietly.

"To tell the truth" said Balthazar more soberly, "when one casts around the fields of so-called knowledge which we have partially opened up one is conscious that there may well be whole areas of darkness which may belong to the Paracelsian regions—the submerged part of the iceberg of knowledge. No, dammit, I must admit that you are right. We get too certain of ourselves travelling backwards and forwards along the tram-lines of empirical fact. Occasionally one gets hit softly on the head by a stray brick which has been launched from some other region. Only yesterday, for example, Boyd told me a story which sounded no less strange: about a soldier who was buried last week. I could, of course, supply explanations which might fit the case, but not with any certainty. This young boy went on a week's leave to Cairo. He came back having had an enjoyable time, or so he said. Next he developed an extraordinary intermittent fever with simply huge maximum temperatures. Within a week he died. A few hours before death a thick white cataract formed over his eyeballs with a sort of luminous red node over the retina. All the boy would repeat in the course of his delirium was the single phrase: '*She did it with a golden needle.*' Nothing but these words. As I say one could perhaps strap the case down clinically with a clever guess or two but . . . had I to be honest I would be obliged to admit that it did not exactly fit within an accepted category that I knew. Nor, by the way, did the autopsy give one anything more to go on: blood tests, spinal fluid, stomach etc. Not even a nice, familiar (yet itself perhaps inexplicable) meningeal disturbance. The brain was lovely and fresh! At least so Boyd says, and he took great pleasure in thoroughly exploring the young man. Mystery! Now what the devil could he have been doing on leave? It seems quite impossible to discover. His stay is not recorded at any of the hotels or army transit hostels. He spoke no language but English. Those few days spent in Cairo are completely missing from the count. And then the woman with the golden needle?"

"But in truth it is happening all the time, and I think you

205

are right" (this to Clea) "to insist obstinately on the existence of the dark powers and the fact that some people do scry as easily as I gaze down the barrel of my microscope. Not all, but some. And even quite stupid people, like your old Scobie, for example. Mind you, in my opinion, that was a rigmarole of the kind he produced sometimes when he was tipsy and wanted to show off—I mean the stuff supposedly about Narouz: that was altogether too dramatic to be taken seriously. And even if some of the detail were right he *could* have had access to it in the course of his duties. After all Nimrod did the *procès verbal* and that document must have been knocking around."

"What about Narouz?" I asked curiously, secretly piqued that Clea had confided things to Balthazar which she had kept from me. It was now that I noticed that Clea had turned quite white and was looking away. But Balthazar appeared to notice nothing himself and went plunging on. "It has the ingredients of a novelette—I mean about trying to drag you down into the grave with him. Eh, don't you think? And about the weeping you would hear." He broke off abruptly, noticing her expression at last. "Goodness, Clea my dear" he went on in self-approach, "I hope I am not betraying a confidence. You suddenly look upset. Did you tell me not to repeat the Scobie story?" He took both her hands and turned her round to face him.

A spot of red had appeared in both her cheeks. She shook her head, though she said nothing, but bit her lips as if with vexation. At last "No" she said, "there is no secret. I simply did not tell Darley because . . . well, it is silly as you say: anyway he doesn't believe in that sort of rubbish. I didn't want to seem stupider than he must find me." She leaned to kiss me apologetically on the cheek. She sensed my annoyance, as did Balthazar who hung his head and said: "I've talked out of turn. Damn! Now he will be angry with you."

"Good heavens, no!" I protested. "Simply curious, that is all. I had no intention of prying, Clea."

She made a gesture of anguished exasperation and said: "Very well. It is of no importance. I will tell you the whole thing." She started speaking hastily, as if to dispose of a disagreeable and time-wasting subject. "It was during the last dinner I told you about. Before I went to Syria. He was tipsy, I don't deny it. He said what Balthazar has just told you, and he added a description of someone who suggested to me Nessim's brother. He said, marking the place with his thumbnail on his own lips: 'His lips are split here, and I see him covered in little wounds, lying on a table. There is a lake outside. He has made up his mind. He will try and drag you to him. You will be in a dark place, imprisoned, unable to resist him. Yes, there is one near at hand who might aid you if he could. But he will not be strong enough.' " Clea stood up suddenly and brought her story to an end with the air of someone snapping off a twig. "At this point he burst into tears" she said.

It was strange what a gloom this nonsensical yet ominous recital put over our spirits; something troubling and distasteful seemed to invade that brilliant spring sunshine, the light keen air. In the silence that followed Balthazar gloomily folded and refolded his overcoat on his knee while Clea turned away to study the distant curve of the great harbour with its flotillas of cubist-smeared craft, and the scattered bright petals of the racing dinghies which had crossed the harbour boom, threading their blithe way towards the distant blue marker buoy. Alexandria was virtually at norm once more, lying in the deep back-water of the receding war, recovering its pleasures. Yet the day had suddenly darkened around us, oppressing our spirits—a sensation all the more exasperating because of its absurd cause. I cursed old Scobie's self-importance in setting up as a fortune-teller.

"These gifts might have got him a bit further in his own profession had they been real" I said peevishly.

Balthazar laughed, but even here there was a chagrined doubt in his laughter. His remorse at having stirred up this silly story was quite patent.

"Let us go" said Clea sharply. She seemed slightly annoyed as well, and for once disengaged her arm when I took it. We found an old horse-drawn gharry and drove slowly and silently into town together.

"No damn it!" cried Balthazar at last. "Let us go down and have a drink by the harbour at least." And without waiting for answer from us he redirected the jarvey and set us mutely clip-clopping down the slow curves of the Grande Corniche towards the Yacht Club in the outer harbour of which was now to befall something momentous and terrible for us all. I remember it so clearly, this spring day without flaw; a green bickering sea lighting the minarets, softly spotted here and there by the dark gusts of a fine racing wind. Yes, with mandolines fretting in the Arab town, and every costume glowing as brightly as a child's coloured transfer. Within a quarter of an hour the mag-nificence of it was to be darkened, poisoned by unexpected—completely unmerited death. But if tragedy strikes suddenly the actual moment of its striking seems to vibrate on, extend-ing into time like the sour echoes of some great gong, numbing the spirit, the comprehension. Suddenly, yes, but yet how *slowly* it expands in the understanding—the ripples unrolling upon the reason in ever-widening circles of fear. And yet, all the time, outside the centre-piece of the picture, so to speak, with its small tragic anecdote, normal life goes on unheeding. (We did not even hear the bullets, for example. Their sullen twang was carried away on the wind.)

Yet our eyes were drawn, as if by the lines-of-force of some great marine painting, to a tiny clutter of dinghies snubbing together in the lee of one of the battleships which hovered against the sky like a grey cathedral. Their sails flapped and tossed, idly as butterflies contending with the breeze. There was some obscure movement of oars and arms belonging to figures too small at this range to distinguish or recognise. Yet this tiny commotion had force to draw the eye—by who knows what interior premonition? And as the cab rolled silently along

208

the rim of the inner harbour we saw it unroll before us like some majestic seascape by a great master. The variety and distinction of the small refugee craft from every corner of the Levant—their differing designs and rigs—gave it a brilliant sensuality and rhythm against the glittering water. Everything was breath-taking yet normal; tugs hooted, children cried, from the cafés came the rattle of the *trictrac* boards and the voices of birds. The normality of an entire world surrounded that tiny central panel with its flicking sails, the gestures we could not interpret, the faint voices. The little craft tilted, arms rose and fell.

"Something has happened" said Balthazar with his narrow dark eye upon the scene, and as if his phrase had affected the horse it suddenly drew to a halt. Besides ourselves on the dockside only one man had also seen; he too stood gazing with curious open-mouthed distraction, aware that something out of the ordinary was afoot. Yet everywhere people bustled, the chandlers cried. At his feet three children played in complete absorption, placing marbles in the tramlines, hoping to see them ground to powder when the next tram passed. A water carrier clashed his brass mugs, crying: "Come, ye thirsty ones." And unobtrusively in the background, as if travelling on silk, a liner stole noiselessly down the green thoroughfare towards the open sea.

"It's Pombal" cried Clea at last, in puzzled tones, and with a gesture of anxiety put her arm through mine. It was indeed Pombal. What had befallen them was this. They had been drifting about the harbour in his little dinghy with their customary idleness and inattention and had strayed too near to one of the French battleships, carried into its lee and off their course by an unexpected swoop of the wind. How ironically it had been planned by the invisible stage-masters who direct human actions, and with what speed! For the French ships, though captive, had still retained both their small-arms and a sense of shame, which made their behaviour touchy and unpredictable. The sentries they mounted had orders to fire a warning shot across the bows of any craft which came within a dozen metres of any battleship. It was, then, only in response to orders that a sentry put a bullet through Pombal's sail as the little dinghy whirled down on its rogue course towards his ship. It was merely a warning, which intended no deliberate harm. And even now this might have . . . but no: it could not have fallen out otherwise. For my friend, overcome with rage and mortification, at being treated thus by these cowards and lack-bones of his own blood and faith, turned purple with indignation, and abandoned his tiller altogether in order to stand precariously upright and shake his huge fist, screaming: *"Salauds!"* and *"Espèces de cons!"* and—what was perhaps the definitive epithet—*"Lâches!"*

Did he hear the bullets himself? It is doubtful whether in all the confusion he did, for the craft tilted, gybed, and turned about on another course, toppling him over. It was while he was lying there, recovering the precious tiller, that he noticed Fosca in the very act of falling, but with infinite slowness. Afterwards he said that she did not know she had been hit. She must have felt, perhaps, simply a vague and unusual dispersion of her attention, the swift anaesthesia of shock which follows so swiftly upon the wound. She tilted like a high tower, and felt the sternsheets coming up slowly to press themselves to her cheek. There she lay with her eyes wide open, plump and soft as a wounded pheasant will lie, still bright of eye in spite of the blood running from its beak. He shouted her name, and felt only the immense silence of the word, for the little freshet had sharpened and was now rushing them landward. A new sort of confusion supervened, for other craft, attracted as flies are by wounds, began to cluster with cries of advice and commiseration. Meanwhile Fosca lay with vague and open eyes, smiling to herself in the other kind of dream.

And it was now that Balthazar suddenly awoke from his trance, struggled out of the cab without a word and began his queer lurching, traipsing run across the dock to the little red field-ambulance telephone with its emergency line. I heard the small click of the receiver and the sound of his voice speaking, patient and collected. The summons was answered, too, with almost miraculous promptness, for the field-post with its ambulances was only about fifty yards away. I heard the sweet tinkle of the ambulance's bell, and saw it racing along the cobbles towards us. And now all faces turned once more towards that little convoy of dinghies—faces on which was written only patient resignation or dread. Pombal was on his knees in the sheets with bent head. Behind him, deftly steering, was Ali the boatman who had been the first to comprehend and offer his help. All the other dinghies, flying along on the same course, stayed grouped around Pombal's as if in active sympathy. I could read the name *Manon* which he had so proudly bestowed upon it, not six months ago. Everything seemed to have become bewildering, shaken into a new dimension which was swollen with doubts and fears.

Balthazar stood on the quay in an agony of impatience, urging them in his mind to hurry. I heard his tongue clicking against the roof of his mouth *teck tsch*, clicking softly and reproachfully; a reproach, I wondered, directed against their slowness, or against life itself, its unpremeditated patterns?

At last they were on us. One heard quite distinctly the sound of their breathing, and our own contribution, the snap of stretcher-thongs, the tinkle of polished steel, the small snap of heels studded with hobnails. It all mixed into a confusion of activity, the lowering and lifting, the grunts as dark hands found purchase on a rope to hold the dinghy steady, the sharp serrated edges of conflicting voices giving orders. "Stand by" and "Gently now" all mixed with a distant foxtrot on a ship's radio. A stretcher swinging like a cradle, like a basket of fruit upon the dark shoulders of an Arab. And steel doors opening on a white throat.

Pombal wore an air of studied vagueness, his features all dispersed and quite livid in colour. He flopped on to the quay as if he had been dropped from a cloud, falling to his knees and recovering. He wandered vaguely after Balthazar and the stretcher-bearers bleating like a lost sheep. I suppose it must have been her blood splashed upon the expensive white *espadrilles* which he had bought a week before at Ghoshen's Emporium. At such moments it is the small details which strike one like blows. He made a vague attempt to clamber into the white throat but was rudely ejected. The doors clanged in his face. Fosca belonged now to science and not to him. He waited with humbly bent head, like a man in church, until they should open once more and admit him. He seemed hardly to be breathing. I felt an involuntary desire to go to his side but Clea's arm restrained me. We all waited in great patience and submissiveness like children, listening to the vague movements within the ambulance, the noise of boots. Then at long last the doors opened and the weary Balthazar climbed down and said: "Get in and come with us." Pombal gave one wild glance about him and turning his pain-racked countenance suddenly upon Clea and myself, delivered himself of a single gesture—spreading his arms in uncomprehending hopelessness before clapping a fat hand over each ear, as if to avoid hearing something. Balthazar's voice suddenly cracked like parchment. "Get in" he said roughly, angrily, as if he were speaking to a criminal; and as they climbed into the white interior I heard him add in a lower voice, "She is dying." A clang of iron doors closing, and I felt Clea's hand turn icy in my own.

So we sat, side by side and speechless on that magnificent spring afternoon which was already deepening into dusk. At last I lit a cigarette and walked a few yards along the quay among the chaffering Arabs who described the accident to each other in yelping tones. Ali was about to take the dinghy back to its moorings at the Yacht Club; all he needed was a light for his cigarette. He came politely towards me and asked if he might light up from me. As he puffed I noticed that the flies had already found the little patch of blood on the dinghy's floorboards. "I'll clean it up" said Ali, noticing the direction of my glance; with a lithe cat-like leap he jumped aboard and unloosed the sail. He turned to smile and wave. He wanted to say "A bad business" but his English was inadequate. He shouted "Bad poison, sir." I nodded.

Clea was still sitting in the gharry looking at her own hands. It was as if this sudden incident had somehow insulated us from one another.

"Let's go back" I said at last, and directed the driver to turn back into the town we had so recently quitted.

"Pray to goodness she will be all right" said Clea at last. "It is too cruel."

"Balthazar said she was dying. I heard him."

"He may be wrong."

"He may be wrong."

But he was not wrong, for both Fosca and the child were dead, though we did not get the news until later in the evening. We wandered listlessly about Clea's rooms, unable to concentrate on anything. Finally she said: "You had better go back and spend the evening with him, don't you think." I was uncertain. "He would rather remain alone I imagine."

"Go back" she said, and added sharply, "I can't bear you hanging about at a time like this. . . . O, darling, I've hurt you. I'm sorry."

"Of course you haven't, you fool. But I'll go."

All the way down Rue Fuad I was thinking: such a small displacement of the pattern, a single human life, yet it had power to alter so much. Literally, such an eventuality had occurred to none of us. We simply could not stomach it, fit it into the picture which Pombal himself had built up with such care. It poisoned everything this small stupid fact—even almost our affection for him, for it had turned to horror and sympathy! How inadequate as emotions they were, how powerless to be of use. My own instinct would have been to keep

213

away altogether! I felt as if I never wanted to see him again—in order not to shame him. Bad poison, indeed. I repeated Ali's phrase to myself over and over again.

Pombal was already there when I got back, sitting in his gout-chair, apparently deep in thought. A full glass of neat whisky stood beside him which he did not seem to have touched. He had changed, however, into the familiar blue dressing-gown with the gold peacock pattern, and on his feet were his battered old Egyptian slippers like golden shovels. I went into the room quite quietly and sat down opposite him without a word. He did not appear to actually look at me, yet somehow I felt that he was conscious of my presence; yet his eye was vague and dreamy, fixed on the middle distance, and his fingers softly played a five-finger exercise on each other. And still looking at the window he said, in a squeaky little voice—as if the words had power to move him although he did not quite know their meaning: "She's dead, Darley. They are both dead." I felt a sensation of a leaden weight about my heart. *"C'est pas juste"* he added absently and fell to pulling his side-beard with fat fingers. Quite unemotional, quite flat—like a man recovering from a severe stroke. Then he suddenly took a gulp of whisky and started up, choking and coughing. "It is neat" he said in surprise and disgust, and put the glass down with a long shudder. Then, leaning forward he began to scribble, taking up a pencil and pad which were on the table—whorls and lozenges and dragons. Just like a child. "I must go to confession to-morrow for the first time for ages" he said slowly, as if with infinite precaution. "I have told Hamid to wake me early. Will you mind if *Cléa* only comes?" I shook my head. I understood that he meant to the funeral. He sighed with relief. *"Bon"* he said, and standing up took the glass of whisky. At that moment the door opened and the distraught Pordre appeared. In a flash Pombal changed. It was the presence of someone of his race perhaps. He gave a long chain of deep sobs. The two men embraced muttering incoherent words and phrases, as if consoling each other for a disaster which was equally wounding to both. The old diplomat raised his white womanish fist in the air and said suddenly, fatuously: "I have already protested strongly." To whom, I wondered? To the invisible powers which decree that things shall fall out this way or that? The words sputtered out meaninglessly on the chill air of the drawing-room. Pombal was talking.

"I must write and tell him everything" he said. "Confess everything."

"Gaston" said his Chief sharply, reprovingly, "you must not do any such thing. It would increase his misery in prison. *C'est pas juste.* Be advised by me: the whole matter must be forgotten."

"Forgotten!" cried my friend as if he had been stung by a bee. "You do not understand. Forgotten! He must know for *her* sake."

"He must never know" said the older man. "Never."

They stood for a long while holding hands and gazing about them distractedly through their tears; and at this moment, as if to complete the picture, the door opened to admit the porcine outlines of Father Paul—who was never to be found far from the centre of any scandal. He paused inside the doorway with an air of unction, with his features composed around an air of gluttonous self-satisfaction. "My poor boy" he said, clearing his throat. He made a vague gesture of his paw as if scattering Holy Water over us all and sighed. He reminded me of some great hairless vulture. Then surprisingly he clattered out a few phrases of consolation in Latin.

I left my friend among these elephantine comforters, relieved in a way that there was no place for me in all this incoherent parade of Latin commiserations. Simply pressing his hand once I slipped out of the flat and directed my thoughtful footsteps in the direction of Clea's room.

The funeral took place next day. Clea came back, looking pale and strained. She threw her hat across the room and shook out her hair with an impatient gesture—as if to expel the whole distasteful memory of the incident. Then she lay down ex-exhaustedly on the sofa and put her arm over her eyes.

"It was ghastly" she said at last, "really ghastly, Darley. First of all it was a *cremation*. Pombal insisted on carrying out her wishes despite violent protests from Father Paul. What a beast that man is. He behaved as though her body had become Church property. Poor Pombal was furious. They had a terrible row settling the details I hear. And then . . . I had never visited the new Crematorium! It is unfinished. It stands in a bit of sandy waste-land littered with straw and old lemon-ade bottles, and flanked by a trash heap of old car-bodies. It looks in fact like a hastily improvised furnace in a concentration camp. Horrid little brick-lined beds with half-dead flowers sprouting from the sand. And a little railway with runners for the coffin. The ugliness! And the faces of all those consuls and acting consuls! Even Pombal seemed quite taken aback by the hideousness. And the heat! Father Paul was of course in the foreground of the picture, relishing his rôle. And then with an incongruous squeaking the coffin rolled away down the garden path and swerved into a steel hatch. We hung about, first on one leg then on the other; Father Paul showed some inclination to fill this awkward gap with impromptu prayers but at that moment a radio in a nearby house started playing Viennese waltzes. Attempts were made by various chauffeurs to locate and silence it, but in vain. Never have I felt unhappier than standing in this desolate chicken run in my best clothes. There was a dreadful charred smell from the furnace. I did not know then that Pombal intended to scatter the ashes in the desert, and that he had decided that I alone would accompany him on this journey. Nor, for that matter, did I know that Father Paul —who scented a chance of more prayers—had firmly made up his mind to do so as well. All that followed came as a surprise.

"Well finally the casket was produced—and what a casket! That was a real poke in the eye for us. It was like a confectioner's triumphant effort at something suitable for inexpensive chocolates. Father Paul tried to snatch it, but poor Pombal held on to it firmly as we trailed towards the car. I must say, here Pombal showed some backbone. 'Not you' he said as the priest started to climb into the car. 'I'm going alone with Clea.' He beckoned to me with his head.

" 'My son' said Father Paul in a low grim voice, 'I shall come too.'

" 'You won't' said Pombal. 'You've done your job.'

" 'My son, I am coming' said this obstinate wretch.

"For a moment it seemed that all might end with an exchange of blows. Pombal shook his beard at the priest and glared at him with angry eyes. I climbed into the car, feeling extremely foolish. Then Pombal pushed Father Paul in the best French manner—hard in the chest—and climbed in, banging the door. A susurrus went up from the assembled consuls at this public slight to the cloth, but no word was uttered. The priest was white with rage and made a sort of involuntary gesture—as if he were going to shake his fist at Pombal, but thought better of it.

"We were off; the chauffeur took the road to the eastern desert, acting apparently on previous instructions. Pombal sat quite still with this ghastly *bonbonnière* on his knees, breathing through his nose and with half-closed eyes. As if he were recovering his self composure after all the trials of the morning. Then he put out his hand and took mine, and so we sat, silently watching the desert unroll on either side of the car. We went quite far out before he told the chauffeur to stop. He was breathing rather heavily. We got out and stood for a desultory moment at the roadside. Then he took a step or two into the sand and paused, looking back. 'Now I shall do it' he said, and broke into his fat shambling run which carried him about twenty yards into the desert. I said hurriedly to the chauffeur, 'Drive on for five minutes, and then come back for us.' The sound of the car starting did not make Pombal turn round. He had slumped down on his knees, like a child playing in a sand-pit; but he stayed quite still for a long time. I could hear him talking in a low confidential voice, though whether he was praying or reciting poetry I could not tell. It felt desperately forlorn on that empty desert road with the heat shimmering up from the tarmac.

"Then he began to scrabble about in the sand before him, to pick up handfuls like a Moslem and pour it over his own head. He was making a queer moaning noise. At last he lay face downwards and quite still. The minutes ticked by. Far away in the distance I could hear the car coming slowly towards us—at a walking pace.

" 'Pombal' I said at last. There was no reply. I walked across the intervening space, feeling my shoes fill up with the burning sand, and touched him on the shoulder. At once he stood up and started dusting himself. He looked dreadfully old all of a sudden. 'Yes' he said with a vague, startled glance all round him, as if for the first time he realised where he was. 'Take me home, Clea.' I took his hand—as if I were leading a blind man —and tugged him slowly back to the car which by now had arrived.

"He sat beside me with a dazed look for a long time until, as if suddenly touched to the quick by a memory, he began to howl like a little boy who has cut his knee. I put my arms round him. I was so glad you weren't there—your Anglo-Saxon soul would have curled up at the edges. Yet he was repeating: 'It must have looked ridiculous. It must have looked ridiculous.' And all of a sudden he was laughing hysterically. His beard was full of sand. 'I suddenly remembered Father Paul's face' he explained, still giggling in the high hysterical tones of a schoolgirl. Then he suddenly took a hold on himself, wiped his eyes, and sighing sadly said: 'I am utterly washed out, utterly exhausted. I feel I could sleep for a week.'

"And this is presumably what he is going to do. Balthazar has given him a strong sleeping draught to take. I dropped him at his flat and the car brought me on here. I'm hardly less exhausted than he. But thank God it is all over. Somehow he will have to start his life all over again."

As if to illustrate this last proposition the telephone rang and Pombal's voice, weary and confused, said: "Darley, is that you? Good. Yes, I thought you would be there. Before I went to sleep I wanted to tell you, so that we could make arrangements about the flat. Pordre is sending me into Syria *en mission*. I leave early in the morning. If I go this way I will get allowances and be able to keep up my part of the flat easily until I come back. Eh?"

"Don't worry about it" I said.

"It was just an idea."

"Sleep now."

There was a long silence. Then he added: "But of course I will write to you, eh? Yes. Very well. Don't wake me if you come in this evening." I promised not to.

But there was hardly any need for the admonition for when I returned to the flat later that night he was still up, sitting in his gout-chair with an air of apprehension and despair. "This stuff of Balthazar's is no good" he said. "It is mildly emetic, that is all. I am getting more drowsy from the whisky. But somehow I don't want to go to bed. Who knows what dreams I shall have?" But I at last persuaded him to get into bed; he agreed on condition that I stayed and talked to him until he dozed off. He was relatively calm now, and growing increasingly drowsy. He talked in a quiet relaxed tone, as one might talk to an imaginary friend while under anaesthetic.

"I suppose it will all pass. Everything does. In the very end, it passes. I was thinking of other people in the same position. But for some it does not pass easily. One night Liza came here. I was startled to find her on the doorstep with those eyes which give me the creeps—like an eyeless rabbit in a poultry shop. She wanted me to take her to her brother's room in the Mount Vulture Hotel. She said she wanted to 'see' it. I asked what she

would see. She said, with anger, 'I have my own way of seeing.'
Well I had to do it. I felt it would please Mountolive perhaps.
But I did not know then that the Mount Vulture was no longer
a hotel. It had been turned into a brothel for the troops. We
were half-way up the stairs before the truth dawned on me.
All these naked girls, and half-dressed sweating soldiers with
their hairy bodies; their crucifixes tinkling against their identity discs. And the smell of sweat and rum and cheap scent. I
said we must get out, for the place had changed hands, but she
stamped her foot and insisted with sudden anger. Well, we
climbed the stairs. Doors were open on every landing, you
could see everything. I was glad she was blind. At last we came
to his room. It was dark. On his bed there lay an old woman
asleep with a hashish pipe beside her. It smelt of drains. She,
Liza, was very excited. 'Describe it' she told me. I did my best.
She advanced towards the bed. 'There is a woman asleep there'
I said, trying to pull her back. 'This is a house of ill fame now,
Liza, I keep telling you.' Do you know what she said? *So much
the better.* I was startled. She pressed her cheek to the pillow
beside the old woman, who groaned all at once. Liza stroked
her forehead as if she were stroking a child and said 'There now.
Sleep.' Then she came slowly and hesitantly to my hand. She
gave a curious grin and said: 'I wanted to try and take his
imprint from the pillow. But it was a useless idea. One must
try everything to recover memory. It has so many hiding-
places.' I did not know what she meant. We started downstairs
again. On the second landing I saw some drunken Australians
coming up. I could see from their faces that there was going to
be trouble. One of their number had been cheated or something. They were terribly drunk. I put my arms around Liza
and pretended we were making love in a corner of the landing
until they passed us safely. She was trembling, though whether
from fear or emotion I could not tell. And she said 'Tell me
about his women. What were they like?' I gave her a good hard
shake. 'Now you are being banal' I said. She stopped trembling

and went white with anger. In the street she said 'Get me a taxi. I do not like you.' I did and off she went without a word. I regretted my rudeness afterwards, for she was suffering; at the time things happen too fast for one to take them into account. And one never knows enough about people and their sufferings to have the right response ready at the moment. Afterwards I said many sympathetic things to her in my mind. But too late. Always too late."

A slight snore escaped his lips and he fell silent. I was about to switch off his bedside lamp and tip-toe from his room when he continued to speak, only from far away, re-establishing the thread of his thought in another context: "And when Melissa was dying Clea spent all day with her. Once she said to Clea: 'Darley made love with a kind of remorse, of despair. I suppose he imagined Justine. He never excited me like other men did. Old Cohen, for example, he was just dirty-minded, yet his lips were always wet with wine. I liked that. It made me respect him for he was a man. But Pursewarden treated me like precious china, as if he were afraid he might break me, like some precious heirloom. How good it was for once to be at rest!' "

II

So the year turned on its heel, through a winter of racing winds, frosts keener than grief, hardly preparing us for that last magnificent summer which followed the spring so swiftly. It came curving in, this summer, as if from some long-forgotten latitude first dreamed of in Eden, miraculously rediscovered among the slumbering thoughts of mankind. It rode down upon us like some famous snow-ship of the mind, to drop anchor before the city, its white sails folding like the wings of a seabird. Ah! I am hunting for metaphors which might convey something of the piercing happiness too seldom granted to those who love; but words, which were first invented against despair, are too crude to mirror the properties of something so profoundly at peace with itself, at one with itself. Words are the mirrors of our discontents merely; they contain all the huge unhatched eggs of the world's sorrows. Unless perhaps it were simpler to repeat under one's breath some lines torn from a Greek poem, written once in the shadow of a sail, on a thirsty promontory in Byzantium. Something like . . .

> *Black bread, clear water, blue air.*
> *Calm throat incomparably fair.*
> *Mind folded upon mind*
> *Eyes softly closed on eyes.*
> *Lashes a-tremble, bodies bare.*

But they English badly; and unless one hears them in Greek falling softly, word by word, from a mouth made private and familiar by the bruised endearments of spent kisses they must remain always simply charmless photographs of a reality which overreaches the realm of the poet's scope. Sad that all the brilliant plumage of that summer remains beyond capture—for one's old age will have little but such memories upon which to found its regretful happinesses. Will memory clutch it—that incomparable pattern of days, I wonder? In the dense violet shadow of white sails, under the dark noon-lantern of figs, on the renowned desert roads where the spice caravans march and the dunes soothe themselves away to the sky, to catch in their dazed sleep the drumming of gulls' wings turning in spray? Or in the cold whiplash of the waters crushing themselves against the fallen pediments of forgotten islands? In the night-mist falling upon deserted harbours with the old Arab seamarks pointing eroded fingers? Somewhere, surely, the sum of these things will still exist. There were no hauntings yet. Day followed day upon the calendar of desire, each night turning softly over in its sleep to reverse the darkness and drench us once more in the royal sunlight. Everything conspired to make it what we needed.

It is not hard, writing at this remove in time, to realise that it had all *already happened*, had been ordained in such a way and in no other. This was, so to speak, only its "coming to pass'— its stage of manifestation. But the scenario had already been devised somewhere, the actors chosen, the timing rehearsed down to the last detail in the mind of that invisible author— which perhaps would prove to be only the city itself: the Alexandria of the human estate. The seeds of future events are carried within ourselves. They are implicit in us and unfold according to the laws of their own nature. It is hard to believe, I know, when one thinks of the perfection of that summer and what followed it.

Much had to do with the discovery of the island. The island! How had it eluded us for so long? There was literally not a corner of this coast which we did not know, not a beach we had not tried, not an anchorage we had not used. Yet it had been there, staring us in the face. "If you wish to hide something" says the Arabic proverb "hide it in the sun's eye." It lay, not hidden at all, somewhat to the west of the little shrine of Sidi El Agami—the white scarp with the snowy butt of a tomb emerging from a straggle of palms and figlets. It was simply an upshouldered piece of granite pushed up from the seabed by an earthquake or some submarine convulsion in the distant past. Of course, when the sea ran high it would be covered; but it is curious that it remains to this day unmarked on the Admiralty charts, for it would constitute quite a hazard to craft of medium draught.

It was Clea who first discovered the little island of Narouz. "Where has this sprung from?" she asked with astonishment; her brown wrist swung the cutter's tiller hard over and carried us fluttering down into its lee. The granite boulder was tall enough for a windbreak. It made a roundel of still blue water in the combing tides. On the landward side there was a crude N carved in the rock above an old eroded iron ring which, with a stern anchor out to brace her, served as a secure mooring. It would be ridiculous to speak of stepping ashore for the "shore" consisted of a narrow strip of dazzling white pebbles no larger than a fireplace. "Yes, it is, it is Narouz' island" she cried, beside herself with delight at the discovery—for here as last was a place where she could fully indulge her taste for solitude. Here one would be as private as a seabird. The beach faced landward. One could see the whole swaying line of the coast with its ruined Martello towers and dunes travelling away to ancient Taposiris. We unpacked our provisions with delight for here we could swim naked and sunbathe to our heart's content without interruption.

Here that strange and solitary brother of Nessim had spent his time fishing. "I always wondered where it could be this island of his. I thought perhaps it lay westerly beyond Abu El Suir. Nessim could not tell me. But he knew there was a deep rock-pool with a wreck."

"There is an N carved here."

Clea clapped her hands with delight and struggled out of her bathing costume. "I'm sure of it. Nessim said that for months he was fighting a duel with some big fish he couldn't identify.

That was when he gave me the harpoon-gun which Narouz owned. Isn't it strange? I've always carried it in the locker wrapped in an oilskin. I thought I might shoot something one day. But it is so heavy I can't manage it under water."

"What sort of fish was it?"

"I don't know."

But she scrambled back to the cutter and produced the bulky package of greased rags in which this singular weapon was wrapped. It was an ugly-looking contrivance, a compressed-air rifle no less, with a hollow butt. It fired a slim steel harpoon about a metre and a half in length. It had been made to specifications for him in Germany. It looked deadly enough to kill quite a large fish.

"Pretty horrible looking" she said, eating an orange.

"We must try it."

"It's too heavy for me. Perhaps you will manage it. I found that the barrel lagged in the water. I couldn't bring it to bear properly. But he was a marksman, so Nessim said, and shot a lot of quite large fish. But there was one, a very big one, which made infrequent appearances. He watched and waited in ambush for it for months. He had several shots at it but always missed. I hope it wasn't a shark—I'm scared of them."

"There aren't many in the Mediterranean. It is down the Red Sea that you get them in numbers."

"Nevertheless I keep a sharp eye out."

It was too heavy an instrument, I decided, to lug about under water; besides I had no interest in shooting fish. So I wrapped and stowed it once more in the cutter's ample locker. She lay there naked in the sunlight, drowsing like a seal, to smoke a cigarette before exploring further. The rock-pool glowed beneath the glimmering keel of the boat like a quivering emerald, the long ribbons of milky light penetrating it slowly, stealing down like golden probes. About four fathoms, I thought, and drawing a deep breath rolled over and let my body wangle downwards like a fish, not using my arms.

Its beauty was spell-binding. It was like diving into the nave of a cathedral whose stained-glass windows filtered the sunlight through a dozen rainbows. The sides of the amphitheatre —for it opened gradually towards the deep sea—seemed as if carved by some heartsick artist of the Romantic Age into a dozen half-finished galleries lined with statues. Some of these were so like real statuary that I thought for a moment that I had made an archaeological find. But these blurred caryatids were wave-born, pressed and moulded by the hazard of the tides into goddesses and dwarfs and clowns. A light marine fucus of brilliant yellow and green had bearded them—shallow curtains of weed which swung lightly in the tide, parting and closing, as if to reveal their secrets suggestively and then cover them again. I pushed my fingers through this scalp of dense and slippery foliage to press them upon the blind face of a Diana or the hooked nose of a mediaeval dwarf. The floor of this deserted palace was of selenite plastic clay, soft to the touch and in no way greasy. Terra-cotta baked in a dozen hues of mauve and violet and gold. Inside close to the island it was not deep— perhaps a fathom and a half—but it fell away steeply where the gallery spread out to the sea, and the deeper lining of water faded from emerald to apple green, and from Prussian blue to black, suggesting great depth. Here, too, was the wreck of which Clea had spoken. I had hopes of finding perhaps a Roman amphora or two, but it was not alas a very old ship. I recognised the flared curve of the poop as an Aegean design— the type of caique which the Greeks call 'trechandiri'. She had been rammed astern. Her back was broken. She was full of a dead weight of dark sponges. I tried to find the painted eyes on the prow and a name, but they had vanished. Her wood was crawling with slime and every cranny winked full of hermit crabs. She must have belonged to sponge fishers of Kalymnos I thought, for each year their fleet crosses to fish the African coast and carry its haul back for processing in the Dodecanese Islands.

A blinding parcel of light struck through the ceiling now and down flashed the eloquent body of Clea, her exploding coils of hair swerved up behind her by the water's concussion, her arms spread. I caught her and we rolled and sideslipped down in each other's arms, playing like fish until lack of breath drove us upwards once more into the sunlight. To sit at last panting in the shallows, gazing with breathless delight at each other.

"What a marvellous pool." She clapped her hands in delight.

"I saw the wreck."

And climbing back to the little sickle of beach with its warm pebbles with her drenched thatch of hair swinging behind her she said: 'I've thought of another thing. This must be Timonium. I wish I could remember the details more clearly.'

"What is that?"

"They've never found the site, you know. I am sure this must be it. O let us believe that it is, shall we? When Antony came back defeated from Actium—where Cleopatra fled with her fleet in panic and tore open his battle-line, leaving him at the mercy of Octavian; when he came back after that unaccountable failure of nerve, and when there was nothing for them to do but to wait for the certain death which would follow upon Octavian's arrival—why he built himself a cell on an islet. It was named after a famous recluse and misanthrope— perhaps a philosopher?—called Timon. And here he must have spent his leisure—*here*, Darley, going over the whole thing again and again in his mind. That woman with the extraordinary spells she was able to cast. His life in ruins! And then the passing of the God, and all that, bidding him to say goodbye to her, to Alexandria—a whole world!"

The brilliant eyes smiling a little wistfully interrogated mine. She put her fingers to my cheek.

"Are you waiting for me to say that it is?"

"Yes."

"Very well. It is."

"Kiss me."

227

"Your mouth tastes of oranges and wine."

It was so small, the beach—hardly bigger than a bed. It was strange to make love thus with one's ankles in blue water and the hot sun blazing on one's back. Later we made one of many desultory attempts to locate the cell, or something which might correspond to her fancy, but in vain; on the seaward side lay a tremendous jumble of granite snags, falling steeply into black water. A thick spoke of some ancient harbour level perhaps which explained the wind-and-sea-break properties of the island. It was so silent, one heard nothing but the faint stir of wind across our ears, distant as the echo of some tiny seashell. Yes, and sometimes a herring gull flew over to judge the depth of the beach as a possible theatre of operations. But for the rest the sun-drunk bodies lay, deeply asleep, the quiet rhythms of the blood responding only to the deeper rhythms of sea and sky. A haven of animal contents which words can never compass.

It is strange, too, to remember what a curious sea-engendered *rapport* we shared during that memorable summer. A delight almost as deep as the bondage of kisses—to enter the rhythm of the waters together, responding to each other and the play of the long tides. Clea had always been a fine swimmer, I a poor one. But thanks to my period spent in Greece I too was now expert, more than a match for her. Under water we played and explored the submarine world of the pool, as thoughtlessly as fishes of the fifth day of the Creation. Eloquent and silent water-ballets which allowed us to correspond only by smile and gesture. The water-silences captured and transformed everything human in movement, so that we were like the coloured projections of undines painted upon these brilliant screens of rock and weed, echoing and copying the water-rhythms. Here thought itself perished, was converted into a fathomless content in physical action. I see the bright figure travelling like a star across this twilit firmament, its hair combed up and out in a rippling whorl of colour.

But not only here, of course. When you are in love with one

228

of its inhabitants a city can become a world. A whole new geography of Alexandria was born through Clea, reviving old meanings, renewing ambiences half forgotten, laying down like a rich wash of colour a new history, a new biography to replace the old one. Memory of old cafés along the seafront by bronze moonlight, their striped awnings a-flutter with the midnight sea-breeze. To sit and dine late, until the glasses before one had brimmed with moonlight. In the shadow of a minaret, or on some strip of sand lit by the twinkle of a paraffin lamp. Or gathering the masses of shallow spring blossom on the Cape of Figs—brilliant cyclamen, brilliant anemone. Or standing together in the tombs of Kom El Shugafa inhaling the damp exhalations of the darkness which welled out of those strange subterranean resting-places of Alexandrians long dead; tombs carved out of the black chocolate soil, one upon the other, like bunks in a ship. Airless, mouldy and yet somehow piercingly cold. ("Hold my hand.") But if she shivered it was not then with the premonitions of death, but with the sheer weight of the gravid earth piled above us metre upon metre. Any creature of the sunlight would shiver so. That brilliant summer frock swallowed by the gloom. "I'm cold. Let us go." Yes, it was cold down there. But with what pleasure one stepped from the darkness into the roaring, anarchic life of the open street once more. So the sun-god must have risen, shaking himself free from the damp clutch of the soil, smiling up at the printed blue sky which spelt travel, release from death, renewal in the life of common creatures.

Yes, but the dead are everywhere. They cannot be so simply evaded. One feels them pressing their sad blind fingers in deprivation upon the panels of our secret lives, asking to be remembered and re-enacted once more in the life of the flesh—encamping among our heartbeats, invading our embraces. We carry in ourselves the biological trophies they bequeathed us by their failure to use up life—alignment of an eye, responsive curve of a nose; or in still more fugitive forms like someone's dead laugh, or a dimple which excites a long-buried smile. The simplest of these kisses we exchanged had a pedigree of death. In them we once more befriended forgotten loves which struggled to be reborn. The roots of every sigh are buried in the ground.

And when the dead invade? For sometimes they emerge in person. That brilliant morning, for example, with everything so deceptively normal, when bursting from the pool like a rocket she gasped, deathly pale: *"There are dead men down there"*: frightening me! Yet she was not wrong, for when I mustered the courage to go down myself and look—there they were in very truth, seven of them, sitting in the twilight of the basin with an air of scrupulous attention, as if listening to some momentous debate which would decide everything for them. This conclave of silent figures formed a small semicircle across the outer doorway of the pool. They had been roped in sacks and leadweighted at the feet, so that now they stood upright, like chess pieces of human size. One has seen statues covered in this way, travelling through a city on a lorry, bound for some sad provincial museum. Slightly crouched, responding to the ligatures which bound them, and faceless, they nevertheless stood, flinching and flickering softly like figures in an early silent film. Heavily upholstered in death by the coarse canvas wrappers which bound them.

They turned out to be Greek sailors who had been bathing from their corvette when, by some accident, a depth-charge had been detonated, killing them instantly by concussion. Their unmarked bodies, glittering like mackerel, had been harvested laboriously in an old torpedo net, and laid out upon dripping decks to dry before burial. Flung overboard once more in the traditional funeral dress of mariners the curling tide had brought them to Narouz' island.

It will sound strange, perhaps, to describe how quickly we got used to these silent visitants of the pool. Within a matter of days we had accommodated them, accorded them a place of their own. We swam between them to reach the outer water, bowing ironically to their bent attentive heads.

It was not to flout death—it was rather that they had become friendly and appropriate symbols of the place, these patient, intent figures. Neither their thick skin-parcels of canvas, nor the stout integuments of rope which bound them showed any sign of disintegration. On the contrary they were covered by a dense silver dew, like mercury, which heavily proofed canvas always collects when it is immersed. We spoke once or twice of asking the Greek naval authorities to remove them to deeper water, but by long experience I knew that we should find them un-co-operative if we tried, and the subject was dropped by common consent. Once I thought I saw the flickering shadow of a great catfish moving among them but I must have been mistaken. We even thought later of giving them names, but were deterred by the thought that they must already have names of their own—the absurd names of ancient sophists and generals like Anaximander, Plato, Alexander. . . .

So this halcyon summer moved towards its end, free from omens—the long sunburnt ranks of marching days. It was, I think, in the late autumn that Maskelyne was killed in a desert sortie, but this was a passing without echoes for me—so little substance had he ever had in my mind as a living personage. It was, in very truth, a mysterious thing to find Telford sitting red-eyed at his desk one afternoon repeating brokenly: "The old Brig's copped it. The poor old Brig" and wringing his purple hands together. It was hard to know what to say. Telford went on, with a kind of incoherent wonder in his voice that was endearing. "He had no-one in the world. D'you know what? He gave me as his next-of-kin." He seemed immeasurably touched by this mark of friendship. Nevertheless it was with a reverent melancholy that he went through Maskelyne's exiguous personal effects. There was little enough to inherit save a few civilian clothes of unsuitable size, several campaign medals and stars, and a credit account of fifteen pounds in the Tottenham Court Road Branch of Lloyds Bank. More interesting relics to me were those contained in a little leather wallet—the tattered pay-book and parchment certificate of discharge which had belonged to his grandfather. The story they told had the eloquence of a history which unfolded itself within a tradition. In the year 1861 this now forgotten Suffolk farm-boy had enlisted at Bury St. Edmunds. He served in the Coldstream Guards for thirty-two years, being discharged in 1893. During his service he was married in the Chapel of the Tower of London and his wife bore him two sons. There was a faded photograph of him taken on his return from Egypt in 1882. It showed him dressed in white pith helmet, red jacket and blue serge trousers with smart black leather gaiters and pipe-clayed cross belts. On his breast was pinned the Egyptian War Medal with a clasp for the battle of Tél-el-Kebir and the Khedive's Star. Of Maskelyne's own father there was no record among his effects.

"It's tragic" said little Telford with emotion. "Mavis couldn't stop crying when I told her. She only met him twice. It shows what an effect a man of character can have on you. He was always the perfect gentleman, was the Brig." But I was brooding over this obscure faded figure in the photograph with his grim eyes and heavy black moustache, with the pipe-clayed cross belts and the campaign medals. He seemed to lighten the picture of Maskelyne himself, to give it focus. Was it not, I wondered, a story of success—a success perfectly complete within the formal pattern of something greater than the individual life, a tradition? I doubted whether Maskelyne himself could have wanted things to fall out otherwise. In every death there is the grain of something to be learned. Yet Maskelyne's quiet departure made little impact on my feelings, though I did what I could to soothe the forlorn Telford. But the tide-lines of my own life were now beginning to tug me invisibly towards an unforeseeable future. Yes, it was this beautiful autumn, with its torrent of brass brown leaves showering down from the trees in the public gardens, that Clea first became a matter of concern to me. Was it, in truth, because she heard the weeping? I do not know. She never openly admitted it. At times I tried to imagine that I heard it myself—this frail cry of a small child, or a pet locked out: but I knew that I heard nothing, absolutely nothing. Of course one could look at it in a matter-of-fact way and class it with the order of natural events which time revises and renews according to its own caprices. I mean love can wither like any other plant. Perhaps she was simply falling out of love? But in order to record the manner of its falling out I feel almost compelled to present it as something else—preposterous as it may sound—as a visitation of an agency, a power initiated in some uncommon region beyond the scope of the ordinary imagination. At any rate its onset was quite definitive, marked up like a date on a blank wall. It was November the fourteenth, just before dawn. We had been together during the whole of the previous day, idling about the city, gossiping and shopping. She had bought some piano music, and I had made her a present of a new scent from the Scent Bazaar. (At the very moment when I awoke and saw her standing, or rather crouching by the window, I caught the sudden breath of scent from my own wrist which had been dabbed with samples from the glass-stoppered bottles.) Rain had fallen that night. Its delicious swishing had lulled our sleep. We had read by candle-light before falling asleep.

But now she was standing by the window listening, her whole body stiffened into an attitude of attentive interrogation so acute that it suggested something like a crisis of apprehension. Her head was turned a little sideways, as if to present her ear to the uncurtained window behind which, very dimly, a rain-washed dawn was beginning to break over the roofs of the city. What was she listening for? I had never seen this attitude before. I called to her and briefly she turned a distraught and unseeing face to me—impatiently, as if my voice had ruptured the fine membrane of her concentration. And as I sat up she cried, in a deep choked voice: "O *no!*", and clapping her hands over her ears fell shuddering to her knees. It was as if a bullet had been fired through her brain. I heard her bones creak as she hung crouching there her features contorted into a grimace. Her hands were locked so tightly over her ears that I could not disengage them, and when I tried to lift her by her wrists she simply sank back to her knees on the carpet, with shut eyes, like a dement. "Clea, what on earth is it?" For a long moment we knelt there together, I in great perplexity. Her eyes were fast shut. I could feel the cool wind from the window pouring into the room. The silence, save for our exclamations, was complete. At last she gave a great sigh of relaxation, a long sobbing respiration, and unfastened her ears, stretched her limbs slowly, as if unbinding them from painful cramps. She shook her head at me as if to say that it was nothing. And walking like a drunkard to the bathroom she was violently sick in the washbasin. I stood there like a sleep-walker; feeling as if I had been uprooted. At last she came back, got into bed and turned her face to the wall. "What is it, Clea?" I asked again, feeling foolish and importunate. Her shoulders trembled slightly under my hand, her teeth chattered lightly from cold. "It is nothing, really nothing. A sudden splitting headache. But it has gone. Let me sleep now, will you?"

In the morning she was up early to make the breakfast. I thought her exceptionally pale—with the sort of pallor that might come after a long and agonising toothache. She complained of feeling listless and weary.

"You frightened me last night" I said, but she did not answer, turning away evasively from the subject with a curious look of anxiety and distress. She asked to be allowed to spend the day alone painting, so I took myself off for a long walk across the town, teased by half-formulated thoughts and premonitions which I somehow could not make explicit to myself. It was a beautiful day. High seas were running. The waves flailed the Spouting Rocks like the pistons of some huge machine. Immense clouds of spray were flung high into the air like the explosion of giant puff-balls only to fall back in hissing spume upon the crown of the next wave. I stood watching the spectacle for a long time, feeling the tug of the wind at the skirt of my overcoat and the cool spray on my cheeks. I think I must have known that from this point onward everything would be subtly changed. That we had entered, so to speak, a new constellation of feelings which would alter our relationship.

One speaks of change, but in truth there was nothing abrupt, coherent, definitive about it. No, the metamorphosis came about with comparative slowness. It waxed and waned like a tide, now advancing now retreating. There were even times when, for whole weeks, we were apparently completely restored to our former selves, reviving the old raptures with an intensity born now of insecurity. Suddenly for a spell we would be once more completely identified in each other, inseparable: the shadow had lifted. I tell myself now—and with what truth I still do not know—that these were periods when for a long time she had not heard the weeping which she once long ago described as belonging to a she-camel in distress or some horrible mechanical toy. But what could such nonsense really mean to anyone—and how could it elucidate those other periods when she fell into silence and moroseness, became a nervous and woebegone version of her old self? I do not know. I only know that this new personage was subject to long distracted silences now, and to unusual fatigues. She might, for example, fall asleep on a sofa in the middle of a party and begin to snore: as if overcome with weariness after an immensely long vigil. Insomnia too began to play its part, and she resorted to relatively massive doses of barbiturates in order to seek release from it. She was smoking very heavily indeed.

"Who is this new nervy person I do not recognise?" asked Balthazar in perplexity one evening when she had snapped his head off after some trivial pleasantry and left the room, banging the door in my face.

"There's something wrong" I said. He looked at me keenly for a moment over a lighted match. "She isn't pregnant?" he asked, and I shook my head. "I think she's beginning to wear me out really." It cost me an effort to bring out the words. But they had the merit of offering something like a plausible explanation to these moods—unless one preferred to believe that she were being gnawed by secret fears.

"Patience" he said. "There is never enough of it."

"I'm seriously thinking of absenting myself for a while."

"That might be a good idea. But not for too long."

"I shall see."

Sometimes in my clumsy way I would try by some teasing remark to probe to the sources of this disruptive anxiety. "Clea, why are you always looking over your shoulder—for what?" But this was a fatal error of tactics. Her response was always one of ill-temper or pique, as if in every reference to her distemper, however oblique, I was in some way mocking her. It was intimidating to see how rapidly her face darkened, her lips compressed themselves. It was as if I had tried to put my hand on a secret treasure which she was guarding with her life.

At times she was particularly nervous. Once as we were coming out of a cinema I felt her stiffen on my arm. I turned my eyes in the direction of her gaze. She was staring with horror at an old man with a badly gashed face. He was a Greek cobbler who had been caught in a bombardment and mutilated. We all knew him quite well by sight, indeed Amaril had repaired the damage as well as he was able. I shook her arm softly, reassuringly and she suddenly seemed to come awake. She straightened up abruptly and said "Come. Let us go." She gave a little shudder and hurried me away.

At other such times when I had unguardedly made some allusion to her inner preoccupations—this maddening air of always *listening* for something—the storms and accusations which followed seriously suggested the truth of my own hypothesis—namely that she was trying to drive me away: "I am no

236

good for you, Darley. Since we have been together you haven't written a single line. You have no plans. You hardly read any more." So stern those splendid eyes had become, and so troubled! I was forced to laugh, however. In truth I now knew, or thought I did, that I would never become a writer. The whole impulse to confide in the world in this way had foundered, had guttered out. The thought of the nagging little world of print and paper had become unbearably tedious to contemplate. Yet I was not unhappy to feel that the urge had abandoned me. On the contrary I was full of relief—a relief from the bondage of these forms which seemed so inadequate an instrument to convey the truth of feelings. "Clea, my dear" I said, still smiling ineffectually, and yet desiring in a way to confront this accusation and placate her. "I have been actually meditating a book of criticism."

"Criticism!" she echoed sharply, as if the word were an insult. And she smacked me full across the mouth—a stinging blow which brought tears to my eyes and cut the inside of my lip against my teeth. I retired to the bathroom to mop my mouth for I could feel the salty taste of the blood. It was interesting to see my teeth outlined in blood. I looked like an ogre who had just taken a mouthful of bleeding flesh from his victims. I washed my mouth, furiously enraged. She came in and sat down on the *bidet*, full of remorse. "Please forgive me" she said. "I don't know what sort of impulse came over me. Darley, please forgive" she said.

"One more performance like this" I said grimly "and I'll give you a blow between those beautiful eyes which you'll remember."

"I'm sorry." She put her arms round my shoulders from behind and kissed my neck. The blood had stopped. "What the devil is wrong?" I said to her reflection in the mirror. "What has come over you these days? We're drifting apart, Clea."

"I know."

237

"Why?"

"I don't know." But her face had once more become hard and obstinate. She sat down on the *bidet* and stroked her chin thoughtfully, suddenly sunk in reflection once more. Then she lit a cigarette and walked back into her living-room. When I returned she was sitting silently before a painting gazing at it with an inattentive malevolent fixity.

"I think we should separate for a while" I said.

"If you wish" she rapped out mechanically.

"Do you wish it?"

Suddenly she started crying and said "O stop questioning me. If only you would stop asking me question after question. It's like being in court these days."

"Very well" I said.

This was only one of several such scenes. It seemed clear to me that to absent myself from the city was the only way to free her—to give her the time and space necessary to . . . what? I did not know. Later that winter I thought that she had begun running a small temperature in the evenings and incurred another furious scene by asking Balthazar to examine her. Yet despite her anger she submitted to the stethoscope with comparative quietness. Balthazar could find nothing physically wrong, except that her pulse rate was advanced and her blood pressure higher than normal. His prescription of stimulants she ignored, however. She had become much thinner at this time.

By patient lobbying I at last unearthed a small post for which I was not unsuitable and which somehow fitted into the general rhythm of things—for I did not envisage my separation from Clea as something final, something in the nature of a break. It was simply a planned withdrawal for a few months to make room for any longer-sighted resolutions which she might make. New factors were there, too, for with the ending of the war Europe was slowly coming accessible once more—a new horizon opening beyond the battle-lines. One had almost stopped dreaming of it, the recondite shape of a Europe hammered flat by bombers, raked by famine and discontents. Nevertheless it was still there. So it was that when I came to tell her of my departure it was not with despondency or sorrow—but as a matter-of-fact decision which she must welcome for her own part. Only the manner in which she pronounced the word "Away" with an indrawn breath suggested for a brief second that perhaps, after all, she might be afraid to be left alone. "You are going away, after all?"

"For a few months. They are building a relay station on the island, and there is need for someone who knows the place and can speak the language."

"Back to the island?" she said softly—and here I could not read the meaning of her voice or the design of her thought.

"For a few short months only."

"Very well."

She walked up and down the carpet with an air of perplexity, staring downwards at it, deep in thought. Suddenly she looked up at me with a soft expression that I recognised with a pang— the mixture of remorse and tenderness at inflicting unwitting sorrow upon others. It was the face of the old Clea. But I knew that it would not last, that once more the peculiar shadow of her discontent would cast itself over our relationship. There was no point in trusting myself once more to what could only prove a short respite. "O Darley" she said, "when do you go, my dear?" taking my hands.

"In a fortnight. Until then I propose not to see you at all. There is no point in our upsetting each other by these wrangles."

"As you wish."

"I'll write to you."

"Yes of course."

It was a strange listless way of parting after such a momentous relationship. A sort of ghostly anaesthesia had afflicted our emotions. There was a kind of deep ache inside me but it wasn't sorrow. The dead handshake we exchanged only ex-pressed a strange and truthful exhaustion of the spirit. She sat

239

in a chair, quietly smoking and watching me as I gathered my possessions together and stuffed them into the old battered briefcase which I had borrowed from Telford and forgotten to return the summer before. The toothbrush was splayed. I threw it away. My pyjamas were torn at the shoulder but the bottom half, which I had never used, were still crisp and new. I assembled these objects with the air of a geologist sorting specimens of some remote age. A few books and papers. It all had a sort of unreality, but I cannot say that a single sharp regret was mixed with it.

"How this war has aged and staled us" she said suddenly, as if to herself. "In the old days one would have thought of going away in order, as we said, to get away from oneself. But to get away from *it*. . . ."

Now, writing the words down in all their tedious banality, I realise that she was really trying to say goodbye. The fatality of human wishes. For me the future lay open, uncommitted; and there was no part of it which I could then visualise as not containing, somehow, Clea. This parting was . . . well, it was only like changing the bandages until a wound should heal. Being unimaginative, I could not think definitively about a future which might make unexpected demands upon me; as something entirely new. It must be left to form itself upon the emptiness of the present. But for Clea the future had already closed, was already presenting a blank wall. The poor creature was afraid!

"Well, that's everything" I said at last, shoving the briefcase under my arm. "If there's anything you need, you have only to ring me. I'll be at the flat."

"I know."

"I'm off then for a while. Goodbye."

As I closed the door of the little flat I heard her call my name once—but this again was one of those deceptions, those little accesses of pity or tenderness which deceive one. It would have been absurd to pay any attention to it, to return on my tracks, and open a new cycle of disagreements. I went on down the stairs, determined to let the future have every chance to heal itself.

It was a brilliantly sunny spring day and the streets looked washed with colour. The feeling of having nowhere to go and nothing to do was both depressing and inspiriting. I returned to the flat and found on the mantelpiece a letter from Pombal in which he said that he was likely to be transferred to Italy shortly and did not think he would be able to keep the flat on. I was delighted as this enabled me to terminate the lease, my share of which I would soon not be able to afford myself.

It was at first somewhat strange, even perhaps a little numbing, to be left entirely to my own devices, but I rapidly became accustomed to it. Moreover there was quite a lot of work to be done in winding up my censorship duties and handing over the post to a successor while at the same time collecting practical information for the little unit of technicians which was to install the radio post. Between the two departments with their different needs I was kept busy enough. During these days I kept my word and saw nothing of Clea. The time passed in a sort of limbo pitched between the world of desire and of farewell—though there were no emotions in very clear definition for me: I was not conscious of regrets or longings.

So it was that when at last that fatal day presented itself, it did so under the smiling guise of a spring sunshine hot enough to encourage the flies to begin hatching out upon the window-panes. It was their buzzing which awoke me. Sunlight was pouring into the room. For a moment, dazzled by it, I hardly recognised the smiling figure seated at the foot of my bed, waiting for me to open my eyes. It was the Clea of some forgotten original version, so to speak, clad in a brilliant summer frock of a crisp vine-leaf pattern, white sandals, and with her hair arranged in a new style. She was smoking a cigarette whose smoke hung in brilliant ash-veined whorls in the sunlight above us, and her smiling face was completely relaxed and unshadowed by the least preoccupation. I stared, for she seemed so precisely and unequivocally the Clea I should always have remembered; the mischievous tenderness was back in the eyes. "Well" I said in sleepy amazement. "What . . . ?" and I felt her warm breath on my cheek as she leaned down to embrace me.

"Darley" she said, "I suddenly realised that it's tomorrow you are leaving; and that today is the Mulid of El Scob. I couldn't resist the idea of spending the day together and visiting the shrine this evening. O say you will! Look at the sunshine. It's warm enough for a bathe, and we could take Balthazar."

I was still not properly awake. I had completely forgotten the Name Day of the Pirate. "But it's long past St. George's Day" I said. "Surely that's at the end of April."

"On the contrary. Their absurd method of lunar calendar reckoning has turned him into a movable feast like all the others. He slides up and down the calendar now like a domestic saint. In fact it was Balthazar who telephoned yesterday and told me or I would have missed it myself." She paused to puff her cigarette. "We shouldn't miss it, should we?" she added a little wistfully.

"But of course not! How good of you to come."

"And the island? Perhaps you could come with us?"

The time was just ten o'clock. I could easily telephone to Telford to make some excuse for absenting myself for the day. My heart leaped.

"I'd love to" I said. "How does the wind sit?"

"Calm as a nun with easterly freshets. Ideal for the cutter I should say. Are you sure you want to come?"

She had a wicker-covered demijohn and a basket with her. "I'll go on and provision us up; you dress and meet me at the Yacht Club in an hour."

"Yes." It would give me ample time to visit my office and examine the duty mail. "A splendid idea."

And in truth it was, for the day was clear and ringing with a promise of summer heat for the afternoon. Clip-clopping down the Grande Corniche I studied the light haze on the horizon and the flat blue expanse of sea with delight. The city glittered in sunshine like a jewel. Brilliantly rode the little craft in the inner basin, parodied by their shining reflections. The minarets shone loudly. In the Arab quarter the heat had hatched out the familiar smells of offal and drying mud, of carnations and jasmine, of animal sweat and clover. In Tatwig Street dark gnomes on ladders with scarlet flower-pot hats were stretching strings of flags from the balconies. I felt the sun warm on my fingers. We rolled past the site of the ancient Pharos whose shattered fragments still choke the shallows. Toby Mannering, I remembered, had once wanted to start a curio trade by selling fragments of the Pharos as paperweights. Scobie was to break them up with a hammer for him and he was to deliver them to retailers all over the world. Why had the scheme foundered? I could not remember. Perhaps Scobie found the work too arduous? Or perhaps it had got telescoped with that other scheme for selling Jordan water to Copts at a competitive price? Somewhere a military band was banging away.

They were down on the slip waiting for me. Balthazar waved his stick cheerfully. He was dressed in white trousers and sandals and a coloured shirt, and sported an ancient yellowing Panama hat.

"The first day of summer" I called cheerfully.

"You're wrong" he croaked. "Look at that haze. It's altogether too hot. I've betted Clea a thousand piastres we have a thunderstorm by this afternoon."

"He's always got something gloomy to say" smiled Clea.

"I know my Alexandria" said Balthazar.

And so amidst these idle pleasantries we three set forth, Clea at the tiller of her little craft. There was hardly a breath of wind inside the harbour and she lagged somewhat, only gathering way by the momentum of the currents which curved down towards the harbour entrance. We stole past the battleships and liners, breasting the choppy main-channel hesitantly, the main-sail hardly drawing as yet, until at last we reached the huddle of grey forts which marked the main harbour entrance. Here there was always a bundle of choppy water piled up by the tide and we wallowed and yawed for a while until suddenly she heeled and threaded herself upon the wind and settled her bowsprit true. We began to hiss through the sea like a flying fish, as if she were going to impale a star. I lay in the sheets now, staring up at the gold sun shining through the sails, hearing the smat-tering of the wavelets on the elegant prow of the cutter. Bal-thazar was humming an air. Clea's brown wrist lay upon the tiller with a deceptive soft negligence. The sails were stiff. These are the heart-lifting joys of small sailing-craft in ideal weather. A speechless delight held me, a mixture of luxuries born of the warm sun, the racing wind, and the light cool touches of spray which dashed our cheeks from time to time. We went far out on an easterly course in order to come about and tack inshore. By now we had performed this manœuvre so often that it had become second nature to Clea: to ride down upon the little island of Narouz and to judge the exact moment at which to turn into the eye of the wind and hang, fluttering like an eyelash, until I had run the sail in and scrambled ashore to make fast. . . .

"Smart work indeed" said Balthazar approvingly as he stepped into the water; and then "By God! it is quite fantastic-ally warm."

"What did I tell you?" said Clea busy in the locker.

"It only proves my point about a thunderstorm."

And curiously enough, at this moment, there came a dis-tinct rumble of thunder out of that cloudless sky. "There" said Balthazar in triumph. "We will get a fine soaking and you will owe me some money, Clea."

"We'll see."

"It was a shore battery" I said.

"Rubbish" said Balthazar.

So we secured the cutter and carried our provisions ashore. Balthazar lay on his back with his hat over his nose in the best of humours. He would not bathe, pleading the indifference of his swimming, so Clea and I dived once more into the familiar pool which we had neglected all winter long. Nothing had changed. The sentinels were still there, grouped in silent debate, though the winter tides had altered their dispositions somewhat, grouping them a little nearer to the wreck. Ironically yet respectfully we greeted them, recognising in these ancient gestures and underwater smiles a familiar happiness growing up in the sheer act of swimming once more together. It was as if the blood had started to flow again in veins long withered from disuse. I caught her by the heel and rolled her in a long somersault towards the dead mariners, and turning expertly she repaid the debt by coming up behind me to drag me down by the shoulders and climb surfacewards before I could retaliate. It was here, spiralling up through the water with her hair coiled out behind her, that the image of Clea was restored once more. Time had rendered her up, whole and intact again—'natural as a city's grey-eyed Muse'—to quote the Greek poem. Swiftly, precisely the fingers which pressed upon my shoulder re-evoked her as we slid through the silent pool.

And then: to sit once more in the simple sunlight, sipping the red wine of St. Menas as she broke up the warm brown loaf of French bread, and hunted for a particular cheese or a cluster of dates: while Balthazar talked discursively (half asleep) of the Vineyard of Ammon, the Kings of the Harpoon Kingdom and their battles, or of the Mareotic wine to which, not history, but the gossiping Horace once attributed Cleopatra's distempers of mind . . . ("History sanctions everything, pardons everything —even what we do not pardon ourselves.")

So the warm noon drew on as we lay there on the hot pebbles: and so at last—to Balthazar's great delight and Clea's discomfiture—the predicted thunderstorm made its appearance, heralded by a great livid cloud which rolled up from the east and squatted over the city, bruising the sky. So suddenly too— as when an ink-squid in alarm puffs out its bag and suddenly fogs clear water in a cloud of black—rain flowed down in glittering sheets, thunder bellowed and insisted. At each peal Balthazar clapped his hands with delight—not only to be proved right, but also because here we were sitting in full sunlight, fully at our ease, eating oranges and drinking wine beside an untroubled blue sea.

"Stop crowing" said Clea severely.

It was one of those freak storms so prevalent in the early spring with its sharp changes of temperature born of sea and desert. They turned the streets to torrents in the twinkling of an eye, yet never endured above half an hour. Suddenly the cloud would be whisked away by a scrap of wind, utterly to disappear. "And mark me now" said Balthazar, inebriated by the success of his prediction. "By the time we get back to harbour everything will be dry again, dry as a bone."

But now the afternoon brought us another phenomenon to delight us—something rarely seen in summer in the waters of Alexandria, belonging as it did to those days preceding winter storms when the glass was falling steeply. The waters of the pool darkened appreciably, curdled, and then became phosphorescent. It was Clea who first noticed. "Look" she cried with delight crushing her heels down in the shallows to watch the twinkling prickling light spark from them. "Phosphorus!" Balthazar started saying something learned about the organism which causes this spectacle but unheeding we plunged side by side and ranged down into the water, transformed into figures of flame, the sparks flashing from the tips of our fingers and toes with the glitter of static electricity. A swimmer seen underwater looks like an early picture of the fall of Lucifer, literally on fire. So bright was the electrical crackle that we could not help wondering how it was that we were not scorched by it. So we played, glittering like comets, among the quiet mariners

246

who sat, watching us perhaps in their thoughts, faintly echoing the twitching of the tide in their canvas sacks.

"The cloud's lifting already" cried Balthazar as I surfaced at last for air. Soon even the fugitive phosphorescence would dwindle and vanish. For some reason or other he had climbed into the stern of the cutter, perhaps to gain height and more easily watch the thunderstorm over the city. I rested my forearms on the gunwale and took my breath. He had unwrapped the old harpoon gun of Narouz and was holding it negligently on his knee. Clea surfaced with a swish of delight and pausing just long enough to cry: "The fire is so beautiful" doubled her lithe body back and ducked downward again.

"What are you doing with that?" I asked idly.

"Seeing how it works."

He had in fact pushed the harpoon to rest in the barrel. It had locked with the spring. "It's cocked" I said. " Have a care."

"Yes, I'm going to release it."

Then Balthazar leaned forward and uttered the only serious remark he had made all that day. "You know" he said, "I think you had better take her with you. I have a feeling you won't be coming back to Alexandria. Take Clea with you!"

And then, before I could reply, the accident happened. He was fumbling with the gun as he spoke. It slipped from between his fingers and fell with a crash, the barrel striking the gunwale six inches from my face. As I reared back in alarm I heard the sudden cobra-like hiss of the compressor and the leaden twang of the trigger-release. The harpoon whistled into the water beside me rustling its long green line behind it. "For Christ's sake" I said. Balthazar had turned white with alarm and vexation. His half-muttered apologies and expressions of horrid amazement were eloquent. "I'm terribly sorry." I had heard the slight snick of steel settling into a target, somewhere down there in the pool. We stayed frozen for a second for something else had occurred simultaneously to our minds. As I saw his lips starting to shape the word "Clea" I felt a sudden darkness descending on my spirit—a darkness which lifted and trembled at the edges; and a rushing like the sough of giant wings. I had already turned before he uttered the word. I crashed back into the water, now following the long green thread with all the suspense of Ariadne; and to it added the weight of slowness which only heartsick apprehension brings. I knew in my mind that I was swimming vigorously—yet it seemed like one of those slow-motion films where human actions, delayed by the camera, are drawn unctuously out to infinity, spooled out like toffee. How many light-years would it take to reach the end of that thread? What would I find at the end of it? Down I went, and down, in the dwindling phosphorescence, into the deep shadowed coolness of the pool.

At the far end, by the wreck, I distinguished a convulsive, coiling movement, and dimly recognised the form of Clea. She seemed intently busy upon some childish underwater game of the kind we so often played together. She was tugging at something, her feet braced against the woodwork of the wreck, tugging and relaxing her body. Though the green thread led to her I felt a wave of relief—for perhaps she was only trying to extricate the harpoon and carry it to the surface with her. But no, for she rolled drunkenly. I slid along her like an eel, feeling with my hands. Feeling me near she turned her head as if to tell me something. Her long hair impeded my vision. As for her face I could not read the despairing pain which must have been written on it—for the water transforms every expression of the human features into the goggling imbecile grimace of the squid. But now she arched out and flung her head back so that her hair could flow freely up from her scalp—the gesture of someone throwing open a robe to exhibit a wound. And I saw. Her right hand had been pierced and nailed to the wreck by the steel arrow. At least it had not passed through her body, my mind cried out in relief, seeking to console itself; but the relief turned to sick malevolent despair when, clutching the

248

steel shaft, I myself braced my feet against the wood, tugging until my thigh muscles cracked. It would not be budged by a hair's breadth. (No, but all this was part of some incomprehensible dream, fabricated perhaps in the dead minds of the seven brooding figures which attended so carefully, so scrupulously to the laboured evolutions we now performed—we no longer free and expeditious as fish, but awkward, splayed, like lobsters trapped in a pot.) I struggled frantically with that steel arrow, seeing out of the corner of my eye the long chain of white bubbles bursting from the throat of Clea. I felt her muscles expending themselves, ebbing. Gradually she was settling in the drowsiness of the blue water, being invaded by the water-sleep which had already lulled the mariners to sleep. I shook her.

I cannot pretend that anything which followed belonged to my own volition—for the mad rage which now possessed me was not among the order of the emotions I would ever have recognised as belonging to my proper self. It exceeded, in blind violent rapacity, anything I had ever before experienced. In this curious timeless underwater dream I felt my brain ringing like the alarm bell of an ambulance, dispelling the lulling languorous ebb and flow of the marine darkness. I was suddenly rowelled by the sharp spur of terror. It was as if I were for the first time confronting myself—or perhaps an alter ego shaped after a man of action I had never realised, recognised. With one wild shove I shot to the surface again, emerging under Balthazar's very nose.

"The knife" I said sucking in the air.

His eyes gazed into mine, as if over the edge of some sunken continent, with an expression of pity and horror; emotions preserved, fossilised, from some ice age of human memory. And native fear. He started to stammer out all the questions which invaded his mind—words like "what" "where" "when" "whither"—but could achieve no more than a baffled "wh——": a vague sputtering anguish of interrogation.

The knife which I had remembered was an Italian bayonet which had been ground down to the size of a dirk and sharpened to razor keenness. Ali the boatman had manufactured it with pride. He used it to trim ropes, for splicing and rigging. I hung there for a second while he reached out for it, eyes closed, lungs drinking in the whole sky it seemed. Then I felt the wooden haft in my fingers and without daring to look again at Balthazar I turned my toes to heaven and returned on my tracks, following the green thread.

She hung there limp now, stretched languorously out, while her long hair unfurled behind her; the tides rippled out along her body, passing through it, it seemed like an electric current playing. Everything was still, the silver coinage of sunlight dappling the floor of the pool, the silent observers, the statues whose long beards moved slowly, unctuously to and fro. Even as I began to hack at her hand I was mentally preparing a large empty space in my mind which would have to accommodate the thought of her dead. A large space like an unexplored sub-continent on the maps of the mind. It was not very long before I felt the body disengage under this bitter punishment. The water was dark. I dropped the knife and with a great push sent her reeling back from the wreck: caught her under the arms: and so rose. It seemed to take an age—and endless progression of heartbeats—in that slow-motion world. Yet we hit the sky with a concussion that knocked the breath from me—as if I had cracked my skull on the ceiling of the universe. I was standing in the shallows now rolling the heavy sodden log of her body. I heard the crash of Balthazar's teeth falling into the boat as he jumped into the water beside me. We heaved and grunted like stevedores until she was out on the pebbles, Balthazar meanwhile scrabbling about to grasp that injured hand which was spouting. He was like an electrician trying to capture and insulate a high-tension wire which had snapped. Grabbing it, he held on to it like a vice. I had a sudden picture of him as a small child holding his mother's hand nervously among a crowd of other children, or crossing a park where the boys had once thrown stones at him. . . . Through his pink gums he extruded the word "Twine"—and there was some luckily in the cutter's locker which kept him busy.

"But she's dead" I said, and the word altered my heartbeats, so that I felt about to faint. She was lying, like a fallen seabird, on the little spit of pebbles. Balthazar squatted almost in the water, holding frenziedly on to the hand at which I could hardly bear to look. But again this unknown alter ego whose voice came from far away helped me to adjust a tourniquet, roll a pencil in it and hand it to him. With a heave now I straightened her out and fell with a thump upon her, crashing down as if from a very great height upon her back. I felt the soggy heavy lungs bounce under this crude blow. Again and again, slowly but with great violence I began to squeeze them in this pitiful simulacrum of the sexual act—life saving, life-giving. Balthazar appeared to be praying. Then came a small sign of hope for the lips of that pale face opened and a little sea water mixed with vomit trickled from them. It meant nothing, of course, but we both cried out at the omen. Closing my eyes I willed my wrists to seek out those waterlogged lungs, to squeeze and void them. Up and down, up and down in this slow cruel rhythm, I pumped at her. I felt her fine bones creaking under my hands. But still she lay lifeless. But I would not accept the thought that she was dead, though I knew it with one part of my mind. I felt half mad with determination to disprove it, to overthrow, if necessary, the whole process of nature and by an act of will force her to live. These decisions astonished me, for they subsisted like clear and sharply defined images underneath the dazed physical fatigue, the groan and sweat of this labour. I had, I realised, decided either to bring her up alive or to stay down there at the bottom of the pool with her; but where, from which territory of the will such a decision had come, I could not guess! And now it was hot. I was pouring with sweat. Balthazar still sat holding the hand, the painter's hand, humbly as a child at its mother's knee. Tears trickled down his nose. His head went from side to side in that Jewish gesture of despairing remorse and his toothless gums formed the sound of the old Wailing Wall "Aiee, Aiee". But very softly, as if not to disturb her.

But at last we were rewarded. Suddenly, like a spout giving in a gutter under the pressure of rain, her mouth opened and expelled a mass of vomit and sea-water, fragments of breadsoak and orange. We gazed at this mess with a lustful delight, as if at a great trophy. I felt the lungs respond slowly to my hand. A few more strokes of this crude engine and a secondary ripple seemed to stir in the musculature of her body. At almost every downward thrust now the lungs gave up some water, reluctantly, painfully. Then, after a long time, we heard a faint whimper. It must have hurt, as the first few breaths hurt a newly born child. The body of Clea was protesting at this forcible rebirth. And all of a sudden the features of that white face moved, composed themselves to express something like pain and protest. (Yes, but it *hurts* to realise.)

"Keep it up" cried Balthazar in a new voice, shaky and triumphant. There was no need to tell me. She was twitching a little now, and making a soundless whimpering face at each lunge. It was like starting a very cold diesel engine. Finally yet another miracle occurred—for she opened very blue sightless unfocused eyes for a second to study, with dazed concentration, the stones before her nose. Then she closed them again. Pain darkened her features, but even the pain was a triumph—for at least they expressed living emotions now—emotions which had replaced the pale set mask of death. "She's breathing" I said. "Balthazar she's breathing."

"She's breathing" he repeated with a kind of idiotic rapture.

She was breathing, short staggering inspirations which were clearly painful. But now another kind of help was at hand. We had not noticed, so concentrated were we on this task, that a vessel had entered the little harbour. This was the Harbour

Patrol motorboat. They had seen us and guessed that something was wrong. "Merciful God" cried Balthazar flapping his arms like an old crow. Cheerful English voices came across the water asking if we needed help; a couple of sailors came ashore towards us. "We'll have her back in no time" said Balthazar, grinning shakily.

"Give her some brandy."

"No" he cried sharply. "No brandy."

The sailors brought a tarpaulin ashore and softly we baled her up like Cleopatra. To their brawny arms she must have seemed as light as thistledown. Their tender clumsy movements were touching, brought tears to my eyes. "Easy up there, Nobby. Gently with the little lady." "That tourniquet will have to be watched. You go too, Balthazar."

"And you?"

"I'll bring her cutter back."

We wasted no more time. In a few moments the powerful motors of the patrol vessel began to bustle them away at a good ten knots. I heard a sailor say: "How about some hot Bovril?"

"Capital" said Balthazar. He was soaked to the skin. His hat was floating in the water beside me. Leaning over the stern a thought suddenly struck him.

"My teeth. Bring my teeth!"

I watched them out of sight and then sat for a good while with my head in my hands. I found to my surprise that I was trembling all over like a frightened horse with shock. A splitting headache assailed me. I climbed into the cutter and foraged for the brandy and a cigarette. The harpoon gun lay on the sheets. I threw it overboard with an oath and watched it slowly crawling downwards into the pool. Then I shook out the jib, and turning her through her own length on the stern anchor pressed her out into the wind. It took longer than I thought, for the evening wind had shifted a few points and I had to tack widely before I could bring her in. Ali was waiting for me. He had already been apprised of the situation, and carried a message from Balthazar to the effect that Clea had been taken up to the Jewish hospital.

I took a taxi as soon as one could be found. We travelled across the city at a great pace. The streets and buildings passed me in a sort of blur. So great was my anxiety that I saw them as if through a rain-starred window-pane. I could hear the metre ticking away like a pulse. Somewhere in a white ward Clea would be lying drinking blood through the eye of a silver needle. Drop by drop it would be passing into the median vein heart-beat by heart-beat. There was nothing to worry about, I told myself; and then, thinking of that shattered hand, I banged my fist with rage against the padded wall of the taxi.

I followed a duty nurse down the long anonymous green corridors whose oil-painted walls exuded an atmosphere of damp. The white phosphorescent bulbs which punctuated our progress wallowed in the gloom like swollen glow-worms. They had probably put her, I reflected, in the little ward with the single curtained bed which in the past had been reserved for critical cases whose expectation of life was short. It was now the emergency casualty ward. A sense of ghostly familiarity was growing upon me. In the past it was here that I had come to see Melissa. Clea must be lying in the same narrow iron bed in the corner by the wall. ("It would be just like real life to imitate art at this point.")

In the corridor outside, however, I came upon Amaril and Balthazar standing with a curious chastened expression before a trolley which had just been wheeled to them by a duty nurse. It contained a number of wet and glistening X-ray photographs, newly developed and pegged upon a rail. The two men were studying them anxiously, gravely, as if thinking out a chess problem. Balthazar caught sight of me and turned, his face lighting up. "She's all right" he said, but in rather a broken voice, as he squeezed my hand. I handed him his teeth and he blushed, and slipped them into his pocket. Amaril was wearing horn-rimmed reading glasses. He turned from his intent study of those dripping dangling sheets with an expression of utter rage. "What the bloody hell do you expect me to do with this mess?" he burst out waving his insolent white hand in the direction of the X-rays. I lost my temper at the implied accusation and in a second we were shouting at each other like fishmongers, our eyes full of tears. I think we would have come to blows out of sheer exasperation had not Balthazar got between us. Then at once the rage dropped from Amaril and he walked round Balthazar to embrace me and mutter an apology. "She's all right" he murmured, patting me consolingly on the shoulder. "We've tucked her up safely."

"Leave the rest to us" said Balthazar.

"I'd like to see her" I said enviously—as if, in bringing her to life, she had become in a way my own property too. "Could I?"

As I pushed open the door and crept into the little cell like a miser I heard Amaril say peevishly: "It's all very well to talk about surgical repair in that glib way——"

It was immensely quiet and white, the little ward with its tall windows. She lay with her face to the wall in the uncomfortable steel bed on castors of yellow rubber. It smelt of flowers, though there were none to be seen and I could not identify the odour. It was perhaps a synthetic atomiser spray— the essence of forget-me-nots? I softly drew up a chair beside the bed and sat down. Her eyes were open, gazing at the wall with the dazed look which suggested morphia and fatigue combined. Though she gave no sign of having heard me enter she said suddenly:

"Is that you Darley?"

"Yes."

Her voice was clear. Now she sighed and moved slightly, as if with relief at my coming. "I'm so glad." Her voice had a small weary lilt which suggested that somewhere beyond the confines of her present pain and drowsiness a new self-confidence was stirring. "I wanted to thank you."

"It is Amaril you're in love with" I said—rather, blurted out. The remark came as a great surprise to me. It was completely involuntary. Suddenly a shutter seemed to roll back across my mind. I realised that this new fact which I was enunciating was one that I had always known, but without *being aware of the knowing!* Foolish as it was the distinction was a real one. Amaril was like a playing card which had always been there, lying before me on the table, face downwards. I had been aware of its existence but had never turned it over. Nor, I should add, was there anything in my voice beyond genuine scientific surprise; it was without pain, and full of sympathy only. Between us we had never used this dreadful word—this synonym for derangement or illness—and if I deliberately used it now it was to signify my recognition of the thing's autonomous nature. It was rather like saying "My poor child, you have got cancer!"

After a moment's silence she said: "Past tense now, alas!" Her voice had a puzzled drawling quality. "And I was giving you good marks for tact, thinking you had recognised him in my Syrian episode! Had you really not? Yes, Amaril turned me into a woman I suppose. O isn't it disgusting? When will we all grow up? No, but I've worn him out in my heart, you know. It isn't as you imagine it. I know he is not the man for me. Nothing would have persuaded me to replace Semira. I know this by the fact of having made love to him, been in love with him! It's odd, but the experience prevented me from mistaking him for the other one, the once for aller! Though who and where he is remains to discover. I haven't really affronted the real problems yet, I feel. They lie the other side of these mere episodes. And yet, perverse as it is, it is nice to be close to him —even on the operating-table. How is one to make clear a single truth about the human heart?"

"Shall I put off my journey?"

"But no. I wouldn't wish it at all. I shall need a little time to come to myself now that at last I am free from the horror.

That at least you have done for me—pushed me back into mid-stream again and driven off the dragon. It's gone and will never come back. Put your hand on my shoulder and squeeze, instead of a kiss. No. Don't change plans. Now at last we can take things a bit easily. Unhurriedly. I shall be well cared for here as you know. Later when your job is done we shall see, shall we? Try and write. I feel perhaps a pause might start you off."

"I will." But I knew I wouldn't.

"Only one thing I want you to do. Please visit the Mulid of El Scob tonight so that you can tell me all about it; you see it is the first time since the war that they are allowing the custom-ary lighting in that *quartier*. It should be fun to see. I don't want you to miss it. Will you?"

"Of course."

"Thank you, my dear."

I stood up and after a moment's pause said: "Clea what exactly *was* the horror?"

But she had closed her eyes and was fading softly into sleep. Her lips moved but I could not catch her answer. There was the faintest trace of a smile at the corners of her mouth.

A phrase of Pursewarden's came into my mind as I softly closed the door of the ward. "The richest love is that which submits to the arbitration of time."

o   o   o   o   o

It was already late when at last I managed to locate a gharry to take me back to the town. At the flat I found a message to say that my departure had been put forward by six hours; the motor-launch would be leaving at midnight. Hamid was there, standing quite still and patient, as if he already knew the con-tents of the message. My luggage had been collected by an Army truck that afternoon. There was nothing left to do except kill the time until twelve, and this I proposed to do in the fashion suggested by Clea: by visiting the Mulid of El Scob. Hamid still stood before me, gravid with the weight of another parting. "You no come back this time, sir" he said blinking his eye at me with sorrow. I looked at the little man with emotion. I remembered how proudly he had recounted the saving of this one eye. It was because he had been the younger and uglier brother of the two. His mother had put out his brother's two eyes in order to prevent him from being conscripted; but he Hamid, being puny and ugly—he had escaped with one. His brother was now a blind *muezzin* in Tanta. But how rich he was, Hamid, with his one eye! It represented a fortune to him in well-paid work for rich foreigners.

"I come to you in London" he said eagerly, hopefully.

"Very well. I'll write to you."

He was all dressed up for the Mulid in his best clothes—the crimson cloak and the red shoes of soft morocco leather; in his bosom he had a clean white handkerchief. It was his evening off I remembered. Pombal and I had saved up a sum of money to give him as a parting present. He took the cheque between finger and thumb, inclining his head with gratitude. But self-interest could not buoy him up against the pain of parting from us. So he repeated "I come to you in London" to console himself; shaking hands with himself as he said the words.

"Very well" I said for the third time, though I could hardly see one-eyed Hamid in London. "I will write. Tonight I shall visit the Mulid of El Scob."

"Very good." I shook him by the shoulders and the familiarity made him bow his head. A tear trickled out of his blind eye and off the end of his nose.

"Goodbye ya Hamid" I said, and walked down the stairs, leaving him standing quietly at the top, as if waiting for some signal from outer space. Then suddenly he rushed after me, catching me at the front door, in order to thrust into my hand, as a parting present, his cherished picture of Melissa and myself walking down Rue Fuad on some forgotten afternoon.

III

The whole quarter lay drowsing in the umbrageous violet of approaching nightfall. A sky of palpitating *velours* which was cut into by the stark flare of a thousand electric light bulbs. It lay over Tatwig Street, that night, like a velvet rind. Only the lighted tips of the minarets rose above it on their slender invisible stalks— appeared hanging suspended in the sky; trembling slightly with the haze as if about to expand their hoods like cobras. Drifting idly down those remembered streets once more I drank in (forever: keepsakes of the Arab town) the smell of crushed chrysanthemums, ordure, scents, strawberries, human sweat and roasting pigeons. The procession had not arrived as yet. It would form somewhere beyond the harlots' quarter, among the tombs, and wind its slow way to the shrine, geared to a dancing measure; calling on the way at each of the mosques to offer up a verse or two of the Book in honour of El Scob. But the secular side of the festival was in full swing. In the dark alleys people had brought their dinner tables into the street, candlelit and decked with roses. So sitting they could catch the chipped headtones of the girl singers who were already standing on the wooden platforms outside the cafés, piercing the heavy night with their quartertones. The streets were beflagged, and the great framed pictures of the circumcision doctors rippled on high among the cressets and standards. In a darkened yard I saw them pouring the hot sugar, red and white, into the little wooden moulds from which would emerge the whole bestiary of Egypt—the ducks, horsemen, rabbits, and goats. The great sugar figurines too of the Delta folklore—Yuna and Aziz the lovers interlocked, interpenetrated—and the bearded heroes like Abu Zeid, armed and mounted among his brigands. They were splendidly obscene—surely the stupidest word in our language?—and brilliantly coloured before being dressed in their garments of paper, tinsel, and spangled gold, and set up on display among the Sugar Booths for the children to gape at and buy. In every little square now the coloured marquees had been run up, each with its familiar sign. The Gamblers were already busy—Abu Firan, the Father of Rats, was shouting cheerfully for customers. The great board stood before him on trestles, each of the twelve houses marked with a number and a name. In the centre stood the live white rat which had been painted with green stripes. You placed your money on the number of a house, and won, if the rat entered it. In another box the same game was in play, but with a pigeon this time; when all the bets were laid a handful of grain was tossed into the centre and the pigeon, in eating it, entered one of the numbered stalls.

I bought myself a couple of sugar figurines and sat down outside a café to watch the passing show with its brilliant pristine colour. These little "arusas" or brides I would have liked to keep, but I knew that they would crumble or be eaten by ants. They were the little cousins of the *santons de Provence* or the *bonhommes de pain d'épices* of the French country fair: of our own now extinct gilt gingerbread men. I ordered a spoon of mastika to eat with the cool fizzing sherbet. From where I sat at an angle between two narrow streets I could see the harlots painting themselves at an upper window before coming down to set up their garish booths among the conjurers and tricksters; Showal the dwarf was teasing them from his booth at ground level and causing screams of laughter at his well-aimed arrows. He had a high tinny little voice and the most engaging of acrobatic tricks despite his stunted size. He talked continuously even when standing on his head, and punctuated the point of his patter with a double somersault. His face was grotesquely farded and his lips painted in a clown's grin. At the other corner under a hide curtain sat Faraj the fortune-teller with his instruments of divination—ink, sand, and a curious hairy ball like a bull's testicles only covered in dark hair. A radiantly beautiful prostitute squatted before him. He had filled her palm with ink and was urging her to scry.

Little scenes from the street life. A mad wild witch of a woman who suddenly burst into the street, foaming at the lips and uttering curses so terrible that silence fell and everyone's blood froze. Her eyes blazed like a bear's under the white matted hair. Being mad she was in some sort holy, and no-one dared to face the terrible imprecations she uttered which, if turned on him, might spell ill luck. Suddenly a grubby child darted from the crowd and tugged her sleeve. At once calmed she took his hand and turned away into an alley. The festival closed over the memory of her like a skin.

I was sitting here, drunk on the spectacle, when the voice of Scobie himself suddenly sounded at my elbow. "Now, old man" it said thoughtfully. "If you have Tendencies you got to have Scope. That's why I'm in the Middle East if you want to know. . . ."

"God, you gave me a start" I said, turning round. It was Nimrod the policeman who had been one of the old man's superiors in the Police Force. He chuckled and sat down beside me, removing his tarbush to mop his forehead. "Did you think he'd come to life?" he enquired.

"I certainly did."

"I know my Scobie, you see."

Nimrod laid his flywhisk before him and with a clap of his hands commanded a coffee. Then giving me a sly wink he went on in the veritable voice of the saint. "The thing about Budgie was just that. In Horsham there's no Scope. Otherwise I would have joined him years ago in the earth-closet trade. The man's a mechanical genius I don't mind admitting. And not having any income except what the old mud-slinger—as he laughingly calls it—brings him in, he's stymied. He's in baulk. Did I ever tell you about the Bijou Earth Closet? No? Funny I thought I did.

Well, it was a superb contrivance, the fruit of long experimen
Budgie is an F.R.Z.S. you know. He got it by home study.
That shows you what a brain the man has. Well it was a sort
of lever with a trigger. The seat of the closet was on a kind of
spring. As you sat down it *went* down, but when you got up it
sprang up of its own accord and threw a spadeful of earth into
the bin. Budgie says he got the idea from watching his dog
clear up after himself with his paws. But how he adapted it I
just can't fathom. It's sheer genius. You have a magazine at the
back which you fill with earth or sand. Then when you get up
the spring goes bang and presto! He's making about two
thousand a year out of it, I don't mind admitting. Of course it
takes time to build up a trade, but the overheads are low. He
has just one man working for him to build the box part, and he
buys the springs—gets them made to specification in Hammer-
smith. And they're very prettily painted too, with astrology
all round the rim. It looks queer, I admit. In fact it looks
arcane. But it's a wonderful contrivance the little Bijou. Once
there was a crisis while I was home on leave for a month. I
called in to see Budgie. He was almost in tears. The chap who
helped, Tom the carpenter, used to drink a bit and must have
misplaced the sprockets on one series of Bijous. Anyway com-
plaints started to pour in. Budgie said that his closets had gone
mad all over Sussex and were throwing earth about in a weird
and unwholesome way. Customers were furious. Well, there
was nothing for it but to visit all his parishioners on a motor-
bike and adjust the sprockets. I had so little time that I didn't
want to miss his company—so he took me along with him. It
was quite an adventure I don't mind telling you. Some of them
were quite mad with Budgie. One woman said the sprocket
was so strong her closet threw mud the length of the drawing-
room. We had a time quietening her down. I helped by lending
a soothing influence I don't mind admitting, while Budgie
tinkered with the spring. I told stories to take their minds off
the unhappy business. But finally it got straightened out. And

now it's a profitable industry with members everywhere."

Nimrod sipped his coffee reflectively and cocked a quizzical eye in my direction, proud of his mimicry. "And now" he said, throwing up his hands, "El Scob. . . ."

A crowd of painted girls passed down the street, brilliant as tropical parrots and almost as loud in their chattering and laughing. "Now that Abu Zeid" said Nimrod "has taken the Mulid under his patronage it's likely to grow into a bit of headache for us. It's such a crowded quarter. This morning he sent a whole string of he-camels on heat into the town with *bercim* clover. You know how horrible they smell. And when they're in season they get that horrible jelly-like excrescence on their necks. It must irritate them or suppurate or something for they're scratching their necks the whole time on walls and posts. Two of them had a fight. It took hours to untangle the affair. The place was blocked."

Suddenly a series of bangs sounded from the direction of the harbour and a series of bright coloured rockets traced their splendid grooves across the night, drooping and falling away with a patter and a hiss. "Aha!" said Nimrod with self-satisfaction. "There goes the Navy. I'm glad they remembered."

"Navy?" I echoed as another long line of rockets tossed their brilliant plumage across the soft night.

"The boys of H.M.S. *Milton*" he chuckled. "I happened to dine on board last night. The wardroom was much taken by my story of an old Merchant Seaman who had been beatified. I naturally did not tell them very much about Scobie; least of all about his death. But I did hint that a few fireworks would be appropriate as coming from British mariners, and I also added that as a political gesture of respect it would earn them good marks with the worshippers. The idea caught on at once, and the Admiral was asked for permission. And there we go!"

We sat for a while in companionable silence watching the fireworks and the highly delighted crowd which saluted each salvo with long quivering exclamations of pleasure. "All—ah!

All—ah!" Finally Nimrod cleared his throat and said: "Darley, can I ask you a question? Do you know what Justine is up to?" I must have looked very blank for he went on at once without hesitation. "I only ask you because she rang me yesterday and said that she was going to break parole today, come into town deliberately, and that she wanted me to arrest her. It sounds quite absurd—I mean to come all the way into town to give herself up to the Police. She said she wanted to force a personal interview with Memlik. It had to be me as reports from the British officers on the force would carry weight and draw Memlik's attention. It sounds a bit of a rigmarole doesn't it? But I've got a date with her at the Central Station in half an hour."

"I know nothing about the matter."

"I wondered if you did. Anyway keep it under your hat."

"I will."

He stood up and held out his hand to say goodbye. "You're off tonight I gather. Good luck." As he stepped down from the little wooden platform he said: "By the way, Balthazar is looking for you. He's somewhere down at the shrine—what a word!" With a brief nod his tall figure moved away into the brilliant swirling street. I paid for my drink and walked down towards Tatwig Street, bumped and jostled by the holiday crowd.

Ribbons and bunting and huge coloured gonfalons had been hung from every balcony along the street. The little piece of waste land under the arched doors was now the most sumptuous of saloons. Huge tents with their brilliant embroidered designs had been set up creating a ceremonial parade ground where the dancing and chanting would be held when the procession reached its destination. This area was crowded with children. The drone of prayers and the shrill tongue-trills of women came from the shrine which was dimly lit. The suppliants were invoking fruitfulness of Scobie's bath-tub. The long quavering lines of the Suras spun themselves on the night in a web of melodious sound. I quested round a bit among the crowd like a gun-dog, hunting for Balthazar. At last I caught sight of him sitting somewhat apart at an outdoor café. I made my way to his side. "Good" he said. "I was on the look out for you. Hamid said you were off tonight. He telephoned to ask for a job and told me. Besides I wanted to share with you my mixture of shame and relief over this hideous accident. Shame at the stupidity, relief that she isn't dead. Both mixed. I'm rather drunk with relief, and dazed with the shame." He was indeed rather tipsy. "But it will be all right, thank God!"

"What does Amaril think?"

"Nothing as yet. Or if he does he won't say. She must have a comfortable twenty-four hours of rest before anything is decided. Are you really going?" His voice fell with reproof. "You should stay, you know."

"She doesn't want me to stay."

"I know. I was a bit shocked when she said she had told you to go; but she said 'You don't understand. I shall see if I can't will him back again. We aren't quite ripe for each other yet. It will come.' I was amazed to see her so self-confident and radiant again. Really amazed. Sit down, my dear chap, and have a couple of stiff drinks with me. We'll see the procession quite well from here. No crowding." He clapped his hands rather unsteadily and called for more mastika.

When the glasses were brought he sat for a long while silent with his chin on his hands, staring at them. Then he gave a sigh and shook his head sadly.

"What is it?" I said, removing his glass from the tray and placing it squarely before him on the tin table.

"Leila is dead" he said quietly. The words seemed to weight him down with sorrow. "Nessim telephoned this evening to tell me. The strange thing is that he sounded exhilarated by the news. He has managed to get permission to fly down and make arrangements for her funeral. D'you know what he said?" Balthazar looked at me with that dark all-comprehending eye and went on. "He said: 'While I loved her *and all that*, her death has

265

freed me in a curious sort of way. A new life is opening before me. I feel years younger.' I don't know if it was a trick of the telephone or what but he sounded younger. His voice was full of suppressed excitement. He knew, of course, that Leila and I were the oldest of friends but not that all through this period of absence she was writing to me. She was a rare soul, Darley, one of the rare flowers of Alexandria. She wrote: 'I know I am dying, my dear Balthazar, but all too slowly. Do not believe the doctors and their diagnoses, you of all men. I am dying of heartsickness like a true Alexandrian.' " Balthazar blew his nose in an old sock which he took from the breast-pocket of his coat; carefully folded it to resemble a clean handkerchief and pedantically replaced it. "Yes" he said again, gravely, "what a word it is—'heartsickness'! And it seems to me that while (from what you tell me) Liza Pursewarden was administering her death-warrant to her brother, Mountolive was giving the same back-hander to Leila. So we pass the loving-cup about, the poisoned loving-cup!" He nodded and took a loud sip of his drink. He went on slowly, with immense care and effort, like someone translating from an obscure and recondite text. "Yes, just as Liza's letter to Pursewarden telling him that at last the stranger had appeared was his *coup de grâce* so to speak, so Leila received, I suppose, exactly the same letter. Who knows how these things are arranged? Perhaps in the very same words. The same words of passionate gratitude: 'I bless you, I thank you with all my heart that through you I am at last able to receive the precious gift which can never come to those who are ignorant of its powers.' Those are the words of Mountolive. For Leila quoted them to me. All this was after she went away. She wrote to me. It was as if she were cut off from Nessim and had nobody to turn to, nobody to talk to. Hence the long letters in which she went over it all, backwards and forwards, with that marvellous candour and clear-sightedness which I so loved in her. She refused every self-deception. Ah! but she fell between two stools, Leila, between two lives, two loves. She said

266

something like this in explaining it to me: 'I thought at first when I got his letter that it was just another attachment—as it was in the past for his Russian ballerina. There was never any secret between us of his loves, and that is what made ours seem so truthful, so immortal in its way. It was a love without reserves. But this time everything became clear to me when he refused to tell me her name, to share her with me, so to speak! I knew then that everything was ended. Of course in another corner of my mind I had always been waiting for this moment; I pictured myself facing it with magnanimity. This I found, to my surprise, was impossible. That was why for a long time, even when I knew he was in Egypt, and anxious to see me, I could not bring myself to see him. Of course I pretended it was for other reasons, purely feminine ones. But it was not that. It wasn't lack of courage because of my smashed beauty, no! For I have in reality the heart of a man.' "

Balthazar sat for a moment staring at the empty glasses with wide eyes, pressing his fingers softly together. His story meant very little to me—except that I was amazed to imagine Mount-olive capable of any very deep feeling, and at a loss to imagine this secret relationship with the mother of Nessim.

"The Dark Swallow!" said Balthazar and clapped his hands for more drink to be brought. "We shall not look upon her like again."

But gradually the raucous night around us was swelling with the deeper rumour of the approaching procession. One saw the rosy light of the cressets among the roofs. The streets, already congested, were now black with people. They buzzed like a great hive with the contagion of the knowledge. You could hear the distant bumping of drums and the hissing splash of cymbals, keeping time with the strange archaic peristaltic rhythms of the dance—its relatively slow walking pace broken by queer halts, to enable the dancers, as the ecstasy seized them, to twirl in and out of their syncopated measures and return once more to their places in the line of march. It pushed its way

267

through the narrow funnel of the main street like a torrent whose force makes it overleap its bed; for all the little side streets were full of sightseers running along, keeping pace with it.

First came the grotesque acrobats and tumblers with masks and painted faces, rolling and contorting, leaping in the air and walking on their hands. They were followed by a line of carts full of candidates for circumcision dressed in brilliant silks and embroidered caps, and surrounded by their sponsors, the ladies of the harem. They rode proudly, singing in juvenile voices and greeting the crowd: like the bleating of sacrificial lambs. Balthazar croaked: "Foreskins will fall like snow tonight, by the look of it. It is amazing that there are no infections. You know, they use black gunpowder and lime-juice as a styptic for the wound!"

Now came the various orders with their tilting and careening gonfalons with the names of the holy ones crudely written on them. They trembled like foliage in the wind. Magnificently robed sheiks held them aloft walking with difficulty because of their weight, yet keeping the line of the procession straight. The street-preachers were gabbling the hundred holy names. A cluster of bright braziers outlined the stern bearded faces of a cluster of dignitaries carrying huge paper lanterns, like balloons, ahead of them. Now as they overran us and flowed down the length of Tatwig Street in a long ripple of colour we saw the various orders of Dervishes climb out of the nether darkness and emerge into the light, each order distinguished by its colour. They were led by the black-capped Rifaia—the scorpion-eaters of legendary powers. Their short barking cries indicated that the religious ecstasy was already on them. They gazed around with dazed eyes. Some had run skewers through their cheeks, others licked red-hot knives. At last came the courtly figure of Abu Zeid with his little group of retainers on magnificently caparisoned ponies, their cloaks swelling out behind them, their arms raised in salutation like knights embarking on a tournament. Before them ran a helter skelter collection of male prostitutes with powdered faces and long flowing hair, chuckling and ejaculating like chickens in a farm-yard. And to all this queer discontinuous and yet somehow congruent mass of humanity the music lent a sort of homo-geneity; it bound it and confined it within the heart-beats of the drums, the piercing skirl of the flutes, the gnashing of the cymbals. Circling, proceeding, halting: circling, proceeding, halting, the long dancing lines moved on towards the tomb, bursting through the great portals of Scobie's lodgings like a tide at full, and deploying across the brilliant square in clouds of dust.

And as the chanters moved forward to recite the holy texts six Mevlevi dervishes suddenly took the centre of the stage, expanding in a slow fan of movement until they had formed a semicircle. They wore brilliant white robes reaching to their green slippered feet and tall brown hats shaped like huge *bombes glacées*. Calmly, beautifully, they began to whirl, these "tops spun by God", while the music of the flutes haunted them with their piercing quibbles. As they gathered momen-tum their arms, which at first they hugged fast to their shoulders, unfolded as if by centrifugal force and stretched out to full reach, the right palm turned upward to heaven, the left downward to the ground. So, with heads and tall rounded hats tilted slightly, like the axis of the earth, they stayed there miraculously spinning, their feet hardly seeming to touch the floor, in this wonderful parody of the heavenly bodies in their perpetual motion. On and on they went, faster and faster, until the mind wearied of trying to keep pace with them. I thought of the verses of Jalaluddin which Pursewarden used sometimes to recite. On the outer circles the Rifaia had begun their display of self-mutilation, so horrible to behold and yet so apparently harmless. The touch of a sheik's finger would heal all these wounds pierced in the cheeks and breasts. Here a dervish drove a skewer through his nostrils, there another fell

269

upon the point of a dirk, driving it up through his throat into his skull. But still the central knot of dancers continued its unswerving course, spinning in the sky of the mind.

"My goodness" said Balthazar at my elbow, with a chuckle, "I thought he was familiar. There's the Magzub himself. The one at the further end. He used to be an absolute terror, more than half mad. The one who was supposed to have stolen the child and sold it to a brothel. Look at him."

I saw a face of immense world-weary serenity, the eyes closed, the lips curved in a half-smile; as the dancer spun slowly to a halt this slender personage, with an air of half-playful modesty, took up a bundle of thorns and lighting it at a brazier thrust the blazing mass into his bosom against the flesh, and started to whirl once more like a tree in flames. Then as the circle came to a swaying halt he plucked it out once more and gave the dervish next to him a playful slap upon the face with it.

But now a dozen dancing circles intervened and took up the measure and the little courtyard overflowed with twisting turning figures. From the little shrine came the steady drone of the holy word, punctuated by the shrill tongue trills of the votaries.

"Scobie's going to have a heavy night" said Balthazar with irreverence. "Counting foreskins up there in the Moslem heaven."

Somewhere far away I heard the siren of a ship boom in the harbour, recalling me to my senses. It was time to be going. "I'll come down with you" said Balthazar, and together we started to push and wriggle our way down the crowded street towards the Corniche.

We found a gharry and sat silent in it, hearing the music and drumming gradually receding as we traversed the long rolling line of the marine parade. The moon was up, shining on the calm sea, freckled by the light breeze. The palms nodded. We clip-clopped down the narrow twisted streets and into the commercial harbour at last with its silent ghostly watercraft. A few lights winked here and there. A liner moved out of its berth and slid softly down the channel—a long glittering crescent of light.

The little launch which was to carry me was still being loaded with provisions and luggage.

"Well" I said, "Balthazar. Keep out of mischief."

"We'll be meeting again quite soon" he said quietly. "You can't shake me off. The Wandering Jew, you know. But I'll keep you posted about Clea. I'd say something like 'Come back to us soon', if I didn't have the feeling that you weren't going to. I'm damned if I know why. But that we'll meet again I'm sure."

"So am I" I said.

We embraced warmly, and with an abrupt gesture he climbed back into the gharry and settled himself once more.

"Mark my words" he said as the horse started up to the flick of a whip.

I stood, listening to the noise of its hooves until the night swallowed them up. Then I turned back to the work in hand.

IV

Dearest Clea:

Three long months and no word from you. I would have been very much disquieted had not the faithful Balthazar sent me his punctual postcard every few days to report so favourably on your progress: though of course he gives me no details. You for your part must have grown increasingly angry at my callous silence which you so little deserve. Truthfully, I am bitterly ashamed of it. I do not know what curious inhibition has been holding me back. I have been unable either to analyse it or to react against it effectively. It has been like a handle of a door which won't turn. Why? It is doubly strange because I have been deeply conscious of you all the time, of you being actively present in my thoughts. I've been holding you, metaphorically, cool against my throbbing mind like a knife-blade. Is it possible that I enjoyed you better as a thought than as a person alive, acting in the world? Or was it that words themselves seemed so empty a consolation for the distance which has divided us? I do not know. But now that the job is nearly completed I seem suddenly to have found my tongue.

Things alter their focus on this little island. You called it a metaphor once, I remember, but it is very much a reality to me —though of course vastly changed from the little haven I knew before. It is our own invasion which has changed it. You could hardly imagine that ten technicians could make such a change. But we have imported money, and with it are slowly altering the economy of the place, displacing labour at inflated prices, creating all sorts of new needs of which the lucky inhabitants were not conscious before. Needs which in the last analysis will destroy the tightly woven fabric of this feudal village with its tense blood-relationships, its feuds and archaic festivals. Its wholeness will dissolve under these alien pressures. It was so tightly woven, so beautiful and symmetrical like a swallow's nest. We are picking it apart like idle boys, unaware of the damage we inflict. It seems inescapable the death we bring to the old order without wishing it. It is simply done too—a few steel girders, some digging equipment, a crane! Suddenly things begin to alter shape. A new cupidity is born. It will start quietly with a few barbers' shops, but will end by altering the whole architecture of the port. In ten years it will be an un-recognisable jumble of warehouses, dance-halls and brothels for merchant sailors. Only give us enough time!

The site which they chose for the relay station is on the mountainous eastward side of the island, and not where I lived before. I am rather glad of this in an obscure sort of way. I am sentimental enough about old memories to enjoy them—but how much better they seem in the light of a small shift of gravity; they are renewed and refreshed all at once. Moreover this corner of the island is unlike any other part—a high wine-bearing valley overlooking the sea. Its soils are gold, bronze and scarlet—I suppose they consist of some volcanic marl. The red wine they make is light and very faintly *pétillant*, as if a volcano still slumbered in every bottle. Yes, here the mountains ground their teeth together (one can *hear* them during the frequent tremors!) and powdered up these metamorphic rocks into chalk. I live in a small square house of two rooms built over a wine-magazine. A terraced and tiled courtyard separates it from several other such places of storage—deep cellars full of sleeping wine in tuns.

We are in the heart of the vineyards; on all sides, ruled away on the oblong to follow the spine of the blue hill above the sea, run the shallow canals of humus and mould between the sym-metrical vines which are now flourishing. Galleries—no, bowling-alleys of the brown ashy earth, every mouthful finger-and-fist-sifted by the industrious girls. Here and there figs and olives intrude upon this rippling forest of green, this vine-carpet. It is so dense that once you are in it, crouched, your field of visibility is about three feet, like a mouse in the corn. As I write there are a dozen invisible girls tunnelling like moles, turning the soil. I hear their voices but see nothing. Yes, they are crawling about in there like sharpshooters. They rise and start work before dawn. I wake and hear them arriving often, sometimes singing a snatch of a Greek folk-song! I am up at five. The first birds come over and are greeted by the small reception committee of optimistic hunters who pot idly at them and then pass up the hill, chattering and chaffing each other.

Shading my terrace stands a tall tree of white mulberries, with the largest fruit I have ever seen—as big as caterpillars. The fruit is ripe and the wasps have found it and are quite drunk on the sweetness. They behave just like human beings, laughing uproariously about nothing, falling down, picking fights. . . .

The life is hard, but good. What pleasure to actually sweat over a task, actually use one's hands! And while we are harvesting steel to raise, membrane by membrane, this delicate mysterious ex-voto to the sky—why the vines are ripening too with their reminder that long after man has stopped his neurotic fiddling with the death-bringing tools with which he expresses his fear of life, the old dark gods are there, underground, buried in the moist humus of the chthonian world (that favourite word of P's). They are forever sited in the human wish. They will never capitulate! (I am talking at random simply to give you an idea of the sort of life I lead here.)

The early hill-barley is being gathered. You meet walking haystacks—haystacks with nothing but a pair of feet below them trudging along these rocky lanes. The weird shouts the women give, either at cattle or calling to one another from hillside to hillside. "*Wow*" "*hoosh*" "*gnaiow*". This barley is laid upon the flat roofs for threshing out the chaff which they do with sticks. Barley! hardly is the word spoken before the ant-processions begin, long chains of dark ants trying to carry it away to their private storehouses. This in turn has alerted the yellow lizards; they prowl about eating the ants, lying in ambush winking their eyes. And, as if following out the octave of causality in nature, here come the cats to hunt and eat the lizards. This is not good for them, and many die of a wasting disease attributed to this folly. But I suppose the thrill of the chase is on them. And then? Well, now and then a viper kills a cat stone dead. And the man with his spade breaks the snake's back. And the man? Autumn fevers come on with the first rain. The old men tumble into the grave like fruit off a tree. *Finita la guerra!* These people were occupied by Italians and quite a few learned the language which they speak with a Sienese accent.

In the little square is a fountain where the women gather. They proudly display their babies, and fancy them as if they were up for sale. This one is fat, that one thin. The young men pass up and down the road with hot shy glances. One of them sings archly *"Solo, per te, Lucia"*. But they only toss their heads and continue with their gossip. There is an old and apparently completely deaf man filling his pitcher. He is almost electrocuted by the phrase "Dmitri at the big house is dead." It lifts him off the ground. He spins round in a towering rage. "Dead? Who's dead? Eh? What?" His hearing is much improved all at once.

There is a little acropolis now called Fontana, high up there in the clouds. Yet it isn't far. But a steep climb up clinker-dry river-beds amid clouds of black flies; you come upon herds of rushing black goats like satans. There is a tiny hospice on the top with one mad monk; built as if on a turntable like a kiln of rusk. From here you can drink the sweet indolent misty curves of the island to the west.

And the future?

Well, this is a sketch of a nearly ideal present which will not

275

last forever; indeed has almost expired, for within another month or so my usefulness will come to an end, and with it presumably the post upon which I depend for my exiguous livelihood. I have no resources of my own and must consider ways and means. No, the future rolls about inside me with every roll of the ship, so to speak, like a cargo which has worked loose. Were it not to see you again I doubt if I could return again to Alexandria. I feel it fade inside me, in my thoughts, like some valedictory mirage—like the sad history of some great queen whose fortunes have foundered among the ruins of armies and the sands of time! My mind has been turning more and more westward, towards the old inheritance of Italy or France. Surely there is still some worthwhile work to be done among their ruins—something which we can cherish, perhaps even revive? I ask myself this question, but it really addresses itself to you. Uncommitted as yet to any path, nevertheless the one I would most like to take leads westward and northward. There are other reasons. The terms of my contract entitle me to free "repatriation" as they call it; to reach England would cost me nothing. Then, with the handsome service gratuity which all this bondage has earned me, I think I could afford a spell in Europe. My heart leaps at the thought.

But something in all this must be decided for me; I have a feeling, I mean, that it is not I who shall decide.

Please forgive me my silence for which I cannot offer any excuse and write me a line.

Last Saturday I found myself with a free day and a half, so I walked across the island with a pack to spend a night in the little house where I lived on my previous visit. What a contrast to this verdant highland it was to strike that wild and windy promontory once more, the acid green seas and fretted coastlines of the past. It was indeed another island—I suppose the past always is. Here for a night and a day I lived the life of an echo, thinking much about the past and about us all moving in it, the "selective fictions" which life shuffles out like a pack of cards, mixing and dividing, withdrawing and restoring. It did not seem to me that I had the right to feel so calm and happy: a sense of Plenitude in which the only unanswered question was the one which arose with each memory of your name.

Yes, a different island, harsher and more beautiful of aspect. One held the night-silence in one's hands; feeling it slowly melting—as a child holds a piece of ice! At noon a dolphin rising from the ocean. Earthquake vapours on the sea-line. The great grove of plane trees with their black elephant hides which the wind strips off in great scrolls revealing the soft grey ashen skin within. . . . Much of the detail I had forgotten.

It is rather off the beaten track this little promontory; only olive-pickers might come here in season. Otherwise the only visitants are the charcoal burners who ride through the grove before light every day with a characteristic jingle of stirrups. They have built long narrow trenches on the hill. They crouch over them all day, black as demons.

But for the most part one might be living on the moon. Slightly noise of sea, the patient stridulation of *cigales* in the sunlight. One day I caught a tortoise at my front door; on the beach was a smashed turtle's egg. Small items which plant themselves in the speculative mind like single notes of music belonging to some larger composition which I suppose one will never hear. The tortoise makes a charming and undemanding pet. I can hear P say: "Brother Ass and his tortoise. The marriage of true minds!"

For the rest: the picture of a man skimming flat stones upon the still water of the lagoon at evening, waiting for a letter out of silence.

o   o   o   o   o

But I had hardly confided this letter to the muleteer-postman who took our mail down to the town before I received a letter with an Egyptian stamp, addressed to me in an unknown hand. It read as follows:

"You did not recognise it, did you? I mean the handwriting on the envelope? I confess that I chuckled as I addressed it to you, before beginning this letter: I could see your face all of a sudden with its expression of perplexity. I saw you turn the letter over in your fingers for a moment trying to guess who had sent it!

"It is the first serious letter I have attempted, apart from short notes, with my new hand: this strange accessory-after-the-fact with which the good Amaril has equipped me! I wanted it to become word-perfect before I wrote to you. Of course I was frightened and disgusted by it at first, as you can imagine. But I have come to respect it very much, this delicate and beautiful steel contrivance which lies beside me so quietly on the table in its green velvet glove! Nothing falls out as one imagines it. I could not have believed myself accepting it so completely— steel and rubber seem such strange allies for human flesh. But the hand has proved itself almost more competent even than an ordinary flesh-and-blood member! In fact its powers are so comprehensive that I am a little frightened of it. It can undertake the most delicate of tasks, even turning the pages of a book, as well as the coarser ones. But most important of all— ah! Darley I tremble as I write the words—IT can *paint*!

"I have crossed the border and entered into the possession of my kingdom, thanks to the Hand. Nothing about this was premeditated. One day it took up a brush and lo! pictures of truly troubling originality and authority were born. I have five of them now. I stare at them with reverent wonder. Where did they come from? But I know that the Hand was responsible. And this new handwriting is also one of its new inventions, tall and purposeful and tender. Don't think I boast. I am speaking with the utmost objectivity, for I know that I am not responsible. It is the Hand alone which has contrived to slip me through the barriers into the company of the Real Ones as Pursewarden used to say. Yet it is a bit frightening; the elegant velvet glove guards its secret perfectly. If I wear both gloves a perfect anonymity is preserved! I watch with wonder and a certain distrust, as one might a beautiful and dangerous pet like a panther, say. There is nothing, it seems, that it cannot do impressively better than I can. This will explain my silence and I hope excuse it. I have been totally absorbed in this new hand-language and the interior metamorphosis it has brought about. All the roads have opened before me, everything seems now possible for the first time.

"On the table beside me as I write lies my steamship ticket to France; yesterday I knew with absolute certainty that I must go there. Do you remember how Pursewarden used to say that artists, like sick cats, knew by instinct exactly which herb they needed to effect a cure: and that the bitter-sweet herb of their self-discovery only grew in one place, France? Within ten days I shall be gone! And among so many new certainties there is one which has raised its head—the certainty that you will follow me there in your own good time. I speak of certainty not prophecy—I have done with fortune-tellers once and for all!

"This, then, is simply to give you the dispositions which the Hand has imposed on me, and which I accept with eagerness and gratitude—with resignation also. This last week I have been paying a round of goodbye visits, for I think it will be some long time before I see Alexandria again. It has become stale and profitless to me. And yet how can we but help love the places which have made us suffer? Leave-takings are in the air; it's as if the whole composition of our lives were being suddenly drawn away by a new current. For I am not the only person who is leaving the place—far from it. Mountolive, for example, will be leaving in a couple of months; by a great stroke of luck he has been given the plum post of his profession, Paris! With this news all the old uncertainties seem to have vanished; last week he was secretly married! You will guess to whom.

"Another deeply encouraging thing is the return and recovery of dear old Pombal. He is back at the Foreign Office now in a senior post and seems to have recovered much of his old form to judge by the long exuberant letter he sent me. 'How could I have forgotten' he writes 'that there are no women in the world except French women? It is quite mysterious. They are the most lovely creation of the Almighty. And yet . . . dear Clea, there are *so very many of them*, and each more perfect than the other. What is one poor man to do against so many, against such an army? For Godsake ask someone, anyone, to bring up reinforcements. Wouldn't Darley like to help an old friend out for old times' sake?'

"I pass you the invitation for what it is worth. Amaril and Semira will have a child this month—a child with the nose I invented! He will spend a year in America on some job or other, taking them with him. Balthazar also is off on a visit to Smyrna and Venice. My most piquant piece of news, however, I have saved for the last. *Justine!*

"This I do not expect you to believe. Nevertheless I must put it down. Walking down Rue Fuad at ten o'clock on a bright Spring morning I saw her come towards me, radiant and beautifully turned out in a spring frock of eloquent design: and *flop flop flop* beside her on the dusty pavements, hopping like a toad, the detested Memlik! Clad in elastic-sided boots with spats. A cane with a gold knob. And a newly minted flower-pot on his fuzzy crown. I nearly collapsed. She was leading him along like a poodle. One almost saw the cheap leather leash attached to his collar. She greeted me with effusive warmth and introduced me to her captive who shuffled shyly and greeted me in a deep groaning voice like a bass saxophone. They were on their way to meet Nessim at the Select. Would I go too? Of course I would. You know how tirelessly curious I am. She kept shooting secret sparks of amusement at me without Memlik seeing. Her eyes were sparkling with delight, a sort of impish mockery. It was as if, like some powerful engine of destruction, she had suddenly switched on again. She has never looked happier or younger. When we absented ourselves to powder our noses I could only gasp: 'Justine! Memlik! What on earth?' She gave a peal of laughter and giving me a great hug said: 'I have found his *point faible*. He is hungry for *society*. He wants to move in social circles in Alexandria and meet a lot of *white* women!' More laughter. 'But what is the object?' I said in bewilderment. Here all at once she became serious, though her eyes sparkled with clever malevolence. 'We have started something, Nessim and I. We have made a break through at last. Clea, I am so happy, I could cry. It is something much bigger this time, international. We will have to go to Switzerland next year, probably for good. Nessim's luck has suddenly changed. I can't tell you any details.'

"When we reached the table upstairs Nessim had already arrived and was talking to Memlik. His appearance staggered me, he looked so much younger, and so elegant and self-possessed. It gave me a queer pang, too, to see the passionate way they embraced, Nessim and Justine, as if oblivious to the rest of the world. Right there in the café, with such ecstatic passion that I did not know where to look.

"Memlik sat there with his expensive gloves on his knee, smiling gently. It was clear that he enjoyed the life of high society, and I could see from the way he offered me an ice that he also enjoyed the company of white women!

"Ah! it is getting tired, this miraculous hand. I must catch the evening post with this letter. There are a hundred things to attend to before I start the bore of packing. As for you, wise one, I have a feeling that you too perhaps have stepped across the threshold into the kingdom of your imagination, to take possession of it once and for all. Write and tell me—or save it for some small café under a chestnut-tree, in smoky autumn weather, by the Seine.

"I wait, quite serene and happy, a real human being, an artist at last.

"Clea."

o   o   o   o   o

281

But it was to be a little while yet before the clouds parted before me to reveal the secret landscape of which she was writing, and which she would henceforward appropriate, brushstroke by slow brushstroke. It had been so long in forming inside me, this precious image, that I too was as unprepared as she had been. It came on a blue day, quite unpremeditated, quite unannounced, and with such *ease* I would not have believed it. I had been until then like some timid girl, scared of the birth of her first child.

Yes, one day I found myself writing down with trembling fingers the four words (four letters! four faces!) with which every story-teller since the world began has staked his slender claim to the attention of his fellow-men. Words which presage simply the old story of an artist coming of age. I wrote: "Once upon a time . . ."

And I felt as if the whole universe had given me a nudge!

WORKPOINTS

Hamid's story of Darley and Melissa.

o   o   o

Mountolive's child by the dancer Griskin. The result of the duel. The Russian letters. Her terror of Liza when after her mother's death she is sent to her father.

o   o   o

Memlik and Justine in Geneva.

o   o   o

Balthazar's encounter with Arnauti in Venice. The violet sunglasses, the torn overcoat, pockets full of crumbs to feed the pigeons. The scene in Florian's. The shuffling walk of general paralysis. Conversations on the balcony of the little *pension* over the rotting backwater of the canal. Was Justine actually Claudia? He cannot be sure. "Time is memory, they say; the art however is to revive it and yet avoid remembering. You speak of Alexandria. I can no longer even imagine it. It has dissolved. A work of art is something which is more like life than life itself!" The slow death.

o   o   o

The northern journey of Narouz, and the great battle of the sticks.

Smyrna. The manuscripts, The Annals of Time. The theft.

NOTES

* *Page 140*

CHE FECE . . . IL GRAN RIFIUTO

To some among us comes that implacable day
Demanding that we stand our ground and utter
By choice of will the great Yea or Nay.
And whosoever has in him the affirming word
Will straightway then be heard.
The pathways of his life will clear at once
And all rewards will crown his way.
But he, the other who denies,
No-one can say he lies; he would repeat
His Nay in louder tones if pressed again.
It is his right—yet by such little trifles,
A 'No' instead of 'Yes' his whole life sinks and stifles.
free translation from C. P. Cavafy

* *Page 40*

FAR AWAY

This fugitive memory . . . I should so much
Like to record it, but it's dwindled . . .
Hardly a print of it remaining . . .
It lies so far back, back in my earliest youth,
Before my gifts had kindled.

A skin made of jasmine-petals on a night . . .
An August evening . . . but *was* it August?
I can barely reach it now, barely remember . . .
Those eyes, the magnificent eyes . . .
Or was it perhaps in September . . . in the dog days . . .

Irrevocably blue, yes, bluer than
A sapphire's mineral gaze.

free translation from C. P. Cavafy

* *Page 39*

THE AFTERNOON SUN

This little room, how well I know it!
Now they've rented this and the next door one
As business premises, the whole house
Has been swallowed up by merchants' offices,
By limited companies and shipping agents . . .

O how familiar it is, this little room!

Once here, by the door, stood a sofa,
And before it a little Turkish carpet,
Exactly here. Then the shelf with the two
Yellow vases, and on the right of them:
No. Wait. Opposite them (how time passes)
The shabby wardrobe and the little mirror.
And here in the middle the table
Where he always used to sit and write,
And round it the three cane chairs.
How many years . . . And by the window over there
The bed we made love on so very often.

Somewhere all these old sticks of furniture
Must still be knocking about . . .

And beside the window, yes, that bed.
The afternoon sun climbed half way up it.

We parted at four o'clock one afternoon,
Just for a week, on just such an afternoon.
I would have never
Believed those seven days could last forever.

                              free translation from C. P. Cavafy

* *Page 204*
  The incidents recorded in Capodistria's letter have been
  borrowed and expanded from a footnote in Franz Hart-
  mann's *Life of Paracelsus*.